STRANGE BEDFELLOWS

KATHLEEN MARSHAL. Once Jean Jacques Charles threw her out of the Cabinet. Now she has his job.

JEAN JACQUES CHARLES. His own rise to the top was meteoric, and Kate was one of his closest friends. But that was before the tides turned.

ANTHONY WHITESIDE. The perfect choice for U.S.-Canadian liaison man. He still loves Kate with a schoolboy's devotion—and thoughts of *liaison* are uppermost in his mind.

U.S. PRESIDENT WILLIAM CONCORD THOMPSON. Behind his square, broad grin is a man with no respect for any woman running any government—even though it's no secret that his wife is the steel butterfly behind his throne.

ANDREW WICKSTROM. Once an enormously successful newspaper publisher and now Kate's husband, he gives her all his love and support—until events drive him packing in a cold fury.

Bantam-Seal Books by Judy La Marsh

A VERY POLITICAL LADY
A RIGHT HONOURABLE LADY

A Right Honourable Lady

A novel by
Judy La Marsh

SEAL BOOKS
McClelland and Stewart-Bantam Limited
Toronto

A RIGHT HONOURABLE LADY
*A Seal Book / published by arrangement with
McClelland & Stewart Limited*

PRINTING HISTORY
*McClelland & Stewart edition published January 1980
A Selection of Literary Guild Book Club March 1980
Seal edition / November 1980*

Front Cover Photo Courtesy of Bruce Coleman, Inc.

To J.G.

A Right Honourable Lady

Chapter One

Kathleen Marshal collapsed into the rear seat of the luxurious car, shaken and breathless. As the car's wheels spun on the icy drive, she checked the damage. Her fingers pinned up the fallen strands of her long black hair, while she glanced down at her coat, noting the large rent along one sleeve. Her expression became rueful at the damage done to the rippling fur. The coat had been an extravagant Christmas gift from Andrew, her husband, and she'd scarcely worn it. There was a wide, unsightly run in her dark hose, and her expensive brown suede boots were badly scuffed.

What a mess! And what a way to arrive at the Prime Minister's, she thought ruefully.

To make matters worse, the whole incident never should have happened. She had left Andrew in their hotel suite and gone down in the elevator with her Mountie escort. The trip through the lobby to the waiting car should have been uneventful since no one knew of her plan to visit the Prime Minister at his official residence.

As she stepped off the elevator ahead of her plainclothes Mountie escort, her thoughts had been on what she would say to Jean Jacques Charles. Only yesterday she had been elected by the Liberal party to replace him as leader, and she knew their first meeting since the convention would not be an easy one.

Not for a moment had Kathleen anticipated the maelstrom that met her in the lobby. A crowd of jostling people filled the marble-floored corridor. Many of them still wore scarves and hats, relics of the leadership convention. They stood in sloppy lines at the registration desk, or clustered in clumps, encouraging each other to stay for one more drink before heading home, back to their families and everyday lives.

Almost as one, they recognized Kathleen, and shouts rang out.

"It's Kate, our Kate!"

"Hiya, Katie! How about a kiss?"

"Gimme an autograph!"

"Three cheers for Kathleen Marshall!"

Hands reached from the crowd, snatching at her. A tall, knobby man in a white Stetson and string tie threw a sinewy arm across her shoulders and breathed beery fumes into her face. As she struggled to free herself, he clumsily planted a heavy cowboy boot on her elegant brown suede instep, and pain immediately shot up her leg. A bird-like woman, her face wreathed in a worshipful smile, plucked repeatedly at her coat sleeve, and as she was in turn jostled from her side, Kathleen heard the sleek fur of her sleeve rip.

Then the crowd engulfed her. She was pulled and pushed as they fought to touch her, to speak to her. An excited young man pounded her rhythmically on the back, while he gleefully chanted her campaign theme song.

"Katie, K-K-K-Katie . . ."

Kathleen clutched her handbag, but felt it slip from beneath her arm. It was lost underfoot, trampled by the milling convention delegates as supporters good-naturedly competed for a place beside her, and the crush became worse. Kathleen was first yanked one way, then half-spun back again, off-balance, to face more grinning faces, pressing ever closer. A wave of panic swept through her.

"Please. Please," she begged, but if they heard her, they ignored her plea.

They were all in great good humour, most of them far from sober this late Sunday afternoon, still riding their high from the exciting leadership convention, spinning out the last few comradely hours before they had to leave the national capital. All they meant was to show Kathleen their pleasure at her selection. All they wanted was to have her join their celebration.

But Kathleen was frightened, her face white-lipped from shock.

The valiant young Mountie had been separated from his charge by the pushing, jostling Liberal delegates. He struggled to reach her, but until other RCMP officers roughly cleared a path to free her, he was powerless to protect the new leader from her boisterous admirers. In a flying wedge, the burly young federal policemen shouldered through the mass of people to hustle her to the hotel's side entrance and the waiting car. One of them retrieved her purse from the floor. It tinkled with the sound of broken glass from her compact.

Now the car was hurrying down Sussex Drive, bringing her closer to her meeting with Jean Jacques Charles.

I can't go back now, she thought. *I won't be late! Jacques will certainly notice—he'll probably make some snide crack in that superior way of his. But there's not a damn thing I can do.* She sighed as she settled back in the seat, brushing vainly at the boot.

But, she consoled herself gloomily, *maybe a joke or two at my expense will put him in a better mood.*

Kathleen fully recognized how important this meeting was for her. She was the leader now, but not yet prime minister. Her problems were complicated by the fact that she had no seat in Parliament; she had not run in the last election, thinking then that she was finished with politics. In order to obtain that all-important seat now she would have to either contest a by-election or launch the minority Government she had inherited into a general election in order to win her own mandate from the people. Soon, very soon, she would have to decide which route she would take.

As the limousine sped along the broad, snow-banked drive, she considered how she would approach Jean Jacques Charles, the man who was still Prime Minister, but no longer leader of his party. The strength of the Liberal's minority Government rested on its overwhelming support from Quebec—and Jean Jacques Charles was the key to Quebec. If he should refuse to support her—refuse to co-operate in healing the divisions opened by the party's rejection of him and her election to leadership.... But he must! she told herself firmly. *Jacques owes it to the party, to the country. And to me.*

Kathleen resolved to appeal, if necessary, to their close personal ties over the years, stretching back to Sandy Sinclair's administration. She would ignore the hiatus of the past two years since Jean Jacques Charles, as Prime Minister, had abruptly banished her from his Cabinet. She must persuade him to stand by her, she must. Her wounds had healed; she could only hope that he himself now felt no bitterness.

The limousine made a left off Sussex Drive, turning in between the low stone gates of Number 24. It edged smoothly around the manicured drive towards the awning-covered entrance of the grey stone mansion. Immediately, several muffled figures stepped from the gathering shadows of the late February afternoon. They moved ahead of a uniformed RCMP constable. Portable lights blazed against the dusk as a television cameraman prepared to record her arrival.

What rotten luck! thought Kathleen. There was no way the press could have known she would be coming, but there they were, ready to record her dishevelled arrival. Then she realized that they were undoubtedly just following that old reporter's instinct—lying in wait for Jacques after his explosive exit from the convention yesterday. So putting on her best smile, Kathleen braced herself to meet the reporters, hoping that they wouldn't notice her appearance.

As the heavy car purred to a stop, a clutch of newsmen ran to her window. Her escort leaped from the car and stepped quickly to assist her, pushing them back roughly.

Kathleen smiled serenely into the full glare of the television lights. She bent her body to step from the car. Then, as her head came up, an errant elbow from the crowding reporters struck the car door, pushing it back towards her face. A freshet of bright blood gushed from her nostril, streaming down her chin and spilling over her clothes.

The young Mountie, still smarting from the memory of his powerlessness against the mob at the hotel, chopped viciously at the offending reporter. His victim dropped to the gravelled drive, writhing and moaning. Stunned, Kathleen herself whimpered with pain and fought to keep her balance. And all the while the television camera ground on, recording the short, ugly scene.

Finally, Kathleen lurched towards the doorway, stumbling on the shallow step. The door swung wide, and the redheaded young maid stood staring in the entrance, her hand to her mouth in horror.

A muscular arm pushed her aside and reached for Kathleen, yanking her headlong into the foyer.

Over her shoulder, blue eyes blazed at the reporters scrambling at her heels. She heard a familiar, gritted voice.

"Get out of here, you scum!"

The door slammed shut behind her.

"Feeling better, now?" Jacques' voice was cool, almost detached, belying the concern of his words. Jean Jacques Charles preferred order. He was almost personally offended by its opposite, although many said that he had often shown his finest mettle when, through some misadventure, he found himself in circumstances of extreme disorder. There was about him now a faint air of disdain, as if it were Kathleen's fault that she had arrived on his doorstep in such disarray and brought in her wake a herd of reporters.

Outwardly calm now, Kathleen fumbled silently for natural conversation to bridge the jarring events of the past half hour and touch upon the purpose of her visit.

"I'm fine now, Jacques. There's no permanent damage, and anyway it was all an accident. God knows how the media will play the whole thing on the news tonight. In the worst possible light, I expect."

He nodded his agreement.

"Let's just forget it, shall we?"

He offered her a brandy, which she sipped; its mellow glow masking the lingering metallic after-tang of blood. The Prime Minister returned to the leather armchair facing her.

They were sitting in the study on the first floor of the mansion, to the left of the entrance foyer. Kathleen's coat and boots had been whisked away for brushing and temporary repairs by the housekeeper, and the little black-clad maid had recently removed the icepack that had been brought to stem the blood. The pain was still there though, and the taste of blood still lingered on the back of her tongue.

Kathleen cleared her throat, mentally putting aside all but her purpose in coming here.

"Jacques, I have to start thinking about the future, about my plans. I would very much appreciate your advice. And your help, of course."

"I'd have thought, Kathleen, that you already had made your decisions. You didn't seem to need my help during the convention."

Kathleen winced. This was not going to be easy, but she plunged ahead, mentally stopping herself from apologizing to this man whom she had so recently toppled from his perch as party leader.

"That's behind us, Jacques. I hope that we will be able to work together now, as we once did." Kathleen glanced at her host, but as he made no response, other than raising an expressive eyebrow, she began to tick off on her fingers. "First is the question of whether to call a snap general election, as you did when you became leader. Should we capitalize on all the convention publicity—catch its momentum, and the enthusiasm of the party members—to try for a majority now?"

At the word "majority," Jacques bristled. He slid deeper

into the well-worn chair, his fingers steepled on his chest, his bright blue gaze on her face.

"Or," she went on, ignoring his reaction, "should we avoid the risk of a general election? The Government," she glanced at him and hesitated, "if you'll forgive me, is not too popular at the moment. Should we try to build a better record before we go to the country? That would mean I would have to go the by-election route before I could take a seat in the House."

"There are no vacancies now; all the seats were filled in last fall's by-elections," he reminded her curtly.

Kathleen brushed his comment aside. "I don't see any problem there. Someone will resign to let me into the House. It will be impossible to go on long as leader without being a member of Parliament. I have to find a seat quickly, one way or the other."

"There's always the Senate," Jacques said cynically. "There's certainly a precedent—Bowell and Abbott, I seem to remember."

"But that was before the turn of the century. I just couldn't get away with it today. No, I'll have to get into the House," she said firmly. "Either way, it will take two months after the issue of the Writ. That's too long as it is, but there's no way around it."

Jacques looked at Kathleen appraisingly. "It doesn't much matter, so long as you don't recall the House," he said.

Kathleen shook her head. "That can't be put off too much longer, either, unless we have a general election. The House last sat in October. And it's February now. It will have to be recalled before the summer, or the Opposition will raise hell."

"The Opposition! Who cares?" he scoffed. "It's a whole lot easier to govern when the House isn't in session, let me remind you. I shouldn't be in such a damn hurry to bring the members back." His tone was dry.

"Then your advice is for a general election now?" Her eyes searched his impassive face for confirmation.

"Kathleen, it hasn't even been two years since the last election." Jacques stirred in his armchair, shifting to a more comfortable position.

"But the Government is in a minority," she argued. "If I don't pull the plug now, I'll be at the mercy of the opposition."

"Well, they haven't tried to bring me down in the past two years," he said loftily.

"But that's because Malloy publicly pledged that the NDP wouldn't provoke another election right away. And their timetable has just about run out, I'd guess. Anyway, I'll have to feel out Malloy, before I decide. And Richard Sherwood, too."

"What do the party people think?" Jacques asked.

"They'll probably favour an election. Some will have reservations. I've asked them to poll the organizations and get back to me. And of course, I want to consult the Cabinet and the caucus." She smiled. "But, being members, I daresay none of them will be too anxious to hit the hustings again so soon."

Characteristically, Jean Jacques Charles shrugged.

Kathleen shifted to a new tack. She was getting no help from the Prime Minister.

"Jacques, I need to know where you stand. Can I count on your support?" she asked forthrightly.

He studied the tall, grave woman, her face a little swollen, her dark hazel eyes steady on his, awaiting his response.

Once, Jacques reflected, they had been close friends, not merely colleagues. Fleetingly, his thoughts touched on those early years when he and Kathleen had been eager, junior ministers, dedicated to their jobs, loving the complexities of governing, stimulated by their own rising influence and increasing power. Those thoughts gave way to a remembrance of Sandy Sinclair's sudden death. The Cabinet had chosen Kathleen to serve as prime minister during the interregnum. Then had come his own meteoric rise to first minister, her years of service in his Cabinet, as one of his most trusted advisors, her closeness to Evangeline. . . . *Evangeline.* Charles' pock-marked skin stretched even tighter over his high cheekbones. The almost oriental cast of his face was intensified, as pain touched the hooded eyes. And in a flash, his mood changed again, remembering. Damn her for an interfering bitch! And then to snatch the leadership for herself!

He gestured with both hands, palms up. In a cold tone, he asked, "What do you want of me, Kathleen?" Then, an edge of hostility creeping into his voice, "Am I to be in your Cabinet? Or am I expected to subside into the back benches and just melt away from public view? Do you want me to quit altogether? Perhaps you would prefer that," he said even more icily, "so that there won't be any odious comparisons."

Kathleen stiffened at the scorn in Jacques' tone. Both her expression and her voice hardened. Sharply, she said, "No, Jacques. I won't worry about comparisons—they'll be made whether you're there or not. I want you to understand, however, that I have no intention of looking over my shoulder all the time, worrying about what my predecessor may be doing to undermine me. This is the Liberal party we're talking about, not the Conservatives. Let's have this clearly understood. If you are going to stay on in the House, I will tolerate nothing but absolute loyalty. I gave it to you as my leader, and I am entitled to expect the same from you."

She continued in a calmer voice, trying to be persuasive. "I don't want you to quit. You've such a wealth of experience. It would be a loss to the Government—to the country—if you were to quit. But it's up to you." She sat back, then added. "If there's anything special you would like to do, I hope you'll tell me. I'm not promising anything at the moment, you understand."

"You mean, do I want a job?" he asked harshly.

"I know you don't need a job," she responded testily. "I don't mean that the way you put it. But you have to do something with the rest of your life. Surely you can say whether you plan to stay on in politics?" Kathleen was becoming exasperated at his noncommittal stance.

Coolly, the rejoinder came. "I hadn't thought much about it. There was really no need, until yesterday," he said pointedly. "But I suppose I'll stay. At least until the election—whenever that is." His features softened at his last words, his eyes lit with inner amusement.

He was trifling with her. Well, she thought grimly, two can play at that game. But that was followed by the disquieting thought that although two could play, only one could win. The winner was unlikely to be she, whose style was so much more forthright, so much less subtle than that of the practised man facing her across the small study. Jacques was a sharp and unpredictable adversary, and obviously, he still considered her an interloper. His attitude spelled out clearly that he was still confident that he was better and brighter than she, and that before long both party and country would recognize their mistake, and turn back to him for leadership. Kathleen grudgingly admitted to herself that perhaps Jacques was right.

Nonetheless, even if she shrank from it, she must make it clear who was in control now.

She paused and deliberately opened the silver box on the low coffee table before her. Drawing out a cigarette she held it in the flame of the chunky onyx table lighter. As she inhaled deeply, she studied her opponent through the smoke.

Jacques did not smoke and did not like others to do so in his presence, although he rarely said so. His displeasure was usually indicated by the wrinkling of his long nose.

She saw now that he understood that she was deliberately staking out her right to smoke if she chose to in this house, where she was once again the rightful chatelaine. Indeed, the Prime Minister moved the heavy crystal ashtray nearer her hand, with a mocking gesture of acknowledgement that she had made her point.

"Would you ring for some tea, Jacques?"

"Certainly. Or would you prefer another brandy? I'm told that it is quite fine."

"Indeed it is. But no, thank you. I would prefer tea. With lemon. No sugar."

The polite little exchange permitted them both a moment of reassessment. The tension appeared to ease somewhat. After the tea arrived, Kathleen broke the silence once again.

"We've come full circle, Jacques. We're back to the question of whether to go to the country now, or not. What do you say?"

"It's entirely up to you, Kathleen," he answered suavely. "As you have pointed out, you're the leader now." He let his remark sink in, then posed a question of his own. "What about the change-over? When do you plan to be sworn in as prime minister? There's no obligation that you must wait until you have a seat—after all the post isn't even mentioned in the constitution."

The man was maddening, so damn professorial. Why couldn't he understand the difference between what was allowed under the law and what people expected? You *could* be prime minister without having been elected in an election, you *could* govern without the Parliament in session, you *could* govern as though you had a majority when you did not—but people did not expect these actions, or the arrogance it took to state them publicly. This brilliant man was his own worst political enemy.

"I assume you'd like to take over as soon as possible?" His question interrupted her oft-made analysis of him.

"Soon, Jacques, but not right away. I have to settle the main question first. If there's to be a general election, there's no reason to postpone our visit to the Governor General. But if I decide on a by-election . . ." Her voice trailed off, while she considered the alternatives.

"Would you be prepared to carry on as prime minister if I should decide to fight a by-election?" she asked, watching him narrowly.

He shrugged.

Damn him! He's impossible!

Then Jacques disarmed her by shifting the subject to something more personal.

"Guess I'd better look for a house for the twins and me," he said. He glanced around him at the familiar, comfortable study, with its many remainders of his tenure here. "You'll be wanting to move in. Here, and at the office too," he said, a bit wistfully.

"I suppose so," she responded, inattentively. Then she realized what he had said, and hastened to reassure him. "There's no hurry, Jacques. I'll stay at the hotel this week, anyway. Maybe I could move in across the street, temporarily, until you're ready to leave."

"Where? At Rideau Hall? Oh, you mean the official guest house. Sure, I don't see why not. I'll have the staff check that out and get back to you tomorrow."

The Prime Minister seemed less wary, more conciliatory, but it was clear that Charles was going to reserve his own options, for now. Kathleen knew she had to choose her own course, without knowing what his intentions were. He had served notice on her that neither she nor the Liberal party that had rejected him could necessarily count on his co-operation and loyalty in the future. Jean Jacques Charles, as always, would remain a free agent.

Kathleen stood, smoothing down her blood-spotted dress in an habitual gesture of which she was entirely unaware. Her host summoned the red-haired maid, who brought in the well-brushed boots and hastily mended coat.

At the door, Kathleen held out her hand to Jacques. He took it, looking first at it, and then up into her face, so that standing close to him she became aware of her height. Quixotically, he pressed his lips to the back of her hand.

Puzzled, Kathleen thought to herself that she would never understand this man of abundant charm, with his graceful gestures, and memorable turn of phrase. He was a chameleon. When one expected to encounter his softer side, one was all too often met with disdain, contempt, or a cutting coldness. But then suddenly he could be warm—all charm and very disarming. She sighed. There was only one Jean Jacques Charles, and he would be forever a mystery.

When the entry door was opened, Kathleen saw the car ready before it, its engine softly purring, the plainclothesman alert to assist her. Outside the Prime Minister's residence the lamps were already lit, holding at bay the night that had so swiftly fallen on this cloudy winter's day. A handful of uniformed RCMP stood about near the mansion's canopied entrance, and beyond, at the edge of the light, she noticed a row of reporters, behind a cordon stretched between two heavy stanchions.

Standing tall in her rich fur coat, and straightening her shoulders, Kathleen smiled and waved to the watching members of the media. She hoped that the image of the now calm and composed leader might somehow replace that of the battered, bloody, staggering woman who had made her entrance here less than two hours ago. But she knew that the dramatic four o'clock pictures would headline the National.

As the shining car rolled out of the driveway to turn up Sussex Drive, carrying the new Liberal leader back to the hotel through the light evening traffic, her thoughts strayed to other politicians, caught by a camera at a moment of disadvantage. The resulting photographs, carried the length of the land, had left an ineradicable image: a Conservative leader fumbling a football; a civic leader whose credibility suffered even more than her dignity when she lost her footing on an icy sheet as she opened a curling match; even a leader who suffered the country's judgment that "he could hardly be trusted to lead" after he had been snapped backing into a bayonet while reviewing an honour guard.

"It's damn bad luck, but it just can't be helped," Kathleen spoke aloud to herself. With determination, she pushed it all to the back of her mind, including the unproductive meeting with Jacques.

I must lead, she thought to herself. I must be seen to be leading. She contemplated the danger of a by-election. That would mean she would have to be out of the capital, fighting to re-enter Parliament, unable for months to put her own stamp on the minority Government. And for that whole period, she would have to rely on the loyalty of the Cabinet —a loyalty she could not yet be sure of. Furthermore, the public would find it hard to accept that Jean Jacques Charles, although deposed as party leader, was still very visibly heading the Government. The party had, after all, replaced him because of his unpopularity.

It seemed best that she should dismiss Parliament at once for a general election, despite the risks. That way, there could be no question that Kathleen Marshal was truly leader. She would have to purge some of Charles' ministers and bring in some of her own people to put a fresh face on the Liberal team. Yes. That way would free her from any taint of responsibility for the sorry record of the Charles' Government. She would have to stand or fall on her own.

Kathleen's entry into the château-like hotel was uneventful. She was led to the lower level elevator, and was soon delivered to her door by the impassive young policeman. She made no comment to him about the uncontrolled events that had marred the last few hours, but she informed him that guests would arrive for drinks shortly.

As Kathleen bathed and dressed, moving from the bathroom to the dressing-table and back, Andrew brought her what they called a "dressing drink." She sipped from it intermittently as she recounted the past hours.

He watched her, aware of an unexpressed current of distress at the dishearteningly unfavourable turn of events. Andrew Wickstrom cared deeply for this woman who had been his wife for little more than a year. He had dreaded all along the kind of hurt she would be sure to encounter in her quest for the party's leadership, and beyond that, her aspiration to become Canada's first woman prime minister. Wickstrom understood well from his own successful career as a newspaper publisher that the world could be heartlessly cruel and inhumane. He knew that where the stakes were high the way was strewn with hurts and disappointments, and, worse, cut throats and stabbed backs. Kathleen Marshal was skilled in the practice of politics but it worried him that he had never detected in her that cutting edge, that instinct for the jugular, that he believed was necessary for successful political leadership. He saw his wife as softer, more vulnerable than other people in politics. He craved to protect her but felt powerless to do so.

Andrew listened quietly, anger smoking in his mind at the indignities offered his wife from the riotous if friendly crowd, from the insistent but clumsy reporters, and from the cool, implacable man who was still the Prime Minister of Canada. The physical incidents he could dismiss fairly lightly since Kathleen had not been harmed and they had, after all, been accidental; but the resolve grew in his own mind that Jean Jacques Charles must be neutralized to protect Kathleen from his hostility. Kathleen could carry on trying to understand Charles if she wanted to—it was part of her nature to keep trying to see people's better side. For himself, Andrew Wickstrom felt free simply to dislike and distrust Charles.

Turning to Kathleen, he let his sympathetic silence speak for him, not interrupting her flow of words.

When the knock came at the door of the suite, Andrew Wickstrom moved swiftly to answer it and cheerfully busied himself with his guests' coats, then their seating. He offered them drinks and quickly brought their choices. By the time the Fraziers had settled, Kathleen made her entrance from the bedroom. Once again smoothly coiffed, she was clad in a clinging black wool cocktail dress. It was accented by creamy pearls at the neckline and a small spray of maple leaves picked out in rubies winking from one shoulder.

Kathleen had dressed with care for this meeting. Hume Frazier was another former Cabinet colleague who had contested for the Liberal leadership. Kathleen had won out over him, but for a while he had led the voting, and it had been touch-and-go to the end. As the second-ranking contender, Hume had showed surprising delegate strength. Kathleen understood that the tall, personable man with the chiselled features had a special constituency—strong support in the business world. That world, despite her marriage to Andrew, had remained wary of her. If she was going to call a general election, she needed Hume Frazier's credibility among the money men.

Kathleen and the handsome Hume had once been close friends. In a sense, he had been her protégé after he entered Parliament—but that closeness had dissolved after his marriage to the cool and subtly manipulative Sybil. The Fraziers now lived in Toronto, not far from the Wickstrom home, but since Hume had become president of SilverTinCo, Andrew and Kathleen had hardly seen the younger couple, who moved so naturally in the tight social circles of money and power.

Kathleen was fully composed as she held out her hands to Sybil, concealing her suspicion of the sleek, blonde woman. They pecked at the air beside each other's cheeks, pretending but avoiding actual physical contact. Such a gesture was expected of them, and they responded in the small ritual greeting to the amusement of both men.

To Hume Frazier, Kathleen offered at first a handshake, but then, drawn by something quizzical in his expression, she moved closer and dropped a light kiss on his firm cheek. His face was tangy with the bracing scent of aftershave. Laughing, he rubbed the faint imprint of her fresh lipstick from his cheek.

Andrew brought Kathleen a crisp martini in a stemmed glass. She glanced at him appreciatively. She wondered if he knew how his strength supported her, wordless as it most often was.

The two couples talked comfortably about the convention highlights of the past few days, exchanging views on how the people of Canada would perceive the party in its aftermath. Then Hume mentioned that while dressing he had been watching the early evening television news and had been startled by the incident at 24 Sussex.

"I can't tell you how delighted I am to find that you weren't seriously hurt, Kathleen. I'm sure it was nothing but an accident, but it was pretty scary to see the Mountie belt that reporter so hard. And the sight of you with your face all bloody was shocking."

"Just a nosebleed, Hume," she reassured him. "Nothing to it. But I confess the blow hurt like hell and I was dazed for a bit. Anyway, all in a day's work."

He nodded. "So you saw Jacques? Did he tell you what he plans to do?"

"No." She hadn't intended to mention her interview with the Prime Minister to Hume but there was no way now to avoid it. "I suppose it's a little early, anyway. I'll talk to him again in a few days, when he's had time to consider. . . ." She let her voice trail away, leaving Hume to speculate just what it was that she had offered to Jacques that he had to take time to consider.

"Speaking of plans, Hume," she went on, getting to the point of this meeting, "what are yours? Or," and here she paused for emphasis, glancing at Sybil, seated primly beside her handsome husband, "do you plan to go back to business again and forget politics?"

Hume Frazier had been sitting forward on the edge of the chesterfield, in that characteristic attitude of intensity, his gaze bent on Kathleen. Now, his glance dropped to his strong, square hands in which he was turning round and round his chunky, now emptied glass. Deliberately, he set the glass on the polished surface of the low table before him and turned his athletic body towards his wife. Placing one hand over Sybil's hands, folded demurely in her lap, he spoke to her as much as to Kathleen. Instead of his usual staccato delivery his voice was hesitant.

"It's up to Syb. She doesn't care much for politics, as you know, and she's been very happy in Toronto since I've been there in business. But she was with me all the way when I decided to go for the leadership, and I won't do anything unless it will make her happy, too. We haven't really had a chance to discuss our future since yesterday. I dunno, Kit," he said softly. Then turning to the ash-blonde woman listening silently at his side, he asked, "What do you say, Sybil?"

Sybil gave her husband a slow look. Turning her sleek head on its long slender neck, she spoke in her light, silvery voice to her hostess. "It is far too early to make that decision, Kathleen. We'll have to consider the alternatives, of course. It would be very disrupting to our lives and the children's lives to have to move back to Ottawa just now in the middle of term. Of course, we knew that would have been necessary if Hume had become leader but," she hesitated, "but under the present circumstances, it would be, ah, disruptive."

Hume cleared his throat. "Just what job would you be offering me, Kit-baby, if I decided to come back?" Hume laughed. "Not Finance again, I hope. I've served my time there. It's a dead end. It could make a difference if the job itself sounded interesting. I really should know, ah, what your intentions are. If I were to decide on Parliament again, that is."

Kathleen nodded. This was what she had expected. Sybil would want to hedge. Hume would want to know what power he might wield. Hume was no longer a team player, if indeed he ever had been. There was no more loyalty here to her or to the party than Jacques had displayed. Although she had anticipated this reaction, she was dismayed to hear it confirmed.

"Hume," she began firmly, "you know that as leader I have to keep my options open. I can't promise you anything definite. Not now, and maybe not ever. I have to look at all the people available and make my decision then. I don't want to promise you something and then be unable to deliver. And," she added silkily, "I don't want to presume that I can *buy* you back into political life. Whether you are prepared to come back or not is your own decision. Yours and Sybil's, of course," she amended.

Hume Frazier started to interrupt, but Kathleen held up her hand, silencing him.

"I won't plead with you or beg you or even bargain with you," she went on purposefully, wanting to say her piece before Frazier could break in. "The convention surely made you realize that you are still held in high regard by the party, and by many in the country. Your return to political life would be welcomed, I'm sure. And if there is any doubt about it, I would be glad to have you on *my* team!" Her emphasis had been slight, but deliberate. Neither Hume nor Sybil missed its significance.

"But, Kit," Frazier said, "you've got to understand that before I would be willing to quit my job and run for Parliament, I'd need some idea of what was in it—of what you had in mind for me."

Hume wasn't about to give in, Kathleen realized, or respond to her appeal to his loyalty.

"Okay," she replied, "suppose you tell me what portfolio *would* interest you? I am not promising anything, remember, but it would be useful for me to know. Is there anything— short of the leadership of course—" she smiled, "that you have thought of?"

"Well," he said slowly, this time not looking at Sybil, "I always thought that External might be fun. But I haven't discussed it with Sybil at all," he warned, "and she might not enjoy all the travelling that it would entail."

Not much she wouldn't, thought Kathleen with amusement. Sybil loved to travel, and would simply adore the chance to move around the world meeting kings and princes and presidents. As if Sybil had read the older woman's thoughts, her clear brown eyes flickered away. But not before Kathleen had caught the gleam of interest.

"Hume and I will discuss it, Kathleen, and let you know our decision," Sybil said coolly. "I do feel that it would be pointless for Hume to return to politics unless he is assured of a very important role. But before he throws over his future at SilverTinCo, I should think he would want more than just a place in your Cabinet."

"Oh?" said Kathleen. "And what would that be?"

"Well, we should know how long you plan to retain the leadership and whether you would pledge Hume your support as your successor."

Her words dropped into the suddenly silent room like pebbles into a pool. Ripples of dismay widened.

Hume was shocked at his wife's blunt statement. He was grateful for her support, but resented the fact that she had chosen this moment to throw down the gauntlet on his behalf. This was the kind of hard-nosed talk he and Kathleen should hold privately. It was against unwritten rules that husbands and wives should be present, much less participate, in such a power-play.

Kathleen's hazel eyes glittered. She was aghast at Sybil's effrontery. Hot words crowded to her lips, which narrowed as she struggled to restrain herself. Try as she might, she could not hide her reaction to the woman's bold challenge.

"No one has the right to make such demands," she chided. "No leader could afford to give such a promise." She swung her gaze to Hume. "Am I to take it that Sybil has expressed your terms correctly, Hume?"

Caught by circumstances, Hume thrust forward his square, cleft chin. His heavy, arching brows drew down over the bright blue chips of his eyes, and he said deliberately, "That's it, in a nutshell, Kit-baby. I know damn well that you need me. And I know you know it. Well, it's a seller's market. My price comes high. Give me External and a free rein. Make me deputy prime minister and dub me your heir apparent. Guarantee that you'll only stay one term, and that you'll back me next time out. Do all that, and I'll run for you."

From beside him chimed his wife's silvery voice. "And it ought to be in writing."

Kathleen sucked in her breath at the audacity of the two of them. She let the silence build. Then, with a gesture of dismissal, she rose and walked to the bar table, setting down her glass with such force that the fragile stem snapped in her hand.

She turned to confront the young couple on the chesterfield and said in a voice totally devoid of warmth or colour, "That's out of the question. I'll give no such hostage to fortune. The fact is, Hume, you're too expensive. I'll just have to get along without you. I think I can manage!"

Hume's clean-cut features were suffused with pink, mirroring a combination of embarrassment, anger, and disappointment. He rose to his six-foot-plus height, drawing Sybil up beside him.

"If that's your final answer, Kathleen, okay. But you'll regret it, more than I will. At least now we know where we stand." He moved aggressively across the room towards the door.

Andrew, the silent witness, rose to see him out.

Frazier's composure eroded and his anger burst, as he said rudely, "No, I'll get our coats," and then, his hand under his wife's elbow, he steered her to the door, opened it and motioned her to leave. He turned in the doorway to face Kathleen and bit off the words.

"You can go to hell—you and the Liberal party—for all I give a damn!" Then he was gone.

Kathleen and Andrew stared briefly at the empty, open door. Then Andrew walked slowly over and shut it.

"I guess we won't be seeing them again for a while," he said lightly to his wife, who looked helplessly at him for a moment, then turned towards the bedroom door.

"Kathleen, wait."

She turned and walked quickly to him, burying her face on his shoulder. Then, pulling herself together she said, "It seems that now I'm on my own."

"Not entirely, dear. The party is behind you. And I'm here."

"Oh, Andrew, I know. It's just been such an exhausting day. Tomorrow will be better. At least I know where I stand, now."

As they walked arm in arm towards the bedroom, Andrew said softly, "I'm sorry about Frazier, darling. He enjoys real respect among people in the financial community. I suspect you're going to need him, or someone very like him. He's a real loss."

"But what he asked was impossible," his troubled wife replied. "He must have known I would refuse. Perhaps it's just as well. There is simply no loyalty in Hume. And he is not indispensable. I'll find someone else, you'll see."

Andrew thought otherwise, but it was too late to argue. People like Frazier were rare. All in all, he thought heavily, this has been a truly disastrous day.

In the bedroom, they undressed silently and fell asleep quickly, clasped in one another's arms.

Chapter Two

The room was a mess. There were overflowing ashtrays, stained coffee cups in sloshing saucers, cloudy rings on the furniture beneath wet-bottomed glasses, and the remains of cardboard-like hotel sandwiches with their edges stiffly curled. The eight people in the room ignored the disarray. They were still intent on their discussion even though there was now a momentary silence.

"This, I suppose, is what one calls a pregnant pause," Kathleen joked mildly, looking at each in turn. It didn't relieve the tension of the weary group.

To her immediate left, Matthew Lyndon, the distinguished party president, was leaning back in the delicate chair. His face wore his usual sardonic grin, his long legs were crossed above the knee and smoke from his ever-present thin cheroot wreathed his fine features.

"We're agreed in principle," he said. "But there are problems."

A female voice chimed in. "I still say that we've nothing to gain by waiting. We should use the momentum of the convention, make it clear that there's a new hand at the helm. Kathleen, you just can't afford to lead the country from outside the House. It makes you dependent on Jacques. It puts you in *his* hands. I say go!" As she spoke, Bonnie Costello's dark eyes flashed. She strained forward from her place on the overstuffed chesterfield, pounding the palm of her hand with her fist. Her ordinarily well-modulated voice was pitched higher than usual, her wiry body tense as she tried to drive her point home.

The silver-haired Senator beside her shook his head.

"Not so fast, Bonnie. Remember we spent a lot on this convention, and the last election is not even two years back. The party's coffers are just about empty and we can't afford to go to the well so often. One of these days we'll come up dry. You can't run elections without money—these days a lot of money. The television spots alone . . ." His voice trailed off as Bonnie again spoke.

"Oh—money! That's all you think about, Jim." She brushed off Senator O'Rourke's admonition. "The money will come once we are into an election. But it won't come if we leave Jacques in control. It'll be just as though the convention never happened. And, don't forget," she looked around at the others, "business people will be glad to be rid of him. They'll be happy to underwrite the new leader. Don't you agree, Davie?"

"I think so." The reply had not been immediate. David Kirke, Senator from Toronto, long-time election organizer for the federal Liberals, was not worried about the money. His job was to spend it, not find it. He was more concerned about the problem of promoting a new leader who was also a woman. He wasn't at all sure how to handle it. It could prove a big plus, or a fatal minus.

"You sound cautious, Davie. Any reservations?" Kathleen knew what was bothering him. His job was strategy and organization. He wasn't sure how to handle the troubling matter of her sex. She wanted to say something to ease his mind then and there, but that wasn't the subject under discussion. Strategy was for another time.

"No," Kirke amended quickly, "no reservations. I favour going now." He knew he still sounded hesitant, so, with the instinctive skill of the politician, he passed. "How about you, Carter?"

Carter Warden glanced at Kirke, his long-time protégé, then slowly turned his eyes to Kathleen. "Bonnie's right. Charles can't stay on as leader. You'll lose credibility if you don't put your stamp on things right away. Of course, O'Rourke's right too. The party *is* broke."

Fernand LeMesurier murmured agreement. "We'll just have to raise the money."

Slowly, all eyes turned to Kathleen. She let the silence build until it became obvious that everyone had already said all each had to say, then finally she nodded her head in agreement.

"I do favour an election right away, for the reasons many of you have stated." She looked up in surprise as Bonnie clapped her hands together in excited approval. "But I can't make the final decision until I consult with the Cabinet and the caucus. I also feel we have to wait for the party executives to test the water at home. I've asked them to do that. I think we have to touch all bases; in fact I should see the Opposition leaders, too. It would be helpful to know their attitude, in case the decision is to meet the House. And then there's Jacques. . . ."

Carter Warden grinned. He suddenly stood and did the perfect Jean Jacques Charles shrug. "Should we care?" he questioned mockingly. They all laughed, breaking the tension. Unfortunately, they all knew that they did care. They had to care.

"You've got to be firm with him, Kathleen. Don't let him get away with anything. He's wily. So far as we on the coast are concerned, the sooner he's out, the better." The party president's tone was unusually sharp. Gone for the moment was the controlled languor that was his trademark. Lyndon brought the front legs of his chair down hard as his body shifted forward for emphasis, and a long curl of gray ash fell over his waistcoat. He brushed it away in irritation.

"You know we've all gone through a hell of a period— nearly a year of damned hard, dangerous, expensive work to get him out as leader. And we did it because we were convinced Jacques was destroying the party. We asked you to become leader to save the Government because we were sure Charles would be defeated at the earliest possibility.

"You've got to put as much distance between yourself and Charles as you can, Kathleen. It's the only way we're going to win an election. Cut him off. Be brutal. Get rid of him! Let the country see that you're turning your back on him and his record. Dump some of his ministers, bring in new people. Canadians have to see that you're the boss."

From the others came murmurs of agreement.

Carter Warden nodded his approval of the president's advice. Now, completely serious, he added, "Don't settle for a by-election. He'll still be there, and a lot of his cronies will be there, like millstones around your neck. I doubt you can trust them, but you'd be forced to."

Kathleen turned her attention to Le Mesurier, the most powerful of her supporters in the Quebec wing of the party. Her expression, too, was serious as she asked, "And Quebec?"

He answered without hesitation. "Charles has been rejected by the party. Quebeckers know it. That damage is done. They will respect you more, I think, if you show yourself to be strong. They won't consider you anti-Quebec just because you defeated him. Remember, when they go to the polls they have

to weigh the alternatives. I doubt that cutting yourself free
from Jacques will cause Quebec to turn to either Sherwood or
Malloy."

Kathleen was grateful for the reassurance, but she was not
totally willing to take the word and opinions of her loyal
supporters only. Fernand's sensible words aside, she still
worried about Quebec. Traditionally, when Quebeckers felt
rejected, or felt the country had rejected their leader, they
found their own alternatives. Was Social Credit dead? The
question remained in her mind. A tiny inner voice whispered
caution.

There was a long pause, then Matthew Lyndon lifted
himself from his chair. Shaking the ashes from his trousers,
he looked at each person in the room.

"Shall we adjourn then? At the call of the leader." As
Kathleen rose to stand beside him, bringing all of them to
their feet, he added, "Don't be too long about it, Kathleen,
but talk to everyone you think you must. Let's have your
decision soon. There'll be a helluva lot to do."

The two who were driving to Toronto moved together
towards the door. Matthew Lyndon and Frank Oldham looked
at each other.

"Going to the airport?" Lyndon questioned.

Frank, who had been almost totally silent during the
meeting, nodded.

"I've got a car coming in twenty minutes. Is that okay?"
pursued Lyndon.

"Sure. I'd appreciate the lift."

Kathleen shook hands with both men as they left, her
eyes lingering on Frank. He was a relative newcomer to the
inner group of advisors. He was a big westerner with leathery
skin and faded hair which was laid in precise strands across
his otherwise bald pate. This silent and agreeable man had
proved, unexpectedly, to be a tower of strength during the
leadership campaign. Without him the support of the prairie
delegates might well have gone to the Edmonton candidate.
He was, strangely, a superb speaker in larger groups and
painfully shy in small groups among friends. She felt he was a
strong man, and was glad he was now part of the team.

These people were the best and they were also the closest
to her. They were the important Seven.

"Let me help you straighten this place up," Bonnie offered
when the others had left. The short, wiry member for Toronto

Beaches stood, hands on her hips, surveying the litter in the smoke-filled room.

Kathleen was already struggling with the heavy window. A blast of icy air ballooned the thick drapes, brining with it the wet scent of a bitter winter's night. Methodically Bonnie began to dump the ashtrays and crumpled serviettes and collect the discarded glasses and cups. Suddenly she looked over at Kathleen, who had collapsed into the only comfortable chair in the hotel sitting room and was kicking off her shoes.

"Where's Andrew?" the younger woman asked, realizing that she had not seen Kathleen's husband all day.

Kathleen shook her head wearily. "He had to go back to Toronto for a couple of days. He's been here since before the convention. Things piled up at his office. He'll be back just as soon as he can get away." She paused. "I miss him. I really miss him. Especially now, at the end of the day. I never dreamed that anyone's absence could make such a hole in my day."

Bonnie was standing in the centre of the room, looking around her with smug satisfaction. The place certainly looked better now. She went to the telephone to call the waiter to remove the debris. As she put down the receiver, she was struck by Kathleen's woebegone expression. A flash of insight told her how much the older woman was dreading the prospect of an evening alone. She was lonely. She must be. She and Andrew had been married such a short time, and they hadn't had much time together in the past six months or so. Bonnie felt a rush of sympathy.

"Would you like me to stay, Kathleen? We could have dinner together. Unless, of course, you'd rather be alone?"

Kathleen brightened. "Oh, stay. I'd like that. And there's something I wanted to discuss with you, Bonnie. This will be a good chance. We can have dinner sent up, if that's all right with you. I'm too tired to get dressed to go out. We can make an early evening of it." Then she added ruefully, suddenly feeling her years, "And at my age, I'll appreciate that."

The two politicians talked of many things over the next two hours as they shared the intimacy of a room-service meal. Then Kathleen broached the subject she had in mind.

"I'm sure it will come as no surprise, Bonnie, that I'm going to ask you to join the Cabinet."

There was instantly a sparkle in the black eyes. Bonnie's

wide lips stretched in an eager grin, her delight wrinkling the heavy nose that marred her beauty, but not her bright personality.

"I thought I'd ask you to take over the Labour portfolio. How would that appeal to you?"

The young woman's face went blank in surprise, but she quickly recovered. "Labour? But why me—and Labour?" she asked, not at all sure she should question her leader's suggestion.

Kathleen stroked her jaw with her thumb. "It's going to be busy over there this year. I'm told that a great many contracts in the public sector are up for renegotiation. There's sure to be a lot of labour unrest. There are the railroad unions, the dock workers, air traffic controllers, ground maintenance crews—and, as usual, the Post Office. Of course, that's the Postmaster General's headache, but sometimes it takes the Minister of Labour to help straighten things out. Any one of those unions striking could spell real trouble. We can't have a protracted strike *this* year, and there are so many contracts coming up that there's real potential for what amounts to a general transportation strike. I don't have to tell you that that would cripple the economy."

Kathleen paused, then sensing Bonnie's interest, she continued. "I think you might bring some fresh insights into the process. Previous governments have always been late getting down to negotiations and the whole process gets so bogged down. I'd be tempted to strike myself. My new Labour Minister will have to be full of energy and enthusiasm, someone who can cut through the process and find new solutions. I think you're the person and I think you'd like the challenge."

Bonnie's thoughts were racing. All she knew of organized labour she knew from her father. He was an old union man. Remembering his repeated complaints, she thought, maybe I can change things. Maybe, as a woman. . . . No. She firmly rejected the beginnings of that offensively sexist train of thought, and began to toy with her dessert fork, polishing it with her fingers to still their excited trembling. Then she looked at her mentor.

"What about Jake Wilson?" she asked. "He's had so much experience in the portfolio."

"That's the trouble," Kathleen said decisively. "He's a good man, but he's been there so long he's atrophied. I think I'll recycle him into a new ministry." Quickly, she continued to urge her young supporter. "Well, Bonnie, would you like to try it? It's an important post at any time, but this year it's bound to be critical. You'll have a high profile. Do you think you're up to it?"

Bonnie flushed and then, abandoning her misgivings, answered. "Yes, I'd like to try—if you think I can do it."

"Thats fine," said Kathleen with satisfaction. "It won't be right away, you know, but soon . . . before the election. For a minute I thought you might refuse—you seemed to hesitate. Did you have your heart set on another portfolio?"

"Well," she admitted modestly, "I hoped you would invite me into the Cabinet, and I had an idea Energy might be interesting, but I wouldn't say I had my heart set on it."

"Energy? Why, I should think you'd find that a bore. I didn't consider you for that ministry, although I am going to make a change there."

Kathleen's thoughts lingered for a moment on the Minister of Energy—Stan Findlay. She didn't like him; he was too much Jacques' man. A yes-man, really. That, she noted firmly, was certainly one Cabinet change that had to be made.

"Like to talk to you, PM."

Jean Jacques Charles looked up from the memo he had been studying. His expression showed some irritation at the big westerner whose frame seemed almost to fill his doorway. Charles always had a faint feeling of distaste at the sight of Stanley Findlay, although he had never bothered to pinpoint the reason. Perhaps it was Findlay's large, rumpled body, which, although powerful and rangy enough, absolutely refused to wear clothes gracefully. Or perhaps it was Findlay's speech. A little slow and methodical, it reflected his reasoning. Or was it something else? Perhaps a faintly false ring in Findlay's almost puppy-dog devotion to his leader. There was something almost obsequious about his manner towards Jacques.

"Come in, Stan," said the Prime Minister without warmth.

His visitor's ordinarily high colour was heightened. He plunked himself into the guest chair facing the desk, scratched the sandy bristle of his head, and moved his butt around, trying to find a comfortable position for his long, powerful legs.

Jacques placed a marker on the memorandum, closed the

file and dropped it into a lower drawer, carefully turning the key in its lock.

"Was it something particular?" he prompted.

"Yeah. I want to talk to you about where we go from here."

"We?" Jacques' eyebrows shot up.

"You and me. Now that the convention is over, I thought maybe you'd tell me your plans. It would kinda help me decide about my own future."

Jacques allowed his brow to furrow elaborately. "How would that help you?"

The big man blinked. "Well, I've followed you pretty faithfully now, for a long time—the anti-abortion fight and the leadership included. I don't think anybody's been more loyal to you, 'cept maybe Senator LaCroix. I've kinda tied my career to your kitestrings, so I thought maybe you'd have some idea of what I ought to do or think about doing."

"What is it you want to do, Stan?"

"Nothing special, I guess. I'd like to just carry on, although that will be up to the Marshal woman, whenever she takes over. I hear rumours she's thinking of taking me out of Energy. I suppose she might even be thinking of dropping me from the Cabinet." He paused and then reassured himself. " 'Course I don't think she'd likely do that. She needs me too much in the West. Anyway, I sort of thought that if she was planning anything like that, you could speak up for me. She gonna take over soon?"

"My guess is, she's planning to call an election shortly. If she does, you'll be safe enough until that's over, Stan. She won't rock the boat when she's looking for support in the West. After that, *if* she wins the election. . . ." Jacques pondered the alternative.

"And if she doesn't call an election?" Although he took his time, Stan wasn't stupid.

"I doubt she'd keep you for long, win or lose." Jacques let his discouraging words hang in the air for a moment. "It's no secret she doesn't like you," he added.

Findlay squirmed in his chair and nodded his agreement. He didn't feel personally insulted. He didn't like Kathleen Marshal either.

"What do you plan on doing yourself, Jacques? Gonna stick around in case she loses the election—try to pick up the pieces?"

"I haven't decided. Perhaps I'll wait out the results of an election—for now I plan to carry on here."

"She's leaving you as acting Prime Minister? Well, then, you're still her number-one man. You're in a good position to put in a word for me."

"I don't think you should count on that, Findlay," said Jacques evenly.

The big man's craggy features creased in puzzlement. "Why not? I've always been there when you needed me." He was protesting, and an edge of anger came into his voice. He felt that an injustice was being done.

Charles wanted to tell Findlay that this was a case of every man for himself. What did Findlay think Jacques owed him anyway? He, Jacques, did not feel he owed anyone anything. The bluff man across from him looked dejected as well as angry, however, and it struck Jean Jacques Charles that he was being too hard on Findlay. Perhaps, it occurred to him, he might still find use for him. And, if ever the chance came for him to supplant Kathleen, he would of course need the veteran member's support in the West.

He relented a little. "Now look, Stanley. All you have to do is keep your nose clean. Don't pick any fights with Kathleen. Just go along, and do what she tells you. And keep your mouth shut."

From under his sandy brows, Findlay's bright brown eyes peered up at him with hope, and Charles went on to say rather more than he had intended.

"But I think you should get busy, Stan. Look around for something other than politics. So long as Kathleen's here, you probably have no long-term future prospects. Once she gets her own crew in, it's likely she'll have no further need of you."

The westerner's face fell. "Jacques, you know I've got eight kids in school. And Joan, who spends money like a drunk. Where the hell am I going to find a job that pays me the kind of money I need? I've cut all my old business ties. I've made politics my life, and I always figured I'd be taken care of. Other people have been appointed to cushy jobs with good pay and lotsa perk—like the chairman of Air Canada, or the Transport Board, or the Capital Commission. Why not me? I just wouldn't know where to begin to look. I can't very well start answering Help Wanted ads," he finished with a kind of touching, simple dignity.

Charles felt a sudden guilty twinge of pity for the man. It was a problem he, with his inherited wealth, had never had to worry about. But, he shrugged mentally, he wasn't responsible for other people's problems. He was about to ease Findlay out with some platitude or another, when a sudden thought struck him.

"All right, Stan. I'll tell you what I'll do. I can't promise you anything, but I'll call a couple of people I know. Maybe they can find something lucrative for you. I'll get back to you. Now"—and he let his face soften into a rather wintry smile—"get out of here so I can get back to work."

When the big man had left, mumbling words of gratitude, Charles leaned across his desk and punched the intercom.

"Christianne, see if you can get me Willis Cranston in Montreal, please. Let me know when he's on the line." While he awaited the call, he unlocked the lower desk drawer and drew from it the memorandum. Although he knew every word on the one page of paper, he reread it for perhaps the hundredth time that day. He devoutly hoped it would never be seen by any other eyes.

The call came Wednesday morning as Kathleen stepped out of her bath. It was Richard Sherwood, the Conservative leader of Her Majesty's Loyal Opposition.

"Congratulations, Kathleen. I know you must be snowed under, but I think it's imperative that we have a talk. Could you and Andrew come here for dinner, tonight? I know it's very short notice but the matter I need to talk to you about is quite urgent. Can you possibly make it?"

"Certainly, Woody. Andrew is coming in later this afternoon and we had planned a quiet dinner for two. But of course, if it's as urgent as you say, we can change our plans. What time? Black tie?"

"About eight and make it informal. Would you mind if I also invited Terry Malloy and a few others?"

"Does this involve Parliamentary business?" she hedged. Kathleen barely knew the leader of the NDP, and she had always found his holier-than-thou attitude in the House very irritating.

"In a way. I'm inviting him as a kind of cover, in case the press should learn of our meeting. Anyway, it could prove useful for you to meet with him informally," he chuckled.

Kathleen had a quick impression of Sherwood, the stooped

lean figure, the sculptured head with its crop of greying curls, the kind eyes. Kathleen and Richard represented opposing political parties, but although they rarely saw one another outside the environs of the House, they had always had a certain rapport. A nice man, Richard Sherwood, Kathleen had often thought; but not tough enough to lead that rambunctious party of Tories.

"Yes, of course," she assured him. "I'm sure Malloy won't bite. And Woody, thank you for the telegram. It was very thoughtful of you."

"Least I could do, my dear. But as for Terry, never make the assumption that he won't bite. The man is a barracuda whenever he sees the chance. Don't *ever* trust him!"

Kathleen was surprised by the sudden venom in Sherwood's voice, but before she could comment, Sherwood said lightly, "Anyway, Martha will stuff him with so much food tonight he won't be *able* to bite."

Andrew was shaving as she towelled herself vigorously.

"You don't mind about tonight, do you, darling? I had looked forward to a quiet evening together, but I could scarcely say no to Sherwood, when he put it on an urgent basis. Anyway, it shouldn't take long. We can have a pleasant evening and slip away early."

She looked at Andrew for confirmation. He didn't like to carry on a conversation when he was shaving—"broke his concentration," he said. He had resisted her suggestion that he switch to an electric shaver, because he "hated the damned contraptions." And truth to tell, Kathleen loved the marvelous smell of him after a fresh shave, and the firm, whisker-free tanned face, the skin softened and smoothed by the billowing shaving cream.

Her tall, distinguished-looking husband had been quiet since his arrival. Andrew looked tired, she thought. He had briefly kissed her hello, then had gone straight away to shower and shave. It wasn't like him to be quite so taciturn. He had probably had a heavy day himself before he flew back to Ottawa, arriving later than he had planned. A pleasant evening with stimulating company would help relax him. It would be just what he needed.

The car moved slowly along Acacia, then turned into the short drive of the opposition leader's official residence, stopping under the protection of the *porte-cochère*. A cold wind was rising, and the sky was menacing with heavy jumbled clouds. Snow was expected before morning.

Kathleen was surprised to be met at the door by her host himself, his quiet wife hovering behind him making welcoming noises. This really was to be an informal evening—no maid, butler, or aide in sight.

Only once before had she been a guest at Stornoway, the official residence of the opposition leader. At that time she had arrived late and alone, after a struggle getting her miniatures—the dress version of her war medals—pinned on straight. The Governor General of the day and his lady had been guests of honour, and Kathleen had been stiff with nervousness. The invitation had made it clear that she was supposed to arrive before Their Excellencies, but her battered taxi had actually followed the vice-regal car into the drive. Kathleen had dropped her wrap quickly and darted into place at the very end of the line of guests waiting to be presented. She had curtsied, at the right time, but on the wrong foot, and felt a fool, her face blushing with embarrassment. She had loved on sight the Governor's wife, who had been so quick to help her regain her composure. That night, unlike tonight, there had been servants all over the place, so many that she had even mistaken one of the GG's aides in his evening livery for a waiter. Kathleen blushed to herself with the memory of how gauche she had once been. She was glad tonight was *not* formal. She looked around curiously.

The rather nondescript furniture in the high-ceilinged living room was almost shabby, but the effect was charming nonetheless. This place looked like a home, not like an official dwelling at all. Kathleen was well aware how difficult it was to accomplish that in one of these barn-like old places, and impulsively complimented her hostess. Martha Sherwood coloured with pleasure.

Richard Sherwood's wife was short and plump. Her grey curls were flyaway; her dark grey eyes small, but usually warm and bright. As always she was dressed in grey, so that the overall effect was a plump, cooing dove. Strangers were inclined to dismiss Martha lightly as being one of those regrettable mistakes made by ambitious politicians in early life, which they simply had no choice but to continue to live with. That early impression would be dispelled if one had the opportunity to observe the Sherwoods together. There was a kind of communion between them that told of two people happy in a relationship that was warm and deep and strong and familiar. Their glances touched often; and even when Richard was bent attentively to a guest, his wife's eyes followed him. Tonight, those bright grey eyes seemed troubled, Kathleen thought.

The dinner was simple but very good. Martha herself, it appeared, had done the cooking and the food was served on an ample buffet. There was a platter of chicken pieces, as well as an assortment of mysterious fragrant casseroles, warm, homemade beaten biscuits, salads and several rich but homey desserts—more than enough for the assembled guests, most of whom Kathleen had met before. Terry Malloy, leader of the NDP, greeted her without warmth, and only grudgingly introduced her to his painfully thin wife. The pair might have been brother and sister. They had in common carrot-red hair, his worn in a stiff military brush, hers in a rough mannish cut first made popular by the flappers of the twenties. Both had hard green eyes of a remarkably similar colour, and both wore expressions compounded of discontent and suspicion. They kept to themselves, disdaining to mingle with Sherwood's other guests.

As Kathleen settled before the fire with a plate of steaming food, she was joined by three young strangers. They introduced themselves and asked her permission to take places near her. The two men, it appeared, were both Conservative members first elected to the House two years ago, and the tense, unsmiling young woman was the new bride of the younger of the two. Adam Sorenson, the older and the more aggressive, took over the conversation. He was inquisitive, pelting Kathleen with questions about her successful campaign for leadership. He had a disconcerting habit of fixing his unblinking black eyes under their brilliantine-slicked cap of black hair, on her lips, rather than on her eyes. It made Kathleen self-conscious as she ate.

"So the outcome was never in doubt, really?" he asked abruptly.

"No, I said that *I* never doubted the outcome," Kathleen corrected. "But I confess I was shaken when Hume Frazier led on the first ballot. You see, normally the first-ballot leader keeps building on successive ballots."

"Yes, yes," Sorenson cut in impatiently. "I know all about that. I've made a study of leadership conventions. We'll be having one of our own, one of these days."

With a wide grin, his Adam's apple bobbing as he spoke,

the very tall, gangling young member in the ill-fitting green tweed suit asked, "You going to be a candidate, Adam?"

"I expect to," admitted the sharp-nosed freshman MP.

"I want Bill to run, too," spoke up the hitherto silent bride, laying her reddened, knuckly hand on her young husband's sleeve.

"Really?" Sorenson gave his young colleague a disparaging once-over. "Well, no reason why not. Good experience for you. It'll be wide open."

Kathleen set down her plate, excusing herself. She went to join Andrew, who had spent the past half hour gallantly making conversation with a couple of tongue-tied women staffers from Sherwood's office.

All too soon, Richard Sherwood rose to break up the little groups chatting together over emptied plates, and suggested, with apologies, that he and Kathleen and the NDP leader retire to the study for coffee.

"This, I hope, won't keep us too long from the others," their host said, as he waved Terry Malloy into a high-backed needlepoint-covered sofa in the small, cluttered room.

"Not sure why you put this meeting together, Sherwood," Malloy began a little testily, loosening his belt. He was a known trencherman, and had been seen to return to the buffet at least twice. "What are you two cooking up?"

"Nothing, I assure you, Terry. I wanted to speak to Kathleen privately for a few moments, it's true, but there hasn't yet been time for that. I knew she would want to meet with both of us, and this seemed a good time to do it. It never hurts to get to know fellow politicians a bit better, does it now?"

Malloy passed a hand over his stiff red brush. He wasn't very tall, and he had the cockiness common to many little men. "A banty rooster" was what he'd often been called, and Kathleen found the description apt. He had a long head with a pugnacious jaw, and carried himself with more than a hint of a swagger. When he walked his right shoulder always led, and he implanted his bowed legs in their heavy shoes with authority. In the echoing halls of the House of Commons no one ever mistook Terry Malloy's distinctive step. He had been a long-time union leader who had scrapped his way to the top. Many were surprised that a man of his aggressive, often abrasive personality had ever been selected to lead a national political party.

"I don't need to tell either of you that I'm not much for socializing with capitalists," he said now, in a surly voice. "We've learned that any time the likes of you start to get buddy-buddy with one of us, we have to look out for ourselves. You always want something."

It was not a very promising beginning, and Kathleen was impatient with Malloy's rudeness. She had come to expect it from him in the House, but had supposed that he would drop the chip-on-the-shoulder attitude while he was a guest in Sherwood's home.

"*I* don't want anything from you, Mr. Malloy," she protested, "I am just another guest here myself; but now that we are all here, it certainly could be useful to all of us to explore the possibilities if Parliament should be recalled."

"*If?* If, you say? So you *are* playing with the idea of a quick dissolution? Afraid to meet the House, are you?"

Kathleen brushed aside the challenging remark. "Of course, dissolution is always a possibility. But assuming the House is recalled, where do you stand on support for the Government? The two years you pledged just after the last election have about run out. Would you continue to support my administration, as you have Jacques'?"

"So that's what you want. I thought so," he sneered. "Well, Madame Leader, that probably depends upon how you go about it. Would Charles stay on as leader till you get a seat? Who would be running things? Would I have to deal with him, or with you?"

His tone was deliberately offensive to Kathleen, who struggled to remain polite.

"That's not decided yet, Terry. If Jacques were to be replaced by someone else—maybe the House leader—until I could get a seat, would you be prepared to pledge your support for, say, another year?"

"Why should I? I've already taken plenty of crap for going along with Charles for this long. Why should I make a deal to let you get established, so you could pick your own sweet time to go to the country? What's to be gained from that for me, or for the NDP?"

Richard Sherwood, their host, lifted a hand, breaking into the two-sided conversation. "Now calm down, Terry. Sure you have to remember your party's interests. Nobody expects otherwise. But how would it look if you pulled the plug right away, before Kathleen had a chance to make her mark as leader? It's one thing for her to decide to call an election, but

quite another thing for you lads to take advantage by preci-
pitating an election while she's fighting for a seat. The
Malloy's lined face flushed pink. His hard green eyes
snapped. He sat up straight in his chair and wagged a stubby
finger at the others. "Dirty pool, is it? Well, what do you two
expect from us, the great unwashed? Politics is no game to us,
even if it is to you. I only know one rule—fight like hell. I'm
not troubled with playing by gentlemen's rules. Or a lady's
either," he tossed at Kathleen. "In politics, you just gotta take
your chances."

"I take it, then, that there is no room for discussion at all
country wouldn't like that. It's just plain dirty pool."
on that point," Kathleen interjected icily.

"That's it, Kathleen Marshal Wickstrom—no deals. No
deals," he repeated. He grinned widely, with something akin
to malice glinting in his stony eyes. "And if you're looking for
a by-election, you may be sure there'll be an NDP candidate
against you—in case you were going to ask us for an
acclamation," he added. With that the NDP leader propelled
himself from his chair and addressed himself to his host.
"Thanks for the dinner, Sherwood. I'm going. No, don't
bother. I can see myself out."

Richard Sherwood rose at once, however, following his
guest from the room while mutely motioning Kathleen to
remain where she was. As he assisted the Malloys with their
coats, he maintained the benign air of the host, cheerily
speeding his guests homeward, but when he reappeared in the
study, he sighed wearily as he lowered himself into a rocker.

"Malloy really is a monumental pain in the ass, isn't he?"
Kathleen laughed.

"Now, Kathleen, at least you know where you stand with
that moral runt. Don't forget, however," he said kindly, "that
support might come to you from other directions. *We* are,
after all, the Official Opposition, and there are a lot more PC's
in the House than there are NDP's."

"But *you* can't make any blanket commitment, Richard.
Your caucus would never stand for it. If you tried to force it
you would face open revolt. I can just imagine the trouble
you'd have—even with freshmen like your young Sorenson."

He nodded in agreement, then said thoughtfully, "But they
might go along—under certain circumstances, Kathleen—and
that's really why I asked you here. We'll have to rejoin the

others soon, but I have something to tell you that just might make the Conservative caucus support you for that year you need. Not, I admit, because they would want to, but because they would have no other choice."

Kathleen's hazel eyes widened, but she said nothing to interrupt his flow of thought. For a moment he fell silent, seeking the right words. His guest lit a cigarette, willing him to continue. Slowly, he pushed himself up from his chair and walked to the window, turning his back to her, his silver grey curls haloed against the night.

"No one knows what I am about to tell you, Kathleen. No one but my wife. And my doctor. I count on you to respect my confidence."

"Of course," she murmured, puzzled.

"It seems I am a sick man. No use beating about the bush—it's leukemia. Nobody knows how long I've got left, but the doctor says I have to get out of politics. My wife has made me promise to quit just as soon as I can; so we can have whatever time there is left together. I'm prepared to quit now, but I can't do that. It isn't that simple," he sighed heavily, taking the few steps necessary to stand squarely in front of her, his troubled eyes looking directly into hers.

"No, don't say anything yet." He raised his hand, restraining her, and Kathleen choked back instinctive words of sympathy. "I could announce my retirement immediately, then carry on until there's a convention to replace me as leader. That would give you maybe six months, and afterwards it isn't likely that my successor would try to bring you down right away. So you'd have your year, do you see? Maybe even longer."

"And if I should decide on a snap election now?" she asked softly, her eyes steady on his.

"Then I would have to stay, and do the best I could, for as long as I could. The doctors won't promise that I could even make it through a campaign. But I would have to try." There was an air of quiet resignation in his soft-spoken answer.

"Oh, Woody!" The cry was wrung from her. "How ... inadequate ... to say how sorry I am. No wonder Martha looks so anxious. You've been so kind to me in the past and I had looked forward to working in the House with you. Now—"

"Kathleen, I know this is unfair of me. But if you hold off on an election, I can go quickly—leave the leadership. I know you have to think of your party's best interests, but maybe you'll find that this isn't the best time for an election anyway. After all, it hasn't even been two years since the last one, and Canada is a bit fed up with them. Maybe you would do better to consolidate yourself in the House—try to build up your own record there—put some distance between you and Charles—before you ask the country to give you a mandate." He reached for her hand, and helped her to her feet. "I'm not asking for any decision right now, of course, but I just thought you ought to know *before* you decide."

Her eyes filled with tears. She brushed them away as he placed his arm round her.

"Come on now. We'd better join the others before they think we're in here making deals—or making love," he joked, as he led her from the room.

Later, Kathleen lay sleepless in the big bed beside her husband. She hadn't yet told Andrew of Richard Sherwood's confidence. Andrew knew that she had already almost decided that her best course would be to call a general election immediately.

But, she asked herself as she restlessly rolled her head from side to side upon the bunched pillows, how can I do that when it means condemning a friend to almost certain death, leaving him no time with his wife? Sherwood would never let his own party know the truth. He would never let them down. And it would kill him. No, *I* would kill him! I would be responsible. Oh dear God, how could I live with that? A sob caught at her throat as she remembered Sherwood's many kindnesses to her.

At 541 Acacia, Martha Sherwood tapped at the study door. Living room, dining room, and kitchen were now tidy again, glasses and dishes stacked in the dishwasher, leftovers carefully wrapped and refrigerated. Their guests were long gone into the blustery night—all, except Adam Sorenson. The young M.P. had been closeted with Richard for almost an hour, and Martha had heard his strident voice raised more than once as she busied herself readying the house for the night. Normally, she would not dream of interrupting her husband while he was talking with his political supporters, but it was already late, and Martha knew how quickly such confrontations could sap Richard's dwindling strength.

At her entrance, Sherwood looked up gratefully. He clearly

had had enough for this evening. He was irritated, even angered, by his one-time protégé's rudeness and argumentiveness with his other guests, and for the past hour, he had been forced to beat back the aggressive young member's demands to call the Liberal's bluff if Kathleen chose to avoid a general election and meet the House. Adam Sorensen, Sherwood's one-time policy assistant, was spoiling for a fight, sure the Conservatives could wage a successful campaign now. He was eager to force a confrontation before Kathleen had time to settle in as the new leader.

Adam ignored his hostess, so intent was he on his argument.

"Woody, I tell you, now's the time. If she goes to the country, we'll all work like hell, and we'll beat her, mark my words. And if she chickens out, then we ought to hit her with everything we can scrape up—never let the public forget she's nothing but a little cosmetic on the face of that old whore—the Charles' Government. We should do everything we can to pull her down, first chance we get. I tell you, she's ripe for the plucking," he continued with obvious relish. "All we gotta do is work our asses off, and you'll be prime minister within the year. I guarantee it," he added brashly.

Martha's hand flew to her mouth to block her protest. Her anguished eyes locked with her husband's who shook his head, negatively. They both knew that if Adam Sorensen had his way, Richard Sherwood wouldn't be prime minister. Not within the year. Not ever. He would be dead if he "worked his ass off," as his colleage urged.

For a moment, Sherwood contemplated Sorenson. Where, he wondered to himself, had the often shy, almost always charming young man he had first plucked from the party's ranks to bring here to work in his office, gone? Sorenson, with the ink still fresh on his master's degree in business administration, had proved indefatigable, a master of detail. He had gradually come to take over liaison with the Progressive Conservative party and, with his wide circle of friends and acquaintances there, had rapidly developed his own power base. Richard had been glad to help him win a nomination, and to render every possible assistance in his freshman outing, glad to have Adam return to Ottawa as a member. But he regretted that somewhere along the way the young man's objectivity appeared to have been lost. Sorenson's frustration, his contempt for the Government, his hatred of the Liberals had increased since he had taken his seat in the House. Now he was unable to see any good whatsoever in the Grits. He was champing at the bit to turf them out.

Sherwood heaved a deep sigh. He wondered whether he should reveal to Adam the precarious state of his own health, and the plea he had made only hours earlier to Kathleen. But he immediately dismissed the idea. No one must know. Nor must he ever reveal his pledge to Kathleen to keep her in office until he was replaced as leader. He sighed again at the thought that he would experience a long hard fight from people like Sorenson in his own caucus, to keep that pledge. But he had sought the favour from the Liberal leader, and he had freely offered the pledge. He must keep to it, no matter how difficult.

Stanley Findlay and his wife Joan were dining out at the invitation of their new acquaintances from Montreal. The stately hotel's Grille Room was panelled, dark, and rather sedate. Even if the food was notoriously indifferent, there was an unobtrusive, mellow dance orchestra. It was much preferred by their generation over the heavy metallic beat of rock or the insensate pound of the all-too-prevalent disco music offered elsewhere in Ottawa's upscale watering holes.

The two couples occupied a plush-upholstered booth along one side of the long, shadowy room, the two dinner-jacketed men bracketing the women in their long, festive gowns. Joan Findlay wore rustling taffeta in a shade of jade just slightly too bright for elegance, her plump pink arms gleaming from the long, slashed sleeves of the oddly unfashionable, although obviously new, gown. Her hair was freshly done, piled on her head in fat auburn coils. As she bent her head to catch a comment from the younger woman beside her, light flashed from the rhinestone clips glinting at her bosom.

She looks marvellous, thought Findlay, with a satisfaction he didn't always feel about his wife. No one would ever guess that she has eight kids and spends half of each day working in my office, without pay. She can really hold her own with anyone, he concluded with a sense of proud possessiveness; but he was suddenly less certain of that when his gaze rested on Giselle Cranston.

His hostess was very stylish, he noticed, and unquestionably a beauty. That long straight fall of lustrous brown hair, those dark, dancing eyes framed in sweeping lashes, that perfect *café au lait* skin, that full-lipped, curving mouth. And what a figure! He suddenly realized that his not-so-covert scrutiny was not going unnoticed. Giselle was looking full at him, in just as frank an assessment. Apparently she liked what she saw.

Stanley Findlay dared a glance at her husband. Had Cranston noticed too? My God, he would have to be more careful. It just wouldn't do to alienate Will Cranston. He was too powerful, too important to Stanley's own future. Still, the big westerner could hardly keep his eyes from roaming to the petite Frenchwoman's décolletage. Although Giselle's brown velvet gown was deceptively simple, its neckline plunged very low, revealing glimpses of a high round bosom, startlingly lush in such a tiny, slender woman. Somehow, compared to Giselle, Joan now seemed ... what? A little vulgar, maybe. Out of date, overdressed, whatever.

Willis Cranston—or "Will," but never "Bill"—enjoyed other men's admiration of his wife. Just so long as they only looked, and never touched. Giselle was an ornament, a possession, bought and paid for, for his own use alone.

Cranston himself was of no more than average height, several inches shorter than his guest, and perhaps a dozen years older. He didn't take care of his body, so that it had noticeably thickened, although superb tailoring hid his more than fledgling paunch. He looked sleek and well cared for, in comparison to the tall, rough-hewn Minister, awkwardly ill at ease in his dated tuxedo. Cranston was smooth. He looked like what he was—a man of money and privilege, the product of a good education, too much good food, the weekly sunlamp and the regular masseur and manicurist.

The older man's forehead was high and dome-shaped. Sharp inroads tracked into his hairline above each brow. His expression was normally bland and his manner affable, but anyone who had ever crossed him in business could attest to the way his mild eyes could suddenly congeal into marbles when he was angered. More than one career had been ruined when Willis Cranston unleashed his power, implacably, against the offender. He could and would with relish break anyone he chose.

The Cranstons were an old Montreal family—now impoverished, some said. But Will had nonetheless made his own success. His business interests were obviously highly remunerative, even if quite mysterious. There were rumours of Mafia connections and worse, but whatever he touched seemed to turn to gold. He was a wheeler and dealer, but in the most discreet and circumspect way. Shady some of his deals might be termed, but the law had never touched him, for he was careful, very careful, and not about to let anyone forget that the soft, manicured hand could, when he chose, become a hurtful claw of steel.

Will Cranston's languid eyes had noted, without appearing to, the glances Findlay seemed unable to resist, but he wasn't disturbed. It didn't impress him that the big westerner was a federal Cabinet Minister. Politicians came a dime a dozen by Cranston's reckoning, especially those that were about to be booted out of the Cabinet, as Jean Jacques Charles had told him Findlay was. No, Stanley Findlay posed no threat to Willis Cranston—he was too hungry. The Energy Minister needed a job where he could make money—lots of money—and quickly, and there weren't many other avenues open to him. Cranston was sure that Findlay's lechery would be bridled by his greed. He'd not nibble in this forbidden pasture. Of if he dared, the Montrealer thought with a flash of savagery, I'll break him. It was as simple as that.

He studied the menu. "The oysters, I think. They should be superb right now, and the hotel at long last has begun to bring in fresh fish from the coast. They damn well had to or lose the last of their old customers. How about the rack of lamb? Probably frozen, but the chef here has a way with it. All right, then. Salads. And vegetables—fresh, mind you, waiter. And afterward, a soufflé—Grand Marnier will be splendid. And some cheese, coffee. For now, another round of drinks, and let me have the wine list."

Cranston waved away the hovering waiter, who was at once replaced by the wine-steward, the silver tasting-cup of the sommelier dangling from a knotted silk neck-cord. Cranston scanned the poster-sized padded wine list presented with a flourish. He chose a wine by pointing to it wordlessly, then dismissed the functionary peremptorily to turn his attention to the others at the table. None of them had been invited to make a selection, nor had they even been consulted. It was like that with Will Cranston—he expected to pay, and to pay well. He expected that his guests would be content to eat whatever he ordered.

There were those who admired his take-charge manner, and others who were annoyed by it. Among the latter was his wife, the beautiful Giselle Cranston. Giselle was the second of Will's wives, fifteen years his junior, although she appeared twenty-five years younger. Giselle appreciated the advantages that had come her way when she became Mrs. Willis Cranston—fine food, lustrous furs, jewels, designer clothes, the chauffered limousine and her own sleek, powerful sportscar. travel (always first class), the beautiful home in Westmount and the villa in the south, each with its carefully trained, discreet staff. But she didn't really like her husband. Will Cranston was dreadfully inept in bed. She met his friends and business associates often, but for the most part, although they were rich and often powerful, they were old and, like Cranston, running to fat. They were almost devoid of witty conversation. They didn't even flirt with her. They were all poor candidates for a satisfactory extra-marital fling. The truth was that, like her husband himself, they bored her.

Stanley Findlay, however, was something else. There was a kind of earthy magnetism about him, a kind of animal intensity beneath his casual, almost rumpled appearance, that stirred her interest. While the Minister of Energy could hardly be called handsome in any conventional way, he had craggy, interesting features, extraordinarily bright, round berry-brown eyes, a slow, disarming smile. Stanley Findlay exuded an air of solid, if rough, masculinity. It was common knowledge that he had eight children and a wife who rarely let him out of her sight. Giselle found him oddly exciting. The big westerner was sexy. Yes, definitely sexy.

Giselle speculated that here was a man who enjoyed women. Or would, if ever released from his wife's constant vigilance. It was clear that he was attracted to her, even if his gaze kept returning, not to her piquant face, but to the swelling curve of her breasts in this new and quite daring dress. Yes, Stanley Findlay was definitely displaying interest, but Giselle was ever conscious that she must be circumspect and careful. Willis had eyes in the back of his head where she was concerned, and she had heard enough about Joan Findlay to know that the plump lady in garish green was determined to protect her own. Go slow, Giselle told herself. I'll get him to dance with me a little later. There's nothing wrong with that. And then, we'll see.

Later, at Giselle's arch suggestion, they did dance. The tiny, curvaceous woman pressed against Stanley, her body moving closely against his to the slow, throbbing rhythm. She could feel him harden against her in an involuntary physical reaction, but he said nothing. Instead, he self-consciously loosened his hold on her slightly. She looked up at the tall man, laughing tauntingly at his obvious embarrassment.

He looked down at her, and roughly pulled her close again. They concluded their dance wordlessly, glued together from breast to knee. As he bowed her into the banquette seat, his gaze stroked her breasts like a hot hand, where they strained against the sumptuous dark brown cloth. Giselle's nipples were erect and obvious. Findlay sank back into his own seat. He hadn't had much opportunity to experience extra-marital liaisons with Joan so constantly at his side, but he recognized a voluptuous invitation when it was offered. If only he dared accept it. Suddenly he realized that his host was speaking to him. He had not heard what was said, his mind still filled with confusion, the imprint of Giselle's sexuality still upon him, her perfume still drowning his senses.

He heard his wife speak. "Of course Stanley is interested, Will. You know, he is a very able man, a brilliant Minister of Energy. It's just that it's time for him to leave politics. We've been here over ten years. He's done his service to his country. Now it's time he began to think of himself, and his family. You know we have eight beautiful children. It's expensive—nannies and good schools and all the right advantages. It's very difficult when you have only a Cabinet minister's salary. And it isn't as if it's easy to settle on the right job offer. You know, he's not supposed to make any job commitments while he's still a Minister. Isn't that ridiculous? As if a man could just quit, when he has nothing lined up to step into."

Stan laid a restraining hand on the plump, bared arm. "I doubt Willis is interested, Joan. After all, he's offering me a job, isn't he?" Turning to Cranston, he said a little uncertainly, "I'm none too sure of the details, but I suppose this isn't the place to discuss them anyway, before the women."

"Stan!" his wife said, indignantly. "You know we always talk over your career moves. I want to know what the offer is all about. After all, it's my future, too—mine and the children's. There is absolutely no sense in your jumping out of the Cabinet before we're sure that the job has a future. It has to be well-paid and, well, dignified. After all, you're a Minister of the Crown, and it wouldn't be suitable for you to take just any old job. And you know, we couldn't afford it," she said, pouting a little.

Willis Cranston looked at Joan Findlay with interest, although his face remained as smooth and expressionless as ever. So this is the one who wears the pants in the Findlay family, he thought to himself. He admired the plump little woman for her nerve. Imagine her, he thought, trying to strike a bargain with me! She has more guts than Findlay has, and maybe more brains, too. She wasn't about to be drawn in by vague promises. She was clearly too hard-nosed. Ambitious. And shrewd. Surprising when she looked like such a country bumpkin, all tarted up for an evening out.

"We really haven't had time to discuss this fully, Will," Findlay interjected. "I haven't absolutely made up my mind to leave politics," he added lamely, glad that Cranston didn't know that it was really Kathleen who was likely to precipitate his retirement.

Joan Findlay leaned forward, placing her plump, beringed hand on the soft fabric of Cranston's black sleeve. "We really appreciate that you've been so kind, Will, and taken such an interest in us. My husband wouldn't dream of doing anything to offend you—I'm sure you realize that. But don't you see, it really isn't fair to ask him to just give you a blanket commitment, to follow you blindly, when he doesn't know what your plans are."

Cranston spoke directly to Joan. "Isn't it enough, the prospect of making money—a lot of money—and for only a few months' work?" he asked, as he bit off the end of a cigar.

"For now, of course, that's an exciting prospect. But there's the future to think of. What would he do after those few months? He has a fascinating job in government now. He can't abandon that for just a few months' work. And isn't a scheme that makes him a lot of money in only a few months likely to be risky?"

The overdressed woman was daring to barter with him, damn it. What nerve! If Joan Findlay had been a man, Cranston wouldn't have stood for it. But she wasn't a man. Just a very stubborn lady, sure of herself and her control over her husband. And not such a bad-looking lady, either, if you liked that slightly faded, Klondike-hooker look.

Stanley Findlay was silent, a little frightened by his wife's habitual boldness. Instinctively, he knew that Will Cranston was just not the man you could talk to that way, for all his surface polish. Maybe, once again, Joan had gone too far. Findlay already, many times over the years, had cause to regret his ambitious, determined wife's interference in his business. She had made him extra enemies in the past, in her zealous pursuit of what she judged best for his career. He really ought to lay down the law with her, but it was already probably too late. If she's queered this, he thought, glaring at Joan. He really didn't like her much, he suddenly realized.

Cranston was amused. "As a matter of fact, I've had some thoughts about what you might do, after your initial assignment. Of course, it depends on how well you do first time out."

Findlay glanced at the other man, trying to conceal his eagerness. An inner feeling told him this whole deal involved big money.

"Your portfolio's been Energy," Cranston continued. "Well, this job ought to suit you to a 'T.' After that, the sky's the limit for a good businessman with the right connections. I'm looking for a man who can move in and make the final arrangements on certain contracts. The contracts involve a lot. The commissions are, well, more than adequate."

Findlay smiled. He didn't look at his wife. He didn't dare.

"Well?" Cranston said. "Do you want a fling at this business? It's sometimes risky, sure, but that's what makes it highly profitable."

Stanley Findlay remained silent once again, balancing the prospect against the present. Why, he could be an instantly rich man, and powerful. Never, of course, as powerful as Cranston, although he might become his heir apparent. But that would mean good-bye forever to politics. He'd have to give up all that—the career he'd worked so hard at, hoped for so much from. It would be back to the dog-eat-dog world of business. No security. No pension. No guarantee. But big money. No need to kowtow to Jean Jacques Charles, or pussy-foot around Kathleen Marshal. The prospect stirred him with a growing excitement, a growing resolve to risk it, but before he could speak, Joan intervened.

"Thank you, Willis, that's quite helpful. It will make it so much easier for Stansie to make his decision, now that you have spelled out your plans for him."

Stanley flinched at the use of her term of endearment, as Joan sat back, well satisfied that she had provoked Cranston as she had others before him, into making a commitment to her husband.

"Of course, we'll have to take a few days to discuss it. We always decide these things together," she said smugly. "We do make such a good team, both at home and at the office, don't we, Stansie?"

Stanley glared at his wife. Why the hell did she have to start using that stupid nickname now?

Cranston leaned forward and stubbed his well-chewed cigar. "Sure, take a week or so, if you like. But I'll need to know soon."

"I've got a Cabinet meeting tomorrow. An important one." Findlay wanted to emphasize the fact that he wasn't out of a job—not yet anyway. "But after that maybe we'll take a week or so off and talk it over."

"Why not use our place in the Bahamas," Willis Cranston offered. "After your important Cabinet meeting, of course. We have a spread down there that we don't use as much as we'd like."

Joan's eyes opened wide at the thought of the Bahamas in February. She and Stan rarely had the time—or the money—for lavish holidays.

"Matter of fact," Will went on calmly, noting the effect his suggestion had on the hitherto reluctant Mrs. Findlay, "Giselle is planning to go down anyway in a day or so, and I'm going to join her for the weekend. Why not go with her? Okay?" He tossed the question at his wife without looking at her, sure of her response.

"Of course, Will," Giselle said eagerly.

And so it was decided. The Findlays would join their hostess in a day or so, on exclusive Lyford Cay, in the siren islands of the Bahamas.

Chapter Three

The last rays of a setting sun reflected into the Oval Office and cast a halo around the head of the man behind the desk. The President of the United States tipped back his chair, his gnarled hands clasped behind his neck. He faced his two aides, both of whom were in their early thirties. The President, who prided himself on "keeping in touch" with the younger generation, surrounded himself with people who were many years his junior.

William Concord Thompson liked this time of day best of all. At home, this was the hour when the workers came in from the fields, tired and dusty after an honest day's work. Sweat stained their worn denims and faded shirts. It was a time when a man could close his ledgers and leave his desk, secure in the knowledge that all was well. Of course, that was back home. The south, he reflected, still practised those values he held dear. William Thompson missed his home. He missed that daily feeling of accomplishment and satisfaction. It was something one only rarely, if ever, experienced in the White House. Besides, he thought ruefully, as President, he found the damned day's work was almost never done.

Billy Thompson was a man of medium build with greying blond hair. He flashed his square, strong teeth in his famous grin as he accepted a dark-gold glass of bourbon and branch water. Taking a long gulp of the drink, he smacked his lips in appreciation.

"Now, what's the story?" he asked. "What's she like, this new leader in Ottawa? What's her name again? Oh, I remember, Marshal, right?"

Larry Conover nodded affirmatively to answer the President's question.

The President shook his head in a gesture of both wonder and exasperation. "Imagine the Canadians picking a woman as leader! What's the world coming to? First England and now Canada! There'll be a helluva passel of coons treed before that'll happen in the good old U.S. of A. You can bet your bottom dollar on that! It's okay to have a few ladies in government, but I just can't imagine one running things here."

Diplomatically, both aides struggled to conceal smiles. It was no secret that the President's own lady was pretty close to running things. She even sat in on meetings of the Thompson Cabinet, a place where she shouldn't be at all since she held no official post and had not been confirmed by Congress as a Cabinet member.

Larry Conover cleared his throat and glanced down at the clipboard in his lap. It firmly held a sheaf of typed papers marked "Confidential."

"Kathleen Marshal is the name she uses. She's married to"—he rechecked the name to be sure—"a fellow named Andrew Wickstrom. He's a newspaper publisher—small weeklies, country and suburban papers mainly, but he's a man of some substance. No children; they've only been married a little over a year."

The President expressed surprise. He had been listening closely as he sipped his drink.

"Go on," he encouraged Conover. "What kind of person is she? Is she as tough as the Steel Butterfly the Limeys elected?"

Conover threw a glance at him, a flash of amusement gleaming from behind the heavy spectacles.

"Probably not, but it's too early to tell. Marshal has fine credentials. She's a veteran in federal politics. Spearheaded a drive to drop abortion as a crime when she was Charles' Minister of Justice. Must be a bit of a feminist. Then she suddenly dropped right out of politics a couple of years ago and got married. It surprised a lot of people when she contested the leadership." Conover paused for a moment and looked at the President. Then he flipped the paper on his board. "Oh, yes, she was acting prime minister for several months after the death of Alexander Sinclair—before Charles was elected leader. Seemed competent enough then, but she was only a caretaker."

The President leaned forward. "You say she's been out of politics? Doesn't a prime minister in Canada have to be elected and have a seat in Congress—I mean, Parliament?" The President was intrigued.

"Yes, sir, Mr. President, that's right. She'll have to appoint herself a senator, or get someone to quit to open up a seat for her so she can run in a by-election."

Robert E. Lee, the more junior of the two aides present,

added another piece of information. "She's got another alternative. She can call an election now. She doesn't have to wait till four years are up, as we do."

"Thanks, Bobby. I'd forgotten that," acknowledged the President. "Which is she likely to do?"

"Our Ambassador says the best guess is that she'll call a general election."

"Will she win it?" asked the older man with professional interest.

"Maybe. The Liberals have been in office for a long time. But Charles hasn't been very popular lately. That's why they pushed him out. Figured he had no chance of winning again."

"I see," said Thompson. For a moment he felt a kinship with the deposed Jean Jacques Charles. Thompson knew there were people in his own party who doubted his chances in the coming election. People who were already sharpening their knives for him, determined to deny him renomination for another term. Still, he had never really liked Charles much—too smooth, too arrogant, too independent. He turned to Lee, who sat attentively in the leather chair to one side of the wide, highly polished desk.

"I suppose I should meet her. Do I invite her down here?"

The young man pressed his lips together thoughtfully, and then offered his advice. "I doubt there's much hurry, Mr. President. Better wait and see whether Marshal is going to last. If she does, it might be the right opportunity to make that visit up to Canada. You haven't been there yet and the Canadians are a little miffed, seeing as you went to Mexico and all."

Billy Thompson nodded, his irritation at the reminder clear for both aides to read. He knew he should have visited the neighbouring capital when Jean Jacques Charles had invited him, but damn it, there were only so many hours in the day and weeks in the year. Besides, Canada would always be there. Sort of a stable place, not like Mexico which was always rocking the boat—or, more aptly, refusing to fuel it.

"Okay," he said, "we'll put that off for now. Is there anything else?"

Conover flipped over another sheet. "Yes, Mr. President. It's about Canada, too. The Ambassador has just about

finished his tour there. Have you thought about his replacement, or should we—?"

"Matter of fact I have," drawled Thompson, interrupting
him. He was glad for once to be a step ahead of his two
bright boys. "Talked to Governor Whiteside the other day.
He tells me he and the Marshal woman were once pretty
good friends. He didn't say just how good. He seemed very
receptive to my suggestion that he take over the embassy in
Canada. Eager, you might even say. Unusually eager for a
Republican. I thought it was a pretty smart idea. Never can
tell when we might need a friend at court up there."

Both his aides concurred. But it was decided that the
announcement of the Governor's appointment be postponed
until events indicated that Kathleen Marshal would last as
Prime Minister of Canada.

The Cabinet met at Harrington Lake. When Kathleen arrived, the drive was already packed with ministers' cars. A
raw, damp wind whistled across the frozen lake, driving
streaks of grainy snow across its corrugated surface. It was
one of those days in Ottawa when one despaired that spring
would never arrive.

Kathleen stepped from her car, muffled in the folds of her
luxurious fur coat. The unsightly rent had now been profes-
sionally repaired, but she found her fingers straying to the
sleeve, as if to remind herself of the incident before her
entrance to 24 Sussex.

She picked her way across the driveway being careful not
to slip in her high-heeled boots. Patches of ice clotted the
stubble of the frozen grass and made the short walk haz-
ardous. A security man hovered nearby, but she waved away
his offered arm.

The door swung open and Jean Jacques Charles stood
waiting to receive her. Kathleen noted in her first sweeping
glance that almost all the ministers were in attendance. They
had obviously been sprawled around the room in a rough
semi-circle, with some of the junior ministers relegated to
cushions on the floor. As their new leader entered, they
scrambled to their feet from their various relaxed positions
on chairs, chesterfields, and footstools.

A fire roared in the fireplace. Dressed as she was in a
brown tweed suit over a belted, long-sleeved turtleneck,
Kathleen was struck by the oppressive heat in the room as

soon as she took the place indicated by the Prime Minister. It was a high-backed, padded rustic rocking chair which faced its twin across the hearth. Both chairs still betrayed, by their gentle continuing motion, that they had been occupied when her arrival had interrupted the gathering.

The ministers were dressed casually in sport shirts and cardigans or heavy pullovers. Nary a tie among them. Only the Prime Minister wore an ascot stuffed into the open collar of his shirt. Kathleen greeted each by name. Even those she hadn't known before she left the Cabinet were already familiar either from the convention or from newspaper stories.

Of the group she had seen only a few since the convention. But she had talked several times by phone with Harry Williams, the bibulous Minister of National Health and Welfare. He was a former Cabinet colleague and a firm and unwavering friend. She acknowledged the presence of Stanley Findlay, formerly Jacques' Minister of Transport, now of Energy, and beside him, his fellow westerner, Bentley Palmer, with whom she had crossed swords at the last meeting of the Cabinet she had attended some two years before. Gabriel LaCroix, Leader of the Senate and Jacques' long-time associate and very close friend, sat at the Prime Minister's left. He wore a multi-striped *ceinture fléchée* belted loosely over his coarse, hand-woven tunic in the *habitant* style of early Quebec.

As Kathleen seated herself, the others also returned to their places. Immediately, a chunky woman in a voluminous starched white kitchen apron, her hair knotted behind her head, silently passed among them, offering each a heavy white cup of steaming, fragrant coffee. Silence followed the homey little bustle created by the serving of the coffee. When the room was completely still, Jacques laid his cup beside him on the hearth and began to speak.

"Welcome back to Cabinet, Kathleen. As always, we keenly await your remarks." There was a sly gleam of amusement in the hooded blue eyes, at odds with the inference of his words.

"Gentlemen," she began—there were no women members in the Charles' Cabinet since she herself had left—"I won't detain you long today. I shall want each of you to prepare for me a synopsis of your departmental plans, and I'll meet with each of you individually as soon as possible. Today, I want your help in party matters, rather than government business. I would like your views on whether this is an appropriate time for dissolution of Parliament. You will recall that Jacques himself went to the people for a personal mandate immediately after he became leader. Is this the time to repeat that strategy?" Even to her ears, the little speech sounded stilted and aloof.

"The alternative being—?" This from Jake Wilson, the veteran Minister of Labour. He was sprawled on the pillowed chesterfield, between the smooth-faced Minister of Finance and the hearty Tod Proudfoot, Minister of Agriculture. Kathleen was on good terms with all three men, even though none had figured largely in the convention result. At this point, she was not sure whether they were for her or against her. That was yet to be learned.

"The alternative being, naturally, that the Government will carry on, until I have won a by-election seat," she said patiently.

"Who would act as prime minister in that period?" barked Stanley Findlay.

"Will it be Jacques?" followed up Senator LaCroix.

Kathleen's gaze lingered on these two ministers, probably the closest of all to Jean Jacques Charles.

Through the years of their past association, she had always found the now-diminished LaCroix a likeable, if highly volatile, colleague. She felt quite differently about Jacques' Minister of Energy, however. Stanley Findlay's plodding, phlegmatic, humourless style had set Kathleen's nerves on edge almost from their first meeting. She had never been able to understand the friendship between the quicksilver Charles and the slow-moving, slow-thinking, sandy-haired westerner. Alone among the Cabinet, Stanley Findlay had joined Senator LaCroix in openly supporting Charles' bid to continue on in the leadership. Whatever the unlikely bonds between Findlay and Charles, the convention had no doubt strengthened them.

Kathleen made a mental note to keep her eye on Findlay, so long as he was permitted to stay around.

"That depends," she answered shortly.

"On what?" asked Stan flatly.

"Partly on what I learn from you. On what my other advisors recommend. On the party's attitude. And on Jacques' own plans." All eyes shifted to the Prime Minister, rocking gently across the width of the fireplace from her.

Jean Jacques Charles lifted his eyes for a moment to Kathleen's and then his glance swept the circle of ministers, aware that each was alert to the undercurrents of tension.

"Well, Prime Minister, are you going to tell us what those plans are?" boomed the voice of Harry Williams.

Good old Harry, Kathleen applauded silently. Maybe he can get a straight answer where I have failed.

"That, my friend, as our leader says, depends." He raised a hand, acknowledging the faint groans that had greeted his remark. "It depends upon what our new leader has in mind, of course. I am entirely at her disposal."

Kathleen sucked in her breath. The effrontery of him, throwing the ball back into her court!

There was a murmur of sound among the ministers, some of whom obviously approved of the Prime Minister's cagey attitude. They settled back to watch what promised to be a heated sparring match between the old leader and the new. But there was a deeper note, almost a growl, from those of the ministers who hoped this meeting would clear the air, not cloud it.

"In that case," Kathleen said, firmly refusing the bait, "I shall have to be blunt. I expect an honest answer from each of you, no matter how embarrassing; what is the likely impact upon the public if Jaques is still visibly heading the Government after losing the leadership? I need your frank appraisal of the situation before I make a final decision." She turned to look at Charles then said, "Perhaps, Jacques, it would be easier for them to be candid if you were to step out for half an hour. Perhaps you could take a walk or something."

Jacques' eyes widened, an expressive eyebrow raised, but he said nothing. He stood up and, making a mocking little bow to Kathleen, announced, "I'll see to lunch," then walked casually from the crowded room to disappear behind the kitchen's swinging door.

The tension in the overheated room eased at once, although Jacques' absence did not dispel it entirely. As each minister expressed his opinion, he and the others were aware that there were among them more than a few pairs of eyes and ears which would shortly carry to the Prime Minister a report naming those who were anxious to see him go.

The attitudes and assessments made by the ministers offered few surprises. The younger, more junior of them unanimously favoured a quick election. Their enthusiasm to mount the hustings was still fired up by the convention. Older heads were more restrained. Most of those, the experienced campaigners, hated elections, although whenever a writ was issued, they managed to enjoy themselves, albeit grudgingly.

They knew that the democratic process was chancy at best. Once launched on a general election, despite advance polls and samplings, no one could ever be certain of the results. Their jobs would be on the line. It was a matter of record that, barring an unforeseen sweep, such as the one that had carried Jean Jacques Charles to his first overwhelming parliamentary majority, in each selection nearly a third of the members would fall by the wayside. They had been through it all less than two years ago, and none was eager to submit himself again to the vagaries of the voters.

A couple of the ministers also pointed out that, as yet, Kathleen had no record of her own to campaign on, and that it was too soon to gauge the reaction of the public to the Liberal party's selection of a woman as leader.

Most of the arguments in favour of an immediate general election were the same as those expressed by Kathleen's inner Seven advisors. The most forceful was the possibility that the Government, in its present minority position, might be defeated if the NDP pulled the plug, or if the Conservatives found an issue on which they could join the NDP.

Kathleen reminded herself of Richard Sherwood's confidence, but kept silent, hugging to herself the knowledge that she could count on support from that quarter, if need be.

"What's the use of talking?" Stan Findlay said recklessly. "We all know you'll wind up doing whatever you want to, anyway."

Even Senator LaCroix winced at the baldness of his colleague's comment.

"I understood that to be part of my job, Minister," Kathleen rebuked him, although her voice was soft.

"Well, why waste our time jawing then?" he said truculently.

"Have you better things to do?" she asked, her expression sweet, a danger signal to those who knew her best.

"We all have," he muttered, suddenly aware that he might have gone too far.

Kathleen's mouth tightened. She was casting about for the right retort, when another minister waved a hand to distract her attention. Time enough to deal with Stanley Findlay later, she promised herself, nodding to Armand Asselin, the thoughtful member from Quebec City who now held the post of Attorney-General. He was firmly against the idea of a general election now, no matter what problems might be encountered if she decided on the alternative.

"In my view, *madame*, if you go to the country now, you will lose Quebec. And without Quebec. . . ." He drew his hand in a short jerky motion across his throat. "You must not discount the fact that the province will be deeply hurt by the rejection of their native son as Prime Minister. It will take time for that initial reaction to fade. And it may *never* fade. It will depend upon you whether the province takes out its anger against the party at the polls."

His words carried Kathleen back to her meeting with the inner Seven. Then, the advice about Quebec had been quite different. Then, her instinct had been to be cautious. Armand Asselin was not one of her close advisors or confidants, therefore his reserve about the mood in Quebec might well be more on the mark. She was glad to have something more to weigh—something that would help her make her decision. Here was a political consideration, one which could go into the same column as her emotional consideration for Richard Sherwood. Now she had three possible reasons for questioning her first instinct to go to the country: her need to establish her own record, separate from that of Jacques' administration; the mood in Quebec; and Sherwood's condition. Nonetheless, Kathleen promised herself, she must remember to make some deeper sampling among Quebec Liberals than she had up to now thought necessary. She had, after all, had fair support from Quebec during the leadership race.

Jacques quietly appeared in the doorway, impassive as ever. He invited them to a buffet lunch which had been laid out on the sturdy bleached-oak trestle table.

As the ministers loaded their plates, Kathleen took the opportunity to talk to each. For the first time since the convention, she spoke at length in French, to the Quebec ministers and the lone francophone minister from New Brunswick who held the post of Fisheries. In almost no time at all it was necessary to bundle into heavy outerwear once more. The Liberal caucus was to assemble at three in Parliament's West Block.

On the drive back through the snow-covered countryside, past the boarded-up cottages, and through the little villages along the spacious parkway, Kathleen pondered somberly on the pros and cons of her political alternatives.

She had not tried to influence the Cabinet. Her purpose was only to consult. Her assessment was that the Cabinet was almost unanimously in favour of an election. Many of the reservations they had expressed, she was sure, were out of deference to Charles. And even the most reluctant of them had been convinced by the need to demonstrate that the Government had undergone a real change. A new direction, a sense of fresh purpose, a revitalized, energetic leadership was what the party had consciously chosen; and the consensus was that the country was just as eager as the party for change. The most cautionary note was the nagging question of Quebec. It troubled her deeply as it had the Cabinet, for if Quebec support eroded, it was unlikely the Liberals could win the election. Whichever route she chose, she would have to be careful not to appear too harsh to Jacques.

Kathleen was vacillating. Her own instinct was to accept her colleagues' advice, but she was haunted by the certainty that in launching the country on a general election, she would be signing Richard Sherwood's death warrant. Perhaps, she thought, I'll get some help from the caucus. But even as she held out to herself that frail ray of hope, it faded. Consulting the caucus was only *pro forma*. It was her job, and only hers to make the decision.

She wrestled with the equation, putting aside for the moment Sherwood's problems, considering the alternatives. On one side, she was impressed with the arguments that the public must see that Jacques was no longer in charge. The answer to that was to lead her troops into electoral battle. On the other hand, if Jacques were seen to be ousted, what would that mean in terms of Quebec seats? Did she dare risk collapse of traditional Liberal support there? If she didn't call an election, how could she make it crystal clear that she was in command, not Jacques?

Was there a compromise? Damn it, but I hate compromise, she thought, even if it is the hallmark of government. I like things black and white, not smudged into grey. But there's got to be some middle way, if I can only think of it.

Maybe Andrew can help. He's good at weighing both sides of the issue. Tonight, I'll talk it over with him, she decided as the car pulled up to the West Block, where the caucus was meeting. Now let's see what they have to say.

"Where the hell is Andrew?"

Kathleen went to the door of the darkened bedroom and snapped on the overhead light. No, he wasn't here. It wasn't like him to go off like that, not telling her where he would be or when he would return. And it was already so late—after six. Kathleen was uneasy. Still fretting, she telephoned the switchboard and asked if there were any messages. The switchboard operator chuckled into her ear, telling her that there was a towering stack. Should she send them up?

"Yes, at once, please, and ask the bellboy to pick up some ice and the evening papers—the Ottawa, Montreal, and Toronto papers, please, both French and English."

At the drink table in the corner, she inspected the depleted liquor supply and poured herself a fairly stiff mixed drink. When the bellboy arrived, Kathleen dropped ice cubes into the glass and absently mixed the drink with her forefinger. Sitting down at her desk, she busied herself for half an hour with her messages, arranging them in priority for answering. Then she weighted the stack on the desk and turned to the first of the newspapers. But her concentration was poor—as she rattled the papers and sipped at her drink she repeatedly glanced at the telephone, as if inviting it to ring.

At last it did.

"Andrew? Oh Drew, darling, I thought you'd never call! Where are you? Toronto! But you were just there. Your things are still here and you didn't leave a note or anything! I've been worried sick. Oh yes, I remember now that you said you had to go back to the office, but I thought at least you would say good-bye. I've been expecting you to walk through the door any minute. Oh, now darling—that's not fair! Of course I have been busy but certainly I missed you. And I was so looking forward to our having dinner alone tonight. I purposely kept this evening free so that we could be together. Of course I'm disappointed. Yes, I know you have your own work, but I thought maybe . . . You could be such a help. . . . No, I understand. Yes. Will you be coming up tomorrow? Not until next week! Yes, of course I'll keep busy. There aren't enough hours in the day to do everything I have to do. But, Drew. . . .

"Yes, all right, Andrew. Wednesday night. Yes. Talk to you tomorrow, then."

She heard the click signalling that he had rung off. Kathleen felt desolate, alone, abandoned. Even a little frightened. The ordinarily very considerate Andrew Wickstrom had flown back to Toronto without a word to her, and then he hadn't called the whole day to explain. His tone, she thought, was detached, cool. That meant Andrew was angry. Angry with her! What for? Of course she hadn't had much time for him and they had virtually no time alone for weeks, but surely he understood.

Kathleen slammed down the telephone receiver, picked up her glass and went to pour herself another defiantly healthy drink. She settled to the newspapers once more, but she was resentful that her husband was not there, now that she had a few hours for him. Should she call someone? No, the delegates would have left Ottawa by now, on their way back to their homes. One of her aides? No, they had to have some time with their own families, and they had been on call at every hour for months. Jacques? No.

There was no one. All right, she promised herself, I'll have a few drinks and dinner here from room service. I'll just have to work things out by myself.

Her mind went back to the alternatives and the seemingly insoluble question of whether to call a general election and satisfy her party, or to wait and give Richard Sherwood the time he needed to enjoy the few months of life remaining.

Okay, Kathleen, first things first. There has to be a solution, and you can find it on your own.

First, make it clear that you're the leader. That means you shouldn't postpone being sworn in as prime minster. Get that done quickly and the power is yours and not Jean Jacques Charles'.

Second, don't get rid of Jacques entirely, for fear of Quebec's reaction. He can still be useful. Give him a senior Cabinet post—maybe External where he'll be out of the mainstream and less visible.

Third, shuffle the Cabinet. Get rid of those of questionable loyalty, but do it in such a way that they won't quit altogether and open up their seats. And bring in as many new faces as possible, to underline the new direction.

If you do all those things there is no need for an election and the risks that would entail.

Feeling pleased with herself and the compromise she had arrived at, Kathleen ordered herself a sumptuous dinner. When it arrived, she dug in, running once more through her mind the actions she had to take.

After the by-election, she decided, she'd recall Parliament. She would have to handle Malloy with kid gloves, but there would be Sherwood's help.... Not for long, though. The scenario she was planning would let him quit quite soon, and his successor might not be so co-operative. But that, she decided, was an uncertainty she would have to learn to live with. She could do it easily, knowing that this way Richard Sherwood would be spared.

Yes, she concluded, that's the way—the classic Canadian compromise. It will work.

There's still a problem though. I'll have to face the Cabinet again, and the party, to tell them my decision. They won't be pleased that I've rejected their advice. I'll just have to win them over to my point of view. And if I can't, they'll still have to accept my decision, like it or not.

"I'm the leader, and the decision is mine," she said aloud to the empty room.

The morning air was fresh with the faintly salty tang of the sea. The sky above was a boundless blue, brush-stroked in white by a contrail which marked the departure of an early morning flight to the north. Sunlight suffused the sparkling air and glittered on the surf that boomed half a mile away on the dazzling expanse of chalk-white beach.

No sound of surf carried here to disturb the almost palpable silence surrounding Joan Findlay. There was only the hum of busy insects as they dipped in and out of honeysuckle, mock-orange, and bougainvillaea, their top-heavy blossoms sagging onto the patio in perfumed profusion. Occasionally, from the tennis court beyond the pool, the droning silence was broken by the plunk of a well-hit ball, the tinkle of feminine laughter, or a deep-voiced yell of masculine triumph. The courts were not visible from the pool. They were shut away by a low stone wall, smothered in masses of fragrant pink, white, and yellow roses.

Joan stretched on the chaise in contentment. Could it really be only yesterday that she and Stan had left the unrelenting Ottawa winter? Now they were here in this tropical paradise. Stan had been so on edge after the Cabinet meeting at Harrington Lake, but now he seemed a totally different person. He was more relaxed than she had seen him in years.

"This is sheer heaven," she said aloud. Oh, it would be wonderful to live like this, to own a refuge from the tiresome Canadian winter, to be able to fly away into the sun whenever one felt like it. It seemed forever since she and Stan had even taken a vacation. Politics was all-consuming. They were always working in the office—she only part-time, of course. Then, too, there was the problem of money. There just wasn't enough. All that tuition! No time!

She looked appraisingly at the large, two-storey white-washed villa. With its black wrought-iron balconies etched along the sun-splashed walls, and the flowers tumbling from niches and containers, it looked for all the world as if it had been transported stone by stone from Malaga. Of course, Will Cranston was born with money—she could never expect to own a house this grand—but she found herself considering what kind of winter retreat she would prefer. A smaller, scaled-down model, perhaps. Or maybe something more modern. *I think when we buy*—Joan was in mid-thought when she suddenly realized she had been lying in the full sun for almost an hour, and on this, her first morning.

Hastily, she dragged her wheeled lounge and its heavy canvas mattress further from the pool into the dappled shade of a citrus-scented tree. Although she had used a sun-screen tanning lotion, she knew what the tropic rays could do to her redhead's pink skin. Warm from her exertions, she dropped her lacy straw sunhat on the mattress, slipped off her thongs and plunged with a heavy splash into the inviting waters of the pool.

As Joan surfaced she was pleased to see Stanley approaching. Her husband certainly looked handsome in his white shorts. His upper body was bare and already bronzing. He had no trouble with sunburn, she thought resentfully. Then, turning her attention to her hostess, she mentally noted that neither had Giselle.

Joan treaded water and watched the handsome pair. Stanley was towelling dry his glistening brow. His chest with its thick mat of curling sandy hair was heaving after the strenuous play in the hot sun. His wife thrilled with pleasure as she never failed to do, when her glance fell upon his powerful thighs and buttocks. She felt a familiar sting of sexual excitement. Without his clothes. the big man's body showed he was fit and well-muscled. Approaching his forty-ninth birthday, he had never looked better.

Their hostess was a pocket mannequin. Her body was golden, slender and clean-limbed against the startling white of her short tennis dress, and her smooth-skinned face bore no trace of makeup beneath the shadow of her bright-green, long-billed tennis cap. Full breasts strained against the crisp linen, as the petite woman dropped into a latticed chair, her racquet clattering to the patio tiles. Giselle laughed with the sheer exuberance of living. It changed her often sulky expression dramatically. Except for the well-developed breasts,

Giselle could have been twenty, Joan thought with envy, conscious of her own body with its flaccid bosom and the bulge of belly.

She climbed from the pool to join them, as a slipper-shod white-coated servant brought to the table tall, frosted glasses tinkling with ice.

"Good game?" she enquired pleasantly.

"Stan is way too good for me," her laughing hostess assured her. "I don't really mind being beaten but this was ridiculous," she added in mock-complaint.

"Don't you believe her, Joanie," Stanley Findlay countered. "Giselle, for all her size, is some tennis player. Never played against a better woman. She really covers the court." He looked at her, the admiration in his bright brown eyes matching that of his words.

Giselle gave him a languid smile. "How about a dip, Stan? Or would you prefer just to shower?"

"A swim for me, for sure. Race you to the pool house!" Grabbing her hand, he pulled his unresisting hostess from her chair, and they pounded off towards the far end of the patio, where the gaily striped awning of the change house soon swallowed them in shadow.

Almost at once, they reappeared, Findlay in flowered swim trunks, a coarse white towel thrown around his neck. Joan caught her breath at the sight of her hostess. Giselle was almost nude, in a black maillot with high-cut legs and a deep-plunging halter. No one with less than a perfect figure would dare to wear it.

It was clear that Giselle was perfectly aware of the effect her appearance created. Carrying herself with assurance, she walked towards the pool, braiding her streaming brown hair into one fat plait, which she tossed casually back over her shoulder. Then, with a fluid movement, she stepped from her high-heeled sandals and glided barefoot to the low diving board. She cleaved the water cleanly, soundlessly.

"Whew." The admiring remark was spontaneous. Stan's eyes didn't leave the golden body until it disappeared beneath the pool's sparkling surface. Then he turned to his wife and unguardedly exclaimed, "Boy, isn't she something?"

Without waiting for a reply, his toes curled around the pool's coping and he, too, dived into the water.

Beside another pool, more than a thousand miles to the north, two men in bathing trunks sat, their feet dangling into the water. The light here was harsh and cold, reflecting through the high windows from the underside of low, snow-threatening clouds. The echoing pool area, tiled in bright turquoise, was hot and steamy, the air redolent of chlorine.

Both men were in their late middle years. Neither was above medium height. The shorter of the two was beginning to show a little flab, and he laughingly admitted to his older and somewhat taller companion that he was getting out of shape. Senator Gabriel LaCroix ran his stubby hand through his shock of greying hair, spangling the pool with droplets of water. His shaggy moustache hid his strong discoloured teeth until he laughed, which he did frequently and whole-heartedly, throwing back the heavy head, the cords of his neck straining.

The Senator was laughing now. He bent his grey-eyed gaze upon his companion, whose slight, almost hairless, well-knit body showed its owner's constant care. It was hard to believe that Jacques was almost sixty, Gabriel marvelled. That is, he corrected himself immediately, until you look into his face. The years are beginning to show there all right. But that's to be expected, after the load he's carried.

"Another ten laps, old friend?" Jacques challenged him.

"Not for me, Jean Jacques, not for me," the Senator demurred.

"A sauna then? Or better still, how about a drink before dinner? I think, for a change, I could use one. How about it?"

"Lead me to it, Prime Minister. No point leaving any of that good liquor around for old Kate, is there?"

Chortling together like a pair of naughty schoolboys, they took the tunnel to the mansion.

The dinner was good, and both men fell to with an appetite sharpened by pre-dinner drinks and their invigorating swim. The thick, dark-green velvet of the pea soup, which was the cook's pride, was followed by generous slices of roast pork in a silky milk gravy accompanied by crisp-cooked slices of pale green cabbage and mounds of buttery, rosy beets. The two men waved away the tossed green salad in anticipation of the sweet dessert that followed—a crusty and authentic sugar pie. Soon nothing remained of it but crumbs, as the two old friends sat back, replete, to savour big cups of fragrant coffee.

The light had fled while they dined, but when the neat, red-haired maid appeared to pull the drapes against the darkened sky, Jacques shook his head, restraining her. Seated still at the table, in the bow-windowed alcove of the formal dining room, each had a view along the river, beyond the snow-humped gardens and the low stone fence at the cliff-edge. A weak February moon illumined tumbling masses of cloud against the distant, frosty sky. There would be more snow before morning to blanket the towns and villages whose lights winked from across the broad expanse of ice-bound river; but while the two old friends dined and joked together, no snow fell, and the dark, roiled air wrapped itself silently about the old mansion.

Jacques and Gabriel LaCroix had been caught up in nostalgic talk of earlier times, times when they had been brothers in a small band of activists in their own province of Quebec. For years, each had fought the oppression of muffling paternalistic governments, trying to let in light and air to the stagnation of Quebec society. Both men had come to public attention through their unswerving attacks on the bosses—whether political or clerical or business—who held their people in thrall. Each in his own way—Jean Jacques as a journalist, and Gabriel as a labour leader—had for more than twenty years kept aloft the banner of freedom and opportunity for their francophone compatriots. Along the way, each had reached the conclusion separately and then together that, for full equality, the francophone presence in the nation's capital must be strengthened and broadened. That belief had brought the pair to Parliament together and into Sandy Sinclair's Cabinet.

From there had begun Jacques' meteoric rise to the prime ministership. Gabriel LaCroix had, in various Cabinet posts of the Charles' administration, remained close to the Prime Minister, relieving him of much of the organizational work in their home province, thus freeing Jacques from days and months of the drudgery needed to keep the Liberal party's fortunes alive in those years when Quebeckers flexed their nationalistic muscles seeking to be masters in their own house.

The now-grey Senator had always been a vigorous, passionate man. Although passionate still—as his increasingly rare oratory bore witness—Gabriel LaCroix's health had gradually deteriorated under the formidable work-load of handling a demanding government ministry while he still shouldered the political burden of crisscrossing Quebec, a constantly reassuring federal presence among his people. Jean Jacques Charles had called LaCroix to the Senate to ease his exhaustion. That had been in the wake of Jacques' soaring electoral triumphs and his marriage to the fragile Evangeline.

Since that time, the two men had spent much less time together. Gabriel LaCroix had been at Jacques' side, however, in his struggle to retain the leadership of the Liberal party. The Senator, perhaps better than anyone else, was aware how deeply the proud Charles had been wounded by the twin losses of his wife and his post as first minister.

Rising, the two old friends strolled through the black-and-white tiled entrance hall, to mount the staircase to the private family quarters. In the sitting room, the fire was freshly lit. Lamps glowed softly, as they made themselves comfortable. Jacques settled in the high-backed overstuffed chair beneath the reading lamp, and the Senator eased his troubled back into the bright-painted rocker that had been Evangeline's favourite haven.

"Have you decided what you'll do now, *mon vieux?*" Gabriel probed gently, mindful that Jean Jacques could not be pressured. He would make up his own mind when he was ready and not a minute sooner.

Jean Jacques Charles drew his finger down his aquiline nose, his hooded eyes thoughtful.

"It depends upon whether Kathleen decides to call a general election right away. But if there's no election for a while, I might just continue on—she has already asked me to think about it. That would give me time to do some of the things I want to do as prime minister."

"If she agreed," the Senator put in.

"Whether she did or not," his companion said with asperity. "If I were to be expected to carry on as prime minister until she found herself a seat, it would be on *my* terms. I would expect a free hand."

Gabriel was uneasy. It crossed his mind that such a scenario could bode ill for the party's fortunes. It would not be the first time a party leader had been sabotaged by his predecessor, but it would be the first such experience for the Liberal party of Canada.

"Do you think Kathleen would go along with that? And would the party? After all, she's the leader now," Gabriel said doubtfully.

"If those are my terms—and they are—what other choice has she?" Jacques raised his hand to forestall his friend's rejoinder. "Oh, I suppose she could call on someone else to stand in for her. But who else is there? I'm still the best."

"Jacques, you mustn't press Kathleen too hard. She might decide that she can't afford you, on your terms. Think what that could do to the Government—an open split between the two of you. The Government, hell," he added, "think what it would do to the party and to our people in Quebec. We could lose everything that we have worked so hard to build up."

"Don't be such a pessimist, Gabriel. Have you lost confidence in me? Surely you think I can handle Kathleen? How could she deal with Quebec without me? The last thing she wants is for me to quit, or, worse, to have to fire me. No, old friend," he said in an abrupt shift of mood, his blue eyes twinkling and his carved face suddenly relaxing as the transforming smile peeled the years away, "leave Kathleen to me. Jean Jacques Charles is not finished yet, not by a damn sight!"

LaCroix was not to be put off so easily.

"Jacques, it's taken a hundred years for our people to get this far in Canada. You and I—and how many others?—have spent the best years of our lives trying to right the imbalance that existed. God knows we've made enormous strides but the *entente* is still so fragile. If you do anything to jeopardize the francophone position you'll throw away everything we've worked for. And I, for one, would denounce you! You could set our cause back thirty years."

Jacques was sobered as much by the Senator's grim look as by his grim words.

"What would you have me do?" He shrugged. "Surely you can't expect me to forget our differences? After all, Kathleen is nothing more than an aberration. She won't last long. I don't think she's tough enough, or smart enough even, to be a real prime minister, and anyway, my guess is that Canada isn't ready to accept a woman as first minister. I don't think she can carry the country in a general election."

His friend said gravely, "If it's apparent that you're not supporting her, she could lose Quebec, and that would be the end of her. Is that really what you have in mind? Do you really think the party would turn to you again, if they judged you responsible? No, Jacques. You know you can't turn back the clock. The party made its choice and you have to accept that, don't you see?"

Jacques was angered by LaCroix's argument. He had come to expect that LaCroix would follow him wherever he chose to lead. He had always been a trusted ally. His opposition came now as a disconcerting surprise. Ordinarily, he would have brushed aside any criticism, confident in his own superior judgment, but when the source of the opposition was one so close, he had to consider its significance. If this was the way Gabriel LaCroix reasoned, he thought with dismay, there would be many others even more critical. It hadn't occurred to him that by staying aloof from Kathleen and cherishing his independence, he could jeopardize his own position. Now he had to examine that possibility.

He rose, picked up the fireside poker and tended the fire. Then he stood, hands in pockets, gazing into its flickering light. The firelight limned his lower face, picking out the strong jaw, the texture of his skin, the tightened lips. But above the high cheekbones, the hooded eyes were shadowed.

LaCroix's eyes had not left Charles' face. He stirred.

"Can't you try to help her? If not for her, then for our people, for the party and for yourself? You could be so influential."

Jacques turned to study his friend's lined face.

"She needs me, she's admitted that already," he said at last. "That gives me some leverage, some scope to bargain with her. If she wants me, she'll have to agree to my terms And they'll include you, Gabriel. If she accepts them, I'll go along. I won't oppose her," he said slowly, reading in his friend's relieved expression, an awareness of his concession. "But that's all I'll promise you. If she won't accept, I won't grovel. I won't be her lackey. I'll feel free to take any action I please."

"That's fair enough, Jacques. Only don't let your terms be too high. Don't be unreasonable."

Jacques laughed. He dropped his hand to his companion's shoulder. "Now let me tell you what they are."

Chapter Four

Kathleen pushed her chair back from the table. They had finished the luncheon, ordered from the Parliamentary Restaurant and served on a heavy white damask cloth with the institutional silver and the distinctive white and gold china emblazoned with the Canadian coat of arms. Except for telling him of her decision to contest the by-election, she had kept the conversation light until they finished their meal. Now she judged the time ripe to get down to business.

"Jacques, I hope you've had time to think over your future plans. You know I'd be very pleased if you agreed to stay on in Cabinet."

Her luncheon guest put down his coffee cup, touching the corners of his mouth with the generous linen napkin.

"Before I answer that, Kathleen, you'd better know that I have some reservations. Are you sure you want me around? If I were to fade away it would give you a freer hand, say, if you should want to reverse some of my actions as prime minister." He caught himself and then added, "Although I can't imagine just what they might be."

"Yes, I admit I had considered that, Jacques," she said softly, deciding not to mention the grim possibilities that she knew would lie ahead if Jacques were to "fade away" and sever himself from the party. The potential for alienating Quebec was a topic neither wanted to bring up, but it remained an unspoken threat, lingering in the air.

She went on. "I decided, however, that your presence and your experience would be invaluable, and that the country could benefit greatly from them."

He nodded. He had given Kathleen an out, an opportunity to disassociate herself from him. He hoped that she wouldn't forget that in the future.

"Then I should be pleased and honoured to stay and to help you in any way I can." He looked up and caught a

66

fleeting look of surprise in Kathleen's eyes. She'd obviously expected a tougher fight. Now was the time to press on. "There are ways in which our arrangement could be made mutually beneficial, however."

Here it comes, thought Kathleen. "If you have any conditions, Jacques, I'd be glad to hear them," she said calmly.

"First, I rather think I'd like External. There would be less possibility of conflict on domestic issues if my principal responsibilitiy was in foreign affairs. Besides, I've built up a good relationship with a number of other heads of state. That could be useful."

Kathleen breathed a sigh of relief. She would easily agree to that condition. She had indeed come to much the same conclusion herself. In External, Jacques would enjoy a prestigious senior post, one that could make him acting prime minister in her absence. That should satisfy Quebec. And the job would require him to be away from Ottawa much of the time, which she felt would satisfy those in the party and the Cabinet who had warned against too close an association with her predecessor. What did surprise her was the change in Charles' attitude. All through lunch he had taken pains to be at his most charming and conciliatory. Where she had expected hard bargaining, she had been met with the most reasonable of suggestions.

"Yes," she said as she reached for a cigarette, "I agree with that. As a matter of fact, there's a NATO meeting in Brussels during the campaign. I can't possibly take time to attend. I had intended to ask you to go. Your appointment would make that very natural."

He watched her light the cigarette. "There's another matter, as well. I want to keep Gabriel LaCroix active in Quebec. We've been a team for a long time, and you'll need him to help out there. He can't do that as Senate Leader; it ties him too much to Ottawa."

Over the smoke from the cigarette, she watched him.

"What did you have in mind?" she asked cautiously.

"I thought—Energy."

Kathleen did not try to hide her puzzlement. "Why Energy?" she asked.

"No particularly strong reason, but I assumed that in a Cabinet shuffle, you would probably want to change Findlay if you are going to keep him on at all."

"But Energy is an important portfolio, although it seems

quiet enough at the moment. Do you think Gabriel is up to it, physically and emotionally? I thought his health was delicate."

"No, it's been much better in the last couple of years. I think he's perfectly able now to take on another portfolio, and I'm sure he could be very helpful."

"But he's in the Senate. That means he couldn't answer for his department in the Commons, and someone would have to understudy him there. That's a problem," she said thoughtfully. "I've already considered bringing in a couple of new people to the Cabinet by way of the Senate. I might get away with one, but the House won't like it if there are two or three ministers representing important departments that they can't get at, even in the Question Period. I'd like to think about this, Jacques," she temporized.

His voice was firm. "I'm afraid it's one of my conditions, Kathleen. If I am to cover for you here while you're running in the by-election, to represent you in Brussels, to try to hold our support in Quebec, I need his help. If you want me, you'll have to take Gabriel, too."

Kathleen's hazel eyes rested on the sculptured face. Jacques' blue eyes were guileless, his expression open and candid. The iron hand in the velvet glove.

All right, she thought, it may create difficulties, but if it's that important to him, okay.

"If that's the case, Jacques, I agree. It'll be Senator La-Croix in Energy. Is that the last of the conditions?"

"That's all. When will you tell the Cabinet of your decision not to call a general election?" he asked, content that he had gained what he wanted.

Kathleen crushed out her cigarette. "Soon. In about two days."

"They'll be surprised. They've been pretty sure you were going to call an election," he commented.

"I suppose so. I suspect there'll be some argument, but that can't be helped. I've made up my mind. I plan to be sworn in as prime minister tomorrow, and I'll speak to the Cabinet and announce my decision publicly the day after that. Then, with you looking after things here, I'll be free to concentrate on winning back my seat. In case I've forgotten to, I want to thank you, Jacques, for deciding to stay with the team."

Faint colour tinged his sallow cheeks. He murmured self-deprecatingly, "My pleasure, Kathleen, my pleasure."

The ceremony was brief. It had been hurriedly arranged, and there would be no public announcement until the next day. To Kathleen's regret, not even Andrew Wickstrom was present.

The Governor General received them in his study. He stood, feebly leaning on his cane, as the Clerk of the Privy Council held out the Bible. Kathleen took the oath of office in a firm, controlled voice. Afterwards, she signed the Privy Council roll.

When the representative of the Queen offered them sherry, Kathleen was reminded again of the old gentleman's consideration when she had temporarily shouldered the responsibilities of this office after Sandy Sinclair's untimely death. She suddenly noticed how much the distinguished former diplomat had aged, and she reluctantly tucked into the back of her mind the unwelcome thought that she might soon need to recommend a replacement.

When the civil servants had retired, the Governor General, Kathleen, and Jacques made polite conversation for a few minutes before first Jacques, and then Kathleen, begged permission to leave.

As the freshly sworn Prime Minister stepped from the door to settle into the warmth of her idling limousine, her gaze followed her predecessor as he trudged down the broad driveway in the thickly swirling snow. Jacques looked somehow diminished, and very alone, she thought sadly, as he made his way towards 24 Sussex Drive and the house that soon again would be hers.

Stan Findlay irritably fixed himself another drink from the extensive selection at the poolside bar, then rejoined his wife and their hosts on the flower-banked terrace.

"Damn it, I don't want to go. I'm just beginning to unwind. I hate the thought of leaving all this to go back to Ottawa's winter. Brrr. My God, the radio said it was nearly thirty below there yesterday! Damn Kathleen, anyway!"

The night was balmy, the heady scent of tropic flowers mixed with the faint salt taste of the sea. The moon swung in a star-studded sky of midnight blue. The four had returned from an evening of dining and dancing and gambling to find a message from the new Liberal leader, demanding the return of her Energy Minister. Findlay wondered briefly what Kathleen Marshal wanted. If it had been a ministry matter, one of his aides would have called. Did she need his advice on something? Perhaps Jacques had backed him after all.

Then the old annoyance returned. Why did he have to leave all this to jump at her whim? He and Joan had talked over the prospects of joining Cranston and accepting his offer. Joan was more enthusiastic than he had expected, although he detected a new note of annoyance in her attitude. His own reservations had to do with the risks he might be taking. Joan seemed less concerned about that, however, now that she had seen some of the rewards.

He had to confess that the display of solid wealth here on Lyford Cay had influenced him as well, although, he admitted guiltily to himself, the prospect of being able to see Giselle again also tantalized him. He knew that the promise of a challenging job with an almost limitless financial future, coupled with the probability that he could see more and more of Giselle, had overwhelmed his lifelong ambitions in politics.

"It will only be for a day or so, Findlay, and it wouldn't do to keep the lady waiting. After all, she's almost the Prime Minister and there's no point in burning your bridges to the government."

"She *is* the Prime Minister! The message came from the Prime Minister's Office. She must have had herself sworn in by the Governor General."

"All the more reason not to anger her. Political contacts are very useful in business, I don't have to tell you. But I want you back here right away. You and I have a lot of business decisions to reach. You'll just have to get this matter of politics over. Clear the air. The sooner the better."

Willis Cranston thought Findlay was being unnecessarily petulant. The big man was making a fuss over nothing. Why, when the summons had come from Ottawa, Findlay had suggested he just make a call to the Marshal woman, telling her he'd return when he was good and ready. Well, said the older man to himself, he's got to develop a better sense of what's seemly. And he'd better learn to face up to people. Can't be allowed to duck out of hard decisions.

"We'll take good care of Joan for you," Giselle assured Findlay with a warm smile. "After all, you'll only be gone a day or so," she purred at her guest.

"I think I had better go with Stansie," Joan said tentatively.

She could feel the current of attraction between this sensuous woman and her husband. It seemed to her that it ran both ways. Until Willis Cranston had arrived, his wife had swallowed up almost all of Stanley's time and attention. Oh, she's the perfect hostess, Joan reminded herself, grudgingly admitting that Giselle had always meticulously made a point of including her in their projected plans each day. But those plans were always so *physical*—swimming and tennis and scuba-diving and water skiing and golfing and sailing. All so exhausting in this climate. And all of them inviting more sunburn. She looked ruefully at her blistered arms, conscious that her nose had peeled unbecomingly. She just couldn't take the sun as those two could.

All the same, it had made her very uneasy, leaving the two of them alone together for so many hours. Joan confessed to herself that she had been relieved when Willis Cranston had flown in to join them—sure that Giselle would be much more circumspect with her own husband present. The last couple of days had proved her right.

"You don't need to come, Joanie," her husband protested. "Why would you leave all this?" With a sweeping gesture, he took in the shadowed terrace, the glinting pool, the view across to the sea, the glowing moon. "Why trade paradise for that bloody cold and snow?"

"The children, dear. I miss them. We've scarcely seen them since the convention. I promised them I'd just be away a few days. They sounded lonesome on the telephone. Don't you long to see them too?"

"Oh yes, the kids," her husband responded vaguely. "Sure I miss them but they're busy at school and with their friends. Anyway, I won't have time for a visit. Just into Ottawa and out again. That's what you want, isn't it, Will?"

"Exactly, Stan. Although I suppose it wouldn't hurt to take another day or two if seeing the children is that important."

"No, not to me. At least," Findlay amended with a glance at his wife, "Joan can explain to them. I never get to spend much time with them anyway. We have some plans for the school break but that's still weeks off. Okay then, Joan, if you insist, I'll arrange for another seat on the plane. But I think you're nuts not to stay here and enjoy yourself."

"What did she want, Stansie?" Joan's voice came faintly over the telephone. There was a lot of static on the line. Maybe something to do with the heavy sheath of ice that covered every bare tree limb, every light standard, every lacy iron fence-picket, as far as Stanley could see from his office window.

While his thoughts bloomed with memories of the sunshine-blessed, flowered islands of the Bahamas and of Giselle Cranston, his glance rested on the frost-coated windowpane. He pulled aside the curtain and stared with disgust at the sleet that pelted the window. It was becoming clearer by the minute that his plane would never take off tonight. He would be stuck here in Ottawa. Damn, damn, damn.

"I haven't seen her yet, Joan. She's here, but she's closeted with a long list of people. She had a Cabinet meeting yesterday, which I missed 'cause our plane was late. But apparently there's something she wants to see me personally about. She's asked me to wait. I don't think we'll get off tonight. I doubt any planes will be flying. I'll let you know later."

"Stan, I can't go back with you. Betsy has come down with pneumonia. She's very feverish—I just can't leave her." There had been an unspoken question in Joan's voice, and now she vocalized it into the pause. "I suppose you can't postpone your return a few days?"

"Joan, don't be an ass!" He was exasperated. First the weather, then Kathleen, now Joan—everything seemed to conspire to keep him in Canada. "You know how important it is just now to jump when Willis Cranston says, 'Jump.' When he said he wanted me back there right away he meant it. I can't stay just because of a sick kid. Betsy will be all right. Why can't the nanny look after her? You could join me tomorrow."

"No, I can't Stanley. She's really sick. It will be days until I can get away. I'm sorry. Apologize to the Cranstons for me, please. They'll understand." She sighed and then said, "And, Stansie, do be careful."

"Careful of what?" he asked, gritting his teeth against the repeated use of that hated nickname.

"Just be careful, that's all. Willis is, well, hard. Don't give him any cause to be angry with you."

"Oh damn it, Joan, don't nag! I know which side my bread is buttered on. Go tuck Betsy in. I'll let you know when I'm coming back. Gotta go now."

He dropped the receiver into the cradle before he heard her say good-bye, then stood up and restlessly paced the room. He buzzed for his secretary, but she had left for the night. He'd better check on planes himself.

He dialled and the telephone rang briefly. The ringing was interrupted by a metallic, recorded voice, telling him that all the lines to reservations were busy. He hung up in the middle of the recording. He wasn't going to hang around here, waiting for his turn on the line. He'd get one of the people in the travel office to look after it for him. A swift check in the mirror. Tie straight. Chin could stand a shave, but he would do that later. He telephoned the Prime Minister's office to leave a message that he would be in the dining room when she was ready to see him.

"Sit down, Stan."

Kathleen gestured towards the armchair facing her across the desk. She sat back further in her own high-backed chair, waiting for her Cabinet colleague to settle his bulk. Stanley Findlay's expression was bland. The sandy-haired man stared past her shoulder to the gilt-topped standard with its red and white flag, but he refused to meet her eyes.

"Sorry I couldn't make the Cabinet meeting yesterday, Prime Minister. My plane was delayed by the weather. Did I miss anything?"

Kathleen controlled her temper. "Yes, as a matter of fact, you missed my announcement that I'll be seeking a seat in the House through a by-election."

"But I thought—" Stan blurted out.

"Yes, I know. You weren't the only one who assumed I'd call a general election. But, as I explained to the others," she went on pointedly, "it is my assessment that this is not the time for an election."

"Does that mean things will go on as they were? Will Jacques be acting PM?" Findlay asked, barely masking the hope in his eyes.

"Jacques will be acting PM, but things will not stay the same. For one thing, I'm going to make some Cabinet changes. They'll be announced tomorrow."

His eyes flicked to hers, but he made no comment.

The Prime Minister coughed. "I'm sure you'll understand that I want to bring in some of my own people. And I want to cut down the size of the present Cabinet. Regrettably, that means I'll have to drop some of the current ministers, as well as change around some of the portfolios."

Now Findlay looked at the Prime Minister. "What about me?" he asked her bluntly.

She was as blunt in turn. "I'm going to be replacing you,

Stan. There won't be room for you in the new Cabinet."

A look of anger passed over his face. Kathleen steeled herself against an involuntary twinge of compassion. "You'll still be a member, Stanley. You'll not be out of a job."

"To hell with that," he said rudely. "Do you think I'll stick around in the House after you shove me into a back bench? No, my Right Honourable Lady," he said sarcastically, "if you're going to pitch me out, I'll go all the way. You needn't expect me to stick around, trying to keep you in office. You need my vote, don't you? Well you won't have it."

Kathleen was silent, controlling her answering spurt of anger. It was a struggle not to reply in kind.

"I've made up my mind, Findlay. I want your letter of resignation to the Governor General here on my desk no later than tomorrow. And don't be too hasty about resigning from the House. Of course, it will make it more difficult for me to lose another vote—minority Government is difficult enough as it is. If you should decide to stay, at least until the next election, I'm sure something interesting can be found for you."

"I'll bet!" he said bitterly.

Kathleen studied the big westerner. She didn't like him, never had, but it was distasteful to her to have him go like this.

"The decision is yours, Findlay. Let me know if you should change your mind. But remember, I want your letter of resignation by tomorrow."

She rose to terminate the interview. He stood automatically, swaying, his baleful glance fully on her at last.

"Go to hell, Kathleen Marshal. I've got bigger fish to fry." He swung away from her and ploughed blindly out of her office.

Kathleen studied her husband's profile. The lips were set, the heavy chin stubborn. Both hands were on the wheel of the powerful car. His eyes were fixed straight ahead. Andrew hadn't really wanted to come to Niagara with her this weekend but she had prevailed upon him. Persuasively, she had pointed out that if he didn't come there would scarcely have been any time for them together. Even if the two or three hours spent driving along the Queen Elizabeth Highway to and from Niagara were all the time they could share, it would give them a cosy while to talk.

So far, there had been nothing very cosy about it.

"But Andrew, I *can't* run in Rosedale. The sitting member is a Conservative and there's no way I can get him to step down to let me win the seat."

"But you'll have to kick someone out of a seat in Niagara and appoint him to something."

"Yes, but he's a Liberal member. He'll have to do as he's told. I know it's inconvenient, adopting Niagara again, but it's the riding I know best, and the people there know me best."

"Why not an Ottawa seat?"

"No. It's too easy as it is to be caught up in that Ottawa attitude that assumes that what's good for the capital is what's good for Canada. In no time, you find yourself out of touch with the rest of the country."

"But, Kate, *when* will we get to see one another? You'll have to be in Niagara when you're not in Ottawa and I'll be in Toronto. I might as well not have a wife," he said truculently.

"Darling, this isn't like you. You went along with the plans. If only you wouldn't be so stubborn about coming to Ottawa to live. You don't *need* to be in Toronto. Tage is looking after the business. That's what we talked about—your retirement and our being together. Isn't that what we planned?"

Her voice was cajoling, and her hand, in the wool-lined leather glove, was resting on his right arm. His stony expression did not soften, although he glanced down at the long-fingered hand whose gentle pressure added to her words of entreaty.

"Kate, I couldn't stand doing nothing. Look," he said, head turning to glimpse her reaction, "I hardly saw you in all those months of chasing the leadership. Then, since the convention, whenever we've been together there have always been other people about. We were never alone. It just won't work. I hate just sitting there, waiting for you to snatch an hour or two for me. Or trotting around behind you to all those formal things. I feel like a gigolo."

"But you planned to have time to yourself. Why can't you do that now and let your son take over all your responsibilities?"

"Of course Tage can take them over. He's ready. I agree—that's what we planned. But what would I *do*? Take up tatting? Or join some ladies' aid, husbands' division? I think our marriage would disintegrate under the pressure of my frustration. I would rather risk our being apart most of the time, if we could *really* be together every so often, alone. Really alone, I mean, not just time sandwiched between your damned everlasting meetings. Can't you see?"

Usually so calm, Andrew's deep voice betrayed the strain of his desire to make her understand how mortifying he found it to have to hang back in the shadows.

Kathleen's heart sank. She loved this big, quiet man. Their marriage had brought her such joy, and she depended upon Andrew Wickstrom for so much. He had brought her self-confidence and a stability she had never known before. Their union had brought her peace and a deep happiness. She knew it had been the same for Andrew, a widower for so long. They got along so well, and had made such splendid plans for their future together. . . .

Exasperated, she protested, "But Andrew, I need you *with* me. I need someone to talk to. This is the loneliest job in Canada. What would I do without you? And it won't always be as rushed as these last few weeks have been. Although," she added reluctantly, but honestly, "until the by-election is over, I will be terribly busy. But, after that, I promise you, we'll get away, maybe somewhere out of the country."

"Kathleen, this sleet is worsening. I'd better keep my mind on my driving. The road is hellishly slippery. I'll think about moving to Ottawa, but I'm afraid my mind is pretty well made up. Let's leave it this way: until you've won your seat, I'll stay in Toronto, unless there is something special that you need a . . . an escort for. Then, after you're in Ottawa to stay, we'll see."

Kathleen knew better than to push Andrew any further just now. Better to leave it on this unsatisfactory, temporary basis, even if she would miss him desperately. Truth to tell, she was even a little relieved. His absence would give her some time to concentrate on getting elected. First things first.

Wordlessly, she slid closer to him on the wide leather seat, communicating her warmth and acceptance, but careful not to interfere with his driving.

The silence now was more companionable, if not quite cosy. Leaning her head lightly on his shoulder, she slipped her hand into his coat pocket, her fingers moving lightly along his sturdy thigh.

"Well, Findlay, how does that strike you?"

A couple of million dollars! For him! His own money! Stanley Findlay was stunned, his thoughts in turmoil. Two million dollars! Maybe as much as three. And tax free! His to do with as he chose. Freedom, financial freedom, at last. Two million dollars! Or three!

Of course it had to be shady. Maybe even illegal. He'd have to look into that. But he doubted that Will Cranston ever came near to getting involved in anything downright illegal. Not himself, anyway. And it wouldn't make sense for him even to set up this deal if it involved breaking the law.

The two men were sitting on the patio, looking out over the pool and beyond it, to the sweep of the distant sea. A swollen moon hung in the velvety sky. A drowsy bird trilled as it nestled into sleep, and the night crickets or frogs—Stanley didn't know which—croaked contentedly. A tiny bright-green lizard flitted over the tip of his shoe, its scarlet ribbon of a tongue darting at the soft leather. From somewhere inside the sprawling white house puled a full-throated operatic aria.

Willis Cranston had broken the languorous stillness of the tropical night deliberately. He had been watching Findlay narrowly, calculating the effect of this latest proposal. He had waited, letting the dangling bait of riches seduce the younger man. Money and sex. Those, he was convinced, were the key to most men.

Money-hunger went deep. It wasn't the first time that Cranston had hung out such a carrot, to watch it be snatched in one eager gulp.

Sex, now, that was another thing. There were some men who could be seduced by sex, and some who could take it or leave it. Willis already knew something of Stanley Findlay's apparent appeal where women were concerned, but for the most part, he concluded, the man himself was careful either because of the watchful Joan—whom Cranston grudgingly admired, although she certainly wasn't his type—or because Findlay really wasn't interested.

Anyway, it was clear that money dazzled Findlay.

Cranston splashed a generous portion of mellow Scotch into his glass, followed by a sparing squirt of soda. He stirred in ice, his eyes still on his guest.

Stanley nodded a silent assent when his host questioningly raised the heavy crystal decanter.

"Thanks," he said absently. "Not Scotch though. I think I'll settle for another rum and coke. The dark rum, please."

Cranston mixed the heavy drink and handed it to his guest. Both were dressed for the evening in creamy well-cut dinner jackets, their black, satin-bound trousers sharply creased, their linen snowy, their slippers polished like mirrors. Willis Cranston had taken the big man shopping. It was amazing what a good tailor could accomplish.

As they sipped companionably, there was a stir at the long windows letting onto the patio. The two men turned as one. Tonight, Giselle was in yellow, as butter-bright as the moon. Her hair was dressed high off her graceful neck, caught by a flight of tiny tiger orchids. Against the brown swell of her breasts lay a tracery of fine gold chains. Aside from that touch of gold, and her golden sandals, she wore no other adornment. None was needed to accent the sun-burnished skin, the sheen of the slender, bare arms, the flash of the bright eyes.

"A drink, a drink," she carolled to her husband, turning flirtatiously for effect. When he handed her a long-stemmed goblet of pale, chilled wine, she danced a few steps towards the pool, her long skirt fluttering about her.

"I am rested, and ready, gentlemen, for a night on the town. Now what have you planned?" she asked gaily, curtseying coquettishly to each in turn.

Willis Cranston appreciated his wife's beauty. He knew how skilful she was in protecting and enhancing her most precious asset. Beauty was the commodity that had won Giselle her present life of ease and comfort, and Cranston expected that she would always look her best. Nonetheless, he conceded, she was looking ravishing tonight.

"Nothing very festive, my dear," he said. "I've taken a table at the club. We can dance, if you like. Then maybe a flutter at the tables. Who knows, we might even run into someone interesting, and finish the evening here or at their place. Just the usual. Not really up to the way you look tonight. I'm sorry." He bowed to accompany his compliment.

"Sounds delicious. Just what I feel like, Will," she bubbled. Turning to their guest, she smiled, "Okay with you, Stan? Just the usual?"

Findlay beamed at his hostess. "Some usual! Perfect, as ever." He lifted his glass to her in salute. "Perfect."

The evening drew to a close earlier than usual. It had gone flat, somehow, like a bottle of champagne too long uncorked. Willis watched his wife flirt with his house-guest, but when Findlay had seemed preoccupied, unable or unwilling to rise to Giselle's usually infectious gaiety, she had danced off with other admiring club members. She was standing now in a circle of white-jacketed men, just inside the long French doors thrown open to the terrace. The silvery cadence of her laughter carried to them across the room.

The two men remained at the table, silent for the most part. Findlay had been thinking, pondering over the proposal set before him by his host. Almost as an extension of his silent thoughts, he posed a question to Cranston.

"It's legal, isn't it, Will? I mean, I couldn't go to jail for it, could I? It's just that the stakes seem so high, if it *is* legal."

"Sure. You'd be breaking no law. It's only a commission we are talking about, after all. They have a right to pay a commission to anyone they want to. It's done every day in business. And the fee, while it's negotiable, has to be that high. After all, the price for nuclear reactors *is* high. Nobody but governments can afford to buy them. There are only so many prospective purchasers, and there's a lot of competition among the trade. If you pull off the deal, you'll be paid. And damned well. That's all there is to it."

The less-experienced man persisted. "That all sounds okay, Will, but this isn't a private outfit. It's a government agency. If anyone learned that I was involved in a sale, it could be damned embarrassing." Findlay's craggy features displayed the extent to which his mind was troubled. He bent closer to his companion. "Can't you see the headlines now? 'Atomic Energy Commission in Multi-Million-Dollar Pay-off to Ex-Energy Minister!' Jesus!"

Testily, his host corrected him. "I don't know why you call it a pay-off. It's a *commission*. A perfectly business-like deal. You know how rarely anyone investigates these sales. And if they do, no one will be able to say you didn't earn the money. Everybody will be happy, including you, as you bank all that cash."

"The Americans won't be happy."

"Why? What's it got to do with them? Cuba wants the Candu for peaceful purposes. That's the only string attached, and Castro knows it. He wouldn't try to pull any funny business. Look, Communists do business just like anybody else. Think of Russia—or China. This is just a straightforward business deal. You were Energy Minister. You're familiar with the field. The fact that you've also met the little cigar-chomper is the clincher—the reason AECL is prepared to deal with you, and not a half-dozen other agents, any of whom would jump at the chance. C'mon, Stanley, it's the chance of a lifetime. And remember, you won't even have to pay tax on it."

"I know you keep saying that, Will, but I don't understand how I avoid the taxes."

"It's perfectly simple. You just form a company here in the Bahamas, and work through it. Or if not here, try Bermuda, or the Caymans, or any of a half-dozen of these tropic islands. No trouble, ever. Companies like that are their bread and butter. It's been done a thousand times, and nobody's the wiser."

It all sounded so plausible. Nonetheless, the big westerner thought he had better hold off. Not accept too soon. Not look too eager. He was uneasy. Until he was actually replaced in the Cabinet it seemed a conflict of interest.

"Give me a couple more days to look at all sides of it, Willis. Do you mind?" he asked his host, suddenly struck by the thought that Cranston might not appreciate his caution and apparent lack of enthusiasm.

"All right. Take your time. The deal has been hanging fire for months. A few more days shouldn't matter." Rising, he patted Findlay on the shoulder. "If you don't want the deal, there'll be lots around who will.

"Now, shall we collect Giselle over there before she causes a riot? Let's take a turn at the tables."

But Giselle protested that she was having too much fun to leave.

In the end, one of her partners promised with unconcealed delight to see her home, and her husband and his house-guest drove back without her, each busy with his own thoughts.

The meeting in Niagara had gone well. Kathleen and Andrew had dined with a round dozen of the Liberal movers and shakers from the various parts of the riding. It was a new constituency now, its borders altered by the latest redistribution. That meant that there were a couple of new faces—executive members from the added area of Niagara-on-the-Lake—and a corresponding blank in the Fort Erie area, where former associates, no longer a part of the new riding, had not been invited.

The sitting Member of Parliament for Niagara was not present. Since the convention, Toby Prentice had taken a new bride and was off somewhere in the south, honeymooning. Kathleen had tried to reach him before meeting with his riding executive, but had been unable to locate him. It was a little embarrassing to meet with his supporters, without his knowledge, but now that she had made her decision there was no time to waste. After all, no one foresaw much trouble in having Prentice resign his seat at the request of his leader. He could count on receiving the requisite *quid pro quo*. His tenure in Parliament was only two years long, and it had so far been a singularly lacklustre one. He would no doubt be grateful for a sinecure in exchange for the daily grind of elective politics.

They were enthusiastic, these Liberal men and women, at the prospect of having a prime minister as their Member. Even those who had initial doubts because Kathleen had declined to run again a scant two years or so ago remembered that she had helped them campaign for Prentice, and that she had, during her earlier career, campaigned long and hard for the party, and not only in her own constituency. They had basked in reflected glory when her colleagues in the Sinclair Cabinet had chosen Kathleen to act as interim prime minister. At that time she had brought Niagara more lasting benefits than a transient glory. As a result of her tenure, the riding could boast aid to local industries, an expansion of the nearby airport, a couple of new post office buildings, and a scattering of important federal appointments. She had never forgotten where her own power base lay.

The supporters were pros, whether young or old, and for one reason or another their eyes glistened at the thought of the well-financed, well-organized campaign to come. It would be fun. "No problem," they told her, and before the series of meetings broke up, they had agreed on tentative choices for her campaign team, from the overall chairman, the official agent, the financial people, and the individuals who would take charge of advertising or arranging meetings and speakers, all the way down the list to a driver responsible to see that, as candidate, she got where they wanted her to be, and got there on time. The skeleton organization was fleshed out, and the riding executive prepared to call up their troops and swing them into line. They promised to bring up to date the lists of potential delegates for the nominating convention, argued about alternate dates for the first crucial public meetings and discussed the likelihood of various candidates the opposition parties might be expected to field against her.

"Please remember that all of this is top secret," Kathleen insisted. "I owe it to Toby to discuss his resignation with him first."

Solemnly, they concurred, each swearing to hold the bursting secret in. That was one of the delicious parts of politics—being privy to secrets. And one of the riskiest—expecting so many people to keep them safe. But the risk had to be taken.

"Then that's it, Kathleen. We'll keep quiet until you give us the word, and then we'll be ready for you. It'll be like old times."

Kathleen hugged John Miles, her riding president, whose ruddy face cracked wide open in a delighted smile. He had been chuckling and grinning to himself non-stop. Ordinarily a rather austere man, he loved election campaigns, and it was clear he relished the prospect ahead.

"Like old times, John," she nodded, "only better."

As it turned out, Toby Prentice was not as easy to deal with as Kathleen had hoped. When he returned, having rushed back from his honeymoon as soon as he received the message, he had protested strenuously at her plan for his resignation as Member for Niagara and had sulked over the suggested appointment. It seemed Toby was more ambitious than she had guessed. Or, as was more likely, he felt himself in a good negotiating position. What he wanted was to be made a senator.

"The price is too high," Kathleen had told him, eyeing the short young man with the flushed face and the rising, angry voice.

She had been firm. He would have to resign. Plans were too far advanced for change. Niagara it had to be, and that meant that the brief career of Toby Prentice as its MP was over. Now it was simply a matter of what she would choose to offer him.

But Toby would have none of it. He had defied her, had actually refused to give up his seat. It was the Senate or nothing, he told her. Not for him a two- or three-year appointment to some public body, to be followed by oblivion thereafter. No, ma'am, he wanted security, and the Senate it would have to be. Even when Kathleen had patiently explained to him that he was not old enough, and that he did not have the property qualification required to become a senator, Prentice remained entirely intractable.

"Then change the qualifications," he said defiantly.

"Don't be a damned fool, Toby. The qualifications are set out in the constitution and if you think I'm going to Westminister to get the UK Parliament to change the British North America Act just so you can qualify, you're out of your mind. It'll have to be something else. Now, think about it overnight and let me know tomorrow what you'd like. But it *cannot* be the Senate."

The interview had left a bad taste in her mouth. Kathleen supposed it would have been simpler to let someone else deal with Prentice, but she had not for a moment anticipated such opposition from him. Well, he knew the alternative. If she couldn't run in Niagara, a lot of plans would go by the wayside. But that, she told herself grimly, would be nothing compared to what young Toby Prentice would suffer at the hands of his leader and the party. Memories are long, when a member deliberately defies his leader. And the defiant one's career is sure to be short. Prentice, she was convinced, would fall in line. She'd given him overnight to sleep on it.

Chapter Five

"And I give you now, the Right Honourable Kathleen Marshal, Prime Minister of Canada, and once again, the Member for Niagara!"

Someone grabbed Kathleen's right hand and raised it above her head, waving it wildly. The noise was deafening. Everyone in the room seemed to be cheering or shouting her name. The Royal Canadian Legion hall was jammed with Liberal supporters and workers, well-wishers, hangers-on, and media representatives. It was oppressively hot and smoky, despite the doors at the back that had been opened wide to the misty spring night. There had been a fine spray of rain throughout most of this election day, and the humidity both inside and outside the hall was high.

When the television lights were turned on, they made it much worse. Kathleen was conscious that her flushed face was glistening in the moist heat. She dabbed at herself with her already damp handkerchief.

As the triumphant candidate stepped forward to express her thanks, she was momentarily blinded by a burst of flashbulbs and the sudden glare of the brilliant TV lights. Recovering, her eyes sought out her chief workers, roving over the hundreds of volunteers who had staffed the polls, the telephones, and the cars that carried voters to and fro. She singled out many by name, recalling some special service during the past three weeks. Nor did she forget to say a few words in Italian for the benefit of the vitally important workers from that cohesive group. There was French, too, and some halting German and a phrase in Serbian. These linguistic forays were greeted by peals of delighted laughter, appreciative handclaps and cheers.

So it was over. They had done it once again—carried her to victory. Her repeatedly expressed gratitude was deep-felt and sincere; several times she was close to tears—of joy and appreciation—and of exhaustion.

At last, Kathleen left the small stage to mingle on the floor of the jam-packed hall with her people. This was a night to celebrate. They had earned the right.

A shout went up near the entrance to the hall, and she turned to face her Conservative opponent. Smiling, she reached out to shake the hand of the local PC candidate. Kathleen could hear nothing of what he said against the background din, but it didn't really matter. It was traditional here in Niagara that the losing candidate always came in person to congratulate the victor.

But Kathleen was not so friendly when, later, the NDP candidate pushed in, in the company of his campaign manager. It was obvious that this opponent was reluctant to come to her. His eyes roved suspiciously over the crowd, making a note of those who showed by their presence there that they had failed to support him at the polls. His glowering looks meant that he intended to remember them, the traitors to his cause.

"Congratulations," he said curtly. "But don't forget—there's always the next time."

His campaign manager, a young teacher Kathleen knew slightly, shrugged his apologies for his candidate's ill grace, then clasped both her hands in his own sweaty grip. He pressed them, murmuring, "It was a good battle while it lasted." Then grasping his candidate none too gently by the arm, he withdrew him from the midst of the celebrating Liberals.

"Can you rest now for a few days, Kathleen?" Andrew asked, as he closed the door on the last of the triumphant few who had accompanied them back to the motel room which had been her home for the past three weeks.

"Not just yet, Drew." She sighed. "I'll have to go round to the various committee rooms tomorrow to thank the workers and make sure everything is cleaned up. Oh—and I may have to attend the returning officer's official count. John mentioned it. Appears the Tories want one."

"Whatever for? You beat them by a country mile!"

"Trying to save their deposit, I guess. They have to get a certain percentage of the winner's total vote, or lose the deposit, you know. Half, if I remember correctly."

"Surely you don't have to be there for that?"

"Well, it's traditional."

"But for God's sake, Kathleen, you're the Prime Minister!

You have simply *got* to make better use of your time. Let somebody else do it. Miles will, certainly."

"But John Miles is the riding president, not my official agent," she began to argue. "Anyway, I'm too tired to think. Shall we turn in?" Kathleen was already on her way into the bathroom, pulling off her dress as she went. "Wake me for breakfast, will you darling?" She spoke to him around the door, but his answer was lost in the rush of steaming water from the shower.

"Kathleen, the telephone." He was shaking her shoulder.

She groaned in protest as she struggled to consciousness, for a moment not knowing where she was.

"It's urgent, they say. The Prime Minister's Office calling."

"Oh damn, I'm not even awake. What time is it?"

"Only eight o'clock. Look, I'll go down and order breakfast while you're on the line. I'll get the papers, too. I won't be long."

Kathleen threw Andrew a smile of acknowledgement as he hurried out of the room, then pulled her thoughts together to concentrate on the call.

"Yes, Kathleen Marshal here. Who is this?"

"Prime Minister, I am sorry to waken you. Congratulations, by the way. Something urgent has come up. It really is important, or else I wouldn't have dreamed of disturbing you. Can you come at once to Ottawa? There is an international matter which I should not discuss on the telephone. I assure you, it's urgent."

"Well, of course, I understand. But it will take me hours to drive to Toronto and then fly up." She abandoned her attempt to guess what the sudden emergency could be.

"We'll send the JetStar. I seem to recall it can land somewhere nearby."

"Yes, I'd forgotten about the government plane. It's St. Catherines' Airport. How long will it take to get there?"

"Perhaps an hour and a half. Can you be ready by then?"

"I don't seem to have any choice, do I?"

"No, ma'am," answered the respectful voice. "Do you have transportation to the airport?"

"Yes, of course, that can be arranged."

"Your car will be waiting when you land in Ottawa, to

bring you directly to the office, then. I think I should not alert the press to your coming. Do you agree?"

"Yes, yes. I had better wait until I learn what this is all about."

"Very well. Safe journey, Prime Minister."

The sleek little JetStar, its tail emblazoned with the red and white flag of Canada landed smoothly. The steward helped her to unbuckle, then he held her coat and led her down the short flight of steps to the tarmac where the long silver-grey bulletproof Cadillac waited. Overhead the brilliant sunshine of a morning already unseasonably hot, one of those false summer days that often came early to Ottawa, had replaced the grey drizzle of Niagara.

The uniformed chauffeur touched his hand to his cap, holding the door for Kathleen's entry. She slid in to greet the car's waiting occupant. It was Helmut Ogilvy, the suave Clerk of the Privy Council, one of the most senior and important of all federal civil servants. On his lap lay a black leather briefcase, and on top of it, a sheaf of scribbled notes. Ready for business. Efficient as always.

"Is your husband with you, Prime Minister?"

"No, he's going back to Toronto for a few days. Now what's this all about?"

"It's the Americans. The President, to be precise. He wants you to visit him. Urgently." He coughed in embarrassment. "Today, if possible."

"Today! That seems somewhat precipitous, doesn't it? The President must have a very good reason," she went on, thoughtfully. "I wasn't aware that such a meeting was even contemplated."

"That's correct, Prime Minister. Of course it's customary to arrange for a new prime minister to meet with the President, but this is something ... unusual. It appears that the President is very disturbed. He has something specific to discuss with you. It's Mr. Charles, I'm afraid," he added cautiously.

"Mr. Charles? Isn't he in Brussels at that NATO meeting?"

"He was. Last week. The meeting is over, but he has taken a few days' private holiday. I believe he is in the south of France somewhere—some special road race, I recall."

"But why should the President want to talk to me about Jacques?"

He coughed again. "There was, I am told, an altercation, an unpleasant incident between the two of them, following the meeting. Some hard things were said between them. Very unseemly. Luckily, there were not many observers. We were able to keep it hushed up. I thought it might blow over. But it seems the President wants to pursue it."

Kathleen sat back, stunned. "A fight! A fight with the President of the United States of America! My God!"

She frowned. "Where is Mr. Charles' parliamentary assistant?"

"Mr. Russell left the Brussels meeting early, ma'am. He is in Buenos Aires at the moment with the Minister of Trade. I doubt he knows anything more about the incident."

"And the Under-secretary for External Affairs?"

"He is waiting for you at the office."

"Has anyone talked to our Ambassador in Washington?"

"Indeed yes. Tellier is very . . . agitated."

"I shouldn't wonder. I'm pretty damned agitated myself," she said grimly.

"Yes, ma'am," he murmured and then fell silent.

The long silver car pulled smoothly up to the Langevin Block opposite Parliament Hill, depositing its passengers at the austere entrance. Kathleen slipped out of the car quickly and crossed the sidewalk head down. She strode purposefully up the steps, across the lobby to the elevator, glad that there had been no press about to mark her arrival. The quieter this could be kept the better.

"Then you agree that I should go? You don't think I should wait a day or so, to let the President cool down? This is such a peremptory summons. It's as though I were being dragged to the carpet, like a child about to be punished. I don't like it," Kathleen said firmly. "And the country wouldn't like it either, if they knew. Which, please God, they never will," she added fervently.

Helmut Ogilvey glanced across at the Under-secretary of State for External Affairs. Unlike most of the carefully turned-out senior members of the Canadian diplomatic service, Menzie MacDonald was habitually unkempt. As someone had once described a distinguished American writer, MacDonald looked like an unmade bed. Nonetheless, he had one of the keenest minds in the public service.

His round, totally bald head sat on a short neck between hunched shoulders. His face, too, was full and round, distinguished by flourishing dark brows, the only punctuation in an otherwise quite ordinary countenance. He affected a moustache, but it was thin and straggly in comparison with the luxuriant growth of those dark brows. The Under-secretary gravely contemplated the gold-wire half-glasses he held in his hand, then squinted up at his Prime Minister.

"Nobody likes it, ma'am," he said mildly. "But the President has such a mercurial temperament that it does seem wisest to, well, swallow our national pride, this once. There is no telling what President Thompson might do, if you should try to put him off. Much less what he would do if you should turn him down flat.

"No, Prime Minister, I think we had better move fast, to contain the situation. I regret that it may not be pleasant for you, but I think you'll just have to let him get it off his chest—whatever it is he wants to say. The United States is far too important to us to risk a real breach."

"But if I just *knew* what the argument was all about. I hate going into this blind. Has no one been able to find Jacques?"

"It seems he has slipped off with some friends for a couple of days. Our people are trying to track him down. I'm sorry."

"Well, please keep trying. Let me know the moment you reach him. In the meantime, better get a call through to Russell in Argentina. I've got to know more than this before I meet the President."

When her call did get through, the line crackled and hummed with static. Hamilton Russell, never, in Kathleen's opinion, one of the brightest of Jacques' assistants, sounded even more obtuse than usual. Kathleen asked for his explanation of the Brussels confrontation, but the tinny, distant voice faded in and out. Her frustration mounted.

" . . . . not much more. Something personal . . . but . . . hear Jacques wouldn't . . . . later. Shouldn't have been . . . . I . . . Foreign Affairs . . . ."

"For heaven's sake, Hamilton, speak up! I can't make out what you're saying." Kathleen found herself shouting across the miles. "What did you say started it?"

There was a veritable explosion of crackling static, and Kathleen held the instrument away from her ear. The distant voice faded again, the line spluttering.

"It's hopeless, Russell. Cable me the details, and do it now. I want your version here within the hour."

Disgusted, she banged the receiver down, unsure whether he had even heard her instructions.

"Damn it, it looks as if I'll have to go, without any real idea of what happened over there. Oh, where the hell is Jacques? What can he have been thinking of, to pick a fight with a man like Thompson? When I see him, I'll kill him!"

She swore, as she snatched up her briefcase and strode to the door.

It was late afternoon when the JetStar rolled to a stop. The sleek eight-passenger plane had been motioned to the far side of Washington's National Airport. As she paused at the door of the aircraft, Kathleen caught sight of a shining black car, its red and white standard fluttering in the wind. Pierre Tellier, the Canadian Ambassador, stood beside the car, turning his black homburg in his hands, strands of his long, iron-grey hair blowing in the breeze stirred up by their arrival. His greeting was muted. Tellier was obviously a worried man. His demeanour did nothing to quell Kathleen's qualms.

"We have an hour or so, Prime Minister. The President has pointedly *not* invited you to dinner, so I have arranged for something light to be set out at the Residence. Is that satisfactory?"

"Yes, perfectly. Perhaps we'll hear from Mr. Charles before the meeting. I only wish I knew exactly what he said or did to provoke the President so," she fretted half-aloud. "But if we don't hear, we don't hear."

She leaned forward, peering at Tellier.

"Now tell me something about President Thompson. I've never met him. Too bad, or we might have smoothed this over by telephone. I hear that he's hot-tempered. Does he carry a grudge, or does it blow over?"

"The President is said never to forget a slight, Prime Minister," said her companion dejectedly. "He's a southerner, fiercely proud of his honour. Things haven't been going all that well for him lately in the opinion polls, although just why that should be is difficult to put a finger on. President Thompson doesn't get along very well with Congress, and some say that he won't be renominated. As you know, his nomination and election three years ago came as a bit of a surprise to most of us. He seemed to come out of nowhere, with no experience in Washington at all. And he doesn't know much about Canada. Never been there, I suspect," he said gloomily.

The Ambassador was becoming ever more morose. He searched his mind for something helpful to tell his new Prime Minister but nothing occurred to him. To the aging career diplomat, this kind of thing was a nightmare. It just wasn't supposed to happen. Tellier sighed deeply. There were no precedents for the leaders of two friendly governments to go head to head like a couple of rutting rams. God and the Prime Minister's own good sense would have to be her guides, he thought ruefully. I can't help.

"The Prime Minister of Canada, Mr. President." The beribboned aide in the Marine Corps uniform stepped smartly aside to permit Kathleen and Tellier to enter the Oval Office. Behind the gleaming desk, framed by tall windows and flanked on one side by the tasselled Stars and Stripes, and on the other by the gold-fringed Presidential banner stood the man she had been summoned to Washington to meet.

President Thompson was not as tall as she. He was slope-shouldered but ramrod straight, slighter than he appeared in photographs. His gaze was steady, his face withholding expression. He paused imperceptibly as though to underline the fact that Kathleen Marshal had come to him. Then the stern lines of his face relaxed somewhat, and he came around the desk to her, holding out his hand.

"Welcome, Prime Minister. Won't you sit here?" He gestured toward a short settee upholstered in gold silk, behind a small coffee table. Across from it were three matching chairs. The room was cheerfully decorated in bright colours—blue and yellow and white. The painted woodwork glistened and vases of artfully arranged mixed flowers stood on either side of the classic mantel. The tall windows stood open to the balmy evening, and beyond them she glimpsed watchful members of the President's omnipresent guards.

"Mr. Ambassador, won't you sit here?" He motioned forward another man, who was hanging back, standing by the enormous whistle-clean desk.

"I believe you know Governor Whiteside? Tony has told me that you have already met. He's here because I intend to send him to Canada as our next Ambassador." He added with a hint of humour, "He's not a Democrat, but a fairly liberal Republican. I'm sure you'll get along."

Kathleen caught her breath in surprise. Anthony Whiteside! She had not seen him in years, not since they had broken off their brief liaison, but the familiar sight of him had power to stir her nonetheless. Their affair had been over long before she had met Andrew. She wondered if he remembered?

But how stupid! Of course he remembered. He couldn't have forgotten, even though they had scrupulously kept to their mutual promise never to see or communicate with one another again.

Whiteside's expression was very proper, but in the intelligent brown eyes under the unruly lock of wavy, grey-blond hair, she caught a hint of mockery. He was not tall but his stocky body was fit and well-proportioned, and he carried himself with a marvellous presence. As always, he was perfectly attired in a well-tailored suit. This was a scion of one of America's richest families. Anthony Whiteside had spent his adult life, not in idle pleasure-seeking, nor in amassing ever greater wealth, but in public service. He had been elected Governor of a midwest border state and since then, had served in a variety of high-profile appointments under succeeding presidents of both political parties. Now he had accepted an assignment which he was well aware would bring him and his one-time lover into frequent contact in Ottawa.

Kathleen Marshal was touched by a shadow of apprehension, swiftly followed by a thrill of anticipation. It would be so good to be with Tony again.

"Prime Minister," began President Thompson, his voice breaking unexpectedly into her careening thoughts, "what do I call you?"

"My name is Kathleen Marshal. Wickstrom," she added quickly, darting a glance at Anthony Whiteside. "Mrs. Andrew Wickstrom."

And then ignoring him she spoke directly to the President. "But call me anything you want. Kathleen. Or Katie. Kate, Kath, Kit—whatever you like. Different people use different diminutives. It doesn't matter—I answer to them all."

"Kathleen," her host said speculatively. "A nice name. That'll be it, then. In the south we like to be formal. But call me Billy. That's what my friends do.

"Now let's get down to business."

Kathleen Marshal concentrated her attention on the President. So far, his manner had been pleasant enough, and she found her tension leaving her. But now, as his expression darkened, she brought herself to an inner alert. Outwardly, however, there was little change in her own expression as she awaited the President's explanation of this peremptory summons.

"I learned some very disquieting things last week in Brussels," he began, gravely, leaning towards her across the coffee table that separated them, his gnarled hands, with their prominent veins, clasped around one knee. "From your minister, Jean Jacques Charles."

Kathleen waited, an eyebrow raised in polite enquiry.

"It appears that Canada is about to make a deal to sell a nuclear reactor. To Cuba." He looked at this unknown woman, Canada's new Prime Minister, narrowly. Surprisingly, he detected no immediate reaction.

"To Cuba!" he said again, with emphasis. Then, goaded by her continued silence, "Now we just can't have that happen! I think you know why. There isn't going to be another Cuban crisis under my administration, I can tell you. It was bad enough in Kennedy's time, with Cuba being supplied by the Russians. We are just not going to let Canada—no matter how friendly a neighbour—build up those Communists right there on our front step," the President said vehemently. "Now what are *you* going to do about that?"

Kathleen's mind raced. She knew nothing of this, had received no advance briefing whatsoever on recent proposed sales of the Canadian reactors. She searched her memory. She *had* read newspaper reports of sales to Korea and to Argentina, even to Japan and Mexico, the latter in exchange for a secure supply of newly discovered oil, but for the life of her, she could not remember any mention of a sale to Cuba. And in the few Cabinet meetings she had attended since the leadership convention, there had not been one whisper from Atomic Energy of Canada Limited, the government agency responsible for nuclear production and sales, both domestic and foreign.

Kathleen was uneasily aware of the prolonged silence following the President's challenging question. Fleetingly, she considered an attempt to hide her lack of knowledge, then wisely rejected that course.

"You catch me entirely unaware, Mr. President. I assure you, I know nothing whatever of any such proposal. If indeed there is any such plan," she added doubtfully. "You say you learned of it in Brussels from Mr. Charles? What exactly did he tell you?"

"Not much, I admit. But then, our entire exchange wasn't

exactly calm and edifying. But perhaps you don't even know about that?" He swung his gaze to the Canadian Ambassador. "Surely they have told you that Charles and I," he searched for the right diplomatic phrase, "had words, I guess you'd call it. Heated words."

That the Canadian Ambassador knew something of that undignified exchange was clear. Tellier fidgeted in his seat, refusing to meet the President's eyes.

Kathleen spoke quickly, seeking to ease the Ambassador's discomfort. "We know only that such an incident occurred. Apparently no one was close enough to hear what was said between you. And I have been unable to reach Jacques—Mr. Charles—to get his version of the *contretemps*. In any event, I readily offer you an apology on my government's behalf," she said evenly, gravely, and obviously sincerely.

The President sat back in his chair, measuring her.

"No, I don't suppose any of your people did hear anything," he admitted. "Well, Charles told me that a Cuban deal is already locked up. He gave me to understand that Canada is pressing on with its sales of the Candu, wherever and whenever possible. Including a number of countries in Central and South America. He said he made some preliminary deals when he took a swing around those countries. And everyone knows how chummy he was with Castro on that trip!

"Look, Prime Minister, I know you haven't been in your job long, but how can it be that you don't know of this sale?" His voice rose. "It is directly opposed to our interests in this hemisphere! Those little Spanish-speaking countries are volatile enough without giving them the wherewithal to create there own nuclear armaments. If you do, it won't be Canada on the firing line. It will be us. And I won't have it," he practically shouted. "Surely you see the danger—that Cuba could gain access to all our nuclear secrets through you?"

"I see," murmured Kathleen, her heart sinking. The President was angry all right and, she admitted to herself, with good reason. By his lights, anyway. "Of course, Mr. President. The reason for your concern is very clear now. But I assure you, I knew nothing of such a sale until this very minute. Even now, I find it hard to believe that it's true. Yes, our agency has been making every effort to sell our Candu reactor abroad. It was very costly to develop, and is potentially a big earner of foreign exchange. And it is important to us to sell our own technology. But the AECL, I'm sure, has always used approved methods to interest foreign governments in a Candu purchase."

Her hazel eyes were calm as she reached towards the cigarette box on the coffee table. She slowly drew forth a long cigarette which she tapped to tighten the tobacco.

"But," she began again, pausing to hold the tip of the cigarette to the flame produced smoothly by Anthony Whiteside, "it has been Canadian policy for more than a decade not to sell any of our nuclear or atomic technology to *any* country, unless it guarantees that it will be used for strictly peaceful purposes. We have even turned down sales to France, as long ago as Sandy Sinclair's administration. We are signatories to the non-proliferation treaty and we adhere to that. We demand safeguards." She turned to her Ambassador for confirmation.

"Yes, ma'am, that's right. Of course there was India," Tellier admitted.

"Yes, India, but that was a regrettable breach of good faith."

"That has always been our position, Prime Minister," the diplomat concurred in a soft voice.

"So you see, Mr. President," she said, turning back to face Thompson, "such a sale would represent a departure from our long-established position. It is almost inconceivable that I would not have been told if one had been made." Her voice was steady, her words persuasive.

"Is it possible that there has been a deliberate attempt to keep it from you?" asked Thompson.

"I find that hard to credit," she replied coldly, "but until I return to Ottawa, and talk to my advisors, and to Mr. Charles, it remains a possibility, no matter how unlikely." And then, resolve firm in her voice, she stated, "You may be sure that I *will* find out, and at once, on my return."

"Well, I guess Charles will know. Tell me, could he as prime minister, have made a personal commitment of some kind that your Cabinet and officials would know nothing of?"

"That is remotely possible, of course. But under our system a prime minister can't do that sort of thing on his own. It would have to be followed up. . . ." Her voice faltered, suddenly lacking conviction. Kathleen remembered that Jacques sometimes took fairly unconventional—some said unconstitutional—shortcuts.

"I can't say I know Charles all that well, but while he was

prime minister he did not always display a sympathetic understanding of our continental concerns. And as the leader of the free world, of course, our national interests are those of many other nations," the President said, somewhat pompously. "And he did tell me that Canada was selling that reactor to Cuba, despite our objections."

"No one could keep that kind of thing secret for long. Not in Ottawa any more than in Washington," she countered wryly.

"Can you give me your word that no such sale will be pursued?" he asked her pointblank, no trace in his voice of the usual soft southern cadence.

Kathleen studied the face of the most powerful political leader in the free world. The intent cornflower-blue eyes rested on her own. Thompson's most distinguishing feature, the one political cartoonists loved to play with, was his wide, flashing grin. The grin was not in evidence now—had not been throughout the interview. President William Concord Thompson was very serious and he wanted an answer. Now.

Kathleen searched for an appropriate response. It was not easy. Her instinct was to set his fears at rest, to give him the assurance he demanded. Yet it nagged at her mind that there might be other factors, factors she was at the moment entirely unaware of, which had to be considered. Canada's own national interests were, after all, her first concern. She concluded that she would have to put him off, somehow, until all the facts were in her possession.

The Prime Minister of Canada glanced at her Ambassador. Tellier's expression was dejected, his shoulders slumped, his head bowed, his gaze on his hands clasped between his well-tailored knees. She could see the bald spot he was usually at such pains to conceal. No help for her there.

"I believe you will understand, Mr. President, that under the circumstances, as much as I would like to give you that assurance, I cannot. Not today. But I promise you that you will be hearing from me shortly. Perhaps even now my people have been able to reach Jacques, and asked him to return. I will get to the bottom of this, and quickly. That, I am afraid, is all I can promise this evening," she said, her voice tinged with sincere regret.

"Yes, I understand, of course. But it is a matter of vital importance to us, as I think you are aware. Otherwise, I would not have asked you here like this. I suppose I'll have to wait, but I hope to hear from you soon," he said with acceptance, his hands flat on his knees. Then looking up at her, his tone lightened. "Now, before you go, would you like a drink? Coffee? Something stronger?"

"No, thank you, Mr. President. It's already been a very long day. I'd like to get back to Ottawa as quickly as possible. If you'll forgive me, I think we should leave now," she said courteously, anxious for the meeting to end. "Unless," she paused, wondering whether she should raise the point, bound to be embarrassing, "there is something else—about the altercation with Charles—you'd like me to know?"

The President stood up, considering the question. Should he tell her about the outrageous action of her predecessor, insulting him, threatening to throw a punch at him, the President of the United States of America? He seethed again at the recollection of the ugly, unprecedented incident. Oh hell, why carry tales? Charles would probably tell her his version soon enough. Leave it at that—an injury to the President's pride, an embarrassment to the new Prime Minister. She'd have enough on her plate, as it was.

As the President recollected the incident, his expression had altered, reflecting those thoughts. With relief, Kathleen saw in his eyes his conclusion not to pursue the matter further.

"No," the President said, as he held out his hand to her. "We'll forget all that, and start with a clean slate. But there *is* one other thing you overlooked."

She hesitated, about to turn to take her leave of Anthony Whiteside. She glanced at the President, her brows raised quizzically.

"What's that?" she enquired.

"You forgot. I asked you to call me Billy, Kathleen." His famous white-toothed grin broke at last, like sunshine after a storm.

Kathleen sipped absently at the drink brought her by the steward almost immediately after take-off. Her gaze was directed out the window beside her at the crescent moon sailing in and out among the silver-edged, high-piling clouds.

She was near the edge of exhaustion. Last night's election triumph after the short but furious campaign, followed by this morning's unplanned flight to Ottawa and then on to Washington, the tension of her first meeting with the United States' President and the shock of seeing Anthony Whiteside so unexpectedly, piled one upon the other, had drained away her energy until Kathleen felt she could scarcely hold up her head.

She lay back wearily against the head-rest, her feet propped on the empty seat opposite, and closed her eyes. The crowded events of the past twenty-four hours unreeled again against her lids.

Her thoughts chased one another in two separate but concentric circles. Jacques and the President. Andrew and Anthony. Jacques and the President, Andrew and Anthony. Anthony—Tony.

It all came flooding back. They had met several times at international meetings. Then one night, over dinner in Paris, they had mutually confessed their compelling attraction to one another. Her infatuation had been overwhelming. She had struggled against it, as indeed had Tony. He had told her about his wife. For a while, Kathleen deluded herself that Tony would break free from his marriage, and she had let herself fall more deeply in love with the sophisticated American. They had met once in Hawaii, once more in Paris, and twice in London. Each time they had had only a day or two together, all they could spare from their heavy schedules. Perhaps a week in all, over more than a year. Then, no longer able to bear the furtiveness of the affair, she had sent him away from her forever. It had been years before Kathleen felt whole again, years before she could hear Whiteside's name mentioned or see his photograph without experiencing a deep pang of hurt. Eventually, however, the wound of loss had healed, and since she had met and loved Andrew Wickstrom, Kathleen had never thought of Tony again. Not until today.

And he was coming to Ottawa soon. She would see him again, often. His embassy office was only a step away from hers on Wellington Street. His Residence was only a mile or so through the leafy groves of Rockcliffe from 24 Sussex. They'd meet officially on intergovernmental business and socially at parties and receptions.

For a moment, Kathleen was afraid. Afraid of stirring up again that total abandonment she had felt with Anthony Whiteside. Afraid of its effect on her marriage. And on her role as Prime Minister.

Her eyes flew open and she swallowed the rest of her drink in a gulp and at once rang for another.

Don't be a damn fool, Kathleen. You're a middle-aged

woman with a marvellous husband, not a romantic young thing in love with love. Whiteside is attractive and intelligent. He can be a friend. And no politician ever has enough friends. Just keep your head. What's past is safely past.

"Prime Minister, Mr. Charles is here."

Kathleen acknowledged the announcement with a grateful nod. Jean Jacques had finally been located and flown home. They had landed in Ottawa only hours apart yesterday—she back from her disturbing trip to Washington—he from his impromptu vacation in Europe.

It was still early and although Kathleen had already dressed and breakfasted, the room remained lit by lamps. The sun's rays had not yet reached her quiet study in the government's official guest house, but Kathleen intended to get an early start.

Before she had left Washington, Kathleen had called her office and ordered that the Cabinet minutes for the past year be searched. No reference had been found to the proposed sale of the Candu to Cuba. She had wanted to go over them herself, but when she returned late last night, she had been too exhausted to go over the big, red-bound books labelled "Top Secret," which now lay before her on her littered desk.

"You sent for me, Kathleen?" asked Jean Jacques Charles, striding jauntily into the room.

"Yes, Jacques, sit down. I've had a rather unpleasant twenty-four hours as a result of your actions in Brussels."

Jacques already knew that she had heard of the Brussels incident and he fully expected to be called on the carpet over that. On his return he had also been told that Kathleen had been to Washington in answer to a summons from the President, but he had not been informed about the substance of their meeting.

"I'll come straight to the point, Jacques. Are we selling a Candu to Cuba?"

Jacques dropped into the brass-studded chair beside her desk. He fingered the sturdy polished fabric of its arm as he looked at her steadily. He was not happy that she had leaped directly to the subject of the Candu. He knew of course that it would come up, but he had hoped to approach it in context or, more precisely, he had hoped to be able to explain the Brussels event and then. . . .

Kathleen stared back at the unblinking blue eyes. "The President is furious about it and I can't find anything here." She gestured towards the Cabinet records. "There's no reference to confirm that there are any such plans."

"Oh, that. So that's what the man in the White House wanted to see you about. I might have guessed," he said with a distinct tone of boredom. Jacques leaned forward in the chair. "He called *me* a Commie bastard, did you know that?" Anger rose in his voice. "Said I was just the guy who would sell out the US to my Commie friends. The guy is unbelievable! Imagine trying to tell Canada who it can sell to? I hope you snapped right back at him. Told him to keep his nose out of *our* business!" Jacques leaned back in his chair. The best defence is a good offence.

Kathleen was about to speak, when Jacques added vehemently, "What's more I expect an apology! It's hardly proper to address a foreign minister the way he addressed me."

Kathleen looked at Jacques in disbelief. "No, Jacques, I did not snap back at him. I think he has every right to be upset. I know I am! And I felt a perfect fool, not knowing what he was talking about. Nor can I find any reference to the sale or anyone who knows about it. The President of AECL is away, our Minister of Energy is away, you've been away, and there are no records!" Her voice rose with her frustration. "So *you* tell me. Have we a deal to sell nuclear technology to Cuba?"

Jacques assumed a position of complete relaxation. He folded his hands and put them on his chest.

"The whole story, Kathleen, the whole truth, but the direct answer is yes and no."

"What do you mean yes and no?" she asked evenly.

"Do you agree to listen to the whole story?" He felt the sequence of events would soften her up. It's all, he reflected, in the telling of the tale.

Kathleen relaxed slightly. "Let's hear it—from beginning to end."

"Well, I did have preliminary discussions with Fidel. He's very keen you know. We've met a couple of times and we get on well. He really wants the Candu—and, as you probably know, it's not easy to sell them. Lots of competition out there, especially from the Germans and the Yanks. Well, anyway, we had a gentlemen's agreement. Now, that all happened when I was Prime Minister. Naturally, someone else has to tie it all down—AECL or one of their agents. The truth is, I haven't heard a thing about it lately. AECL may be following it up, or they may have let it drop for one reason or another."

"Why is there no mention of this in the Cabinet minutes?" she asked.

"Because things just weren't into that stage yet. In the early stages this sort of thing has to be kept to only a few people. The competition's rough. When the deal is ready to be signed is *plenty* of time to go to Cabinet, Kathleen." He said it with firmness. His tone implied that she was new in the job and didn't know the ropes yet. Kathleen sighed inwardly. Walking a tightrope with the United States was some way to learn the ropes!

"It's all premature," Jacques added in order to drive his point home. "Look, we don't bring External or Industry, Trade and Commerce in until later. Anyway, this all happened long before the leadership convention. For all I know AECL may have put the whole thing on the back-burner. I've had no enquiry from Castro lately."

"Then why? Why, Jacques, in the name of heaven, did you tell the President the deal was set?" Her voice was frigid.

Jacques looked taken aback. "I don't think I told him *that*. Not so specifically, anyway. I admit I intended him to *think* it was a *fait accompli,* but I certainly didn't say so in so many words." He shifted in his chair. "Look, maybe you'll understand better if you let me finish telling you what happened."

Kathleen stared at him.

"You really must calm down. This whole thing is stupid. It just got out of hand, but I hardly think any real harm's been done. Maybe it'll make that cracker in the White House understand he can't take us for granted."

Kathleen drew in her breath sharply, prepared to lash out at Jacques. He went on, forestalling her.

"After the NATO meeting in Brussels, there was the usual reception, all very formal and stuffy. I didn't even talk to Thompson until just before he was leaving. Then he sort of ambled up for a few words. Everybody was either gone or in the process of leaving, so there wasn't anyone around. Billy-boy was friendly enough, just wanted a word or two about our new military purchases. Started out asking what kind of planes we wanted, if any, then started going on about some proposals he was going to send along about 'sharing' our water in the future—the usual kind of stuff—all those bloody continental assumptions where everything becomes 'ours' instead of Canadian or American.

"Well, you know how I feel about continental plans for survival—water, energy, all that. I guess I was pretty non-committal."

Kathleen did indeed know. As Jacques had proven to her on a number of occasions—when he wanted to be non-committal, he most certainly could be non-committal.

"Then all of a sudden Thompson flashed that big grin and he said, 'Maybe I shouldn't be talking to *you* anymore, seeing as you've been beaten by a *woman*.' He was really contemptuous, you know. Said he was sure you'd be easier to handle, said he knew how to get to you. I didn't like that much, so I started needling him right back. Said we had some other friends we were doing business with, including Castro. Talked a little about our 'third option' and more or less said we might not need the United States as much as he thought. That's when he called me a Commie bastard. Hell, I've had that thrown at me more than once, but Thompson ought to have known better. Now, Kathleen, you know I do have a temper."

At this understatement, Kathleen almost smiled but the seriousness of the situation held her back. She allowed him to continue.

"I just saw red! I called him a 'nobody'—an amateur who had only been elected by a fluke. Told him he couldn't even control his own Congress and that he wouldn't be renominated, much less re-elected, so he should go look after his own shop and let us look after ours. Of course, he blew right up. His aides hustled him out of there. That's all there was to it, I swear. Nobody knows about it."

Kathleen stared at him. Incredible! He really didn't seem to think it was very important. Yet she knew the President's temper, had experienced the extent of his power to summon her to Washington, knew the depth of his concern. It wasn't an unimportant brush. If it wasn't handled properly it could sour their relationship with the powerful Americans for years to come. And for what? A deal that wasn't even set?

"So the deal isn't set?" She honed in on the principal problem, just to confirm again what Jacques seemed to be telling her.

"I overstated it somewhat," he admitted.

"It can be stopped?" She wanted very definite answers.

"I imagine," he answered reluctantly.

"Jacques, if, as you say, the Cabinet doesn't know about this proposed sale, how did you intend to do it? How could you expect to get it through Cabinet, much less the House? This is still a minority Government. An announcement like that would bring down the Opposition like a wolf on the fold. Can you just imagine one of the bright young PC members like Sorenson with something like this?" Kathleen fought to hold herself in check.

"Sorenson?" Jacques said the name with contempt. "Sorenson's a red-baiter, a young pup. Who cares about him? Kathleen, we need the sales. They provide us with billions in foreign exchange, hundreds of jobs, international prestige. Castro isn't so bad you know. Canada has always kept up contacts with Cuba. We've got banks there; thousands of Canadian tourists vacation there. Castro assured me that he only wanted the power for peaceful purposes. Can't the Cubans have electricity? I trust him. What's so wrong about selling a Candu to Cuba?"

Kathleen wanted to scream. She took a deep breath. "The Americans are hyper about Cuba, you know that. It's only ninety miles from Florida! Look what happened when they found out about the Russian troops! Jacques, you dropped a clanger in the White House. Thompson is facing renomination soon. He just can't risk the spectre of Cuba with *our* nuclear technology. You know that, Jacques. What in the hell were you about?"

"Just putting him on notice that we run our own show here. C'mon Kathleen. Every time the President of the US hollers, you don't have to cringe. We are our own masters, don't forget. The USA doesn't own us!" Jacques was indignant, defensive of his position.

This she found believable. Jacques had invented—well, exaggerated—this whole thing just to twist the tiger's tail—to make Thompson mad, to rub in Canada's independence, to make a point. And, she had to admit that what he now said did make some sense. There was always that balance between defending Canada's sovereign right to follow her own path, and the all-too-necessary accommodations that had to be made from time to time with the neighbour to the south. Canada always had to be aware of the effects of her actions on the politicians in Washington, although the years had demonstrated that there were not too many American politicians who were as careful of Canada's sensitivities.

Kathleen sighed deeply, her anger melting. Well, now she knew how to handle this mini-crisis, at least for the present. All it needed was a reassuring message to the President, thank God!

Jacques watched Kathleen's mobile features. She was easy to read for someone who had known her as long as he had.

The tall woman picked up the red-bound books before her, replacing them in the capacious black leather valises in which they had been delivered by special messenger. She rang for the butler, asking him to send her secretary to her.

Barbara Hepburn appeared at once, a notebook and sharpened pencils in her hand, her pert face cheerful and bright-eyed. As she entered the small study she nodded to Jacques pleasantly, immediately sensing the strain in the room. She walked directly to the deskside and stooped for the heavy valises.

"I'll send for the messenger to return them to the Privy Council Office," she said. "And, Prime Minister," her eyes flicked from Kathleen to Jacques and back again, "there's fresh coffee. Interested?"

As they sipped the hot brew, Jacques raised another, more personal matter.

"I've found a house for myself and the children. I can be out of Number 24 by the end of the week. Will you want some redecorating done or do you expect to move in right away? I haven't much in the way of furniture there. Most of it belongs to public works," he said wryly. "I don't know anything about shopping for furniture, so I've called in a decorator who knows such things. The new house is pleasant enough—not far away, in Rockcliffe, of course. But no pool," he said regretfully.

"Please use the pool as often as you like," she offered courteously. "I haven't really thought much about moving across the street but this is a little cramped," she admitted, looking about the small study, with its piles of papers and toppling briefing books. "Jacques, I appreciate your handling of the government while I've been campaigning. Now that I'm back, I want to complete the Cabinet shuffle—and, I must admit, I'm having second thoughts about putting you in External. Frankly, after this, it may not be such a good idea. I have to consider the implications—especially the reaction of the White House. I should think your appointment would be badly received in Washington just now. Have you any suggestions?"

His look froze. "Kathleen, you can't allow the Americans to make your Cabinet. Frankly, the only other alternative would be to appoint me to an embassy somewhere. I don't want that and I should think you would want to avoid it."

The unspoken question of how Quebec would view his going hung in the air. Kathleen tried to read Jacques' face, but she couldn't guess what he was thinking.

"Kathleen, this is really such a nothing affair. You *have* more important things to deal with. Phone the President or the Ambassador and tell him there's nothing to the deal. Let the Energy Minister find out what's happening. Put him on it, he'll keep you informed. Prime ministers shouldn't be chasing paper." Jacques paused. "You *are* going to keep your promises. You are going to appoint LaCroix to Energy, aren't you?"

She nodded in the affirmative and acknowledged that he did have a point. If she appointed him to External, Thompson would be madder than ever; if she didn't she might lose support in Quebec.

"External it will be," she said at length. "But, Jacques, keep a low profile for a while and stay out of Billy Thompson's way. Perhaps you need a vacation?" She never thought she would hear herself say that, but right now she really hoped he would disappear for a few weeks.

He smiled brightly. "Well, perhaps I will wing down to the Club Atlantica for a bit." Jacques rose and with a jaunty smile left her.

Kathleen lit a cigarette and turned to look out the window. At length she rang for her secretary.

"Barbara, will you get me the American Ambassador please. Set up an appointment here. This afternoon, if you can. I'll see him alone."

Moments later the satin-skinned black face reappeared at the doorway.

Kathleen looked up.

"They report that there is no Ambassador in residence, Prime Minister. He was recalled recently and his replacement is expected momentarily. The new one is to present his credentials to the Governor General later in the week. Is there anyone else there you'd like to speak to?"

Kathleen blinked. Of course, Anthony Whiteside was being sent here by the President. But there had been no mention of how soon. Tony would be here this week. Her heart lifted at the thought and she smiled. Then frowned. It would be a complication of her life, but one she had decided she welcomed, nonetheless.

"Let's see," she pondered aloud. "I think maybe our Ambassador in Washington then. No. Barbara, is there a hot-line telephone here in the guest house? To the President?"

"I don't think so, but I'll find out right away. You're going to call him?" was the ready rejoinder. Nothing surprised Barbara Hepburn.

"Yes. If there is no hot-line, arrange it through the PMO and have them patch the call through to this line, as quickly as possible."

"It's just after eight. Do you think it's okay to call so early?"

"I think the President will take the call." He'll no doubt be happy, she thought to herself, to find out how fast I jump to his command. Although it may not always be so. But it can't hurt to do a little stroking of the eagle's feathers this first time. She smiled at the thought.

"Mr. Wickstrom on the line, Madam."

The butler carried the extension phone to Kathleen in the high-backed flowered chair, one of a pair flanking the fireplace in the pretty drawing room. She was alone in the firelit room, its drapes recently drawn against the pearly mist of a swiftly approaching fog-swathed night. Her back ached from bending all day over the piles of papers that had accumulated on her desk, all crying out for attention, and often for prompt decision. Barbara Hepburn had left, pleading exhaustion with the day's work, and the last of the day's visitors had ultimately been ushered out. Kathleen had called for a large, icy martini, and the round silver tray with its crystal shaker, an oversized stemmed glass, and an accompanying bowl of salted nuts, had only just been placed on the gleaming lamp-table beside her, when her husband's call was announced.

Kathleen laid aside her reading glasses, nodding her appreciation as the manservant poured her drink and discreetly withdrew before she spoke into the mouthpiece.

"Andrew. Where are you? In Toronto, of course. How I miss you, Drew. Are you coming up? The house will be ready this week or next. Jacques has found a place for himself and the twins. The staff is arranging everything. What? Furniture? I don't know. There should be enough there for now anyway. I'll look into it later.

"Yes, I guess I am tired. I have the Washington thing straightened out. For now, anyway. I'll tell you all about it when I see you. Or as much as I can, anyway. Yes, I am dining alone and then to bed early. Also alone," she teased.

Andrew had no more than rung off and Kathleen had just raised her glass for a first sip of the icy gin, when she heard the peal of the doorbell.

Oh no, her tired mind rebelled. Not tonight. I'm beat. Her thoughts lingered on the anticipated long hot bath, the tray of dinner in her room, some music and then, blessed sleep.

She looked up as the butler stepped into the room, closely followed by a figure still shrugging his way out of a mist-spangled raincoat.

"The American Ambassador, Madam. He says that he is expected."

Anthony Whiteside emerged from behind the servant and strode energetically across the room to her. His words tumbled out.

"I got your message, Kath. They said a call had come this morning and that you wanted to see me. I only got in an hour or so ago and they almost forgot to give me the message. You see, they didn't expect me until tomorrow or the next day."

Dazed at his unexpected appearance, she rose from her chair and held out her hands to meet his. He clasped them both, then dropped them as his arms went around her in a bear-hug. He whispered into her hair.

"Oh God, it's so good to see you, to touch you, to hold you again. It's been so long. That meeting in Washington was terrible. To be so near and unable to say anything. I could hardly wait to get to Ottawa to see you again. And I was so glad when your message was waiting. Oh, Kath, it's so wonderful." His lips sought hers.

Kathleen stood trembling within the circle of his arms. She intended to stiffen her body, to repel his embrace, but when he kissed her she found herself responding against her judgement, against her will.

When Whiteside released her and stepped back to look into her face, her hazel eyes were luminous, vulnerable. Kathleen caught her lower lip between her teeth, to stop the trembling. She fumbled with her hair, smoothed her dress, anything to distract her from the confusion of her thoughts. She turned away from her unexpected visitor, groping for her chair. Her eyes blinked back sudden tears.

In a choked voice she offered him a seat across from her,

on the sofa. He ignored the invitation and moved to her side. He bent over her and caught up a hand. He brought it to his lips for a lingering caress.

"What is it, Kath? What's the matter, darling? Tears? Why tears? Of happiness, that must be it. I've felt a little weepy myself, ever since I saw you in Washington. Oh my dear, think of the years we've missed. Think how much time we'll have together, now. Glorious time."

Kathleen fought for composure. She dashed the tears from her eyes, appalled at her own reaction, then withdrew her hand from his, and tried to steady her voice.

"Tony, please sit down. Over there. Give me time to get myself under control. This visit—your presence—is such a surprise, I . . . ."

"But you were expecting me, surely. You'd left a message."

"There has been a misunderstanding, Tony. My office did call the Residence, earlier in the day, to speak to the Ambassador. I wanted him to transmit a message to the President about our discussion yesterday. I never for a moment thought it would be you. I had no idea you were coming so soon. I never dreamt—" She was beginning to regain some semblance of her poise. "It was a matter of business—between our governments, Tony. It was nothing personal."

On his tanned face an expression of disbelief dawned. It was followed by the realization that he had made a fool of himself, rushing to her like a schoolboy to his long-lost love, making an assumption that her own feelings remained as deep as his.

She saw the wave of pain cross his face. "Please, Tony. I'm really very glad to see you. Really. Let me tell you why I wanted to see the Ambassador and then we'll have a drink and talk."

He sat back in the chair and nodded—of course she couldn't have known he was here—he had to let her recover.

"What is it?" he asked calmly. "What's my first assignment?"

Kathleen relaxed now. "I had wanted you to give a message to the President, Tony. To tell him that there's no set deal. When I couldn't reach the Ambassador—you, that is—I called him myself."

Tony smiled broadly. "He must have been impressed with your efficiency."

"He did seem relieved, but I don't think he was entirely convinced."

"Well, that will be my first assignment, to convince the President of your sincerity." His smile faded. "Now let's discuss something more personal—us."

She looked at him more calmly now. "I'm terribly sorry about the misunderstanding."

He nodded, but still looked intent. "I watched you in the Oval Office when the President introduced us. I saw your eyes. I thought you felt just as I did. I watched you struggle to hide it just as I had to hide my feelings. I scarcely dared to look at you for fear of giving away what I felt. That's why I came to Ottawa early. I hoped to see you privately. You've no idea how I've been floating since I got that message. I remembered all our times together. How you sent me away those years ago. There were tears in your eyes then, too. Are you honestly telling me now that I've made a terrible mistake? That you no longer care for me?"

Kathleen was aghast at his revelation.

"Tony, dearest," she said gently. "Of course I'm glad to see you. Terribly glad, just as I was in Washington. That was a shock. I thought you had forgotten me, forgotten us. But I saw that you remembered and I remembered, too.

"But everything has changed. You're no longer the Governor with the fragile wife. I'm no longer an ordinary Member of Parliament. I'm married now, to a fine man, and we are happy together." Kathleen paused for a moment, the words she had just said echoing in her head. "We are happy together." Fleetingly, she wondered whether that was really true, anymore.

"And now I am Prime Minister," she continued, swiftly, "and you are one of the most important men in our national capital—our link to our most powerful and important friend, the United States. It's all changed." She hesitated again, groping for words. "Of course we'll see one another often. I look forward to it, my dear old friend. But it never occurred to me, I never thought of anything personal, Tony." She lapsed into silence, watching him.

"Kath, I only heard recently that you had left politics and married. If I'd known that you were on your own in the time before you married, I would have come to you. Pauline—my wife—died a year ago. She was ill for a long time, and she was proud. You know I could never have left her. But when I was free, I found that you hadn't waited. You were married. I thought it was over forever. Then you came back and won the leadership of your party. There was very little in our papers about a husband, and you were using your maiden name. He didn't come with you to Washington and I understand he isn't even in Ottawa. Surely that's no kind of marriage? I assumed it was over between you and this ... Wickstrom?"

"Andrew Wickstrom. And however it may appear, no, the marriage is not over, Tony. Andrew is in Toronto. He doesn't like Ottawa. Nor does he really care for politics. But he cares for me. And I for him. It's just the way we have arranged things between us."

"I can't believe it, Kath. That's not like the woman I remember. It sounds so cold-blooded. An 'arrangement.' Living in different cities. Not using his name. Not being together, every possible moment. That isn't the way I feel about you. It isn't good enough for you, Kath! I can give you what you want and need. Now we'll be together, just as we once dreamed. Kath, look at me. Remember what we had. What we had to give up, once. Don't send me away again, Kath. I love you. I always have. And damn it, I'm determined to have you. Whether this Wickstrom likes it or not, I'm determined never to lose you again."

She looked at him sadly. "Please, Tony. Not tonight— maybe not ever. Please understand that I have to have time to think. You should do some thinking as well. It's been a long week for me—crisis ridden. I can't deal with an emotional crisis too."

He touched her hand. "I'm sorry, Kathleen. I do understand. Can we talk in a few days then?"

"Yes," she replied. "In a few days."

Kathleen stood quietly as the members of her Cabinet stepped up one after another to the Book. Each swore allegiance, repeating the oath after Helmut Ogilvy. Then in turn, they signed the book of register of the Canadian Privy Council, and shook hands with the Governor General.

She wasn't very happy about the Cabinet line-up. It was still essentially Jacques' old Cabinet. She had brought in a few new faces but her options were sharply limited. She had given Jacques External Affairs and Senator LaCroix the Energy portfolio. She had brought Carter Warden back to Ottawa as Minister of Finance. She had to appoint him to the Senate, so that now two of the more senior ministers would be unable to report to the House. The situation made her uneasy. She had previously dropped Findlay and now Palmer. Findlay had resigned his seat but Palmer had not. She had let Proudfoot go and promised him an appointment later when an election was called. On the affirmative side, there were two new women in the Cabinet, Bonnie Costello in Labour and Mary Margaret McMahon in Health and Welfare.

Cabinet-making was difficult at the best of times but especially when you're trying to give a new look to the same old bunch, she thought desperately. Then, as the last of the ministers completed the ceremony, she straightened her shoulders and led them to the ballroom for the traditional group photograph. Afterwards, they would lunch at 24 Sussex, and the real work of her government could begin.

As they sauntered in groups of two or three down the long drive from Rideau Hall, Kathleen walked between Jacques and Gabriel LaCroix. She told the Senator that she was particularly interested in being kept posted on sales of the Candu reactor, especially any to Cuba.

"Keep me advised if anything at all comes up, please, Gabriel."

"Of course, Prime Minister," he said as he exchanged an uneasy look with Jean Jacques Charles.

Adam Sorenson stood at the far end of the Press Club bar, giving only half his attention to the garrulous young cub reporter who had asked him here for an interview over lunch. He hunched his narrow shoulders, trying to shut out his hostess' aimless chatter, tuning his ears to the big, sandy-haired man who was holding forth, further down the bar.

Most of those present, including Sorenson, were talking about the new Cabinet line-up. Reporters, each with a glass in hand, clustered about the former Minister of Energy, who was leaning on the bar, one foot up on the brass rail.

"So I told the bitch I've got bigger fish to fry," the big westerner concluded. He took a gulp of his drink, emptying the glass. "And I have," he insisted, putting the glass down with a thump beside the two others he had already drained dry. "Yes, sir, much bigger fish to fry." He grinned to himself.

There was a respectful silence from the reporters.

Stan Findlay looked a little sad, as he contemplated his empty glass.

"Have another, Stan?" one of the reporters offered.

He brightened. "Don't mind if I do," he said affably.

"You decided what you're going to do?" ventured another, not really interested in the answer.

"Yeah." Findlay looked around him craftily. "Got a little something cooking," he admitted.

He looked into the faces of the reporters nearest him. They didn't seem to care what he did. "Gonna make some real money," he bragged, sure that would catch their interest.

"Moving to Toronto, are you?"

Findlay hooted. "Naw. Can't you just see me with that Bay Street bunch? Who needs them? I got myself a good deal."

The reporters exchanged disbelieving glances. Stan Findlay was certainly into his cups, no doubt about that. One by one, they drifted off, leaving him alone at the bar.

Left alone, the ex-minister morosely addressed himself to his drink. So that Marshal bitch thought she could get along without him, did she? Well, he'd show her—and all the others, too. All he needed was for someone to set up a little appointment with that bearded Commie, and he'd do the rest. He'd be on his way to a bundle! Good ole Jean Jacques Charles—he was a real buddy to have set it up. After all, Jacques owed him some favours and he and Castro were as thick as that. . . .

Adam Sorenson sidled down the bar to stand next to Findlay.

"Hear you quit the Cabinet for a big job, Findlay. Congratulations! I'd like to stand you a round on that."

The sandy-haired man peered down at him owlishly.

"Oh, ah, Sorenson. Yeah, thanks."

His hand closed around the wet glass as soon as it was placed before him, and he drained it in one swallow, wiping his mouth on his sleeve as he replaced the empty glass.

"Well, gotta get going," he said, pushing himself away from the bar. "I've got a plane to catch."

"Where's the new job, Stan?" asked Sorenson.

"Wouldn't you like to know, though," Findlay tossed over his shoulder. He lurched and then steadied himself.

"I wonder why that guy doesn't mind his own business?" he muttered as he made for the exit.

Chapter Six

Stanley Findlay toyed absently with the remainder of his steak. Had he asked all the right questions?

His luncheon partner laid his cutlery precisely on his plate, wiped his lips and shoved himself back from the table. Carefully the president of the AECL made a selection from his monogrammed alligator carrying-case, and his sharp, stained teeth bit off the end of the thin cigar. Then he flicked the lighter that formed one end of the expensive case, inhaling deeply before he spoke again. Billows of aromatic cigar smoke floated about his head.

"Then it's a deal." It was a statement rather than a question. "You'll act as our agent with Dr. Castro."

"At the fee of two million dollars," Findlay reiterated, maintaining a steady gaze towards the president, although his mind was still filled with the wondrous thought that so much money could really be his.

"Agreed. After your contract is signed, of course."

Obviously, dealing with such figures was an everyday matter for the president of AECL, but in spite of the man's attitude the former Minister of Energy still had reservations.

"Will that be made public?" he asked anxiously.

"No, I don't see why it should," came the reassuring reply. "Of course, the agency has to make an annual report to Parliament, but then nobody ever reads the report, so far as I can tell. Anyway, this won't be an isolated item. It will be included with several others of a similar nature. As a matter of fact, the chairman and the board of directors don't even have to know that it's you."

Findlay thought for a moment.

"How can you avoid that?"

"I simply won't mention it. The board members have never displayed any interest in our agents—not in their names at any rate. They only care about results. They want to sell the

Candu," he said flatly, "and all know how strong the competition is. That's why we're prepared to pay so handsomely. It's just a routine matter of business. The details they leave to me."

Findlay found it difficult to believe that such huge sums of public money could change hands so routinely without public accountability. On the other hand, his own tenure as Energy Minister bore out the president's claim. The AECL Annual Report although regularly tabled, had never come up for discussion in Parliament. Certainly, he had never read it. Then, too, there were so many Crown corporations and government agencies. If anything, people were more concerned with those agencies that showed no return. As he recalled, the only one to ever come under real scrutiny was CIDA, the international assistance agency. AECL handled billions. More or less without questions. Still, Stanley could not help but wish that this opportunity had been offered by some corporation in the private sector. Much less risky, he reasoned.

The president seemed to be reading his mind.

"No one need know. It's a thousand to one that anyone would pry into just this one of our many transactions."

"For a million dollars, let alone two, those odds are pretty good," Stanley muttered under his breath.

"I beg your pardon? Did you say 'odds'?"

Findlay was embarrassed. He had not realized he had spoken aloud.

"Nothing. Not important." He brushed it aside. "All right, you've got yourself a deal. Now, is there any special approach I should take? Any rules?"

"None at all. " The president of the Crown agency was a little surprised at the question. "The way it's done is up to you. That's part of what you're being paid for—access. Access to Dr. Castro. You have connections, and that's why we expect you to be successful. Old boy's club, and all that. Results, that's what we want to see, just results."

He looked at Stanley and then withdrew a folded piece of paper from his pocket. "Here. The rest when you deliver the authorized order."

Stanley unfolded the paper and looked at it incredulously. It was a bank draft for $500,000 made out simply "To bearer." It was the largest cheque he had ever held. It was more than ten times his previous yearly salary.

Stanley liked the fact that it was made out to the bearer. It might be a strange way of doing business, but at least it limited the number of people who knew of his involvement to five: Willis Cranston, Jean Jacques Charles, the president of AECL, his own wife, Joan, and Giselle Cranston. Of course, the latter two knew no details. Better to have nothing on paper. Even when Joan asked for details, as she surely would, he resolved to be vague. He smiled to himself. What she didn't know wouldn't hurt her.

"It's for expenses," the president said quietly.

Stanley shook his head. "It sure as hell can't cost that much for a few trips to Cuba."

The dapper president took a long pull on his cigar. He studied his host through the veil of smoke, surprised that the big man was so obtuse. Finally he laid the cigar in the ashtray at his elbow, rubbed his nose with the fingers of his left hand, and explained.

"No doubt you'll need to do some entertaining, and," he coughed delicately, "you'll perhaps be expected to make certain gifts—to show your appreciation for their assistance—in advance." Surely, he thought, I needn't spell it out any clearer.

"Gifts? Who am I to give presents to? I don't know any-body in Cuba but Castro himself and I've only met him a couple of times with Charles. Will he expect a present?" The big man's brow had furrowed. Suddenly it cleared. "Oh, I see. You're talking about greasing the wheels, aren't you?" He looked to the president seeking confirmation.

His luncheon guest sighed. Thank God Findlay finally understood! Nodding, he went on to explain that kickbacks, or gifts, as he chose to call them, were a way of life in the Spanish-speaking nations to the south. They were expected; and without them to smooth the way, Findlay might encoun-ter unexpected roadblocks.

"How do I show them on my expense account? As gifts?" the former Minister asked. He'd fiddled an account or two be-fore in his life, but he had never handled anything approach-ing this sum.

"Oh dear, no. You don't have to account for your ex-penses. Just give us the total when you know it. We'll understand what it covers." The president was faint at the thought that Findlay might send him a detailed statement, naming names. Willis Cranston certainly wouldn't appreciate that. Nor would he. He would have to shred it, but by then his secretary and maybe others would have seen it. Such a disaster must be averted.

"How will you know how much it's actually cost me, if I don't send in a statement? After all, we're talking about half a million bucks!" Findlay persisted.

"Don't worry about it," the president said impatiently. "We've had experience in these things. We've estimated from experience that you'll have to spend around that much to pull off the sale. It would be a mistake not to go first-class."

"Suppose I spread it around, but I don't clinch the sale?" Stanley asked doggedly, unable to leave the subject alone.

"I think that's highly unlikely," the president responded, reflecting that AECL had first been approached by the Prime Minister's Office, and at Fidel Castro's request. Negotiations had gone swimmingly until the first of this year. Since then the Cubans had unaccountably become reticent and allowed the deal to languish. AECL had been casting about for months for just the right person to tie down the last details, and the president was confident that he'd found him when the former Energy Minister, a notoriously close supporter of the deposed Jean Jacques Charles, had been suggested to him by Willis Cranston.

Stanley Findlay was flattered by his guest's display of confidence. Nonetheless, he liked to get things straight in his own mind.

"What will I do if I've used up all the money, and Cuba refuses to buy?" he asked again.

"We'll just have to accept that," the president said grudgingly, "as a cost of doing business."

With that answer Findlay was at last satisfied.

"And if I am successful—" Catching the president's grimace, he began again. "And when the deal is clinched, what about my fee? How do I get paid, and when?"

"When we have the agreement—signed, sealed and delivered—you tell us how you want to be paid, and where. Many agents prefer to have their fees deposited somewhere outside the country. Sometimes in another name. I understood from Willis Cranston you were setting up a Caribbean company and would want your commission paid there."

"Yeah, that's what Willis suggested. I guess I'd better see to that right away."

"Fine, then. Here, in this briefcase, is the file. Study it. It lays out our proposal, our contacts, everything."

He passed over what was clearly a very costly briefcase. To Findlay's surprise his own initials, in bold gilt characters, were already affixed to it.

His guest levered himself from his chair and thrust out his hand. "Thank you for lunch. *Bon voyage,* and good luck."

Stephan Ludvic judged it was time to begin. He rose, shaking out the folds of his long black robes. Standing before his carved oak throne, the Speaker waited for the House to come to attention, and almost at once the restless sounds of a reassembled Parliament—the murmur of private conversations, the rustling of papers, a sudden gust of laughter—were stilled expectantly.

Kathleen Marshal swung around in her front-row seat, checking that the ranks of the Liberal members behind her and to each side along the Government side of the chamber, were filled. To either side of her, the first two rows of her Cabinet showed no gaps except for the seat beside her, which remained empty. That was Jean Jacques Charles' seat. He was out of the country, and the Prime Minister had not insisted that her predecessor return for the first session of her administration.

The ritual was brief. In less than five minutes, the past session of Parliament died, and with it, the last of the Charles parliamentary program. From here on, the responsibility would be Kathleen's alone.

Into the anticipatory hush, the peremptory knock at the great, carved door to the chamber sounded hollowly. There was a resounding second knock, and the double doors swung wide, revealing the presence of the official known as the Gentleman Usher of the Black Rod, the Senate's formal messenger to the Commons.

The slight, black-clad figure strode forward with a deliberate, though awkward, pace. Black Rod was a much-decorated veteran, who had lost both a leg and an arm in the wartime service of his country. Sensing all eyes upon him, he walked with conscious care and dignity, swinging his artificial limb stiffly from the hip, as he moved past the arched doorway, beyond the brass railing designed to restrict entry to those elected to a place in the House, and onto the sacrosanct floor of the green-carpeted chamber.

He moved perhaps ten paces more towards the Speaker.

"Monsieur L'Orateur," he intoned. Then, first in French and then in English, in his high, carrying voice, he announced that His Excellency, the Governor General, had arrived at the Senate and had instructed him to command the members of the Commons to attend upon him.

On behalf of the House members, the Speaker gravely acknowledged the summons. Then, placing on his head the black cocked hat, he descended the short flight of steps to the House floor. Followed by his senior staff, Ludvic paced the length of the vast chamber, wheeled left at the massive open doors and proceeded along the south corridor towards Confederation Hall, and beyond, into the east wing of the Centre Block, along its south corridor. Passing the offices of members of the upper, appointive, chamber of Parliament, he finally arrived at the carved and gilded Senate Lobby.

Behind him, Kathleen Marshal and her ministers strolled in no particular order, chatting among themselves. Both Opposition leaders had fallen in behind the Cabinet, and the ordinary members of the House, of all parties, straggled along behind.

At regular intervals along the corridors lined with members of the public, uniformed commissionaires were discreetly stationed, to ensure that the parade was uninterrupted. Each commissionaire snapped a salute as the party leaders passed by.

The Prime Minister dropped from the long shambling line before it entered the Senate Lobby to hurry along an intersecting corridor, bound for the suite reserved for the Speaker of the Senate. Behind her, the line of members compressed as it reached the Senate Lobby and passed through the small, mullion-windowed anteroom and beyond, to crowd into the upper chamber itself. The Speaker stepped up to his appointed place on a small platform facing the length of the red-carpeted room, towards the Senate Throne. He would have to remain standing throughout the ceremony. The crush of members behind him squeezed to either side, seeking room to stand within the narrow three or four feet allotted them— the only encroachment on the territory of the Senate permitted to Commons members.

Those who had brought up the rear half of the long, meandering line had to content themselves with jostling for standing room within the small antechamber. It was already filled with rows of chairs for those of the members' spouses who were prepared to endure the hour or so of the ritual reading of the Speech from the Throne. In the anteroom no one was able to see or hear anything that transpired beyond the uncomfortably crowded, chattering ranks of the House members. As a consequence, a disturbing babble soon rose.

Despite the red chamber's lofty ceilings, the room was already overwarm. Sunlight streamed through the high windows, its focused heat augmented by the powerful television lights. The chamber smelled of dust and age, and the intermingled perfumes and fragrances of the carefully dressed, hatted and white-gloved women, wives and guests of ambassadors, senators, and members.

The Governor General and his wife were ushered into the Chamber by the diminutive black-robed Senate Speaker, who then retired to a chair placed to one side. The Governor mounted the short flight of steps, then turned to face the assembly. His wife took a carved chair, placed on a slightly lower level to his immediate left, and Kathleen Marshal, as Prime Minister, took another, less ornate chair, at floor level, to the Governor General's right.

Facing the official representative of the Queen of Canada were clusters of chairs occupied by the fur-trimmed, scarlet-robed Justices of the Supreme Court of Canada, more comfortable than their predecessors had once been when the traditional seating for jurists had been a circular, red-velvet bench known as "the woolsack" after its counterpart in the House of Lords at Westminster.

Beyond the members of the Supreme Court, in front of the facing Senate benches, chairs had been placed for foreign ambassadors and other high officials.

The Governor General was uncomfortable in his Court dress. Privately, he thought it a ridiculous get-up. He fervently wished that he had never adopted it. The black satin pants were tight to the knee, finished with flat black satin bows. Sheer black stockings covered his skinny shanks, and shining patent slippers with big gold buckles cramped his toes. His swallow-tailed coat was wool and too heavy and itchy for this day of early, sticky heat. The gold braid encrusting it bore down on his frail shoulders like a yoke. His formal hat, plumed and beribboned, bound his brow painfully. It was giving the Queen of Canada's representative a headache, and he had to move with care, as he fumbled for his reading glasses so that he wouldn't knock the ungainly headgear askew.

With a sigh, he glanced towards his wife. His lady sat serenely beneath the scrutiny of the hundreds of pairs of watching eyes. She wore a pale-blue chiffon dress, ribbons and medals bright on her left breast. Her hands were folded peacefully in her lap, her feet crossed demurely at the ankles, a gentle, abstract smile playing about her lips. She was prepared for her part of the ordeal which was to sit for the next hour, almost motionless, displaying nothing more contentious than this neutral, pleasant expression.

The resplendently costumed old gentleman looked significantly to his left, over his half-glasses, giving a barely perceptible nod. An alert, uniformed aide snapped to attention, then advanced to the Throne, to hand the Governor General a sheaf of stiff cream vellum pages, bound together with narrow scarlet ribbon. Straightening his back, the Governor General coughed once to clear his throat, and began to read the first Speech from the Throne of the Marshal administration.

Kathleen calmly listened, following the much-worked-over opening paragraphs. At first, she tried to assess the reaction to her proposed legislative program as it unfolded in the Governor's scratchy voice, paragraphs alternating first in English and then in French, but soon her attention wandered.

As her glance drifted along the ranks of the formally dressed ambassadors, her eyes caught those of Anthony Whiteside. It was obvious that the tail-coated American had been watching her keenly. The Prime Minister smiled involuntarily. Amused, she speculated what the Republican's reaction might be at his introduction to the Canadian version of the opening ritual developed through centuries of usage by the Mother of Parliaments, far across the Atlantic.

Kathleen nodded slightly, acknowledging Whiteside's frank stare, and then, suddenly aware that the gesture might have been noticed, she darted a quick glance to where her husband was seated.

Andrew Wickstrom sat nearby. He seemed relaxed, although his bulk was folded uncomfortably into a wooden armchair. His face was in shadow but his gaze had been resting steadily on his wife. He had not failed to remark her smile and nod, and his glance had shifted briefly to take in the man to whom it had been directed. Wickstrom's expression did not change, but he felt a prickle of panic. Andrew had already picked up a disturbing Ottawa rumour that Kathleen had known the new American Ambassador years ago. When he had asked Kathleen about it she had laughed and said that it was ancient history. She had explained that although she had indeed seen Anthony Whiteside, their meetings had been strictly business.

Now, catching the exchange of glances, Andrew was momentarily uncertain that his wife had actually been telling him the entire truth. He readily conceded that he had perhaps been foolish in refusing to move to Ottawa, often leaving Kathleen alone, but he truly did not like the role into which her post had cast him. She really had very little private time, he thought, justifying himself, and it was better for him to leave her free to get on with her responsibilities. Besides, he had agreed to make the effort to be in the capital for these interminable, boring, formal occasions when he was required to make an appearance; and he would travel with her whenever it was possible, so long as he wasn't made to feel like a fifth wheel. For the rest, he had resolved to keep busy with his publishing business. Deliberately, he shook off the renewed suspicion about his wife's relationship with the American.

The Governor General's reedy voice quavered to a stop. He flipped the stiff pages, shuffling them together, before he held them out to his aide. Mindful of his hat, he carefully pulled off his spectacles. Then, as he looked about him a bit absently, it was clear that he had forgotten what was to follow.

"Ah yes," he breathed as he caught his aide's signal. He only had to wait until the original copy of the document was duly registered, and then he would rise to signify the conclusion of the parliamentary ceremony.

"Won't be a minute too soon, either," he muttered to himself. How he longed to return to Rideau Hall and get out of this archaic costume! But there was still the reception to come, he remembered. Determinedly, the Queen's representative promised himself to cut his attendance short. He was already looking forward to the moment when the Prime Minister would formally escort him out of the building, to the waiting landau with its patient horses. Only fifteen minutes of clip-clop travel along Sussex Drive and he could get out of this heavy, prickly coat and these damned silly breeches. He could hardly wait.

The Standing Committee was chaired by Wilbur Tolliver. In civilian life, "Doc" Tolliver was a veterinarian and part-time hog farmer from a small hamlet in southwestern Ontario.

Despite the vagaries of his party's fortunes, he had been repeatedly re-elected for more than twenty years.

Wilbur Tolliver was a good family man, a good church-man, and a valued constituency man. He was patient and painstaking with his neighbours. Moreover, he was as careful when dealing with a complaint from the most rock-ribbed Tory farmer or impatient young leftist student as he was with his own Grit followers. It was said of Doc Tolliver that he hadn't an enemy in the world.

Doc was rumpled and cheerful, full of droll, back-country stories. Despite the fact that he wore both belt and braces to keep his pendulous belly under control, his creaseless trousers always seemed to droop. His bald pink skull shone, its white fringe habitually awry, as though he combed it each morning with his facecloth. His eyes, under wayward ginger brows, were protuberant, his nose heavy and veined, his short thick neck creased. Although Tolliver rarely participated in House debates, he had proved that he was of the breed of the most appreciated of back-benchers—loyal and reliable. Every election, with no help at all from the national party, he managed to be comfortably re-elected. He could be trusted never to make waves in caucus, or get into trouble with the press. And he was always there when he was needed, affably making up part of the quorum. As a reward, Wilbur Tolliver had been given this chairmanship for his very own fiefdom.

It was a job calculated never to be too taxing Each session, Doc and the appointed representatives of the other parties—most of them also veteran members—were expected to pick over the bones of one or two Crown corporations. Not for them the high-profile agencies like the CBC or the CN or Air Canada. They were perfectly content to plod along at their own ruminative pace, probing gently into out-of-the-way corners, pursuing their own part of parliament's housekeeping. True, the Standing Committee never attracted much press attention, but that was the way Wilbur Tolliver liked to operate, and as a reward, each session he was able to arrange a modest junket or two for its members somewhere in Canada. Occasionally, there was even a trip abroad, if he could think of some halfway reasonable justification for the expenditure.

This year, there had been some changes in the membership of Tolliver's committee. From the time Adam Sorenson appeared at the first steering committee meeting, a lot more began to change.

"Why not look at something new?" the new member had argued persuasively. "There's a whole raft of things we might look into. For instance, there's that Atomic Energy thing, the AECL. Why not take a look at it, for a change? Atomic Energy and nuclear reactors have been a controversial issue lately. Let's show the public we're earning our keep."

No one else on the committee cared much what they looked at next fall. Government members were there only to make sure the Opposition gave the Government no trouble. NDP members could generally be counted upon to dig into anything laid before them. If anything, they were happy with the prospect of scrutinizing something new. Conservative members—those few who bothered to be in attendance— couldn't care less what they were to study. They were quite content to go along with their more gung-ho colleague.

"Okay, Adam," said the chairman. "It's all right by me. I'm in the hands of the committee. If that's what the steering group wants to do, I don't see any reason why not. Any objections?"

No one spoke.

"It's agreed then. I'll set the staff to work on it. They can set up a tentative schedule, and we can get right to it in the next session, when the House is recalled after the summer." Maybe by that time, this eager beaver will have calmed down, thought Doc Tolliver.

"Why not get started earlier?" asked Sorenson, emboldened by the success of his earlier suggestion. "We've hardly done a thing over the past six months and this session isn't going to last long. What do you say we meet through the summer?" He was pleased with himself. Showed a nice touch of concern for the tax-payer, he thought, sure that if there was any argument, he was going to enjoy it. He might even get some political mileage out of it.

Doc Tolliver blinked. Sit in the summer in Ottawa's notoriously humid heat? Hell, nobody in his right mind wanted to stay here all summer! He'd counted on taking it easy, poking around his own constituency, meeting folks and keeping his political fences mended, maybe getting in a little fishing.

The NDP member who represented an Ottawa seat perked up. Ottawa was a boring wasteland in the summer, emptied of parliamentarians, and given over to hordes of tourists. He himself had no special plans for the season, and he might as well be working. More importantly, he could perhaps get noticed by the press, who would have to scratch hard for news whenever the House wasn't sitting.

"Yeah, Doc. That's not a bad idea. I like it. Why don't we get started right away?"

Tolliver eyed the NDP member with distaste—another eager beaver!

A Liberal committee member who had just begun a satisfactory affair with his new and highly accommodating research assistant and who had not the slightest interest in returning, just now, to his wife, saw in the Opposition member's suggestion a legitimate excuse to remain in the capital. To Tolliver's disgust, he added his voice in support.

"Adam's right, you know, Doc. We haven't spent much time in Ottawa this year—since before the leadership convention. Wouldn't hurt to set an example for the other committees. Yeah. I'd be prepared to sacrifice some of the summer for committee hearings."

The chairman looked around the room, willing some of the others to voice an objection, but they said nothing, although he was sure that they must be as reluctant as he to work after the House rose.

He stroked his hairless pate, considering whether he should try to argue Sorenson and his unlooked for supporters out of it himself. Tolliver weighed his chances of success if he did. If he opposed the summer sittings, it was likely Sorenson and the Tories would dig in their heels and the NDP members would ritually support them, just for the pleasure of going against the Government's chairman. He couldn't even be sure that the Liberal committee members would automatically back him, now that one of them had voiced their shared prickle of guilt at being so long away from government business. It wasn't likely he could carry the day, he concluded.

"Okay," he conceded, reluctantly. "We'll gear up for the summer. But if it gets hotter'n the gates of hell around here, remember it was your idea, not mine. And you fellas had better show up for the meetings, hear? There'd better be enough for a quorum every time."

They kept abreast of developments all morning. Bonnie was in and out of Kathleen's office with regular bulletins, reporting on the progress of the Day of Protest. For months, organized labour had been planning this, and the Government had done its best to contain the damage. Bonnie Costello, as

Minister of Labour, had borne the brunt of the effort to encourage organized workers to ignore their leaders' exhortations to stay at home. Kathleen had helped and encouraged her gifted young Minister but mainly behind the scenes. The Cabinet had judged that the time was not yet ripe for the Prime Minister to intervene. It began to appear that the strategy had worked.

"It's not too bad at all, Bonnie," the older woman said, rifling again through the pile of messages. "Not even in Quebec. And it looks as if Ontario is going to be okay. There are lots of people who didn't show up for work—it's causing a slowdown. But it's nothing industry can't live with for a day."

Bonnie nodded. "Of course it's too early yet in BC for anything but very scattered figures. I hope it's no worse out there."

Kathleen thought of the traditional militancy of some of the west coast unions. "Of course that's important, but this"—she tapped the latest to the Ontario reports—"this is the industrial heartland, and it looks as if it's holding, thanks to you."

The younger woman flushed, grateful for her leader's acknowledgement of her day-and-night efforts to appeal to the workers over their leaders' heads. It had caused her heartache at home where her own father had denounced her as a union-buster and forbidden her ever again to enter his house.

Kathleen's aide knocked and entered, announcing, "Two o'clock!"

The two dark-haired women quickly gathered up their papers and hurried down to the House for Question Period.

In the House, Terry Malloy jumped immediately to his feet, and remained standing until recognized out of turn by the Speaker.

"Mr. Speaker, my question is for the Prime Minister. I want to know when she's going to fire her Labour Minister for her conduct over the past weeks, conduct that amounts to an attempt to divide organized labour against itself."

Kathleen cast a glance at him, but refused to reply.

"If she's not going to answer, let me rephrase the question for the Minister of Labour," he said. "Will the Minister of Labour explain how she's fit to hold that portfolio when she's been doing her best to set worker against worker? She ought to be ashamed of herself," he shouted, as his NDP supporters banged their desks in delight.

Stung, Bonnie Costello jumped to her feet.

"Mr. Speaker, what I am proud of is the reaffirmation of the traditional independence of the Canadian worker and his refusal to be intimidated by his own leadership when he can see how harmful such action would be for Canada." She sat down, pleased with her retort.

But Malloy was up again. "You're a disgrace to that portfolio. You're nothing but a union-buster!" he roared.

"Or-der," the Speaker intervened. "This is not the time for debate. Have you a supplementary question?"

"Yes, I have, for the Secretary of State for External Affairs. How does he explain his speech last week to the United Nations, attacking the American government for its traditional ties with organized labour?" The short red-headed parliamentarian waved a newspaper clipping in the air. "How dare he call President Thompson a 'lackey of the unions'?"

Jean Jacques Charles rose. "Is the Honourable Member disputing the facts or complaining about my drawing attention to them?" he asked laconically.

Malloy hesitated. "Perhaps the Minister can say what he finds so reprehensible in close ties between organized labour and the Democrats? Or perhaps he thinks it preferable to be a lackey of the Communists of China—or Cuba?" He flung the words at the former Prime Minister.

Jacques' face darkened at the insinuation.

"It's better than allowing yourself to be a tool of the American trade unionists. My honourable friend should know all about that."

Malloy's face flamed at the reference to his well-known penchant for supporting the powerful American-dominated international unions against the struggles of the smaller and weaker Canadian-controlled unions. Before he could frame a reply, the Speaker recognized another member.

Malloy took his seat from which he continued to glare in Jacques' direction.

Kathleen was nettled. Why did Jacques have to keep himself embroiled in controversy? She hadn't liked his reported remarks at the UN. She considered them belittling to the touchy US President. Nor did she like his running feud with Malloy. As long as Jacques continued to antagonize the feisty NDP leader, there was nothing Kathleen could effectively do to try to win his support. It was true that there was nothing to fear while Richard Sherwood led the Official Opposition. But when the House reassembled in the fall, the Marshal administration could find itself in a whole new ballgame against an implacable NDP enemy and a fresh new leader of the PC's. Anytime they chose, the two parties could combine to defeat her.

As they left the House after Question Period, Kathleen beckoned to her Minister of Labour.

"You did well, Bonnie, but I think it's going to be a dangerous summer. I suggest we work together closely. Remember, I want you to call on me if there's anything you think you can't handle. We must avoid crippling transportation strikes at all costs. If there's anything I can do, just tell me."

Richard Sherwood had called a press conference in the theatre of the National Press Building on Wellington Street, across from Parliament Hill.

Beside him at the small table on the platform sat the president of the National Press Gallery, who formally introduced the Conservative leader to the audience of reporters crowding the room. Latecomers stood against the walls along the sides of the press theatre.

From an inner pocket Sherwood drew a few folded sheets of paper. He spread them carefully on the table before him, running his thumb along the creases to flatten them. He looked up at his audience, blinded by the clustered television lights. When he cleared his throat, the rustling room fell silent. Sherwood began to read into the microphone:

"I have today tendered my resignation as leader of the Progressive Conservative Party of Canada. My resignation will take effect upon the election of my successor. The National PC Executive has issued a call for a leadership convention. It will be held in Toronto within three months." He paused, and then went on, in a level tone. "I should like to express my thanks to all those Canadians who have supported me during my long public career." Sherwood choked slightly, and then, looking up at his audience, departed from his text. "And to you of the press—you've always been very fair."

Eyes again on the paper, he continued. "Mrs. Sherwood and I have enjoyed public life, but the time has come for me to step down."

A buzz of sound swelled at once. The Opposition leader's secret had been well-kept. His announcement had come as a surprise to most of those in the media audience.

A hand shot up from the crowd. The Gallery president recognized its owner by a nod.

"Do you care to tell us the reason, Mr. Sherwood?"

"For reasons of health" was the short reply.

From another part of the room—"What part will you take in selecting your successor?"

"None whatever. Of course," he added with a smile, "I expect to be a delegate and to vote."

"Care to speculate who it will be?"

Sherwood grinned, acknowledging the game. "Now, Theo, you know better than that," he gently chided the veteran columnist whose pipe was clamped firmly in his prominent teeth. "So far as I'm concerned, the race is wide open."

No other questions were directed to him. After a suitable pause, he nodded at the Gallery president, then rose to shake hands and leave.

All at once, one after the other, the members of the media audience, from hard-nosed veteran to the newest greenhorn, stood up, applauding. In their own way, they were saluting his career of public service, and affectionately saying their good-byes.

Unaccustomed tears gathered in Richard Sherwood's eyes. He stood for a moment, head down, blinking, and then strode to the doorway, speechless with sudden sadness.

"Let me freshen your drink, Woody," his hostess suggested, as she picked up the empty glass.

"Thank you, Kathleen. But make it light, please."

Richard Sherwood relaxed in a wicker chair on the narrow, glassed-in terrace on the river side of the old stone mansion. He and Kathleen were in casual dress. The day had been warm—unseasonably so—and on this late Sunday afternoon, most of the mansion's servants were enjoying a day off.

It had been two weeks since Sherwood had announced his retirement. He had been beseiged ever since with invitations to formal dinner and farewell parties. This had been the first opportunity the two leaders had had to get together for a relaxed evening. Now Sherwood watched as Kathleen mixed their drinks herself from the tray previously wheeled in on a glass-topped tea cart.

"It's so pleasant here, Kathleen. So quiet."

Kathleen nodded. Her eyes lingered on the view across the lawns, from which the colourful ranks of tulips and daffodils had been stripped, the beds ready now for the summer's planting of annuals.

"Yes, it is restful," she replied, absently, her glance continuing on to the rolling river beyond the low stone fencing, the huddled towns on its far bank, the distant Gatineau Hills, the arching, pellucid sky.

"Too bad Andrew couldn't be here," Sherwood commented.

"Yes. Well, something came up. He may arrive later tonight."

To cut off further discussion she quickly offered her guest a bowl of salted almonds.

"I love them," she said guiltily, popping two into her mouth. "But I've got to give them up. I'm putting on weight, and I can't afford to."

She looked down, smoothing her dress, then suddenly, to Sherwood's surprise, returned to the subject she had tried to avoid just a moment before.

"Politics is pretty hard on marriages, isn't it, Woody? This job's certainly putting a strain on mine. Andrew and I never seem to have enough time to be together. Tell me, what's your secret? You and Martha always seem so close. It's clear you've beaten the statistics."

"Well, some statistics, maybe," he said, reminding them both how short his own future was likely to be. "I don't think there's really any secret, Kathleen, except . . . . Well, you have to take time—*make* time if necessary—for your marriage partner. You have to give the relationship time to grow, day by day. It's very hard to do that when you live in different cities. Parliamentary marriages are more troubled than most, I suspect—especially where the members' spouses stay home in the riding. The members are bound to get lonely and to look for companionship in their off hours. I've always encouraged my people to bring their partners to Ottawa whenever possible. And if we've got a secret, I suppose that's it. Martha's always been right by my side," he said simply.

"I can't convince Andrew of that. He refuses to move to Ottawa," she said, in obvious agreement with the older man's theory.

"Then, if your marriage is important to you, Kathleen—and I think it is—you should take every opportunity to go to him or travel together." He paused and then suggested,

"Things seem to be quiet enough in the House; why don't you and Andrew try to get away for a few days together?"

Kathleen brightened. "We might just manage that, Woody, thanks to you. I really appreciate your co-operation. The Throne debate went so quickly! I think we'll probably wind up all the business I have ready within the next couple of weeks, and then we can recess for the summer. There's that Commonwealth Conference in Africa. Maybe we can squeeze in a little time, then."

"But that's months away, Kathleen. Why wait so long? Go and see the Queen. That's always a good excuse. And go before the House closes. A few days will do you good. They can get along here without you," he urged.

"I suppose that's true, although I'd hate to be away if there was any trouble," she said slowly.

"What kind of trouble?"

"It could be anything. I really am worried about the labour situation," she confessed. "Spokesmen for the unions seem unusually militant. I can't help but be sympathetic, but it's a little unnerving. They seem to be orchestrated this year, and I didn't like that scare about a general strike at all."

"I shouldn't worry about it, now. They're always waving a red flag. The unions in this country have never had a very strong alliance. Half of them take their orders from the States, anyway. And no matter what their leadership says, the union members don't pay much attention. Why, you know, I'm sure that most of organized labour supports your party or mine, not the NDP, no matter where their leadership sends their union funds.

"No," he concluded, persuasively, "forget the unions. They're just crying wolf as usual. Bonnie Costello's doing a good job in the department and I assure you, if she gets into any trouble, I'll keep my people in line as I promised. So long as I'm there as leader you're perfectly safe. Now, why not go off to England for a few days? Maybe you could ask the new Prime Minister how she intends to handle her unions. They're a whole lot tougher than ours. I'm sure she remembers that they broke her predecessor. She may have some helpful suggestions."

Kathleen promised to consider his suggestion, then changed the direction of the conversation. "Who do you think is likely to succeed you?" she asked.

Sherwood sipped at his drink.

"It's too early to tell, of course, but I understand a couple of the premiers are giving serious thought to running—not that Tory premiers have a very good track record in the federal house," he smiled, poking fun at himself. "There'll be half a dozen of the more ambitious of my colleagues, as usual. I understand even young Adam Sorenson is planning to toss his hat into the ring."

"Sorenson? That young man I met at dinner at your house? Why he's only a freshman! What chance would he have?"

"Don't underestimate Adam. Remember that although he's young, his whole career has been spent in politics of one kind or another. He's smart, determined, and very ambitious, and he's got a lot of credits built up—favours owed to him from Conservatives all over the country. I don't think it very likely he can win, but he could be a sleeper."

"I thought he was awfully rude," his hostess said, in a tone of dismissal.

"Ah yes, I remember," he grinned. "But Adam Sorenson can lay on the charm when he cares to, all the same. It's just that he doesn't often care to. But make no mistake, Kathleen, Sorenson is a comer. Maybe not this time, I admit, but whenever it is, you Liberals will have to be on your guard. I've never met anybody who is such a good hater. And his prime target is the Grits."

"Thank you, Woody, I'll remember your warning," she said. But she thought privately that the chances of Adam Sorenson ever becoming a PC leader seemed as remote as, well, as the chances of that other young greenhorn she had met that same night. The fellow with the bobbing Adam's apple and the pug ears and the intense wife. Bill Something. Bill Who? No, Bill Watt, that was it.

The Prime Minister sank into her chair, her back to the view, and gazed thoughtfully down into her drink.

Richard Sherwood left shortly before eight. After his departure, Kathleen carried their trays and glasses back to the kitchen, rinsed them off, and loaded them into the dishwasher. Right away, she discovered that she was restless, with a long evening before her.

"Oh Andrew, please come." She found herself voicing her wish aloud. Of course, she could always go into the study, and bury herself in the never-ending pile of paperwork, but Kathleen knew she wouldn't concentrate. She walked through the silent rooms, pausing in the formal drawing room to twitch the drapes together, while her thoughts continued to linger over Richard Sherwood's advice.

Eventually, she drifted back to the glassed-in terrace, where she punched up the canvas cushions on the wicker furniture, emptied the ashtrays and straightened the bar table. Because she could think of nothing further to do, and not really because she wanted it, she built herself another drink from the tea-cart tray. She carried it with her as she stepped outside, to wander over the lawn towards the embankment. She stood there, sipping her drink, her unfocused gaze on the tumbling river below.

As the light faded, mosquitoes came out in force, and after slapping her arm once or twice she retreated to the house. When she passed through the terrace and into the black-and-white floored foyer, she saw that Marilou, the red-haired maid, was just replacing the telephone receiver.

"Oh Madam." The girl turned to her. "I'm sorry, I thought you might have gone out. That was Mr. Wickstrom calling. He asked me to tell you that he won't be able to come this evening, and perhaps not tomorrow, either."

Kathleen looked at her dully in disappointment. There had been no explanation, nothing.

"Did he say where I could reach him, or whether he would call again?" she asked hopefully.

"No, Madam. There was no other message." Marilou's voice was soft, a little sorrowful. It grieved her to see the tall, black-haired woman so sad.

"Can I get you something, Madam?" she asked, reluctant to leave her mistress alone in the silent room.

"No, Marilou, nothing, thank you. I won't be needing anything later, either, so you might as well have the evening to yourself," she added dispiritedly.

"Thank you, Madam. If you should want anything, there are several of us in, upstairs in our quarters. You have only to ring."

"Yes, all right."

The trim maid disappeared towards the kitchen, looking forward to these extra hours of her own time.

Slowly Katheleen climbed the staircase to the second-floor family quarters. A book, she supposed, although there was nothing that she was especially eager to read. Or some music. Or a long cool bath.

Was there anyone she could call?

No, no one. Everyone she knew would be busy with family, many of them out of town.

Damn it, *why* hadn't Andrew come? she thought crossly. It seemed that every time Kathleen arranged her schedule so that they would have a day, or a few precious hours together, something interfered. The Wickstroms had been seeing less and less of each other these past weeks.

For a wild moment, she thought of flying to her husband. If Andrew couldn't spare the time to come to her, then she would go to him. But no. She couldn't just jump on a commercial flight—the Mounties would never permit it. Nor could she summon up a government aircraft at this hour on a Sunday night. The on-duty crews would all be occupied, and besides, she ought not to use a government aircraft on entirely personal business, even though she was firmly convinced that it should be a Prime Minister's prerogative to use one of the planes any time she chose, for any purpose— partisan, political, or private—since her job was a seven-day- a-week, twenty-four-hour-a-day responsibility. She couldn't call Andrew and ask him to send up his company plane. *I don't even know where Andrew is,* she thought in self-pity.

In her bedroom, she picked up the telephone and placed a call to their Rosedale home. It rang a long time. Just as she was on the point of dropping the receiver back into its cradle, Mrs. Gorman, Andrew's stout, longtime housekeeper came on the line.

"No, Mrs. Wickstrom. He isn't here, ma'am. No, I'm sure I don't have any idea," she said unhelpfully. "To tell the truth, ma'am, I thought he was spending the weekend there in Ottawa, with you."

Kathleen put down the instrument slowly, doubt creeping into her mind. Not at home. Not here. Not en route. Where —and with whom—could Andrew be?

After a pause she picked up the phone again, dialling firmly.

"Tony?"

The disembodied voice at the other end of the telephone assured her it was he. His voice was rich with natural vitality, but it betrayed no hint of emotion. Since that first visit a month ago, they had not seen one another alone.

"Are you free to come over for a swim and a drink, with me?" she asked in a slightly plaintive tone.

He caught just the faintest slur in her pronunciation.

"Kathleen, have you been drinking?"

"Sure. But not much," she added, deliberately enunciating more clearly. "I'm not drunk, if that's what you're asking."

"Are you sure you hadn't better just catch up on your sleep?"

"No. I'm not tired. I just thought you might like a swim. It's been so sticky today, and I know your embassy has no pool."

"Love to. I'll just get my suit. I'll be there in ten minutes. Okay?"

"Yes, that's fine. Have you eaten?" But before she could complete the question, she heard the connection break.

Elated, Kathleen replaced the telephone and danced to her closet, pulling from it the new bathing suit she had been saving to wear for Andrew.

"If Drew can't come, at least there's Tony. He'll be more appreciative, anyway," she told herself, as she applied a brush to her glossy black hair, and stroked on fresh, bright lipstick.

"Serves Andrew right!"

Chapter Seven

"This Adam Sorenson?" The voice was muffled, the words indistinct.

Adam himself was groggy, his mind fuzzy. He and some of his colleagues had gone over to Hull for a late dinner. He had had too much wine and when he got home he had fallen asleep on the chesterfield while watching the National. As he shook his head to clear his thoughts, he was aware that the television screen was blank, although it was still on. It must be late.

"Yes, this is Sorenson. Who is this?"

"Not important. I hear you're on a committee that's going to look into AECL. That right?"

"Yes, it is, but how did you know? And what's it to you?"

"Let's just say I know," his caller chuckled. "I have a tip for you. Why don't you take a good close look at the Candu sales? You'll turn up a lot of surprises. If you're interested, you could give the Government a real black eye."

"The what? Candu sales? Is that what you said? What about them?"

"That's for you to find out. Dig around a little. I promise you, you won't be wasting your time."

"Look, whoever you are, can't you give me some details? What am I supposed to be looking *for?*"

Sorenson's head was clearing rapidly now. This sounded worth exploring. Like many other Opposition members, he was occasionally plagued by nuts with a grudge against the Government. Sometimes information appeared in the mail in a plain envelope with no return address. You had to be careful how you handled such material—it had to be checked out completely. But every now and then, one of these unidentified tipsters came up with something damaging to the opposing party.

"C'mon, Sorenson. From what I hear, you're no dummy. I tell you, look at the Candu sales."

There was a click. The connection was broken. As he put down the receiver, Adam glanced at his watch. Three o'clock. What a helluva time for a phone call, he thought wearily. But he might as well follow it up. He doubted the tip would lead to anything. Still, as he reminded himself, you never can tell.

The Standing Committee's research staff had done its work meticulously. They had dug into libraries and old files and collected together every scrap of published information about AECL and its workings. Carefully collated, copies of that material had been provided to each of the committee members. Some of them had read it, but most simply filed it away, bringing it forth only to be carried to committee sessions for quick reference.

Adam Sorenson was made of different stuff. He pored over the research reports, marking anything he thought might bear fruitful investigation. He was a digger, trained as a researcher, and he knew where to look. He capitalized on his extensive acquaintance with the media, probing for tidbits of information about the AECL. Even so, he was now damned frustrated. A sixth sense told him his mysterious phone caller really had something; still the muffled voice had not passed on sufficient information. Adam didn't really know what he was looking for.

One afternoon he decided to make use of some of his foreign contacts. He telephoned Washington to discuss the field of nuclear energy with several relatively obscure Congressmen he had met at interparliamentary conferences whose acquaintance he had since cultivated. The first phone call didn't pay off, but with number two, Adam Sorenson picked up the scent.

"Sure, Adam, there's a lot of ruffled feathers around Washington. There's a lot of people here that just aren't keen about the way you Canajun's operate." The thick Louisiana accent was sometimes hard to cut through. Sam Smithers was a Democrat, a member of the House of Representatives. He was young, and he was a southerner—one of the new breed, from the new South. He was close to the President, but maintained a low profile.

"Oh? Why is that?" Adam answered with surprise in his voice. He had heard nothing of any dissension between

Canada and the United States. Probably nothing important, but still, one could never tell.

"Well, we hear your nuclear safeguards may be too flexible —that you might make exceptions. You know that sort of thing puts a lot of noses out of joint down here."

Adam toyed absently with the pencil and paper he had ready just in case.

"We don't sell unless the buyer agrees to sign—" He hesitated and Sam Smithers interrupted.

"Well, I've heard there's been an exception and the exception was for someplace we don't want to have nuclear technology."

As Adam listened, names of nations America was on the outs with buzzed through his head.

"What country?" he asked bluntly.

"Don't know myself," Smithers answered. "I get the impression it's someplace in Central America or the Caribbean —someplace too close for our comfort."

Adam Sorenson was stunned. Jamaica, maybe. Canada had a lot of ties with Jamaica and certainly that country was headed left. Cuba? Castro and Jean Jacques Charles? My God, what a scandal that would be! Still, it was useless unless he could prove it.

"You really don't know?" He questioned Smithers again.

"Nope," came the reply. "I'm close, but I'm not that close. Your new Prime Minister knows though. I heard Thompson called her down here and gave her hell about it."

"When was this?" asked an astonished Sorenson.

"Oh, months ago. There were only rumours at the time."

"Well, thanks, Sam. I'll look into it," the puzzled Canadian Member of Parliament promised.

"While you're doin' that, you might have a look-see at who handled the deal. Musta walked away with a bundle in commissions."

Sorenson's ears perked up, his intuition working overtime. "Well, that's all handled by our Crown corporation, so far as I know," he said doubtfully.

"Naw, they use free-lancers. And this time they used a coupla big ones," he said.

"Who?" asked Adam Sorenson sharply, his pencil poised.

"I don't know for sure, but your old Prime Minister—Gene Charles, is that his name?—has a lot of connections down there. Why don't you ask around. Check anyone who comes into a lot of money all of a sudden like."

As Adam mumbled agreement, followed by a hurried good-bye, the pencil fell to roll unnoticed on the floor. This was it! This was what he was looking for, he knew in his bones.

My God, what a scandal! he thought. And it's all mine to break. This will *make* my career! It's just what I need for the leadership.

Adam Sorenson scowled.

There were only a handful of reporters present, and among them, as far as he could see, not a single national television commentator, not one of the widely read, highly influential print columnists.

The Gallery president stalled the start of the quickly called press conference for the best part of half an hour, hoping more stragglers would appear, but it was clear that there was little interest in anything the ambitious freshman Tory member would have to tell them. Sorenson's face was a familiar one around the National Press Club. When he wasn't button-holing some newsman, trying to pry out nuggets of information for a new attack on the Government, he could be found hanging around the bar, holding forth on one topic or another, buttering up the media stars. Sorenson was habitually parched for publicity.

In the newsmen's collective opinion, the sharp-featured member was a pain, and anything he chose to announce they could just as well catch up on later. They had better things to do on this humid day.

Finally, the Gallery president called the sparse audience to order, and introduced the member from Petrolia.

Sorenson leaned forward to the desk microphone, his meagre jaw shadowed by the thrust of his long, prominent nose.

"I've got a release here for you fellows." He gestured to a neat stack of mimeographed sheets at the edge of the platform.

"What's it say, Adam?" a lazy, disinterested voice called from the rows of nearly empty seats.

"I'll read it to you," he answered eagerly, picking up his own copy in a hand that trembled so violently he couldn't begin. "No, on second thought, I'll just tell you what's in it. Then you can read it yourself. It's an announcement that I'm going to be a candidate for the PC leadership. That's it, in a nutshell. There's a couple of pages with my bio and some excerpts from my most important speeches. Some stuff from the Standing Committee—you'll need those for your stories. And there's a new photograph, too," he finished rather lamely. "Any questions?"

An awkward five minutes followed, broken only by the clattering exit of a pair of young reporters who stifled yawns as they left. The Gallery president slid a sideways glance at the sweating member, whose fixed smile was frozen with embarrassment.

Mercifully, he touched him on the arm, and then gavelled the press conference to a close.

Andrew Wickstrom sat in the VIP lounge at Toronto International. Kathleen's plane from Ottawa was just landing and soon the two of them would be on their way across the Atlantic.

The months of seeing each other infrequently and the last few weeks of total separation had created a mood of great loneliness for him. He now wanted very much to hold Kathleen.

I've been wrong, he thought. I should have gone back to Ottawa, I should have been there.

The face of the new American Ambassador slid into his imagination. There'd been more rumours, rumours that spread quickly through Ottawa and reached him in Toronto through a variety of sources, about Kathleen and Anthony Whiteside. He put the thought out of his mind. That was before he met Kathleen; it was none of his business. After all, he had known other women. Old flames could turn up, but that didn't mean they were rekindled—necessarily.

Of course he had also heard that Kathleen had seen the new American Ambassador several times. It was business, he told himself. She could hardly avoid seeing him.

All at once the door of the lounge opened and Kathleen burst through. "Drew, it's so good to see you!" She threw her arms around her husband and tilted her head to lay her face on his chest.

"Just imagine," she bubbled, "we'll have almost a whole week together! London! Shopping, theatres, the countryside —the anonymity! Such bliss!"

He looked down at her with mock sternness. "No work at all?"

She smiled. "Well, practically nothing. We are to meet with the Queen, and I must drop in to say hello at 10 Downing, but that's all, I swear." She raised her eyes in time to catch his grimace.

"C'mon, Drew. You've met Her Majesty before. I've never been to the Palace, but it's certain to be interesting. And you needn't come with me to Number 10 Downing. It's just a courtesy call. Shouldn't take more than half an hour. All the rest of the time is ours—alone. We'll have the whole rest of the week, just as I promised."

As they leaned back in their seats, their safety belts fastened, Kathleen closed her eyes and thought about the coming week. If their marriage had had its rocky moments lately, the promise of the days ahead, far from the cares and pressures of her office, held hope that they could re-establish the closeness that was the hallmark of their relationship. I want it to be as it was, Kathleen thought. I want it to be as it should be.

And if Kathleen Marshal Wickstrom thought of Tony Whiteside all during the long flight across the Atlantic, it was only fleetingly. She was with Andrew, her dear husband, and no shadow, past or present, would be allowed to intrude on the sunshine of their days.

As it turned out, things were not all that easy. The Wickstroms were met by the Canadian High Commissioner to the Court of St. James. Heathrow Airport was crowded with summer travellers, but the Canadian Prime Minister and her husband were whisked through customs and were soon rolling through the lush green countryside. Wisps of early-morning fog rose from the road unwinding before them, but the hazy sun was visible and offered the promise of a clear summer day.

Politely, they declined the High Commissioner's offer to stay with him at the Residence, and asked instead to be dropped at the Dorchester, where Andrew had reserved a suite.

Once before, Kathleen had stayed with the High Commissioner, who was a former colleague from the days of Sandy Sinclair's administration. She was fond of the aging politician-turned-diplomat. She knew that he would go out of his way to entertain her properly. But she and Andrew had promised one another that she would keep clear of the time-consuming trappings of a formal state visit, and she intended to keep that promise as much as was possible for a prime minister.

Saul Martineau, the Canadian High Commissioner, was clearly disappointed, but gave way gracefully in the face of their determination. He went on to discuss Kathleen's appointment to meet the new British Prime Minister and her audience with the Queen. To these, he added the possibilty of a dinner party at the Residence at which the Queen Mother would be a guest, a meeting with the new Foreign Secretary, a parliamentary reception offered by the Speaker of the House of Commons, and an appearance at the Canadian Club. Then, he raised the question of a press conference. The press, he stated, was particularly curious about the fact that the only two formal engagements scheduled were with women—the Monarch and the UK's Prime Minister.

Kathleen firmly rejected all of his suggestions. No press conference, no reception, no dinner, and no meeting with the Canadian Club. No. No other engagements; not even the dinner for the Queen Mother. This was to be a private visit. She was adamant.

Kathleen was exhausted from the long overseas flight and the time-loss. She was eagerly looking forward to a hot bath and the fresh, faintly lavender-scented sheets she knew awaited her at the hotel. Guiltily aware that she was being unnecessarily curt with her old friend, she reached over and took Andrew's hand. No, she insisted, one last time, a hot bath, a sleep and a quiet evening with her husband. That was what she wanted.

By the time they had been led to their rooms by an elegantly dressed hotel manager the feeling that they could not escape unwanted attention had made them both glum. They scarcely appreciated the hovering hotel functionary and quickly dismissed him.

The appearance of their suite lifted their spirits. Sunlight washed the small sitting-room. It was filled with flowers and there was an overflowing bowl of fresh fruit and a plate of cheese and biscuits. Kathleen smiled as she noted the napkin-wrapped bottle chilling in the silver bucket. Now that the over-anxious innkeeper had departed, she felt as though she and Andrew were on their honeymoon. At the moment, however, all that the two of them wanted to do was sleep.

In no time at all, Kathleen splashed steaming water into the deep antique tub. She bathed quickly and gratefully slipped into a warm terrycloth robe. Then she sat, smoking, barefoot and wrapped in the thirsty robe, until Andrew joined her.

He rubbed ruefully at his chin. "I won't shave now. I'll do

it later this evening when we get up. Shall I arrange for a dinner reservation and some theatre tickets for tonight?"

Kathleen shook her head. "Oh, darling, let's not. Let's just play it by ear, depending on how we feel. If we leave a call for six o'clock that should be all right." She held out one hand to Andrew. "Let them leave the luggage in the foyer. I don't think I can stay awake until it arrives!"

In the bedroom, she pulled the heavy lined drapes across the wide windows that overlooked Hyde Park. The welcome darkness urged them into their high, too soft, twin beds and almost at once, they were both in a dreamless sleep.

That evening in the lingering twilight, Andrew and Kathleen strolled arm in arm in the blessed anonymity of the teeming city. They walked past shops and houses and through nearby parks before returning to the sedate hotel for an excellent dinner in the luxurious dining room.

They talked of what they would like to do if the weather remained clear. A boat trip to Hampton Court, a drive to the Surrey countryside, or perhaps a quick trip to Stratford-on-Avon. They talked of going to one of the old university towns of Cambridge or Oxford. If the weather did not hold—as it often didn't in England—there was the prospect of the Victoria and Albert Museum, the exciting art galleries and the good food, shopping and, naturally, the theatres and concerts. Andrew was amused that Kathleen wanted to visit the Tower to see the crown jewels and the Beefeater guards. To him, it sounded touristy, but indulgently, he agreed to go—on one condition: that she would go with him to Regent's Park and the famed London Zoo. A zoo person herself, Kathleen gladly agreed to his "condition."

That night, rested and happy, they made love leisurely and fell asleep, both knowing satisfaction and the joy of their return to one another's arms.

Next morning, they dawdled over the papers and the theatre notices and decided on two "must-see" dramas and a much-lauded intimate revue. They looked in vain for a ballet. It was not the season. Nor were there any concerts listed which interested them.

Later, after a satisfying lunch at a pub near the law courts they strolled as far as the Strand, and then to the Embankment, where they walked along the leafy banks of the Thames. At an ancient winebar they stopped to savour tiny glasses of a pale, rich sherry, served to them atop tables that had once been wine barrels.

Nearby, Andrew hailed a passing cab and they climbed into the roomy rear seat, stretching their legs, as the cheery cabbie chatted them up through the open glass barrier. Only minutes later he deposited them before the wide glass entry door of their hotel.

Messages awaited them. Several from the High Commissioner, increasingly urgent. Kathleen sighed in despair, but she dutifully placed a call to him.

"Tomorrow? Already?" she wailed, then, decisively. "All right, best to get it over with, I suppose. What time, and where? Yes, I'll be ready when you arrive. Thank you. No, I haven't changed my mind about dinner. Just let the Queen Mother think I have left town. What? Messages from Ottawa? Damn, I told them to leave me alone this week. Anything pressing? Well, tomorrow will do then. I'll be ready by ten-thirty. Good-bye, Saul."

Andrew Wickstrom lifted his eyes from his newspaper. The concierge had arranged for a subscription for this one week. It had always been an irritation to the Canadian publisher that it was impossible to buy *The Times* or *The Guardian* from a street vendor or stall, as one could freely buy the lurid sex-and-sensation tabloids. It was his custom to arrange for delivery of the more serious papers as soon as he checked into his hotel room.

"Well, what now?"

"Tomorrow, darling. I'm seeing the Prime Minister at eleven, at 10 Downing. And we have an audience at four o'clock, at the Palace. Tea with the Queen. And there are some messages from home. Nothing pressing, though."

"That should just about blow the whole day, damn it. Well, it can't be helped, I suppose. Get those appointments out of the way and then we'll have the rest of the week to ourselves."

"What will you do tomorrow, Drew?"

"Haven't thought about it. Maybe look up a couple of the press 'barons' I've met. Maybe visit my tailor. I could use new shoes—or maybe I'll wear some out, and just wander around some more!"

The meeting between the two women prime ministers was stiff and formal. Kathleen had not hitherto met the bright-haired woman who greeted her at the entrance to the historic building which contained both the offices and the residence of the elected head of the British government. Saul Martineau, who had escorted Kathleen, introduced the tall Canadian to the shorter, well-coiffed British leader. He then discreetly left the two of them together.

Kathleen took in the room. Highly waxed floors and dark furniture greeted her. Various pieces of silver and crystal winked in the artificial light and dark portraits in ornate gilded frames crowded the walls. To her disappointment, her hostess made no offer to show her the rest of 10 Downing.

They drank weak English coffee, poured from a heavy silver pot of Georgian design into fragile Crown Derby cups.

The British Prime Minister was trimly clad in a full-skirted navy silk suit. At her throat she wore a soft polka-dot jabot, and on her feet were high-heeled strapped sandals, higher than any Kathleen would, or could, wear. The Prime Minister's skin was pink and white, her bobbed blond hair was arranged in careful waves; her dark grey eyes were remote and covertly appraising.

Kathleen felt over-large and a little clumsy in this woman's neat presence. Her own dark-grey flannel dress seemed too plain, too business-like for this gracious room. Its crisp white linen collar and cuffs made her look more like an efficient secretary than a prime minister, and try as she would she couldn't manage to establish a rapport with her oh-so-cool hostess.

On the political level they had little in common—on the personal level even less. They never got beyond small talk—"Is this your first trip to London?" Or, "You really shouldn't miss. . . ."

Kathleen regretted that she had spurned a suggested briefing before she left Ottawa. There had been only enough time to settle high-priority matters before the Wickstroms departed on this spur-of-the-moment trip. Her hostess seemed reluctant to open any serious subject, and it was abundantly clear from her rather aloof manner that she would not welcome any woman-to-woman chatter comparing the problems of leading a largely male government. Kathleen wanted to ask her how she intended to handle the militant British unions, but couldn't find the words.

The Canadian Prime Minister crossed and recrossed her long legs, irritated that she was probably broadcasting her lack of poise.

"Of course you will be attending the Commonwealth Conference?" asked her hostess in a precise, not-quite Oxonian accent.

"Yes. Yes, of course. Although I'm not looking forward to the heat of Africa," Kathleen replied. "I've never been there and I really don't know what to expect. Except that it will be hot." She felt she sounded like a simpleton.

The British Prime Minister looked down her nose. "But, my dear, that part of Africa is semi-tropical—quite pleasant really. Rather like California."

Kathleeen cringed inside. Why can't I think of something profound to say? She thinks I'm an idiot.

In chilly tones Prime Minister Plunkett continued, "Of course, if you plan on visiting the west coast—Nigeria or Ghana—well, the heat can be a problem there."

She looked as though she had never felt heat. Kathleen imagined her in one-hundred-per-cent humidity without a hair out of place—and probably wearing a suit, to boot.

"I understand, Mrs. Wickstrom, that you're going to the Palace later in the day. I'm sure you'll find her Majesty very gracious. Have you met before?"

It was obvious that she had given up on her guest. Kathleen glanced at her watch: only fifteen or twenty minutes more to get through, then she could make a proper exit. Although, at this moment she thought of it more as an escape.

"Yes," she answered, "I've met her several times. Members of the Royal Family come quite frequently to Canada. We don't have long, exhausting royal tours across the country any more, but they do come, to different regions, every year or so. I met the royal couple several times, mostly in Ottawa. And I certainly agree, they *are* very gracious." She could hear her own voice rambling on—trying to use up time by talking about something obvious. Naturally, the British Prime Minister knew exactly how often the royal family visited Canada and what the arrangements were.

"Have you met the Prince?"

"Oh, yes, Philip. I find him a fascinating man. Very handsome. Very amusing."

This was getting worse and worse. Kathleen knew she sounded inane. Like a hero-struck schoolgirl.

"I meant the Prince of Wales," the Prime Minister said.

Kathleen cursed herself for her stupid mistake. But how was she to know?

"No, I haven't met him, or the other children for that matter."

Prime Minister Plunkett smiled a frozen smile. "Hardly children. The Princess is married and a mother, Charles is thirty, and Andrew's getting on towards his twenties! They're very charming, very lively."

Kathleen wanted to disappear, dissolve or just plain run. She murmured a rejoinder and a silence followed, a silence broken by the butler. Mercifully, he announced the arrival of Kathleen's car. Both women were immensely relieved. Whatever either had anticipated before the brief meeting, neither had expected to find herself bored. Nonetheless, both were.

Kathleen ducked into the back seat of the car, where she sat wordlessly all the way back to the official residence. When she and Martineau arrived she passed through the stone doorway with its heavy door and into the foyer where she was swept into a hug by the waiting mistress of the house.

Nelda Martineau was attractive, spritely, shrewd, and fun. She had a high bark of a laugh, bold eyes and a habit of calling a spade a spade. She had been a favourite of Kathleen's in the old days—one of the few Cabinet wives who had made the newcomer welcome. Even now she enfolded Kathleen in warmth, as she led her into the long study to the left of the doorway, chattering like a magpie all the way.

The room was inviting. A long chesterfield divided the floorspace, facing comfortable stuffed chairs upholstered with a paisley print in faded tones of old rose and blue and gold. Behind them, sunlight was diffused by the sheer curtains which shut off the view of the cobbled city square beyond.

Kathleen was barely seated, her glance touching the shining tables crowded with clusters of silver-framed photographs of the High Commissioner and the notables of the world, when Saul Martineau himself placed in her hands a stubby crystal glass bearing an etched maple leaf. Kathleen recognized the official crystal. It was a staple in every Canadian diplomatic residence.

"It's a martini. I believe I've remembered how you liked them—extra dry. Am I right?"

"Yes, indeed, Saul. Although I imagine it was Nelda who remembered. Am *I* right?"

Nelda laughed with her distinctive bark. "You can't fool Kathleen, Saul. She knows us too well," she chided her husband, affectionately.

He lowered his portly figure into a chair, ruefully glancing at his wife of almost half a century, and from her to his Prime Minister.

"You women might allow an old man his pretensions," he complained. "What *is* the world coming to? Anyway, the point is, a martini is what she likes. Isn't it, Kath ... Prime Minister?" he recovered.

" 'Kathleen' will do just fine, Saul," she said. Her eyes twinkled at him over the glass. "And the drink is perfect. Very thoughtful of you. I certainly need it."

"Oh," he said, his brows arching towards his well-receded hairline. "Did the interview with the Prime Minister not go well?"

"Nothing to be alarmed about, Saul," she said reassuringly. "I doubt that I have worsened relations with the UK government, or anything of that kind, but I have to confess we didn't seem to hit it off." There was regret in her voice.

"Wasn't the Steel Butterfly friendly?" asked Nelda sympathetically.

Her husband cleared his throat in warning.

Nelda looked at him. "Well that's what the papers call her," she retorted, defensively.

Kathleen interrupted. "No, I wouldn't call her unfriendly. Just—I don't know. I guess 'remote' is the word. But I doubt that I covered myself with glory, either. Couldn't seem to think of anything to say to her. I don't know why." Kathleen's high brow was creased with concern, her voice puzzled. "Oh well, it was only a courtesy call. Next time I'll do better. Let's put that aside. Nelda, I'm starving. When's lunch?"

"When you have the other half of your drink. I'll just go and check. Saul, you have some messages for Kathleen, don't you?"

She left the room, and as she moved towards the rear of the house they could follow her progress by the sound of her quick step on the parquet floor.

"Let's have them, Saul," Kathleen said with a sigh, and for the next fifteen minutes, the two bent together over the half-dozen messages. They were still talking about the darkening labour scene at home when Nelda summoned them to lunch.

Kathleen and Andrew trod the richly carpeted stairway in the wake of the beribboned naval aide who had collected them upon their arrival at the entrance to Buckingham Palace.

The Canadian Prime Minister was nervous. About what,

she was not sure, since she had met her royal hosts previously and had invariably found those experiences pleasurable.

There would be no burden upon her to make conversation. It was protocol that she await the royal pair's opening gambits, and then follow their lead. She was not expected to change the subject, either. That was the prerogative of her sovereign.

Nor was she concerned about the appropriateness of her dress. She had brought with her the short-sleeved, raw silk afternoon dress with its matching full-length straight coat just for this occasion. Her shoes and bag had been dyed to match the rich turquoise of the ensemble. Her white gloves—*de rigeur* when meeting royalty—were immaculate, and she wore only her pearls and the spray of ruby maple leaves. She knew the rich colour was becoming. Andrew had told her so.

No, the butterflies in her queasy stomach probably fluttered because of the fact that hitherto Kathleen had been hostess, at home on her own ground, and this time, she was the guest. A guest in a royal palace.

They were ushered into a large, square sitting room, and had only moments to wait before the diminutive Queen, in a very plain, coral silk dress, its only ornament a diamond maple leaf—a Canadian gift from an earlier visit to the Dominion—entered the room. Behind her strode the tall figure of her Consort, his face split in a welcoming grin. This time, Kathleen dropped her curtsey to each of her royal hosts perfectly. She had practised it while dressing, afraid that she would, as usual, put the wrong foot forward. Andrew's bow had been just right.

So far, so good, she thought with satisfaction.

The audience was a great success. Her Majesty and her Consort kept the conversation light and lively, recalling a number of amusing incidents from their many Canadian visits. They had touched only very lightly on the Canadian political scene, including a request that their greetings be passed on to Jean Jacques Charles, on her return. It appeared that Kathleen's predecessor had been a great favourite of Philip's, who had keenly enjoyed their frequent encounters.

A liveried servant wheeled in a tea-cart. It held a lavish spread of hot scones, tiny sandwiches, petit fours, bowls of pale rose-hip jam and sherried jelly, and a shining ornate tea service. Kathleen accepted the beautiful cup and saucer, the crisp ciphered napkin, and a tiny sandwich. To her delight, it was peppery watercress on plain bread and butter. It reminded her of English novels in which watercress and thin-sliced cucumber sandwiches had been the mainstay of the nobility's afternoon tea.

The audience lasted a little more than an hour, but it passed so quickly that Kathleen was startled when Andrew, who had promised to keep an eye on the time, nodded to signal that they should prepare to leave. The signal was not lost on their experienced hosts, who rose at once to indicate the close of the audience.

In moments, the Wickstroms had been shown to the waiting embassy car, its bright Canadian standard fluttering in the rising afternoon breeze.

As they sat back in the soft cushions, Kathleen contentedly squeezed her husband's arm.

"Wasn't that *nice*, Andrew? And think of it, I curtsied four times. Four times, and every time on the right foot!" she said, proudly.

He looked at her—her hazel eyes shiny with pleasure. Absurd that she should care so much about such a little thing. But then, he supposed, as in so many other things in life, it was often the little things that counted. He smiled at her fondly, taking one white-gloved hand in his.

"Now, Mrs. Wickstrom, you can stop being Kathleen Marshal, Prime Minister. From now on, for the rest of the week, you're mine. Okay?"

"Okay, Mr. Wickstrom. I'm all yours. A whole week to ourselves," she exulted. "Now. Tell me what you have planned."

"What th' hell's wrong with Adam Sorenson?"

Wilbur Tolliver was striding rapidly through the underground tunnel connecting the West and Centre Blocks, deep below the surface of Parliament Hill. He and his companion had just left a meeting of the committee. They were hurrying to ensure a good table in the Parliamentary dining room.

"Who can ever figure Sorenson?"

"Why is he in such an all-fired tear to get started? Hell, if it hadn't been for him, all this coulda waited 'til fall," grunted the chairman. "Now he wants us to have a hearing every day. And didja see the list of witnesses he wants called? Why it could take us to Christmas to listen to 'em all! If he has his way, we'll never get to the other agencies," he went on grumbling. "And that ain't the way I like to run my committee."

"Surprised you didn't cut him down to size, Doc," his companion wheezed.

"I woulda, if we'd had the votes. That's one of the damned troubles with this minority Government. We gotta rely on Opposition support, and I sure didn't have any of that today." He shook his head dolefully. "It sure ain't like it useta be."

His companion struggled to keep up, their footsteps echoing hollowly on the tunnel's tiled flooring as they neared the elevator which would take them to the surface.

"What a mean little bastard that Sorenson is! Why he as near come to accusin' me of protecting the agency. Coverin' up! Made me sound like Nixon and that Watergate! What th' hell's he talkin' about, anyway? AECL's got nothin' to hide that I ever heard about." The chairman's indignation was enhanced by his puffing, his reddened face, his bulging eyes. "*You* know what he's gettin' at?" he jabbed a pudgy finger at his companion's vest.

"How would *I* know? But my guess is the little weasel is just grandstanding, looking for support for the Tory leadership. Nobody takes him seriously. You can tell that bugs him. He's looking for headlines, trying to prove his own importance."

"Mebbe so. But he's got no call being so rambunctious in my committee. I guess I can afford to give him a little more rope, but he better watch his mouth. I just won't stand for any little old two-bit freshman member trying to take over *my* committee."

But Wilbur Tolliver was still uneasy. The hearings weren't going according to Hoyle. The committee had first summoned the chairman of the AECL. That gruff, rough-hewn scientist had come with his carefully prepared statement, and a phalanx of his officials, on hand in case the distinguished but inattentive professor had need of more detail to answer the committee's enquiries.

The chairman had been very open with the MPs. He left the impression that he was a harried academic with too much to do. Nonetheless, he convinced them he was transparently honest, with absolutely nothing to hide. As Tolliver confided to his minister: "The chairman seems like a nice guy, but not so swift up here," and he had tapped his temple.

It had been made clear that the chairman and his fellow members of the board of directors left the day-to-day running of the agency to its suave president. The committee had let the scientist go unscathed, after he assured them of his readiness to reappear later if they had need to recall him.

Later that day it was the AECL president's turn. The too-neat, almost dapper man with the hairline moustache and the round, opaque eyes was supremely confident of his ability to deal with these parliamentarians, whatever they might decide to throw at him. He prided himself on being a true professional. He had a long career in government service behind him, and he fully expected that the committee's scrutiny would be little more than cursory. He would be more than a match for them.

He presented a long, comprehensive statement on the operations of the agency which included both a history of the Atomic Energy Commission and its plans for the future.

"Mr. President, I suppose you know every little detail of what goes on over there at AECL?" began Adam Sorenson, with proper deference.

The president preened a bit. "Well, not everything, of course—it's a pretty big organization. But yes, I suppose, sooner or later, I know almost all that goes on there."

"Maybe you can tell us how the sales of the Candu are going, then?" asked his interrogator, unexpectedly.

"Why yes, I can. Although you understand I wouldn't want to be too specific. Mustn't reveal our secrets," the witness responded archly.

"My responsibility is largely administrative," he continued. "Of course, as the chairman of the board has told you, *they* are responsible for broad policy. I just carry out that policy." He seemed to have forgotten the original question.

"What *is* the policy regarding the sale of the Candu?" the sharp-featured Opposition member asked.

"Why to sell the reactor, of course—just as many as we can. It isn't easy. The field is very competitive. But we are very proud of our technology. It's a top-flight reactor—better than the American model, we think. We're very proud of it. We think the heavy-water type is quite superior in every way."

"How many have we sold, so far?"

"I—I'm not absolutely certain, but I must have the figures here somewhere. If you'll give me a moment. . . ."

Sorenson allowed the witness time to search, unsuccessfully, through the papers before him, before he broke in.

"You can get the exact figures later for the committee. In the meantime, let's have some ballpark figures. Fifty? A hundred?"

"Oh no," the president said, abandoning his futile search. He knew precisely the number sold, but he could see no reason to make the figures public. After all, his agency was in competition with many others who would be eager for any scrap of fresh intelligence. "Not nearly so many as that," he conceded reluctantly.

"Twenty-five? A dozen?" persisted his questioner.

"That's about right. We often sell more than one to a customer."

"And what's the price?" asked Sorenson, making a note of the witness' answer.

"What—of a Candu?" The president was determined not to get into this in any detail. Perhaps he could just obfuscate a bit. "That depends," he hedged.

"On what?"

"Oh, a lot of things. How eager the customer is, for one. How many reactors they'll need. Whether we are the only bidder, or whether our competitors also have the entrée. The relative values of our national currencies. Delivery schedules. The difficulties and costs of transportation. How long our people have to be onsite, setting the reactor up and getting it working. Whether we train their nationals to operate it there, or here in Canada. Whether we'll supply heavy water and enriched uranium. There are dozens of variables. They all have to be considered in pricing the package."

"Would I be right in assuming that the usual price is in the millions?"

"More like hundreds of millions," corrected the president. "They are *quite* expensive."

He stroked his thin moustache to conceal a secret smile. He knew that MPs were accustomed to speaking in millions of dollars. The words tripped easily off their tongues, although he doubted that any of them really had any concept of what the string of zeros meant. In their private lives, he thought with contempt, they were nobodies accustomed only to dealing in nickels and dimes.

"The cost," he decided to add, "of the Candu itself, is only the beginning—"

"Have there been any recent sales?" Adam Sorenson interrupted pointedly.

The president narrowed his eyes.

"Argentina."

"No. I mean since that one?"

The president was silent.

"Is it possible that we have recently sold a reactor to a Caribbean nation?" prompted Sorenson smoothly.

"Yeees. We've been negotiating with several."

"Why haven't we heard of this?"

"Well, it's not good business practice. We may have a deal, but with a few details remaining to be worked out. When everything is set, it's customary to permit the purchaser nation to make the public announcement. The customer is always right, you know." He essayed a weak joke, but it elicited no answering smile from his intent questioner.

"Which Caribbean nations are you negotiating with?" asked Sorenson.

"I'd rather not say. It would be premature," fenced the president.

"I want to know—premature or not. This is the country's business, and we are here to do it," said Sorenson firmly, giving way to his instinct to grandstand a little.

"I'm afraid I'm not at liberty to tell you," said the president, somewhat defiantly. He didn't like this upstart's tone at all.

There was a pause.

"Let's leave that for the moment, then," Sorenson said unexpectedly. "Please tell us *how* you sell a Candu."

The president appeared a little confused. "But *I* don't sell them, as I told you," he began.

"No, no," his questioner waved off the answer. "Just tell us how a sale is made. Who picks the prospects? How do you make contact? Who do you deal with? That kind of thing," he said, helpfully.

"Well, I don't think I ought to reveal details about any particular sale, but I think I can tell you how it goes, in general."

The president launched into his talk, an earnest expression on his face.

"Sometimes, we learn a nation is contemplating going nuclear. More commonly, the initial contact is made when a prospective purchaser approaches us for a bid. Sometimes, their preliminary investigations will have led them to decide already that they want a heavy-water-type reactor. That makes it much easier for us, since, as I said, the Candu is superior, both technically and economically, to our chief competitor, West Germany.

"Sometimes, the purchaser nation hasn't yet made that preliminary decision and the field is then wide open. We have to start from scratch. But our American friends, whose reactors don't employ heavy water as a moderator, may have an edge. Americans are very aggressive salesmen. Industrially developed nations seem to prefer their technology, sometimes for political or other reasons. You'll note that we have been most successful with relatively unadvanced nations who are seeking an integrated, self-sufficient energy system."

"Yes, yes, go on," said Sorenson impatiently. He found this testimony boring but he wanted it on the record.

"The purchaser provides us with its specifications—like how many reactors they need initially, how many ultimately, how big they're to be. They tell us whether they want to buy a reactor only, or whether they'll need a heavy-water plant, too. Sometimes they want to buy our enriched uranium. Or they may want to buy our expertise in exploration and mining technology and equipment, to develop their own uranium sources. Maybe they'll want a fabrication plant to produce natural uranium for fuel. AECL controls the Canadian technology, and we license Canadian companies who bid to do the actual construction to manufacture the fuel and the heavy water.

"Sometimes the customer is interested in buying project management from us, or wants our help in nuclear research. If they want to hunt for their own uranium, we bring in Eldorado Nuclear Limited, which, as you know, is another Crown corporation. And sometimes, because these things are so very expensive, the purchase nation may need a loan to help pay. If they do, they have to negotiate that independently with the Export Development Corporation.

"You mean we lend them money to buy the Candu? Why should we do that?" was the interjection of one of the committee members.

"Because such a sale produces a lot of Canadian jobs, now and in the future," said the president reasonably.

The member nodded his understanding, and the president continued his explanation.

"Let me repeat, the sale of the first Candu is terribly important. If the purchaser buys one Candu, it's more than likely that he'll keep on buying from us. These industrially developing nations are interested in fully integrated systems, to make themselves as self-sufficient energy-wise as possible, whereas many of the better-developed industrial nations have a variety of systems. Even Argentina bought a small German heavy-water model as well as a Candu."

"What did you say the cost was?" another member enquired.

"As I tried to explain, that depends upon the variables. But let's take Argentina, for an example. They bought a 600-megawatt reactor. It's under construction now. The heavy-water plant alone will run three or four hundred million dollars. The whole package might be worth—oh, between a billion and a billion and a half to Canada, by the time Argentina completes its six-billion-dollar program over the next twenty years. We hope to sell them more reactors, but the Germans also have a toe-hold there."

"What was the price of the Candu we sold them?" asked, Adam Sorenson.

"I'd rather not say. You'll appreciate, I'm sure, that this is an extremely competitive business. These deals take a very long time to negotiate, and then sometimes they'll fall apart at the last minute—like Japan. We had high hopes there, but.... And then on the other hand, they'll hang fire for months. Sometimes just one little thing will help to wrap up the deal." He smiled, thinking that "that one little thing" might be, for instance, a two-million-dollar commission to the right agent, with the right connections.

The chairman put his own question. "We don't sell the Candu and our nuke technology to just anybody who comes around, jinglin' the coin in his jeans, do we?"

The president smiled benignly. "No, Mr. Chairman, we don't. It is the long-standing policy of Canadian governments that, as a signatory to the non-proliferation treaties, we insist that our purchasers sign too, and be subject to regular international inspection. Although, sometimes, if they won't go that far, we have negotiated a bi-lateral agreement with what we call 'full-scope' nuclear safeguards. It amounts to the same thing. The point is we assure ourselves that the purchaser intends to use the nuclear technology we are selling for strictly peaceful purposes."

"Has insisting on that ever lost us a sale?"

"Indeed it has. General De Gaulle refused to accept such a condition when we were close to closing a sale with France, back in the sixties. He was adamant. We refused to sell. That was when France was developing its own *force de frappe.*"

"What about India? I seem to remember. . . ."

The president bit off his words like a reprimand. "That was regrettable. But they bought a research model, not a commercial model." He pursed his lips. Obviously, the Indian sale was a sore point.

"What about our competitors? Do they lay down the same conditions?" asked a hitherto silent although attentive NDP member.

"The Americans do. West Germany's conditions have been less stringent, but lately, after some considerable international pressure, they have, ah, fallen into line," the president replied, with a cautious choice of words.

In the momentary pause, Wilbur Tolliver seized the opportunity to break in.

"Six o'clock, gentlemen. Thank you, Mr. President. You have been most helpful."

He rose to shake the relieved witness' hand, and with a last glance at Sorenson, the president of the AECL left the room.

"When's the next meeting, Doc?"

The chairman studied his schedule. "Next week."

"Will the president be recalled?" This from Adam Sorenson, busily scribbling notes of the last of the testimony.

"I don't expect that'll be necessary," Tolliver said. "Appears to me he's covered all the ground."

"Not to me, it doesn't. I've hardly started," argued Sorenson. "And I don't like the pace of these hearings. I think we ought to have him back here tomorrow, and keep him coming back till we're finished with him."

The rotund chairman's eyebrows drew together. He resented Sorenson's latest challenge to his authority. With one swift glance he swept the hearing room, noticing that some of the committee members had already hurried off, while others were crowding towards the exit. He gavelled for their attention.

"When do you want to meet again? I'm in your hands."

The remaining members hesitated, mentally juggling their schedules of commitments.

"Tomorrow morning," demanded Sorenson.

"No way!" interjected one of the Conservative members.

Tolliver was happy to have some support. Other members of the committee looked to him for a settlement.

"Look, Adam," he said. "How about a compromise? We'll recall the president, but not right away. Why don't we wait until Parliament recesses for the summer. We've all got other responsibilities. What about next month?"

The other members nodded and looked relieved. Tolliver brought down his gavel.

Sorenson swore under his breath. He needed more information now, not next month. But then, as his anger subsided, he realized that he just might have enough now—if only he asked the right questions.

"Mr. Speaker. My question is for the Minister for Energy. But since the Right Honourable Lady has seen fit to appoint to that very important ministry a person from the 'other place,' I'll direct my question to her."

Kathleen pulled the earpiece from her ear. Adam Sorenson had spoken in English. The instant translation into French was disconcerting.

Although she was still a little tired after her return trip from England yesterday evening, she had managed to get a good night's sleep. In the morning, the daily briefing from her staff pad included mention of Sorenson's work in the committee. She was glad that she had taken time to call in Gabriel LaCroix.

"You're sure, then, Gabriel," she had asked, "that there's nothing to these allegations of a Candu sale to Cuba? You've checked it out carefully?"

"Prime Minister, I tell you, the president of AECL assures me that we have no contact with the Cubans. The foundation for the stories is probably the negotiations that were undertaken last year. There were talks with Mexico and Venezuela as well. The Mexican deal has firmed up but the other two are in limbo."

Sure of her facts, Kathleen waited now for Sorenson to pose his question.

"Will the Prime Minister inform the House of the details of the sale of a Candu heavy-water reactor without obtaining our usual safeguards?"

Kathleen pushed aside her chair and stood up, the earpiece dangling from her head.

"Mr. Speaker, there has been no such sale. Canadian policy on that matter is unaltered."

Adam Sorenson jumped at once to his feet.

"A supplementary question, Mr. Speaker. Can the Right Honourable Lady then explain the basis for persistent rumours of such a sale?"

Kathleen waved away the question, not bothering even to attempt an answer.

Before the Speaker could nod to one of the half-dozen other members already on their feet, seeking his recognition to pose their prepared questions, Adam Sorenson shot another question at Kathleen.

"Will the Prime Minister confirm or deny that the President of the United States has expressed his concern to her over these persistent rumours?"

There was a stir among the members.

Kathleen considered whether she should reply. She couldn't deny it—that would mean deliberately misleading the House. But if she confirmed it that would only lend credence to the rumours. She decided in a few swift seconds that she had better try to quash the rumour now.

She propelled herself from her chair. "Let me assure the House that Canada has not sold nuclear technology without safeguards. There is no deal, whatever the rumours may be." That should do it, she thought, resuming her seat.

But Adam Sorenson was back on his feet. His piercing voice rose.

"Mr. Speaker, Mr. Speaker. On a matter of personal privilege," he insisted.

Stephan Ludvic stood before his throne. A question of privilege took priority over routine business of the House. It was impossible to rule whether the point was a genuine matter of privilege until he had heard what the Member had to say.

"The Honourable Member for Petrolia, on a question of privilege," he acknowledged and sat down to hear Sorenson out.

The freshman member drew a deep breath, then facing Kathleen across the green-carpeted aisle, he said grimly.

"I charge that the Prime Minister of Canada has *deliberately misled* this house in what she has just said. It is contrary to private information in my possession, and to information being elicited from witnesses before a Standing Committee of this House. I charge her with deliberately misleading the House about the proposed sale."

The House reacted by falling into shocked silence.

The charge of lying was one of the most serious which

might be levelled against any member of the House. It was unparliamentary even to use the word. "Deliberately misleading" was the euphemism of hoary parliamentary tradition. If a member persisted, he would in effect be laying his own seat on the line, for it could lead to an enquiry before the House Committee on Privileges and elections. If the evidence there did not support the charge, the member who had made it would be forced to resign. But if the evidence supported the charge, the member who had been caught lying to the House must resign. Not in modern history had such a charge been made against a Prime Minister.

The Speaker was on his feet.

"I ask the Honourable Member to reconsider what he has just said. It may be that he has not had the experience to fully understand the meaning of his words. I invite the Member for Petrolia to withdraw the word 'deliberately.' It is contrary to parliamentary usage."

Adam Sorenson had taken his seat, as the rules required, as soon as the Speaker was on his feet. Although his face flushed and his jaw set stubbornly, he refused to acknowledge Ludvic.

The Speaker remained standing, giving the freshman member time to reconsider. When it was apparent that Sorenson had no intention of withdrawing, Ludvic sighed, reluctant to do what House Rules required him to do as a result of the freshman member's intransigence. He would have to "name" Sorenson, and demand his withdrawal from the sitting of the House.

He did so.

Sorenson remained in his seat, defying the Speaker. In the spacious green chamber, no member moved, as at the Speaker's nod, the Sergeant-at-Arms got to his feet and moved with deliberate tread towards Adam Sorenson, prepared to oust him, with force if necessary, from the House.

Sorenson eyed the approaching figure uncertainly. Just before the house official reached him, he flung himself from his seat and stamped out of the chamber.

The gold curtain fell back into place behind him. The Speaker recognized the next question and the interrupted business of the Commons resumed.

Kathleen found it difficult to sleep that night. Repeatedly, the ugly scene in the House was replayed in her mind. She had been appalled at Sorenson's accusation, and the gravity of her own situation. It was unthinkable that a Prime Minister might be called before the bar of the House on a charge of lying. She shuddered at the prospect. She would probably have to resign if that happened, even though she was confident that she would be ultimately vindicated. But she could never forget how vulnerable she was. The Liberals had no majority in any of the House Committees. If Sorenson persisted in his charge, there was always the possibility that the Opposition would seize that opportunity to destroy her and her Government with her.

"It's so damned unfair," she muttered to herself. "It's got nothing to do with me at all. It's Jacques who's a friend of Castro, not I, and LaCroix *says* there is no deal. And certainly not one without safeguards. I don't know what else I can do."

One thing you had better do is stop worrying and get some sleep, she told herself grimly. One day at a time. Let tomorrow take care of itself.

As the members resumed their seats after prayers, the public was admitted to the galleries. Kathleen's glance roamed around the upper level. Once again, the capital's residents were demonstrating their almost uncanny sense of a moment of high parliamentary drama. They swarmed in, quickly occupying all available space, as though they had divined that in the future they would want to be able to brag, "I was there when it happened."

Adam Sorenson was on his feet, waiting.

Stephan Ludvic had observed the freshman member in the company of Richard Sherwood when he entered the chamber for prayers. Of all those present in the chamber, the Speaker was one of the few who had been previously advised of Sorenson's decision.

The Speaker stood, and acknowledged Sorenson.

"The Honourable Member from Petrolia."

Sorenson cleared his throat nervously. In his hand, which trembled visibly, he clutched his prepared statement. He was very reluctant to do what he was about to do, but after the interview with his leader, he felt he had very little choice.

"Mr. Speaker, on a question of personal privilege."

Ludvic nodded and resumed his seat.

"Yesterday, Mr. Speaker, I made a charge against the Prime Minister that she had deliberately misled this House. I suggested that she must have known of the sale of a Candu reactor without safeguards."

Sorenson paused, raising his eyes from the paper in his hand to glare across the aisle at Jean Jacques Charles. Jacques sat upright in the green leather armchair to Kathleen's right. He returned Sorenson's look calmly. Beside him, Kathleen was tense.

"Your Honour asked me to withdraw the word 'deliberately' from my remarks." He paused again, remembering how he had been forced into ignominious retreat from the Chamber. "I have given deep thought to the matter overnight, and consulted with some of my more senior colleagues."

"I wish t' hell he'd get to the point. What's he decided to do, anyway?" The growl came from Kathleen's left. It was Harry Williams, who appeared as apprehensive as she.

"The Prime Minister has vigorously denied any knowledge of any such sale. Mr. Speaker, after long and careful consideration of parliamentary tradition, I have decided that I must accept the Right Honourable Lady's word. I withdraw the word 'deliberately.' " Sorenson sat down.

There was a long sibilant sigh as members collectively released pent-up breaths, and a rustling wave of reaction from observers in the galleries.

A clatter began from Opposition benches. At first, a few scattered Conservative members banged their desk-tops, acknowledging Sorenson's far-from-gracious, but correct, apology. More members of his caucus followed, thumping their desks in approval, as Richard Sherwood turned to nod briefly at Sorenson, who had slumped in his seat, his normally sallow colour high. With his leader's approbation, Sorenson became aware of the insistent drumming arising now from all sides of the chamber. A glow of delight began to spread through him, as it dawned upon him that although he had been forced to eat crow, his peers approved of his action.

Kathleen felt drained, sapped of energy. She had listened intently to Sorenson's words. Although she was overwhelmingly relieved that he had withdrawn the charge, she had an uneasy instinct that there would be more to be heard of this matter.

As the galleries emptied and Question Period began, she turned to her seatmate. Jean Jacques Charles' hard blue stare met her gaze from less than a foot away. He raised his eyebrows and shrugged elaborately, then rose, and without a word, left the Commons chamber.

Chapter Eight

Stanley Findlay's voice betrayed his excitement. "It's done! I've got the contract right here with me. Yes, signed by Castro himself! All sealed and witnessed. In both Spanish and English. They've bought the Candu! What? Oh yes, it was sticky for a bit, but they finally agreed to our delivery date. No, you'll get confirmation through the Cuban ambassador. It should be in the diplomatic bag later this week."

There was a loud crackling on the telephone line. Stan waited for the static to clear up. "Hello? Hello? Are you still there?" The voice on the other end answered in the affirmative.

"Look, I've been down there three times, and this last trip it took all week to nail the deal down. God, is Havana hot this time of year! None of the air conditioning works, and no one is in a hurry to do anything. You know, it's always *mañana*. Anyway, thought I better let you know right away. Now, about the commission . . ." He listened intently to the suave voice on the other end of the phone. "As soon as you get the official copies of the contract and the deposit from the Cubans? Right. You know where to make payment?" Again the voice answered in the affirmative. Stanley bid it good-bye and replaced the phone on the hook.

Stepping out of the phone booth, he moved into the small VIP lounge at the Toronto Airport. Still an hour till his flight west would leave. Stanley slumped into a chair, then restlessly pushed himself to his feet again. He didn't really feel like flying west; he wasn't prepared to see Joan. Perhaps, he thought, it might be wise to phone Willis Cranston as well.

He placed the call to the unlisted Montreal number. It rang and rang. Stanley could picture the empty house, probably they were off at a lake somewhere. A mental picture of Giselle Cranston in her tiny, tight bathing suit teased his imagination. He was about to hang up when the telephone was answered in French. Stanley asked for Mr. Cranston.

When the maid told him that the master was unavailable, Findlay hesitantly asked for the mistress of the house. After a wait of several seconds the familiar, sultry voice was in his ear.

Giselle seemed to welcome his call and, not realizing that he was in Toronto, she urged him to come by for a drink. Willis, she purred, would be back in a few hours and would be able to discuss their business then. Perhaps the three of them could have dinner on the town?

It was a crazy idea, but Stanley felt more like flying to Montreal than flying west. He could certainly be with Giselle in two hours, talk to Willis, and then stay in Montreal overnight before flying home. Stanley quickly accepted Giselle's invitation. Then, not even wanting to hear his wife's whine, he sent Joan a perfunctory telegram: "Unavoidable delay stop will arrive p.m. tomorrow."

Stanley Findlay caught the next plane to Montreal.

Bypassing the private stone wall, the taxi deposited Findlay before an ornate oak door set into the facade of a high, cut-stone mansion. On either side of the door were huge stone urns filled with geraniums in shades of pink, coral, crimson, and white. A gaunt serving man in a neat black jacket admitted him into the cool hallway and silently led him through the impressive high-ceilinged rooms to the rear of the house. There, in a glassed conservatory, Giselle rose to greet her guest with a delighted welcome.

"It's so good to see you again, Stan. Do sit here, beside me."

She gestured to a white-painted chair cushioned in piped green linen which was drawn up near the low lounge from which she had risen.

"What can I get you? Tea? Coffee? Wine? A drink? You must be thirsty. It's such a warm afternoon. What will it be?"

"Whatever you're having." He pointed to the tall, bedewed glass beside her.

"Oh, I'm sure you wouldn't like that," Giselle smiled, as she rang for the servant. "That's Vichy—just mineral water."

She was right. Stan wanted more than water, and more than the strong drink he finally ordered. Ever since he had arrived he couldn't take his eyes off Giselle. He had never seen a woman so seductive. She was dressed in a white, gauzy garment that looked very much like a strapless harem suit. The material was opaque and subtly emphasized the presence of warm flesh beneath. When she moved, the fabric clung to her. Above the draped neckline her perfect tanned shoulders and the slender column of her strong throat were the same even golden bronze as her piquant face. Except for the widow's peak and a few loose curly strands, her rich abundant hair was hidden by a turban made from the same cloth as her harem suit.

Giselle reminded Stanley of a Turkish temptress—or at least what he imagined a Turkish temptress would look like. She was exotic, almost unreal. Although he sipped the scotch that had been placed in his hand, he was hardly aware of it; and only gradually, as they laughed and talked together, did he finally begin to relax. Previously, on the way to Montreal, he had felt guilty and apprehensive at the knowledge that he would be alone with his mentor's dazzling wife. He had never before done anything so wild or extravagant as flying from Toronto to Montreal for an hour alone with a woman. It was definitely reckless.

Giselle herself was enjoying the situation. Her large, brown-velvet eyes gleamed with mischief at the effect she was having on her guest. The undisguised longing on his face flattered and excited her, and although she tried to hide her own attraction to him, something, perhaps the promise of things to come, caused her to radiate a special warmth. Willis, after all, rarely looked at her this way anymore.

An hour sped by before they were suddenly interrupted by the thin servant. Giselle excused herself, gliding from the room like an odalisque. She returned shortly, her smooth forehead creased with a frown.

"That was Willis, Stan. He's sorry to have missed you, but he can't be back in the city till noon tomorrow. He suggested that, if you have time, perhaps you might stay over and see him then."

This was more than Stan had hoped for.

"You've saved me from a long evening alone," Giselle said. She waited for his reaction. "Of course, if you must go—" she paused.

Stanley shook his head. "No, I was planning to stay over tonight, anyway. I'll get a hotel room."

"No, no. We wouldn't hear of that. There are dozens of empty rooms here! I'll have one aired for you." Her protest was genuine. The Cranstons were quite used to providing for unexpected guests.

"I'd love to take you out for dinner," Stan said. He had made up his mind. "Of course, I don't have anything to change into." Beside Giselle he was only too aware of his traveller's appearance. He had left his bag at the airport, and this was the suit he had worn from Havana.

Giselle smiled at him. "We'll do something not too dressy, if you like."

It was late, very late. In the distance, the twinkling city lay sprawled under the night sky. The thick summer air threatened a storm, and the closeness caught the scent of the blades of grass that had been crushed beneath their bodies. Contentedly, they breathed the deep verdant smells of fresh, green, growing things and the moist damp earth.

The gay dinner in the candle-lit murk of a tiny basement restaurant in the old quarter had been followed by a *pousse-café* in yet another darkened cellar, crowded with young Québécois rapt before a favourite *chansonnier*. When they left, well after midnight, they had wandered, hands entwined, along the cobbled streets.

Neither one of them could have said whose idea it had been to come up to the slope of Mount Royal where the splendid city could be seen like a jewelled cape thrown at the feet of some conqueror. Their coming together was the result of their mutual desire. As flashes of heat lightning played on the horizon, the same flickering heat had flowed through their veins. Without guilt and without thought of the possible consequences, they had succumbed to the longing they had felt since their first meeting. Perhaps later, one or the other would feel embarrassed that they had made love like this, in the open, in the fashion of a sailor tumbling his girl, but there was no such thought between them now. Now the danger of the setting excited them. Stan had at long last felt the warm flesh of Giselle's body and enjoyed the mysteries which so long had tempted him. His daydream had become a sudden reality and the reality was not in the least disappointing.

At first Adam Sorenson was infuriated by the length of the delays. Committee members failed to show up and there was no quorum. The researchers seemed to be taking forever sifting through the technical documents and translating them into the lay language necessary for the members to understand. And now—the president of AECL was grumbling, insisting that he couldn't appear until he received clearance to discuss the various topics he was being questioned about. All in all, Adam Sorenson concluded that with or without summer meetings, it would be late August or early September before he could wrench what he wanted from the reluctant AECL president. His first reaction had been anger and frustration, but now he began to see an advantage in the delays—this was the time for him to consolidate support for the coming convention.

In between meetings—meetings which often seemed to have no purpose—Adam Sorenson flew west to gain the support of influential delegates in the forthcoming leadership election. It was an election Adam Sorenson felt certain he could win if he was able to break the scandal he was now sure existed.

In Ontario, he had called on a number of people whom he knew from his days in Sherwood's office. He was disappointed to find that most of them were away for July or too busy to see him. But one man had received his call with unexpected enthusiasm and had suggested that Adam meet him for breakfast at a downtown hotel.

"You've been doing a good job, Adam, in that committee. Been getting a lot of press on it. But you have to be careful about muck-raking. As my old man used to say, 'You can't kick a cowflap without getting shit on your own shoe.' If you're serious about this leadership business, you've gotta remember a couple of things. The first is that you better have the goods on these guys. If you're just on a fishing expedition, and there really isn't anything important to uncover, the whole thing will fizzle like a damp squib, and they'll say you were only grandstanding—headline chasing. That'll hurt."

"No need to worry about that," Sorenson interrupted, eagerly. "This isn't any damp squib! There'll be an explosion all right, never fear. My only worry is that we'll never get to it before the convention, the way the chairman is dragging his feet over scheduling the hearings."

His breakfast companion mopped up the last of the sticky egg on his plate with a piece of bread and chewed it appreciatively. He nodded to a passing waitress to refill their coffee cups. While she did so, he pulled out his pipe and briskly packed it, struck a kitchen match on his thumbnail, and holding it to the tobacco, puffed until it glowed. When the waitress had left, he leaned back in the banquette with a contented sigh, his eyes playing over Adam's face.

"Glad to hear it," he said around the pipe. "Both that you're really on to something, and that Doc Tolliver isn't in any hurry to finish up with your hearings. That brings up the other thing you should bear in mind—your image, I guess you'd call it."

Sorenson's face reflected his surprise. "What's wrong with my image?" he said, bristling. "It was good enough to get me elected handily a couple of years ago. I'm still young, aggressive."

"Maybe too agressive. Even a couple of years ago you seemed more—well, more reasonable. Now people see you as a pretty one-dimensional Grit-baiter." He held up his hand to forestall the younger man's protest. "Adam, hear me out. Look, you've got a good crack at the leadership. There are so many people in the field, it's anybody's guess who'll win. I don't say how much first-ballot support you'll have, but I'll bet you'll be high on everybody's list as a second-ballot choice if their favourites get wiped. You've got no real enemies in the party and a lot of friends—a lot of IOU's you can call in. But you'll scare that support away if you come on as a johnny-one-note. After all, they want to choose someone who can convince the public to elect him PM—not a perpetual leader of the Opposition. What I'm telling you is that they won't pick someone who comes across as nothing more than a hatchetman."

Adam Sorenson listened intently, weighing what was being said. His mind rebelled against the implied criticsm. He was ready to defend himself, to remind his tutor of the years of back room effort he'd put in for the party, the solid work he'd done in Sherwood's office and the way he had wholeheartedly thrown himself into his parliamentary role since the last election. But he didn't voice his protests. The man across from him was much his senior in party service and highly successful. Howard Kant was a key advisor to Ontario's Big Blue Machine, which had, against all odds, continued to return a Conservative government to Ontario over a period of almost forty years. His very presence here indicated that the Premier of Ontario was backing Sorenson's run, even if he hadn't yet made that support public. Kant's advice was to be respected. His long string of PC election victories in Ontario was proof of his credentials.

The young member pushed his plate away and leaned forward over the small, littered table. His prominent nose wrinkled in concentration.

"Tell me, Howie," he said, deferring to his companion, "what should I do to improve that image? I haven't got a lot of time."

Kant puffed at his pipe, eyeing Adam Sorenson appraisingly. "I'd shelve this committee thing for a few weeks. Don't look so anxious, and get out of Ottawa. I think you'd be well advised to do a little spade-work in both New Brunswick and Newfoundland. Wouldn't be surprised if both premiers would support you with some encouragement. Maybe Alberta, too. How's your French?" he paused, puffing.

"Not very good," Adam admitted uneasily.

"Well, that can't be helped at this late date. May as well write off support from Quebec delegates. They're likely to go down to the wire with their own men, anyway. You should whip your own team together right away. Put somebody in charge of raising money. We'll help—maybe even lend you a couple of bodies. But you're going to need all the time you can squeeze over the next month or so, so I'd drop the committee stuff for the moment and concentrate on the leadership race."

"But the committee. . . . I thought it would help to have a high profile," Sorenson said doubtfully.

"Yeah, a high profile is good." Relenting, Kant said, "Maybe schedule a hearing in mid-summer, just to remind people, but you really can't afford more time than that."

Adam was mollified, ready to accept the compromise.

His breakfast companion pushed the table away and stood, collecting his briefcase and folded newspaper.

"One other thing, Adam," he suggested. "Quit using that greasy kid stuff on your hair. Get it styled by somebody good. Every little thing counts," he said with a chuckle.

The threat of strikes had been in the air ever since Kathleen had won the party's leadership; but when Bonnie Costello took over the Labour portfolio, she had displayed a freshness of approach, and a willingness to listen and sympathize, that had gradually won over all but the most militant of Canada's leaders of organized labour. Under her direction, the frustrating delays in negotiating contracts in the public sector that had so poisoned the atmosphere were minimized. Bonnie seemed to welcome invitations to appear before union con-

ferences and meetings. She exposed herself willingly to initial
hostility from both union executives and rank-and-file membership. Gradually she convinced them that not only was it
her responsibility in government to speak for the workers, but
it was also her personal inclination. Once they came to accept
that the Labour Minister was on their side, the climate
improved dramatically.

Bonnie had been modest about her success, but there was
one aspect of it which she recounted to Kathleen with shy
pride.

"My dad called me, Kathleen, and asked me to come home
for Labour Day. Seems he wants to show me off to some of
his cronies. I guess that means he's pleased with me."

Kathleen had appreciated how unhappy her father's anger
had made her young minister, and she was glad that the
close-knit family had repaired the breach. But while Bonnie
Costello had concentrated on the public service unions, which
were often located close to Ottawa, she had not had time to
make much impact on negotiations between private management and their workers. Kathleen herself had kept in touch
with the private sector, and she had been relieved when the
two big automotive companies, heavy employers of labour,
had resolved their differences, forestalling threatened indus-
try-wide strikes. But the most troubling area of labour dispute
was far from the nation's capital. Perhaps Canada's most
militant workers were found on the west coast, and to
Kathleen's annoyance, Terry Malloy was frequently reported
among them, stirring up dissent.

Grain-handlers working those important western ports
were spoiling for a fight. There had already been sporadic
walk-outs and one or two violent confrontations followed by
slowdowns, before workers finally left their jobs and threw
picket-lines around the docks. Public pressure mounted.
Canada's granaries were full, and there was a back-up all
down the line, right to the farmers themselves. In Vancouver
and Prince Rupert, the harbours were filling with foreign-
registry ships, riding high and empty, as they waited to fill
their holds with the golden cargo. As much as possible, grain
shipments were diverted to Churchill, Manitoba, to take
advantage of the few summer months of open water there,
but day after day, Canada's vital grain exports were slowing
to a trickle. There was no other single strike that could so
quickly cripple the economy.

Bonnie and her officials had done their best, but the Labour

Minister who kept in daily touch with Kathleen, had finally asked her leader to intervene personally. Quickly, Kathleen had done so. Ordinarily a prime minister kept aloof from such explosive situations, not wanting to risk personal association with failure, but the Cabinet judged that Kathleen's intervention might be just what was needed to halt the strike before the economic damage was irreversible.

The Minister of Labour and her Prime Minister had refused to give in to press demands that they knock heads together in order to force one side or the other to back down. Instead, they had gambled on wearing the participants into submission, refusing to release either negotiating team until sheer exhaustion had led them to a compromise.

It was not a compromise to make anyone cheer. It had cost dearly in higher wages, fewer hours, better working conditions, more health benefits, and higher pensions. Kathleen was apprehensive about the inflationary settlement itself, but even more concerned by the prospect of its effect upon future negotiations with other groups of workers. The package agreed to had moved the workers into an even higher bracket than workers in the neighbouring states of Washington and Oregon. But it couldn't be helped—grain shipments simply had to go through.

"Ah, Tony. Care for a drink?"

Ambassador Whiteside strode into the room. He went at once to the President and shook hands. Although the aides scrambled to their feet, the President hadn't bothered to rise when Whiteside was shown in. He good-humouredly waved the diplomat to an armchair vacated by Bobby Lee, who pulled up a sidechair beside his colleague, Larry Conover. It was that late afternoon hour that was the President's favourite time of day, and he was in an expansive mood.

"Well, how are you getting along with the Right Honourable Lady? Are you enjoying your assignment?" he asked mischievously.

Since Anthony Whiteside's appointment to Ottawa, Billy Thompson had learned more of that earlier association. He was inclined to be amused at the surprise he had delivered to his northern neighbour when he appointed Governor Whiteside, but he was also ready to take advantage of any extra leverage the situation could afford him.

The Ambassador admitted that he found Ottawa enjoyable, particularly now that it was basking in summer weather, and he added that he couldn't complain about his reception by the Prime Minister. "Although I must say I find the pace of government in Ottawa much slower than in Washington. And, if you'll forgive me, politics is considerably less levantine than our own. On the whole, it's a pretty good country, Canada. Yes, I'm enjoying it, Mr. President."

Billy Thompson beamed his approval. "Glad to hear it, glad to hear it." He paused to sip at his drink.

Whiteside glanced at each of the President's aides. He could read nothing from their expressions. He kept silent, sure that the President had asked him to drop over after his debriefing at the State Department for something more than a social drink.

"We seem to be getting more than our share of trouble from Canada these days," Thompson finally remarked, in a casual tone.

Uncertain where the President was leading, Whiteside remained silent.

"Look at their latest labour settlement out west. Our unions will start making noise about that soon enough."

"Yes," Whiteside admitted, "but the Canadian economy depends heavily on those unions."

"Could be. Anyway there's not much we can do about that." Abruptly, President Thompson sat forward, placing his glass firmly on the desk before him. He bent his gaze on his guest, his expression serious. "You know what I can't figure out about that woman prime minister, though? I can't see why she keeps Charles in her Cabinet. I should have thought she'd take the chance to get rid of him when she had it. Believe me, I didn't like it when she made that uppity bastard her Foreign Minister, after the way he lit into me in Brussels. Even thought of calling her about it, after the appointment. I guess I should have, at that. Did you hear what he said about me and this country in his UN speech? A helluva nerve, I thought—we all thought, didn't we?"

Both aides nodded, and without hesitation, Thompson came to his point.

"Do you suppose you could tell the lady to get rid of Charles? Just as a friendly gesture, I mean?"

Anthony Whiteside flinched at the President's suggestion. "The Prime Minister can be quite obstinate, Mr. President," he said slowly, "especially if she thinks she's within her rights, as she clearly is in the matter of choosing her own Cabinet. I know that she must have considered how Charles' appointment would look to you, so soon after your discussion here in Washington. It wouldn't, I'm sure, have been intended as a gratuitous slight to you. I'm convinced that there must have been quite important considerations that led her to keep him in her Cabinet."

"Maybe so, but how do you explain his UN speech?" the President said, his ire rising at the recollection.

"I thought it intemperate," said the Ambassador promptly and sincerely. He remembered how his own eyebrows had risen when he'd read the brief reports, wondering whether Kathleen had known about the speech in advance, and fully expecting that he would hear from Washington about it. "But he wouldn't be the first diplomat to embarrass his government by unauthorized remarks at the UN."

"Yeah," said the President, missing the implication in the barbed comment. "He's an arrogant son of a bitch, that Charles. Too damned independent for my taste. And I don't like being the target for his public attacks. I've got my hands full here at home as it is. Can't you persuade her to get rid of him? Or at least see that he keeps his mouth shut about me—at least until the primaries are over?"

"Do you really mean that, Mr. President? Do you want me to make a formal complaint to the Prime Minister?" Whiteside asked.

"Not one of those stuffy State Department things, no. But you're friendly with her, Tony. Just let her know how annoyed I am and that I'd consider it right neighbourly if she'd deep-six old Jacques Charles for me."

The Ambassador considered his instructions. Clearly, President Thompson wanted no formal written record of his attempts to interfere in Canada's business. But he did want results. Whiteside knew the President well enough to recognize that his message was far from a spur-of-the-moment suggestion. Billy Thompson often allowed himself to appear to be spontaneous and impulsive, whereas in truth, most of his actions were carefully calculated in advance.

"And there's another thing, Tony. You know she assured me there was nothing at all to this talk of supplying Castro with nuclear technology. But we keep picking up confirmation that the deal is all but closed, and there's not a word about safeguards. There must be fire where there's so much smoke! I've asked the CIA to find out what they can. I decided it's too risky just to rely on her word. And I'm warning you, if they turn up anything, there'll be hell to pay! I want it clearly understood—I'll not put up with any hanky-panky with Castro. You keep your ear to the ground up there in Ottawa, and call me direct if you learn anything. I'm convinced your Prime Minister is either playing games with me, or she's too damn dumb and trusting to be capable of doing her job. Either way, it could be dangerous for all of us."

Tony Whiteside's expression remained bland and deferential, but inside his mind he felt a coldly coiling snake of apprehension. This posting wasn't turning out as he had envisioned it, at all.

"Look, Tony, I don't give a continental damn whether William Concord Thompson likes it or not. This is *my* responsibility, and you can just tell him, as diplomatically as you like, to butt out of my business!" The Prime Minister's voice was uncharacteristically shrill.

The American Ambassador stared at her, appalled. He had known this interview wasn't going to go well. Kathleen had always had a stubborn streak, as he had warned President Thompson, and she wasn't likely to brook interference into what clearly was her own prerogative. Nevertheless, he was here, on the very specific instructions of his own Chief Executive, doing the best he could to ward off another of those abrasive little *contretemps* that sometimes flared up between ordinarily friendly nations. No one could ever be sure when some apparently minor incident might mushroom into a serious breach. It was the diplomat's job to put out brush fires before they could spread.

Kathleen was already sorry that she had raised her voice, but, she thought in exasperation, enough is enough. All day long, people had been registering their objections to her actions or proposed actions. Ottawa was a rumour-mill. Everyone seemed to know everything even before she herself had actually come to a decision. If she wasn't under attack for something she *had* done, she was attacked for something she had only thought of doing, or something she had no intention of doing. It scarcely mattered, she thought. Whatever she did was criticized.

In the aftermath of the west coast settlement, the size of the settlement package had spurred a new wave of unrest. It had been exactly as she had feared. And now this. This was the last straw! She had scarcely returned to the Sussex Drive mansion from the office when Anthony Whiteside's call had come, asking for an urgent meeting. Reluctantly, Kathleen had invited the American Ambassador to come over to join her for a drink.

She had not seen Whiteside alone since June. Her cheeks burned when she remembered their intimacy, and she had fretted frequently over what attitude she should adopt the next time she saw him. Now she knew that she need not have given that awkwardness a moment's thought. The Ambassador had come on a diplomat's business, passing on that presumptuous message from his President.

"This is just a tempest in a teapot, Tony. Jean Jacques Charles and Billy Thompson got along reasonably well while Jacques was P.M. It's only silly pride on the President's part, stemming from that quarrel in Brussels. It's petty—quite beneath him. And I tell you, I won't have him interfering like this! The President doesn't have to deal with Jacques as External Affairs Minister. He'll deal with me, as Prime Minister. What's it to him but offended pride—and unmitigated gall!"

"I don't deny that it looks pretty, Kathleen," Whiteside responded in a conciliatory tone. "But I assure you, there's more to it than that. The President is under a lot of pressure these days. His popularity has fallen 'way off, and he can't seem to find any magic solution to bring it back up. There's trouble with Congress, and the press is really hounding him. Thompson has done his damnedest to cast himself as a peacemaker—pretty successfully, too, I think you'll have to agree. Look at his courageous initiatives in the Middle East. And remember that he cared enough about the Spanish Americans to stick out his neck over the Panama hand-over. He had to use real muscle to get that passed by the Senate! On top of that, he's gone out of his way to get SALT II signed, and it's touch and go whether Congress will even ratify the treaty.

"The one thing he *is* terrified about is another threat from Cuba. Russian support of Cuba is not particularly a problem anymore, despite the hullabaloo over the build-up of combat troops, but the President has nightmares over aid to the Communists from *friendly* sources. You understand why— you can threaten your enemies with troops and planes, but you can hardly do that to friends. You know how sensitive we are to leakage of our secrets through the back door. The President explained all that. Thompson can't bring himself to trust Castro, and he's scared stiff that Jean Jacques Charles and that bearded devil have cooked up something between them that threatens American security."

"But, Tony, I *told* him there was nothing to that." Kathleen stood up and moved nervously about the room. "I gave him my word. Doesn't he trust *me,* either?"

"Well. ..." He averted his eyes. "The President doesn't really know you." He decided to put it to her straight. "The fact that you actually made Charles your Secretary of State for External Affairs, doesn't help. And now there's this latest speech of his, attacking us at the UN."

Kathleen's back stiffened. "Yes?" she said ominously.

"I wish you'd think that appointment over again, Kathleen. Let me tell the President you'll reconsider it. It would help if you could toss him a bone of some kind. The President has a very uncertain temper just now. He thinks you should replace Jacques. He thinks you're allowing Charles to launch a personal vendetta against him. I beg you, don't send me back with a flat denial."

"What if I do?" she challenged, facing him across the chesterfield where she had been sitting.

Whiteside raised his shoulders in an eloquent gesture.

Unspoken between them was the knowledge that although military action was unthinkable, there was a whole range of economic reprisals which might conceivably be invoked by the US against Canada. It might be anything from a forced revision of the auto pact, to a green light on plans—blocked up until now by the President for a mid-western dam in the US, which, if proceeded with, would inundate thousands of acres of fertile Canadian farmlands across the nearby border. There could be new restrictions on trade between the two nations, or fresh travel regulations for Canada-bound US tourists and conventioneers. The President could arbitrarily impose new barriers against the import of Canadian agricultural and fisheries products, or clamp down hard on crucial American investment. If President Thompson considered the provocation sufficient, he could, with a stroke, severely damage, even destroy, the vulnerable Canadian economy in scores of ways, ways totally unrelated to the actual cause of his displeasure.

"Surely Charles isn't all that important to you," Whiteside urged.

But Kathleen was incensed enough to ignore the risks.

"What *is* important is that I be free to name anyone *I* want, to any post *I* want. Canada is a sovereign nation. Jean Jacques Charles has been Prime Minister of Canada. He remains one of the most important political figures in Canada, especially to the people of Quebec. He knows personally every head of state in the world—far better than I or any other Canadian—and he has their respect, as well. I consider his experience far too great to lose. I have asked him to accept External and he has done so. He's been sworn in, and that's an end to it. The subject is not open to discussion. And *I* consider it a personal affront that your President should dare to tell me who I can appoint to my Cabinet, or what we can do in labour or international policy!"

Kathleen bit off each word of the last sentence as though her strong white teeth were snapping threads. As her eyes blazed at him across the room, her fingers unconsciously clutched into the back of the chesterfield, her knuckles pale with the pressure.

Anthony Whiteside was alarmed at the extent to which their interview had deteriorated. Covertly, he studied the Prime Minister. This wasn't the young Kathleen Marshal he had once known and loved so well. Nor was it the same woman who had so recently welcomed him to her bed. The angry, flushed person facing him was clearly in no mind to listen to reason, despite the possible consequences. He had never seen Kathleen so reckless, so determined not to listen.

Was there some other way to get her to change her mind? Whiteside could anticipate the blast he would get from Washington if he had to report her adamant refusal. And he hated to fail in his mission, after coming to office here in Ottawa with such high hopes of success in working with her. There must be a way to get around her stubbornness. Perhaps he could try a more personal appeal.

"Your position is clear enough, Prime Minister," he said now, returning for the moment to the formal address.

Kathleen's expression relaxed. Surely Tony could have remembered that she didn't like threats; that she refused to be bullied. Relieved that he wasn't going to persist, she unclasped her fingers, and was suddenly aware that she had been trembling. Hoping that she had been the only one to notice she walked around the end of the chesterfield, yanking at the bell-cord as she passed it.

"I'm going to have a stiff drink, Tony. Care to join me?" she asked in a more normal voice.

"Thought you'd never ask, Kathleen." His endearing, well-remembered triangular grin flashed at her. "I'm free for dinner, too," he added suggestively.

She looked at her guest, an answering grin tugging at the corners of her wide mouth, free now from the tight-lipped anger of a moment ago.

"I think we can handle that. I'll ask cook to lay another plate." She excused herself to go to the kitchen. A thought struck her, and she poked her head back into the study. "On one condition, Tony—no more business talk tonight. Okay?"

His brown eyes measured her. He hesitated, and then with a smile in his voice, he said, "Okay, I promise. Just talk of old times, tonight."

Old times. Happy times. And painful times. Maybe, she thought, not such a good idea after all. Another thought struck her. "Oh, and Tony."

"Yes?"

"You'll have to leave early. Okay?"

"Of course, Kathleen," he said, hiding his disappointment.

Kathleen fastened her seat belt and closed her eyes. The plane lifted off smoothly. She was on her way. In only a few hours, she would be meeting Andrew in Vienna. There was only one formal engagement there—a rather *pro forma* speech before a meeting of the International Atomic Energy Agency. It was relatively rare for a head of state to make an appearance before that low profile group, but the Canadian Prime Minister had been invited months ago, and Kathleen had readily seized the opportunity to visit again the baroque grandeur of the Imperial City. In Austria she and Andrew would have four days plus the Labour Day weekend to themselves, and then, for what remained of the week, they would fly to Venice, then to Rome for a day and on to Canada nonstop.

She sighed wearily as the plane levelled out. Against her closed eyelids there appeared a kaleidoscope of the past weeks. Two state visits, one to Senegal and one to Ghana and then nine days in Kenya at the Commonwealth Conference.

In her briefing sessions the word which had come up most often was *contrast*. Social contrast, cultural contrast, contrasts in the developments of the various regions—it was an apt word, she thought. Africa was indeed a continent of contrasts. Tiring as it had been, the trip had whetted her appetite. Three African nations were simply not enough; she would have to find time to visit them all. She thought of Hemingway's contention that "Africa got in your blood," convinced, now, that it was true. Smiling to herself, she fingered the tiny bottle of anti-malaria pills she would still have to take for two weeks. Africa got into your blood in both the literal and non-literal sense!

She had expected heat in west Africa, but even so she was unprepared for the furnace-like blast that greeted her in Senegal. The temperature was nearly 34°C and the humidity was totally wilting. Still, the sights were unbelievable. She had briefly felt as though she were on the set of some gigantic and spectacular movie.

The plane had come in over the ocean and glided smoothly to a stop, coasting to the smallish modern structure which was the Dakar airport terminal. The building had a low slung roof, windows on all sides which allowed what breeze there was to flow through, and green manicured lawns. The aged President of Senegal had not met her, but all other high-ranking members of the government had. A red carpet glared in the strong sunlight and hordes of gaily dressed women and tribal musicians danced and sang. Colour was what first struck Kathleen. Many onlookers were dressed from head to toe in dazzling white. These were the desert people in traditional Moslem dress. Their coal black skin appeared all the darker next to the gleaming white of the encompassing costume. The Senegalese women were stunning. They too were coal black, but they dressed in bright golds, magentas, flaring reds and shimmering yellows. Great silver earrings glistened and inches of bracelets clung to their arms. Kathleen couldn't take it all in—the music, the people, the scenery.

The trip into Dakar was a long one, and on the way they passed huge red termite hills standing like gaunt castles on the barren savannah grasses. The city of Dakar, surrounded by teeming slums, was a veritable Paris with modern skyscrapers and great white buildings reaching towards a cloudless, clear blue sky. In minutes Kathleen seemed to have passed through the ages of man: the primitive huts on the savannah, the low, crowded dwellings of people living in some middle passage, and finally the wide tree-lined streets with their modern transportation and new buildings. And everywhere a profusion of colour—flowers, lawns, and brightly dressed inhabitants. Contrast seemed too mild a word.

French rolled from the tongues of all she met, and Kathleen was relieved to find that she had no problems with any local dialect. Most, if not all, of the government ministers had been educated in Paris, while some of the older ones had been sitting ministers in the French Parliament.

The people of Ghana were as diverse as the people of Senegal, their dress equally colourful. The Accra airport was much closer to the city, but again, the ever-present termite hills rose from the flat ground. Kathleen was taken on a long motor trip to the site of the Volta Dam. She passed through the plain with its low flat grasses and headed into the lush hills where the road was carved out of the jungle. From a hilltop café she and her hosts peered out on the great high Volta Dam with its huge man-made lake. This was the pride and joy of the country. Over ten years in the building, it had required massive environmental studies and delicate resettlement plans for the people who had once inhabited the valley that was now a lake.

There was even contrast in the food, Kathleen thought. Hot curries seemed most common, but the beverage was all too often weak English coffee. At one point she ventured to try the national dish—ground nut stew. It was made with lamb, cooked slowly in a rich gravy prepared from ground peanuts. She could not, until she tasted it, imagine the two flavours together. But she was delighted by its unique taste and she pleased her hosts by eating it with obvious enjoyment.

If she had been taken aback by the soaring temperatures in Dakar and Accra, she was definitely surprised by Nairobi. Mrs. Plunkett had been quite right. Nairobi had a far more pleasant climate than the west coast of Africa. The humidity was gone and, while the sun was warm, cool breezes blew.

What she saw of Nairobi showed her an incredibly clean city of white buildings, rather like an English holiday resort. There were well-cared for lawns and formal gardens everywhere. Huge hotels filled the downtown centre, and new cars crowded the streets. Nairobi, in fact, was a tourists' paradise, with endless shops and Indian restaurants. Nothing she had ever read about Kenya prepared her for the country itself, and she was delighted when the delegates were bundled off for a day trip to the game park. Here, elephants, lions, and giraffes—all absent in west Africa—roamed the plains at will.

The conference itself had been hectic. Canada's traditional role of "honest broker" required considerable backroom negotiation. To her surprise, Mrs. Plunkett proved more conciliatory than she, or most of the African delegates, had anticipated. Questions which had plagued, and nearly destroyed, other Commonwealth Conferences met eventual agreement. In the end, Prime Minister Plunkett had conceded certain unexpected compromises.

Now, totally exhausted, Kathleen looked forward to Vienna. No more meetings for a while, she thought—no more meetings. On that peaceful thought, she dozed off to sleep, anticipating Andrew's approaching welcome.

Kathleen had insisted that the Austrian government treat this as a private visit. As she descended from the first-class compartment, somewhat refreshed from the past few quiet airborne hours, she was relieved to see a waiting Andrew, and beside him, only the Canadian Ambassador. There were other shadowy figures about, which she rightly assumed to be security people, but there were no flower-laden officials in sight with whom she would have to exchange the traditional formal courtesies.

When the tall middle-aged couple embraced, the Ambassador diplomatically averted his eyes. He was competence itself as Kathleen was spirited through customs. Her baggage appeared magically, and the gleaming Mercedes was soon speeding them towards the city and the Bristol Hotel. Kathleen snuggled up to Andrew, insisting that he unfold his plans for the next few days.

Andrew complied with enthusiasm. "We have tickets for the opera. And for the Spanish Riding School for Sunday morning—courtesy of the Ambassador, I might say. They are almost unobtainable, but he has somehow managed it."

Kathleen was enchanted at the prospect. "You have no idea how delighted I am," she told the Ambassador, beaming. "I have always wanted to see the Lippizan stallions. I want you to know you have simply *made* my trip."

Her praise made the retiring diplomat glad that he had been so adamant with the ministry when her request for the precious tickets had arrived. Normally, they were spoken for six months ahead in the summer months. He didn't know how the Austrians had arranged it. The pair of tickets was not just for any old seats, either, but for those once reserved for the Emperor and his Empress! He mustn't forget that he owed that harassed official a big return favour for accommodating him.

"Oh, and the Opera! How grand! I love that rococco building. I've never seen a performance there, though. Tell me more, Andrew," she cajoled.

"The Ambassador has offered his car and driver so that we can get around and see the palaces and gardens in comfort."

She smiled again, and reached to pat the arm of the diplomat as he sat, half-turned towards them from the passenger's seat in front.

"Surely that's a terrible imposition."

"I insist, Prime Minister," he said firmly.

Kathleen relaxed, her half-hearted protest stilled.

"And he's already suggested a list of places to dine, so you may have your fill of favourites from venison to Wiener schnitzel," Andrew went on. "If the weather holds, a trip into the Wienerwald, and if you absolutely insist, a ride on the Giant Ferris Wheel." He gave Kathleen a teasing smile then explained to the Ambassador: "My wife has been dying to ride it ever since she saw *The Third Man*. Is the experience really all that special?"

"I don't know," replied the Ambassador doubtfully. "I've never tried it, although of course, I've been to the amusement park. It doesn't look very exciting. It's a very high wheel— sixty-five metres—but you don't sit in little open seats like at home. You stand in a largish glass car, something like a small streetcar. I hear," he added more encouragingly, "that there *is* quite a spectacular view from the top."

"We'll let you know if it's worthwhile," she promised solemnly, hugging Andrew's arm. "Anyway, I want to try it. What's the name of the park again?"

"The Wurstelprater. Or just the Prater," he said. "But you don't have to remember that. Just tell the driver. He'll know where you want to go. Ah, and here is the Bristol."

The car drew off the Ringstrasse and pulled up at the canopied hotel entrance. The baggage was whisked away in the custody of a man in a long white apron, and the party of three was led to the antique, walnut-and-brass passenger elevator by a suavely polite hotel night manager.

The Ambassador lingered only long enough to be sure that the Wickstroms were content with their flower-filled suite, and that the store of duty-free embassy liquor and Canadian cigarettes piled on the delicately scrolled desk was satisfactory, before he took his leave. On his way out, he propped a stiff card typed with telephone numbers and addresses in a convenient place by the telephone, just in case they should wish to contact him. Kathleen followed the diplomat to the door, promising to keep in touch.

As she turned back into the room, the tall woman suddenly whirled into an ungainly looping pirouette of joy. Giggling, she flung herself backwards on the wide bed, arms spread across the silken coverlet. She closed her eyes to savour her delight. Vienna. With Andrew. Together—no one else.

Her hazel eyes flew open. Andrew was bending over her, amusement and some of her own high pleasure reflected in his fond lake-blue eyes. He held out a brimming, stemmed glass from which tiny bubbles sprang into the flower-scented air.

"Champagne, Mrs. Wickstrom," he said formally. "The drink of emperors and kings—and even lady prime ministers!"

At mid-week the Canadian Ambassador returned to escort Kathleen to the old Grand Hotel, now the headquarters of the International Atomic Energy Agency. There she was received with the meticulous politeness befitting the elected head of one of the important member nations, but afterwards, Kathleen thought that she detected a certain coolness in the audience's reception of her speech. Admittedly, her remarks had contained nothing new, except a reaffirmation of Canada's policy against proliferation. She hadn't really expected the speech to be considered a barn-burner—discreet speeches prepared by officials in the External Affairs Department rarely were—but it seemed to her that her audience had reacted with a kind of wary skepticism. Puzzled, and wanting to confirm her impressions, she questioned the Ambassador as they walked back to the hotel.

"I confess that I thought their reaction a little, ah, restrained," he agreed in his careful diplomat's way. His brow wrinkled as he went on. "I'm at a loss to explain it, Prime Minister. *I* thought it was a good, straightforward statement of the traditional Canadian position. Yes, on the whole, a good, solid speech," he finished loyally.

"But don't you think their attitude was a bit unusual?" Kathleen pressed the point.

The Ambassador fell silent, then offered, "There has been a rumour circulating that Canada is going soft on the safeguard conditions ever since it lost that sale to Argentina."

"But that's preposterous. Of course, we were disappointed that the sale to Japan fell through and badly shaken when we lost the Argentina contract to Germany over our insistence on safeguards. Senator LaCroix did question whether we need to stick by them. But there's no truth to the rumour."

"I'm sure it will die out, as rumours do, Prime Minister."

"Yes, probably," said Kathleen thoughtfully, "but I'd appreciate it if you would follow it up and let me know if you can discover its source. Do everything you can to kill the rumour in any case. We can't have anyone thinking that we're getting soft on the safeguards issue."

"Certainly, Prime Minister. By the way, have you ridden the Ferris Wheel yet?" he enquired politely.

"Not yet. Tomorrow, Andrew has promised me. We're going to drive to the Vienna Woods, up to Leopoldsberg, and then we'll definitely visit the Prater. And I want to stroll through that park back there, where the casino and the Strauss memorial are, and to sit and listen to the orchestra playing waltzes on the terrace. What's the name of the park?"

"The Stadt Park—yes, it's very popular."

"Then there's the Opera on our last evening. And Demel's of course. We must go there for the Sachertorte."

"Not the Sacher hotel?" he asked, surprised. "That's where the Sachertorte was invented, you know."

"No, we must see Demel's. It's such a famous coffee house, and I am afraid the old waistline can't take two of those fabulous chocolate confections. As it is, everything in Vienna seems to be smothered under *schlagobers*. I've never had so much whipped cream in my life!" she said ruefully, patting her hips. "But it's so *good!*" she added wistfully.

"It's a problem, I admit. Every diplomat who comes to this post has trouble with his weight, at first. Austrian sweets must be the best in the world, but. . . . Ah, here we are. May I see you in?"

"Thank you, but it's not really necessary. Andrew will be waiting in the little bar off the lobby. Would you like to join us for a drink?"

"No. But thank you. I am sure that you two would prefer

to be alone. I'll be here on Monday to take you to the airport, but please call me if there is anything—anything at all—I can do for you for the balance of your stay."

Kathleen murmured her thanks, shook his hand briskly, and hurried through the lobby to find her waiting husband.

"Such peace," Kathleen breathed in contentment.

They were sitting on a rustic wooden bench in the shadow of the partly restored stone keep, at Leopoldsberg, the remains of their simple lunch before them on the scarred picnic table.

Taking another deep breath of the warm, sunny air, Kathleen expelled it slowly. Her gaze roved over the muted green hills and valleys, falling away far beneath them, the meandering flat silver ribbon of river glinting below and then twisting away to be lost in the low-hanging mist of the distance. Silence enfolded them, except for the excited voices of children playing in the car-park behind the huddled stone chapel, or the occasional clink of a glass or plate as a waiter disappeared towards the kitchen.

Kathleen turned to smile at her husband, but he was looking away from her, preoccupied, withdrawn. Impulsively, she squeezed his sweatered arm.

"A penny, darling?" she said coaxingly.

He stirred. "What?"

"Nothing, Andrew. It's just that you suddenly seemed so far away."

He took a deep breath. "Kathleen, do you mind if we talk?"

"Talk? Of course, Andrew," she said, puzzled at his serious expression. "What is it?"

"Kathleen, are you happy with our marriage? I mean, are we all right?"

She was startled. "Drew, what a question!" she smiled uncertainly. "Of course I'm happy." A thought struck her. "Aren't you, Andrew? Aren't you happy?"

"No," he said, "I can't truly say that I am. I don't mean just now, but most of the time. Do you realize how little we have been together in a year—ever since you decided to run for the leadership? I've hardly seen you since the convention in February?"

"Yes, I know. But Drew, we could see one another much more often if you'd only move to Ottawa. Darling, we've talked about this before. I wish you would reconsider, Andrew. I hate to nag, but I miss you so."

"Do you?" He searched her eyes as if from them he could compel the truth.

Kathleen caught her breath. "Whatever do you mean? You know I do! Andrew, what *is* this?"

"I know you missed me at first, Kathleen," he explained slowly, "but ever since the by-election, I haven't been as sure."

"It's just that I've been busy, Andrew," she protested.

"No, it's more than that. I feel that you're somehow different when we're together."

"Different? How different?"

"It's hard to explain. Maybe more remote, more impersonal."

"Darling, this job does give me a lot to worry about. It isn't exactly nine to five, five days a week," she reminded him.

"That has something to do with it, I'm sure," her husband said quietly. "But I sense there's something else. Or someone else." He brought himself reluctantly to say it.

Kathleen withdrew her arm from his and sat up very straight.

"What are you saying?" she asked, a tremor in her voice.

Andrew remained silent. Did he really want to know? he asked himself. The rumours he'd heard could just be gossip. He looked at the fear and hurt in Kathleen's eyes, and slowly, his arm rose to encircle her.

Her tears came, then, and reaching out she pulled him close. Wordlessly they reaffirmed their marriage, pledging their love for each other. Then Andrew gently placed his hand under her chin and tilted her face up to his. He wiped the tears from her cheeks and gently put his lips to her forehead.

"All right, Kathleen. You win. I'll clear up things at the office and then I'll come to Ottawa. And then, please God, the Wickstroms will live happily ever after."

They left Vienna with regret, winging their way to Venice, the romantic city of canals. For two days they relaxed. In the morning, after breakfast under broad, brown-striped canvas beside the Olympic-sized pool, they took the complimentary speedboat to the city. There they wandered the narrow crowded streets, shopping and soaking up sounds and sights and smells. At the Cipriani, their island hotel, they rested or swam or sunned themselves during the siesta hours. In the evenings, they returned to the gilded city to dine on grilled scampi, to linger in St. Mark's Square sipping coffee, and to listen to the outdoor orchestras and watch the throngs of milling tourists. Both evenings, they clambered into a swaying black gondola for the return journey. A perfect end to perfect days.

Andrew bought Kathleen table linens of organdy, hand-embroidered in silk threads in renaissance hues; and as they flew to Rome, for the last day of their holiday, he shyly presented her with a precious miniature of Michelangelo's *Pietà*, threaded on a supple gold chain, worked by the miraculous goldsmiths of Florence.

Chapter Nine

While the Wickstroms had been enjoying their last days in Vienna, the last meeting of the Standing Committee had been held. The Conservative leadership convention was only a week away, and then, shortly after that, Parliament would open. This was Adam Sorenson's last chance at the AECL President and he was ready—very ready.

"All right, Sorenson, go ahead," the chairman said in a stony voice, the usual smile missing from his broad country features.

"Now, Mr. President, I assume you've arranged whatever permission you felt was necessary, so that we can get some straight answers?" began the sharp-featured member in a condescending tone.

The president nodded curtly.

"Good. Well then, what about Cuba? Let's have the story," he demanded.

The president was prepared for the question. Over the summer, the deal had been closed, and so he made the admission quite readily. "Negotiations which have been carried on for about a year have recently been successfully concluded."

"You mean we've actually sold a Candu to the Commies?"

"Yes."

Sorenson was staggered. He hadn't really believed the tipster, but obviously the man had been right. At the press table reporters scribbled madly.

Sorenson recovered. "For how much?" he asked. Mustn't show his surprise, he cautioned himself.

"I can't disclose that."

"Why not?"

"For reasons I have already explained," said the president primly.

"Now look—" began his questioner, all set to blast the witness.

He was interrupted by the chairman.

"I've already warned you, Adam, that I don't hold with you badgerin' the witness," said the now steely-eyed Tolliver, in a manner very different from his usual affable self. "Do I need to tell you again?"

"But he was supposed to get permission," Sorenson sputtered in protest.

"I have the customer's permission only to acknowledge the fact of the sale. Not the details," the witness volunteered.

"You mean we've wasted all this time?" Sorenson was angry.

"Or-der," said Wilbur Tolliver sternly, banging his gavel. "Have you got any more questions?"

"I sure have, plenty of them. Like this: who arranged the deal, Mr. President?"

"Why, ah, agency people for the most part."

"Anybody else?"

"Export Development, I believe."

"You mean we're lending *Commies* the money to buy our nuclear secrets?" asked his questioner, unbelievingly.

"It's not unusual. It's been done before—with Romania," said the president quietly, his face impassive.

"Jesus," said an NDP member. "What next?"

There was a rustle around the U-shaped table, as committee members shifted uneasily. It was apparent that they shared his disapproval. Reporters' pencils flew. Sorenson noted their gratifying reaction and then returned to the attack.

"Anybody besides government people involved?"

"Not initially," the president conceded.

"Anytime?"

"Well, we were having a little trouble firming up the deal. It just wouldn't jell. Towards the end we employed an agent, an expert, to, ah, expedite it," he said with obvious discomfort.

"What kind of expert?" Sorenson felt an inner excitement now. This was more like it. He vowed he'd crack it wide open.

"An ... expediter, as I said."

"With what qualifications?" insisted Sorenson.

The president raised his brows at the question, and turned to Wilbur Tolliver. "Is that really important?" he asked.

Before the chairman could reply, Sorenson slipped in his next question.

"I suggest to you that this 'expediter's' sole qualification was that he was a buddy of Castro's. Am I right?"

The president hesitated. "No, I don't think that's strictly true," he said slowly. As far as he could remember, neither Willis Cranston nor Stan Findlay could fairly be called a "buddy" of the Cuban leader's.

"What then?" asked Sorenson, concealing his disappointment.

"I don't understand. What was the question?"

"What were your 'agent's' qualifications?"

"Sufficient for our needs. After all, he *was* successful," the president pointed out.

"What's his name?" snapped Sorenson, close to losing his temper.

"Is that really germane?"

Sorenson decided to take a short-cut. "I put it to you that Jean Jacques Charles was your expediter. Everybody knows how thick he is with Fidel Castro, and that he dropped in to see his buddy there not long ago."

The reporters scratched noisily, their pencils a blur of motion.

"No." The flat denial hung in the air. "Although I believe that Cuba's first approach was made to him when he was Prime Minister," added the president helpfully, glad that his interrogator's information had proved so wide of the mark.

"Are you trying to tell me that Jean Jacques Charles had nothing to do with the Candu deal?" asked Sorenson, incredulous.

"Not to my knowledge, except as I've explained.".

This was a blow. Surely the Congressman couldn't have been so wrong. Well, he'd fire his second shot. "Well then, let me try another name. Was Stanley Findlay involved?"

Everyone saw the witness wince. Reporters' pencils poised to record his reply.

"Briefly, yes," came the president's reluctant response.

"Explain that," demanded his inquisitor, inwardly grateful that this time his question had not misfired.

"I talked with Mr. Findlay some months ago. I explained our problem. I believe he was acquainted with . . . senior people . . . in Havana." The witness was obviously picking his words with care.

"And?"

"Mr. Findlay proved very helpful. I believe he was instrumental in setting up some meetings . . ." the president's voice trailed off.

"Was he paid?" pounced Sorenson.

"Mr. Findlay? No, not by AECL," said the president, the picture of wide-eyed innocence.

"You mean he did it for nothing?"

The witness shrugged.

"Now isn't that rather rare?" Sorenson pursued him. "I mean, I understand these 'expediters' earn pretty heavy fees."

"Our agents often do, but then very large sums are involved in the sales, as I've explained," said the president, quite reasonably.

"Isn't it usual business practice to pay a commission? And what about expenses?"

"Of course. We cover necessary expenses."

"And how are they accounted for?"

The president looked disdainful. "That's hardly necessary when one is dealing with this type of people."

"Then how do you know what you have to pay?"

"It's usual to make an advance to cover expenses."

"An advance? How? In cash?"

"Of course not. By bank draft."

"Payable to the agent?"

"Not usually."

"No? Then to whom?"

"Usually, to the bearer."

"I see. Was it, in this case?"

"Which case? Cuba?"

"Mr. President, I was under the impression that we were talking about the Cuban sale. Please don't try to play games with me."

Turning to the chairman, the witness protested, "I assure you, Mr. Chairman. . . ."

The chairman harrumphed, but said nothing.

"Well, witness. I'm waiting."

"Yes, Mr. Sorenson. You were asking?"

"I asked whether you handed over a bank draft made payable to the bearer as an advance on expenses regarding the sale of a Candu to Cuba."

"Yes, that's right."

"For how much was the draft?"

"The usual. Expenses run higher in some countries than in others, but this was about the usual."

"And how much is 'the usual'?"

"About five."

"Five what? Hundred? Thousand?"

"Yes." The voice was faint. "Hundred thousand."

"Speak up please! Did I hear you say five hundred thousand dollars?"

"Yes, sir."

"Who got the money?"

"Well, I gave the draft to Mr. Findlay. But I don't think he spent it himself."

"You don't think? Don't you *know* who spent it?"

"Not exactly, no." He was defensive.

"Now wait a minute. I can hardly believe this. Are you telling the members of this committee that you handed over half a million dollars of the taxpayers' money, as good as in cash, to be spent by somebody on some sort of expenses, but you don't know who, or what? And am I right that you seem to imply that this was just routine practice?"

"Yes, sir."

Sorenson sat back, genuinely stunned. For once, he didn't have to resort to histrionics. There was a stir as two reporters scrambled to their feet, racing one another from the room. Around the committee table, more than one member's mouth had dropped ajar in disbelief at the witness' revelations.

The chairman came to with a start. Mercifully, he recessed the hearing until the next day.

When, next morning, the chairman gavelled the committee session to order, the television cameras were present and reporters crowded into every available space and then competed for standing room. Doc Tolliver had never before had so much attention paid to the hearings of his Standing Committee. He decided he definitely didn't care for the circus atmosphere this enquiry had generated.

Sorenson plunged in where he left off yesterday.

"Now let's get back to this bank draft, made out to the bearer for half a million."

The witness waited with trepidation for the question.

"Who did you say you handed it to?"

"Mr. Stanley Findlay."

"The former Energy Minister?"

"The same."

"But you told us before that he didn't get paid. How do you explain that?" A number of the committee members nodded. The point had puzzled them, too.

The president beamed.

"Mr. Findlay is not our agent of record. I think he was a sort of go-between at that point."

"He wasn't your 'expediter' on the Cuban deal?"

"I didn't say that. I said he wasn't our agent."

"Then who was?"

"Originally, a gentleman from Montreal. I doubt you'd know the name, but we have employed him before."

"Who? Tell me the name!" insisted Sorenson.

"Mr. Willis Cranston."

"Did you pay *him?*"

"Of course."

"And he would pay Findlay?"

"I don't know that, of course. You'd have to ask Mr. Cranston what his arrangements were with Mr. Findlay."

"How much did you pay Cranston?"

"The usual negotiated commission." The president pursed his lips. "Of course, strictly speaking, payment hasn't yet been made, but it is in the process of being paid."

Sorenson was becoming very annoyed at the necessity of dragging everything out, bit by bit, from this witness.

"You say the 'usual negotiated commission.' How much is that?"

"I'd rather not say."

The young member exploded. "I don't give a damn what *you'd* rather do. Tell me, *what was the commission?*"

The witness hesitated, glancing at the chairman, but on Tolliver's broad features there was no sign that help would be forthcoming from that quarter.

"Three million dollars," he said at last, helplessly.

"Three. Million. Dollars?" repeated Adam Sorenson.

"Yes, sir."

A hush fell over the room, then Sorenson asked, "And that's standard—'the usual'—I think you said?"

"Considering the sums involved, the commission isn't all that great," the president said defensively.

"Not. All. That. Great. Three million? I see. Well, I suppose it's all relative, as you say."

To the president's relief, Sorenson sat back in his chair, glancing significantly at the rank of watchful reporters. The witness' relief evaporated at his next question.

"Now Findlay, you said, worked for you free. Then who got the money?"

"Why—Mr. Cranston, as I said. Or at least, it will go to him when it's processed."

"Yes, I see." Sorenson pounced again. "Would this Cranston be another of Jean Jacques Charles' buddies?"

The witness remained silent. When he responded, it was in an inaudible monosyllable.

"What? Speak up! Isn't this Willis Cranston known to be a friend of the Secretary of State for External Affairs?"

"Yes," the muffled reply was repeated.

"And Mr. Findlay is the former Energy Minister, a man who just lately left the Government? A known friend and errand boy for Mr. Charles, who's a known friend of Dr. Castro?"

"Yes, I believe so," the president said faintly.

"You *know* so, don't you?"

"Yes, sir. That's common knowledge."

"Did Findlay get the money?"

"Well, he earned the commission. I don't know what his arrangements are with Mr. Cranston, our agent."

Circling back to an earlier question, Sorenson asked, "And tell me, witness, what were Mr. Findlay's other qualifications?"

The president fell silent, confused as to just how to answer.

There wasn't a sound in the crowded room until Sorenson himself provided the answer.

"I put it to you that the AECL is paying some three million dollars to a former Minister of Energy whose sole qualification is as a go-between for the Secretary of State for External Affairs and Fidel Castro. Isn't that the nature of Findlay's so-called expertise?"

The witness sat mute.

Sorenson steamrollered on.

"And this Willis Cranston put the deal together. Isn't that correct?"

"Yes," came the admission.

"And that is why you are paying him the commission?"

"Yes."

"But you don't know where the money will wind up?"

"No. How could I be expected to know that? It isn't my business!"

"Not even if it lines the pockets of the Cabinet?"

The witness was aghast at the innuendo, but Sorenson, with

inner glee, watched the explosion it set off among the media types.

The chairman gavelled for silence against the clamour of the instantaneous outbreak that had followed Sorenson's question.

"Have you had instructions from Cranston about how payment is to be made?" Sorenson's next query closely followed the blows of the gavel.

"Yes."

"What are those instructions?"

The president turned to the chairman, silently appealing for help, but Wilbur Tolliver refused to meet his eyes.

"I'm waiting, witness, for your answer," said Sorenson in a dangerous tone.

"The money was to be paid to an offshore company," came the low-voiced admission.

"Where?"

"In the Caymans, I believe."

"Is that near Cuba?"

"Fairly near, as distances go in that part of the world."

"What company?"

The president hesitated, suddenly struck by the possible significance of the name conveyed to him by Stan Findlay. When he had first heard it he had thought that it was a sentimental, but otherwise meaningless, salute to Findlay's long-time mentor. Now he wasn't so sure. He expelled a long breath before he answered.

"The Evangeline Company."

Adam Sorenson sat back, a grim smile of triumph wreathing his sallow features. No one could miss his point—the significance of the well-remembered name of the tragically dead wife of Jean Jacques Charles.

The room erupted as reporters raced one another for the exits, desperate to be the first to break the scandal.

"Drew, look at this. The Tories' leadership convention has started and Adam Sorenson, of all people, placed high on the second ballot. Imagine him as leader," she said with distaste, remembering his attack on her in the House.

Andrew Wickstrom wearily rubbed his eyes. It had been a long flight from Rome and he was feeling his years. The Wickstroms had been met on their arrival and whisked from their big commercial jet aircraft across the tarmac to the

government JetStar for the last lap of their flight to Ottawa.
The small executive jet was comfortable, if perhaps a little
cramped for his height. He had dozed off without tasting the
drink the steward had prepared after take-off, while Kathleen
had immersed herself in the inevitable books of clippings and
briefings awaiting her on the plane.

"Sorenson, eh? That's a surprise. I wouldn't have thought
he'd have had a chance, with so many more experienced
candidates in the running. And I always thought he was too
nakedly ambitious to go far—not a very attractive person at
all."

"Hmm. Look at these newspaper photos. He's hardly
recognizable. He's done something to his hair. Remember it
always looked like patent leather." She passed the file to her
husband, who studied it for a moment.

"He's certainly got himself a better tailor, too," Andrew
murmured, genuinely struck at the change in the young
Conservative's appearance. "Wonder how he managed to win
so much support?"

"Apparently he may be a compromise candidate. The two
front runners were stalemated for the first vote, and then
some of the low-running candidates and their people moved
to Sorenson on the second ballot. It's amazing! The columnists think he may win. Some of these editorials and columns
are really quite funny. All the pundits are trying to explain
why they didn't pay any real attention to his candidature."

The Prime Minister was quickly scanning the thick sheaf
of clippings. Her tired husband was a little stung at the tone
of amused scorn she directed at the media. After all, he was a
newspaper publisher, and as far as he was aware, no one in
his organization had ever mentioned the possibility that Sorenson could win.

"Were your people any more prescient? Did any of them
guess Sorenson would do so well? If they did, I don't recall
your speaking of it," he said drily.

Kathleen looked up at Andrew, considering his question.
"No, I must confess the possibility was never discussed, but
then I've been out of touch."

"What kind of a leader do you think he would make?"

"I'm not sure at all. I barely know him, but I've never liked
him since he as much as called me a liar in the House." She
paused for a moment, and then remembered a comment
made to her by Richard Sherwood. "Woody once told me

that Sorenson was a confirmed Grit-hater, and that if he should one day become leader, the Liberals had better watch out. I never paid any attention to that, since it seemed so unlikely he'd ever make it. I wonder. . . ." She lapsed into silence for a moment, and finished her drink. As she replaced the glass in the receptacle at her elbow, she glanced back at the clippings.

"Apparently Sorenson got a lot of publicity from his investigation of the AECL," she said, reading hurriedly through the papers in front of her. Then she turned abruptly to another file.

Her husband looked at her quizzically. "What is it? Is something wrong?"

"I'll say there is! Look at this, Andrew." She handed him the file. "Apparently there was a meeting of the committee while we were in Italy and they came up with some rather damning stuff. Stanley Findlay of all people was involved in a Candu sale. And to Cuba! Thank God I got rid of him when I did. He sure didn't waste any time finding himself another job."

Andrew looked up from the file. "Won't this be making things difficult for you? There are some pretty strong innuendoes in some of these columns."

"Yes, but this sort of thing blows over. Findlay is the one who's in hot water."

"But Sorenson could call him before the committee, couldn't he?"

"If he doesn't become leader he could. But if he does, he'll have to drop the committee *and* his muck-raking."

"But surely he could raise it in the House?"

"Oh, I suppose so, but he'd be easier to handle there. I think Doc Tolliver has been letting him get away with murder. My ministers wouldn't let him cause too much trouble, and the Speaker will see that he stays in line. Anyway, there's nothing to this talk of Candu sales without safeguards. I've checked it out and Senator LaCroix has checked it out. I'm convinced it's nothing but rumour."

"Did you know there was a sale to Cuba?" Andrew asked.

"I'd heard there might be—but nothing was being actually done about it. Damn that Findlay! He must have gone off on his own. Apparently the sale only just went through. I guess AECL couldn't turn it down once Castro was willing to buy."

"Are you sure that's what happened?"

"It's the only thing that makes sense. I did check into it last spring."

"It never hurts to check again, Kathleen."

"Yes, darling, but how else *am* I to check it?"

"I suppose you could call up Castro."

"Oh, Drew," she laughed. "Can't you just see me calling him up and asking how we sold him a Candu? He'd think I was out of my mind. Anyway, there's the airport. We're home. I'm even looking forward to getting back to work, aren't you?" She handed the books and files to the steward to return to their valises, and busied herself checking her lipstick and hair, making herself presentable for the inevitable welcoming committee of ministers, staff, and reporters. The Prime Minister of Canada was back in the capital.

Richard Sherwood advanced through the cheering crowd and moved to young Adam Sorenson's side. He put his arm around Adam and with his free hand reached out to shake the young man's hand. The crowd erupted into a burst of applause. The Tories had a new leader.

Richard Sherwood had felt reluctant as he had moved towards the platform, slowly edging his way through the crowd. His thoughts were confused. He hadn't expected this, he hadn't expected it at all.

Throughout the leadership campaign he had remained aloof. He had not supported anyone, he had not passed on the mantle of power as had so often happened before. Now, standing next to the brash young man who had only recently been a junior member of Parliament, he wished that he *had* chosen an heir apparent. Adam Sorenson was far from the type of person Richard Sherwood would have chosen, but now there was no choice at all—now he had to congratulate the winner for the sake of party unity.

Still, he reflected, the man had built his bridges well. He had pulled in the support of the two provincial premiers who were most often at one another's throats, he had quietly married the red Tories to the blue Tories and he now emerged as the great compromiser—but, alas, a compromiser with a burning issue, a crusade as it were. Perhaps, he hoped, Sorenson would mature with the job. Perhaps, as he began to work through the intricate mesh of government, he would be less quick to jump without reason. He thought back to

Sorenson's grandstanding in the last Parliament. The young pup had barked too soon. He had not had the grace to go to the Prime Minister and talk to her privately. On that occasion he had not had enough to go on and he had not acted properly. He was a most unlikely leader for the Tories to have chosen; still he *was* now the leader.

Briefly, Sherwood thought of Kathleen. He felt sorry for her. The gloves would definitely be off next session. He hoped she could handle it. Sherwood looked out across the sea of faces and found his wife sitting where he had left her. Their eyes met. Well, it was over for him and he was glad. Now he could keep his promise to Martha. They would have their last months together, away from the fray, away from the constant pressures. Perhaps, he thought, he would call Kathleen. She would hear the news soon enough of course, but somehow he felt he wanted to say good-bye, to prepare her for what was coming.

He waved to the crowd and shook Sorenson's hand once again. Then Richard Sherwood moved sadly away and back through the crowd to his anxiously waiting wife.

"Willis, it's Stan Findlay. I've been trying to reach you!"

"Hello," the voice on the other end of the phone was cool. "I thought I told you not to use the telephone. If you have to talk to me you had better come here."

"Come off that cloak and dagger stuff, Willis. You told me this was just a straightforward deal. Now look what's happened."

There was a pause and then Cranston answered. "Well, you can't call them all the time. I'm sure it will blow over."

"I don't like it," Findlay shot back. "It's my reputation and I don't like it one bit. I want to see you, I want to see you now!"

"Then get yourself down here and we'll see what we can work out."

"I'll be there," Findlay said; and hung up the phone.

As he threw a change of clothes into his suitcase, he felt empty and drained. All the publicity—God only knows what would happen next, he thought. Joan would be furious. She would accuse him of lying to her, and not just about the money. Of course he had, but now he had been caught. Right now Stan Findlay was angry at himself and at the whole world. Well, what the hell! He had been caught with his hand in the cookie jar. If he went down, he thought, he would damn well take the rest of them with him. That arrogant Willis Cranston, Jean Jacques Charles who had involved him in this mess, and Kathleen—mostly Kathleen.

He dashed into the kitchen to grab a bite to eat before he left the house for the long drive to Montreal. The refrigerator was empty and most of the shelves were bare. Joan and the children were still out west. They had spent the summer at Joan's parents' remote summer house. Stan had joined them for the month of August, but had escaped back to Ottawa on the pretext of looking after the sale of their Ottawa home, rather than stay and help Joan get the kids started in new schools. He had hated it at the cottage. There had been nothing to do except swim, read, and sleep. There was no TV, no radio, not even a newspaper—just the children and their ever-lasting demands. He had been glad to leave.

But when he had arrived in Ottawa last night, his phone had immediately started ringing with calls from reporters. At first he didn't know why they were calling, but as soon as he realized that word had somehow leaked out on the Candu sale, he took the phone off the hook and began checking through the stack of weeks old newspapers that had accumulated during his absence. It hadn't taken him long to find the story he was looking for.

First thing in the morning he'd started trying to reach Cranston.

Stanley Findlay arrived in Montreal in an even worse mood than when he had left. The drive down had done nothing to calm his temper. Willis Cranston's voice rang in his ears. To think he had been grateful to Cranston for doing him a favour. Now it turned out that he had received half as much money as Stan himself! Except he didn't have it yet. It wasn't fair! Willis Cranston did none of the work and Willis Cranston didn't have *his* reputation on the line.

Findlay followed the butler through the Cranston house. He felt like brushing the old thin servant aside and yelling. He resisted the temptation, but was surprised to be ushered into the large living room only to find it occupied by a solemn and solitary Giselle.

The sight of his lover melted away some of his anger. He could never yell at Giselle, he couldn't even explode in front of her.

"Where's Willis?" he said evenly. "He told me to come."

Giselle shook her head. "I know," she said softly. "He told me."

"Well, where is he?"

Giselle looked into his eyes. "I'm sorry, Stan. He had an urgent call. He's left town for four days. He told me you should stay in Montreal, and be here when he gets back."

Stanley was furious. Damn the arrogant behaviour of the man! At this moment Stan Findlay hated Willis Cranston even more than he hated Kathleen. He felt like an unimportant errand boy, a dupe in some gigantic, horrible plot. His eyes narrowed. Well, he knew how to get even. After he finally saw Willis Cranston he would call Adam Sorenson. He still had his copy of the contract. If they were going to leave him holding the bag, he was going to pass the blame right down the line to where it belonged.

He didn't say anything to Giselle. He met her eyes and felt only longing. And then it came to him. Willis would be gone for four days. He took Giselle's hands in his and drew her to him.

"Let's go away for a few days," he said. "Maybe to Vermont. No one has to know."

She knew from past experience that his invitation didn't come from the desire to get even with her husband. Stanley Findlay wanted to be with her. She smiled and squeezed his fingers.

"Yes," she said simply, "let's."

They were threading their way along mountainous country sideroads. They had hoped to find a vacant motel room, but accommodation was scarce. Whenever he slowed down at an inviting prospect, it was to be met by a "No Vacancy" sign. Findlay cursed himself silently for not phoning ahead. But then this whole trip had been spur of the moment. After Giselle's quiet acceptance of his invitation to drive to Vermont for the weekend, he had been behind the wheel of his big car, first through Montreal and the Quebec countryside, then across the border and into Vermont. He had been too excited by her presence, too conscious of the warmth of her bundled close in the curve of his right arm to think of making a reservation ahead, even if he'd had any idea where to phone.

"Getting tired, love?" he whispered into the glossy, perfumed hair.

Giselle stirred and muttered drowsily, "Mmm, hungry too," as she lifted her head.

For just a moment the big man took his eyes off the lonely stretch of road to touch his lips to hers. Neither of them had noticed the dusty, anonymous car following behind them. Suddenly it accelerated wildly and struck them violently from the rear, propelling their car over the side of the twisting mountain road. It crashed and rolled and crashed again. Gasoline spewed and spurted. There was a flickering light against the dark country landscape, then a flame caught and spread in sheets across the crumpled, upturned automobile. Flames licked at the bulk of Stan Findlay, crushed behind the wheel, and reached for the small, sprawling body that had been flung through the windshield, tossed into the tall grass like a broken doll. Suddenly, with a burst of fire and smoke, the car exploded.

Chapter Ten

SORENSON NEW PC LEADER—
PROMISES NEW DISCLOSURES IN WAR ON GOVERNMENT

Jean Jacques Charles read the headlined account with rising concern. It had never occurred to him that Adam Sorenson might be elected leader of the Official Opposition. Knowing nothing of the young member's earlier background, Jacques had judged him only on his performance in the House. It seemed to Jacques that Sorenson had let himself become the hatchetman for the Opposition. And while political parties were more than ready to use hatchetmen, they rarely, if ever, chose one as leader. Parties usually preferred a leader who could be offered to the voting public as less partisan and more objective and statesmanlike. The Conservatives' choice of Sorenson broke all the rules.

He was about to discard the newspaper when his eye was caught by a boxed, late-news flash below the centre fold:

CRASH VICTIMS IDENTIFIED

The report was datelined Vermont. It briefly reported that after extensive efforts, identification had been made of the charred bodies of a man and woman found beneath the remains of a burned-out automobile in an overgrown gully below a remote mountain road. The report went on to say that the deceased, both Canadians, were Stanley Findlay of Ottawa, a former official of the federal government, and Giselle Cranston of Montreal, wife of a well-known businessman and entrepreneur. An investigation of the cause of the accident had been ordered.

Jacques was jolted by the news. His hooded eyes narrowed, as he considered the implications for him of both stories.

Sorenson, in the first flush of leadership, would no doubt redouble his attack, and because of Findlay's death, Jacques would be unable to show that he had never before heard of the Evangeline Company and had never received a cent from the Candu sale commission.

Now, more than ever, he had to be sure that the memorandum was never uncovered.

Her colleagues interrupted their informal discussion and fell silent as Kathleen entered the Cabinet room. She strode purposefully to her place. She had no more than sat down in the central high-backed chair at the oval table, when she turned to her Minister of Energy.

"How is it that you knew nothing of this sale?" she asked, tight-lipped.

Senator LaCroix gulped audibly, as the hazel eyes bored into his. He raised a hand, as though to ward off his leader's accusing look.

"Negotiations started long before I took over the portfolio," he protested; but another glance at the stony-eyed Kathleen convinced him that this was no time for excuses. He began again.

"Atomic Energy of Canada and Eldorado Nuclear are quite independent of my department, Prime Minister. They only come to me if there is a question of policy to be decided. I would have to bring that to Cabinet for discussion. I have no responsibility at all for Export Development. As far as I know, there isn't even a regular channel of communication with my officials. Under the system, there is no reason why I should know about the Cuban sale, any more than any other." This time he raised both his knotted hands in a helpless gesture, aware how hollow his explanation sounded in the light of the extraordinary interest the public had shown in the revelations elicited by Sorenson before the committee.

"What kind of policy decisions would be involved in order for the discussion to be brought to Cabinet?" asked Kathleen.

The grey-thatched Senator's rugged but mobile features mirrored his concentration.

"Certainly, if there was any question of relaxing our conditions on safeguards they'd have to clear that with the Cabinet."

"Is that all?"

"No. If there's something unusual involved in the package they're bidding on, they would probably ask my ministry to approve it in advance."

"Such as?"

"Oh, it could be anything. Anyway, the point is that AECL says it hasn't had to get any clearances from the Cabinet on the sale to Cuba, beyond the initial go ahead."

Kathleen sat upright, surprise evident in her voice. "Go ahead? You mean Cabinet *was* consulted at some time before negotiations started? And approved an approach to Cuba? But what about safeguards?"

The Minister of Energy spoke up. "About two years ago, if I remember correctly, just before Jacques' trip to the Caribbean, we had a full-dress discussion in Cabinet about safeguards, although I don't remember that we came to any definite conclusions. AECL was putting a lot of pressure on us to withdraw, or at least modify, our conditions. The agency wanted the Prime Minister to actively support their sales efforts during his trip, especially in Mexico and Venezuela. They protested against the policy of not even being able to open negotiations until the prospective purchaser had agreed to inspections. They said adherence to that policy was shutting us out of a lot of potential markets. Negotiate first and *then* impose restrictions when the deal was ready to be closed, was what they wanted. And they argued that our conditions were too stringent, especially when compared to those demanded by our West German competitors. There was some suggestion we be more realistic in our demands for safeguards."

"But why haven't I heard of this before?" Kathleen asked. "I checked over the Cabinet minutes myself, months ago, and found nothing!"

"Perhaps you didn't check back far enough?" LaCroix suggested. "Or there may be no Cabinet minute because we didn't take any firm decision. My impression is that we left it to Jacques to play it by ear, but I may be mistaken. After all, I wasn't Energy Minister then—Stan Findlay was."

"Well, we can't ask Findlay now," she replied, coldly. Her eyes flitted from the face of one colleague to another around the oval table. "Is that everyone's understanding—that the matter was left in the air?" Four or five nodded.

"I don't even remember such a discussion at all," said Harry Williams. "I must have missed that meeting of Cabinet."

Bonnie Costello said, "Of course some of us weren't ministers then and know nothing at all about it."

"I confess I have only the vaguest recollection that there

was such a discussion. I was pretty occupied with that business of the RCMP at the time," said the Solicitor-General.

No one else offered a comment.

Kathleen looked across the green baize table and beyond to where one of the Cabinet secretariat was taking notes. She raised her voice. "Will you search the minutes again. Go back to the last election this time. See if there is any notation at all."

The man nodded, but it was Helmut Ogilvy, his superior, who left his seat behind Kathleen to slip into a padded phone booth to order the new search.

Against the Cabinet Secretary's *sotto voce* instructions into the receiver, Kathleen continued her enquiry. "Are you sure that's all? Was there never any follow-up on the question of safeguards?"

"None. AECL says the subject has never even been broached by the Cubans," LaCroix said positively.

"You mean, Castro has accepted the usual conditions, and will sign the non-proliferation treaty?" the Prime Minister asked.

"Apparently."

Kathleen's brow furrowed as she said thoughtfully, "I don't know Castro personally, but it seems out of character with everything I've heard about the President that he would permit international inspection." The Prime Minister turned to Jean Jacques Charles, who was seated to her right as the most senior of the Privy Councillors.

"You know Castro, Jacques. Is it likely that he would agree to international inspection?"

Charles collapsed his steepled fingers. He straightened in his chair, and then said carefully, "I doubt that he intends to do that."

"Then how can he expect us to sell him our nuclear technology?" she said, puzzled.

He glanced at Kathleen, and then at his colleagues around the table. The attention of each was riveted on their exchange.

"We have sometimes made other, alternative, arrangements, you know," he said at last.

"But we can't have made any other arrangements, Jacques, if Cabinet has never been consulted on it. Isn't that what you said, Gabriel?" she asked.

The Senator confirmed her understanding.

"And you're certain there's been no approach from Castro to modify those conditions?"

"That's what AECL tells me. I suppose Findlay might have had some knowledge of the conditions, but he didn't mention any and, of course, we can't ask him now. Very strange, his accident."

"Yes," agreed Kathleen, "especially since neither we nor the RCMP can reach Willis Cranston. It seems he's left the country."

There was a pause as the ministers considered the implications of this news. Then the Minister of Finance said, "Prime Minister, why did you have the Cabinet minutes checked out 'month's ago'? I understood you to say to the House that you knew nothing at all about the sale?"

Kathleen turned to Carter Warden.

"And I didn't *know*. There was a rumour. Actually, President Thompson asked me about it," she said, with a fleeting memory of that confrontation. "I investigated it then, and gave him my assurance that there was absolutely no basis for it. . . . My God," she blurted, suddenly. "I told Thompson not to worry—that there definitely was no Candu sale to Cuba."

"Then you *did* mislead the House when you said you knew nothing of a sale," said Mary Margaret McMahon, appalled as she heard her accusation resonate in the murmur of the others at the table.

"No, no," protested Kathleen, "I said I knew nothing of a sale *without safeguards*." The distinction was an important one, and she stressed the phrase to emphasize the care with which the words had been chosen—now and last spring. "And I asked Senator LaCroix to check it out just after he was appointed. You remember, Gabriel. And you assured me that there was no deal with Castro at all. And no deal with any nation without safeguards. That's why I said what I did in the House." Her eyes demanded his confirmation.

"Yes, that's what I told you. And I did investigate, that very day. And there was nothing. What I didn't know then was that there had been negotiations with Cuba, but they had been stalled for so long that AECL considered it unlikely there would ever be a sale."

"But there must have been a record somewhere," protested Warden.

"You would think so," agreed Kathleen. "But I actually

looked through the records myself and there wasn't anything."

"And you've heard nothing about it since?" her Minister of Finance asked.

"Well, yes. When I was in Vienna, I learned that the members of the International Agency seemed to think we were backing down in our insistence on safeguards. They seemed suspicious."

"And you didn't have that followed up?" Geoff Pratt, the House leader asked in a faintly accusing tone.

"No—or at least, yes, I did. I asked our Ambassador to do what he could to put such rumours to rest. I was convinced they were no more than rumours," she answered. "And I'm still convinced of it."

"But the rumours of a sale to Cuba proved to be true," Carter Warden reminded her gently. He turned to Senator LaCroix. "How is it that the sale went through so quickly—after it was supposedly stalled?"

"Apparently it was Stan Findlay who got the deal back on track and actually got Dr. Castro's signature on the contract. But that was only very recently," the Energy Minister replied.

"How recently?" Kathleen asked.

"I'm not sure, but it seems it was not long after the House recessed for the summer. You were away when I learned of it."

"So Sorenson is right. There is an actual binding contract with Cuba."

Kathleen's heart sank. There was an uneasy silence in the room.

"But with the usual safeguards?" she asked hopefully.

"I assume so—yes. But AECL isn't able to tell us for sure. They haven't received the contract yet. Findlay had a copy but. . . . They've had confirmation from the Cuban Ambassador, but only by telegram. They've asked him to get them another copy but as of today it hasn't been received. The only conclusion is that it must contain Castro's agreement to standard safeguards."

"Well, that's something, anyway," she said.

But she was quite aware that not even that condition would mollify President Thompson. At least it should satisfy the House when it reconvened at the end of this week. It had better, after the flat denial she had given the Commons before they rose for the summer.

"Sorenson's been hinting that there are more revelations to come. Does anyone have any idea what they can be?" she asked.

Senator LaCroix looked enquiringly at Charles behind her back, but saw no response in his friend's enigmatic face.

"Sorenson won't be able to use the committee any longer as a platform, will he, now he's leader?" asked Bonnie Costello trying to be helpful.

"Not likely, but he'll shift his attack to the House," said the House Leader, darkly.

"We'll have to be ready with our explanations, then," Kathleen said, and turning to LaCroix added, "You'll have to answer in the Senate. Jacques and I will do our best in the House."

"No problem with that, PM," LaCroix said. "I don't anticipate any real trouble there. After all, we have a huge Liberal majority in the Senate. My colleagues won't give me a hard time, and there aren't enough Tory senators to worry about. Oh, they'll put me through my paces, of course, and they can keep it going for quite a while every day—remember we have no time limit to the daily question period in the Senate—but we won't be in any danger."

"I wish the same were true of the House," the Prime Minister sighed. "Well, Jacques, it will be up to us, then, in the Commons. Maybe it won't be so bad with two of us to handle it. We've got nothing to hide, no matter what they say. I'll simply repeat the truth—that there was no sale to Cuba when I spoke in the House, with or without safeguards. And now that it's gone through, there's been no departure from policy. Castro has accepted our conditions on safeguards. You can tell the House of the President's approach during your visit to Havana, and how the negotiations were stalled until just lately. That will give you a chance to clear the air and set the record straight. As you once pointed out to me, whether the Americans like it or not, there's nothing wrong with doing business with a Communist state. Between the two of us, we can weather this. The Government will be okay, when you and I explain."

"Not I," said Jacques. "I told you. I have not seen or communicated with Fidel since my trip there over a year ago. I've taken no part in negotiations since. I'm damned if I'm going to let that weasel Sorenson put me on the defensive. I have no intention whatsoever of making explanations in the House. My conversations with Dr. Castro are not for the record."

Jolted, Kathleen stared at him, and it was Bonnie who finally spoke up.

"But, Jacques, surely you must at least formally deny that you're involved," she protested. "You can't leave the Prime Minister alone to make explanations."

He swung his eyes to hers. "That's the PM's job, my dear Minister. She doesn't need any help from me."

Into the strained pause, Bonnie spoke again.

"I hate to ask, Jacques, but what exactly do you know about this Evangeline Company in the Cayman Islands?" The young Labour Minister had been reluctant to pose the question, but someone had to.

Jacques' nostrils flared. "Nothing whatever," he snapped, and his jaw clamped. Then he relented. "I swear to you all. I never heard of it until I read of it in the press. I have nothing to do with it. Nor—although I shouldn't need to tell you—with any commission money, if that's what your question implies."

"Surely Jacques," put in Kathleen, "you'll want to make such a statement in the House to defend your honour."

"My honour should speak for itself. I have never previously had a need to defend it and I refuse to do so now. I won't dignify a charge that I have used public office for private gain by answering it. My mind's made up." He closed his Cabinet book with a snap, and swept it from the table. "I refuse to discuss this further!" Pushing back his chair he strode out of the Cabinet room, his high-cheekboned face set and furious.

Behind him Jacques left a pall of dismay. His colleagues could understand and even grudgingly admire his attitude, but what they were unable to condone was his refusal to pull with the team. What about Cabinet solidarity? Did he expect them to close ranks and defend him when he absolutely refused to defend himself?

Not long after, Kathleen brought the meeting to a close. As she walked back to her office she continued to grapple with the problem. She had an uneasy conviction that she had missed something important. Could there be more to Jacques' refusal to defend himself? She told herself it was idle to speculate. It was clear that she would get nothing more from him. Only unfolding events could cast further light on the reasons for Jacques' obstinacy—but Kathleen devoutly hoped that there was nothing more to come. Her task in the House would be difficult enough. She would have to face Sorenson alone.

"I wasn't sure you were still at that number. Afraid you might have already moved to Stornoway."

Adam Sorenson tensed. It was that same muffled voice. He was sure. How could he forget it?

"You've done pretty well with the lead I gave you, young fella," his caller went on. "Made quite a name for yourself. Got to be leader. Now, how would you like some more ammunition? Maybe enough to take you to the lady's seat, clear across the chamber?"

Sorenson breathed deeply to hide his instant excitement. "What have you got?"

"Now, let's see. You uncovered Findlay. Too bad you can't question him. Know what his fees and commissions were?"

"Yes," said the Opposition leader with disappointment. "Three million. Half a mill in expenses. I got that out of the president."

"Ah," said the voice in his ear, "but he was only going to get part of that, even if, by laundering it in the Caymans, he got it tax-free! Now, what do you know about the safeguard conditions of the deal?"

"Not much. I never had time in the committee to get into that," Sorenson explained.

"That's about what I thought. Now listen carefully. I've got a memo for you and it's very important—just what you need to wrap this up. The problem is how to get it to you? Have you got a car?"

"Yeah, sure. It's down in the apartment garage. But what—?"

"Just be quiet a minute, boy. Have they got Mounties on you? Can you get out without them?"

"I dunno—never tried. Probably. Why?"

"I want you to meet me. Now. But you'll have to give the redcoats the slip."

"Why can't I just say I'm going over to Elgin for a pack of cigarettes?"

"No—too many people around there—too many lights, too."

"How about my office? I could meet you there."

"No. I'd have to explain my business to the Commissionaire on duty. No, this is better. You know the Supreme Court building on Wellington?"

"Sure."

"Drive into the parking lot in, say, twenty minutes. There shouldn't be anybody there at night but if there are any cars, just pull up and douse your lights. Cover your rear mirror and make sure the back door on the driver's side is unlocked. Don't look around and don't try to follow me afterwards. Got all that?"

"Sure, but—"

"What kind of car you got? What's the license number?"

After Adam Sorenson had described his car, the mysterious voice grated, "Good luck, boy," and the connection was abruptly broken.

Sorenson was confused. He was indignant at being called "boy," yet consumed with curiosity about the origin of the anonymous voice and the motive behind these late calls. Questions crowded into his mind, now that it was too late to ask them. He admitted to himself that he found the instructions he had just received pretty bizarre, even by Ottawa's current standards. Why couldn't the memo be left at his office in the usual plain brown envelope favoured by most informants? He'd had lots of tips like that in the past—mainly from aggrieved civil servants anxious to pass on something derogatory to their minister. A sixth sense told Sorenson, however, that it was unlikely that his mysterious caller was a mere civil servant.

Who was he? And why was he doing this? The Conservative leader puzzled over the ownership of the obviously disguised voice as he noted that the hands of his wristwatch had just touched 11:30. Stealthily, he let himself out of his apartment.

Sorenson strode silently down the hall towards the elevator. No, he couldn't use it. The constable on duty would be facing him when he reached the street floor. He went on past the elevators to the staircase, trudged down ten floors to the basement garage. He was already worried that he would be late for the rendezvous.

Quietly, he pulled the car out, keeping the lights dimmed until he reached the cross street where he gunned the motor and sped off, traversing the quiet blocks towards the Supreme Court building.

On his arrival, a quick glance confirmed that there was

no one about. He pulled into the broad forecourt of the classic building, and parked as far as possible from the light standard, deep in shadow. He checked the catch of the rear door, then draped a chamois cloth from the glove compartment over the mirror, as instructed. He waited, smoking quietly.

Suddenly, the rear door clicked and the car springs shifted with the weight as an unseen body slid inside the car, directly behind him.

"Good boy, Sorenson. Here's your dynamite." He heard the gravelly voice and felt an envelope slip to the seat beside him.

"Who are you, and why are you doing this?" Sorenson demanded, but the man was gone, out of the car, melting into the shadows. Nothing about him seemed familiar. Sorenson turned on his lights and slit open the envelope, devouring the contents at a glance.

Dynamite he'd called it and dynamite it was.

"Mr. Sorenson is here, Prime Minister."

Kathleen's tumbling thoughts were penetrated by her secretary's soft-voiced announcement. Barbara's pert features reflected her concern over the Prime Minister's obvious distractions. She was uneasy as she closed the door to the anteroom, leaving the new leader of the Official Opposition alone with Kathleen.

Kathleen stood to greet her visitor. She smoothed down her dress in her habitual gesture, and nodded Adam Sorenson into a chair across the broad desk from her own. She made a determined effort to corral her scattered thoughts in order to concentrate on the interview at hand. It was relatively rare that an Opposition leader sought a private chat. It was probably for something quite important.

For a long moment, she studied the younger man opposite. This was their first private encounter since he had become leader, and Adam Sorenson seemed changed. He seemed older, steadier, more sure of himself; but not so cocky and obstreperous as he had appeared last spring, when he attacked her in the House.

The change was more than cosmetic. Of course there was the newly styled hair, and the better-cut clothes, but it went deeper than that. It was as if he had grown with his new responsibilities. The Opposition leader's eyes were clear and untroubled, his expression polite.

With a start, Kathleen became aware that her wordless scrutiny was causing her visitor embarrassment. He was beginning to shift uneasily in his seat. She rearranged her features into an enquiring expression, willing him to begin.

Adam Sorenson cleared his throat, betraying that he was, after all, nervous. Then he said, in his high, carrying voice, "Thank you for seeing me so quickly, Prime Minister. I have no doubt you're very busy, but I hope not to impose too much on your time. This matter is, however, important. And urgent."

The young man, Kathleen thought with surprise, was displaying dignity and an appropriately firm presence, unusual in one so untried. She nodded, encouraging him to continue.

"It's about this Cuban business." He hesitated.

"Oh?" Kathleen's eyebrows rose. "I thought that was over. And by the way, Adam"—she used his given name for the first time—"my thanks for your withdrawal last summer. I confess, you gave me a sleepless night over the whole thing." She smiled, ready to let bygones be bygones.

He acknowledged her thanks, but his expression remained grave. "No, it's not over. In fact, that's why I'm here. I'm going to have to insist upon an immediate, full-scale debate of the Candu sale to Cuba."

"Insist? And how do you propose to do that?" It was unnecessary to spell out that it was the Government which ordered the daily business of the House.

"In either of two ways," he responded at once. "The choice is yours. I would prefer that you call the Estimates of External Affairs at once."

The Prime Minister's eyebrows climbed again. Sorenson paused to let her consider the first alternative.

External Affairs! That meant he planned to concentrate on Jean Jacques Charles.

"I'm afraid I don't understand. You want Mr. Charles' Estimates to be called. But why External? If you want a debate on the Candu sale, I should think you'd want the Energy Minister's Estimates called. He's responsible for AECL."

"Ah, but the Energy Minister is a Senator. There's no way we can get him before the Commons to make an accounting. Besides, LaCroix is unlikely to know much about this, in spite of the fact that he's a close friend of Charles. No," Sorenson said firmly, "it's Charles we're after. In my opinion, he's a disgrace to Canada and he should be made to resign from the Cabinet and the House."

"Made to resign? By whom?"

"You, of course, as First Minister," he answered, a trifle loftily. "But since you don't seem disposed to fire him, we'll have to do it ourselves when we debate his Estimates. We propose to move to reduce his salary to one dollar. I'm sure we'll have enough support to carry the vote against him, and then he'll have no recourse but to resign."

"I understand the procedural point, Mr. Sorenson," Kathleen said icily. "But I am still at a loss to understand why you are attacking Jacques. He has assured me he has had nothing to do with the sale except for the initial negotiations with Dr. Castro. Surely you don't believe that he has anything to do with that offshore corporation—the Evangeline? Or that he shared in the commission on the sale? You can't believe that a former Prime Minister of Canada could be so dishonourable as to use his office for private gain? I tell you, Jean Jacques Charles had nothing to do with that sale!"

Sorenson made no response.

"How could I ask him to resign when he's done nothing wrong? Why should I throw him to the wolves when he's got nothing to answer for?"

Kathleen suddenly realized that her voice had been rising along with her indignation. She resolved to keep both under better control. Sorenson, however, gave no indication that he had noticed, even though his brilliant black eyes had remained unwaveringly on hers all the time she was speaking.

"So you insist upon defending him?" he said, his lips compressed into a thin line of disapproval. "Even when he refuses to defend himself?"

"It's a matter of honour with him," she said flatly.

"Honour!" her visitor spat contemptuously.

"Yes, honour," she retorted evenly. "He refuses to dignify such an outrageous charge with a reply."

"And you'll stand behind him?" said Sorenson. "Then we'll have to resort to the alternative."

"What is the alternative?" she asked, hoping it would prove more reasonable.

"We'll use the first Opposition day for a full-scale confidence debate, and this time, the whole Government will be the target, not just Charles. And I shouldn't be surprised, Prime Minister, if we don't bring you down. If you persist in shielding Charles, that's no more than you deserve." Realizing that the last phrase had been said with unconcealed relish, Sorenson paused to collect himself. "Of course, I'm candid enough to tell you that I'm no more prepared than you are for an election just now. But if you force me into it, I'll be ready." He spoke with confidence which approached a sneer.

Kathleen stared at her opponent, appalled to realize that Sorenson meant the threat. She remembered that Sherwood had warned her, but she had ignored him. It was clear that the apparent newfound dignity and responsibility was only a veneer masking Sorenson's ferocious hatred of the Liberals. She recoiled at the depths of dislike revealed in his glittering black eyes.

The Prime Minister stood up. "Your readiness is plain enough, Mr. Sorenson," she said. "I assume it would be useless to try to dissuade you."

Her visitor did not respond to her signal that the interview was over. It was apparent that he had more to say. Kathleen resumed her seat. Adam Sorenson's manner underwent a marked change. Now he spoke as an equal— one leader to another, with a new, undisguised compassion.

"Why don't you get rid of Charles, Prime Minister? He did as much to you, I seem to remember. Surely you don't need to risk your Government's life over a has-been? What's one minister more or less? If you should fire him, you could save yourself. And isn't that the first lesson in politics: to sacrifice anybody else necessary if it will only save the leader?"

Kathleen was puzzled by the sharp-featured man's new approach. It almost seemed as if he regretted the prospect of her defeat. He continued in the same conciliatory vein.

"Nobody thinks you're involved personally in this, you know. It's only that you're letting Charles shelter behind your skirts." His voice hardened. "Kick him out—make it clear you're repudiating him. I admit, you'll still have a fight on your hands, but you'll survive. I've got no love for any of you Grits, but it seems to me that you're better than most of your kind. I'd rather defeat you on something that *is* your responsibility instead of on something you inherited. And I'm sure, knowing Grits, that another opportunity will come along soon enough."

Kathleen nodded her understanding, but remained silent.

When she said nothing further, Sorenson reluctantly got to his feet and prepared to make his exit. At the door, he turned back.

"I'll need to know your decision by Monday at the latest, Prime Minister. Earlier, if possible—and I hope you'll take my advice, Kathleen," he added softly.

When he had gone, Kathleen buzzed her secretary on the intercom.

"Barbara, will you get me Mr. Charles, please."

A moment later, mentally framing questions for her Secretary of State for External Affairs, she lifted the receiver in answer to the intercom buzz.

"He's gone for the weekend, Prime Minister," her secretary reported.

"Where?" she asked shortly, exasperated that Jacques was never around when his presence was needed.

"They didn't say. I have his office on the other line. Will you wait, while I enquire?"

"No, Barbara. Tell them to track him down and bring him back," she said testily. "I want to see him as quickly as possible It's important."

"Okay."

"In the meantime, ask the House Leader to come in. He was in the chamber earlier."

"Yes, right away," was the crisp rejoinder.

Shortly thereafter Geoff Pratt appeared, out of breath, at Kathleen's door. His leader was sitting at her desk, deep in thought, her fingers drumming on the blotter. She looked up at his entrance and then explained to him the content of the Opposition leader's message.

The canny Maritimer who was the Government's expert on House procedure heard her out without comment.

"Thought there was something up. I haven't been able to get agreement from the other parties on the order for business for next week. It's not just the Tories; the NDP are obviously in the know, and if I'm any judge, they are likely to support them. I'd better alert the Whip to make sure he has a full complement of our members present. We'll need every last vote, if I'm right."

"No matter what we do, we don't have enough if they combine. They have the numbers to outvote us," she said in a distressed voice.

The House Leader nodded. There was no use denying it. This was the curse of minority government. Any bend in the road might disclose the hidden landmine of defeat, primed to explode.

"What does Jacques say?" he asked.

"He doesn't know yet. I can't reach him—again. But I'm having him brought back. I'll see him before Monday, just as soon as he's found."

"Will you want a Cabinet meeting?" he asked.

"I suppose. Sunday night? No, better make that Monday morning, first thing. There'll be no point unless I've talked to Jacques. But I have to give Sorenson his answer by Monday. You'd better have the ministers alerted."

Geoff Pratt made a notation, and then asked her, in a tentative, voice. "Do you think Jacques will resign?"

"No, I don't. That would be an admission of guilt. But I must get him to break his silence, to spell out that he wasn't involved. The country will never believe him if he persists in his refusal to defend himself."

"I agree. What about you?" he dared to ask her.

"Me? What about me?" she looked at him, unable to fathom the meaning behind his question.

"Surely if there's a general debate, you will have to defend the sale and reveal that President Thompson warned you about it. I don't see how you can escape that."

"But I've got to! The sale was made without my knowledge. I never approved it. And I didn't intend to mislead the President—although I suppose neither he nor the House will believe that." Kathleen's eyes had widened in fright. "Oh, no. I won't stand for that. If I have to face the House, I'll resign." She left her desk to pace the room. "Don't you see, I couldn't carry on."

"I understand that. But there may be no way of avoiding it. They'll never let up, till they have Jacques' head. Or yours."

With a sinking heart, Kathleen acknowledged that he was right.

It was not quite seven a.m. and beyond the long windows of the panelled room, the laggard sun had not yet dispelled the early-morning haze although the gloom outside appeared to be lightening.

Not so the gloom in the Prime Minister's parliamentary office, where she confronted her Cabinet colleagues. Their mood was heavy—dispirited, defeated almost. In vain, she searched the faces of her ministers for a sign of optimism.

Kathleen had already recounted Adam Sorenson's ultimatum, and the House leader had explained the implications of each alternative. Most ministers knew very little about the rules, but they could all understand the seriousness of this latest of crises.

"So after they tear us to pieces in debate, then they'll vote to reduce Jacques' salary to a dollar?" repeated Senator LaCroix.

"And if Jacques should resign?" asked Bonnie Costello, the question hanging in the air.

"That might satisfy them, and save the Government," Pratt said, but doubt was obvious in his voice.

"Where *is* Charles?" Carter Warden asked, peering around the crowded room where some ministers sat, and other, later arrivals, had to stand for want of seating.

"He can't be found. His housekeeper expected him back last night—he's off skiing somewhere. His office says he'll be back this afternoon. But we can't wait. We must decide now, so that I can tell Sorenson my decision this morning."

"If you refuse to call Jacques' Estimates, how soon will it be until the Opposition can find an opportunity for a full-scale debate and a confidence vote?" asked LaCroix, searching for some way to help extricate his longtime friend.

Geoff Pratt said wearily, "Not long. Then there's no way of stopping them from opening up the whole Cuban deal."

"And," he continued, "undoubtedly, Kathleen would have to take part in such a wide-ranging debate. She'd have to defend Jacques, if he refuses to defend himself. She'd have to defend the actual deal. *And* she'd have to defend herself—she'd have to explain that she did have some prior knowledge, despite what she's already said. I think the end result will be a defeat of the Government whichever way it happens," he concluded, contributing to the depressed mood of his colleagues.

Loyal Bonnie Costello was scared. "We have to protect the PM as far as possible. That means she *can't* speak in a general debate."

Senator LaCroix broke in. "And *that* means throwing Jacques to them like a bone to a pack of hungry hounds," he said bitterly.

Kathleen was saddened that not even Bonnie had found her account acceptable. The younger woman's political sense was almost unerring. If she didn't believe her leader, it was unlikely that any less fierce partisan would, much less the public.

"Let me be sure I understand this." Senator LaCroix pushed back the hank of grey hair that was forever falling over his eyes. His face reflected his concentration. "Is there no way to avoid sacrificing Jacques? It seems to me that you could just refuse to put up the Estimates for External Affairs for debate. Make them take something else—even my department, if they want to talk about the Candu."

"Huh!" said Mary Margaret McMahon. "That's a great idea—to call the Energy Estimates, Gabe. *You* wouldn't be under the gun. You could just sit up there in the Senate, safe as a churchmouse, while poor Harry would get dumped on in the House."

Harry Williams, one of Kathleen's oldest friends among the Cabinet, stirred uncomfortably. When he had accepted Kathleen's assignment to speak in the Commons as LaCroix's acting Minister, it had never occurred to him that he would be in danger of having his head chopped off for a department over which he had no authority at all. He voiced his objections.

"Hell, I don't mind taking the rap for whatever goes wrong in my own Ministry. That's my responsibility. But I'm damned if I want to answer in the House for foul-ups in *your* department, Gabe."

The Government House Leader heaved a deep sigh. "I might offer them Energy, but they'd laugh at me. They wouldn't accept a department whose minister can't appear in the House. There really is no choice. Under the rules, the official Opposition has the right to say which Estimates are to be withheld from Standing Committees for debate by the Committee of the Whole House. If they choose External Affairs, we've got to go along with them."

The sombre atmosphere of the meeting deepened perceptibly.

"Is there any way we can postpone the decision?" asked Senator Warden. The Minister of Finance was perched on the wide window ledge behind Kathleen. He stood up, craning his neck as he sought to catch the eye of the House Leader.

"No, Carter," Geoff Pratt said in an expressionless voice. "The motion to refer the Estimates to Standing Committee has to go on the order paper tonight. It has to spell out which Estimates are being retained for debate in the chamber."

"When would the debate be held?"

"Wednesday. It's a short day. It would be over by six. But the PC's have asked for one of their Opposition days the next day, Thursday. And that's a long day, to ten o'clock. They could use it for a confidence motion, if they wanted to. So they've got us over a barrel. Either we let them at Jacques on Wednesday, or they'll do their damnedest to vote out the whole Government on Thursday."

"But the debate on the Estimates would be in the House Committee," said an obviously puzzled Bonnie Costello. "The Government can't be defeated then, can it? I always find it very confusing, but I thought the House had to be sitting as the House with the Speaker in the chair, and not as a Committee of the Whole House, for a motion of non-confidence to defeat the Government."

"Strictly speaking, that's true," replied Pratt. "But remember, the Estimates are part of Supply. That's the basic purpose of Parliament—to control the supply of money to be spent by the Government. If a majority of the House refuses to approve a department's estimated expenditures, then that department is just shut down. In fact, the Government can't go on because it's lost the confidence of the House."

"But," interrupted the Minister of Health and Welfare.

The House Leader's voice over-rode hers. "Let me finish, please, Mary Margaret," he said curtly. "Now on Wednesday let's say they debate all day. Normally, a debate on Estimates would start with item number one—the Minister's salary. But they'll defer that item until the last. They'll hammer Jacques all day on anything they feel like on External's proposed spending, and then sometime before six o'clock, they'll go back to item number one—his salary. And if they outvote us, as I think they will, unless he satisfies them he's in the clear during the debate, he'll have to resign. In effect, *he* will have lost their confidence. But the *Government* wouldn't have to resign. It would take another vote, after the Committee of the Whole House rises and reports back to the House itself, t defeat the Government. That could take the form of a refusal to approve the department's whole Estimates or an actual motion of non-confidence. Understand?"

All of his colleagues had been listening hard. Most of them had never tried to understand the House Rules. They relied on their colleague. Now several nodded their comprehension.

"But, Geoff, what's to prevent them from doing that on Thursday?" asked the Solicitor-General.

"Nothing," responded the House Leader patiently. "But it doesn't look as if they are out to defeat the Government, from what Kathleen has told us of Sorenson's conversation with her. They're in no better shape for an election than we are. My judgement is that once they've got Jacques' head on a platter, they'll be satisfied."

"But they'll still have their Opposition day on Thursday?"

"Yes, but they'll talk about something else. The labour situation would be my guess. And that's a lot less dangerous to the Government right now."

"Can't you postpone the Opposition day?" asked Harry Williams.

"They're entitled to six of them in this trimester, up until mid-December, by the rules. We'll have to give them one pretty soon, this week or next. And there's no good reason to put it off. No. I think we'll have to bite the bullet and do as they ask. It's really less risky that way," he concluded, glancing at Kathleen.

The Prime Minister sat in her high-backed chair, a lone shaft of morning sunlight spilling over her strong features. Her chin was propped in her hand, her eyes fixed steadily on her House Leader. She remained silent for a few moments more, as her ministers murmured among themselves, absorbing the House Leader's explanation.

"Well, Kathleen," said Senator Warden. "The time has come to cut yourself loose from Jean Jacques Charles. If it's not already too late."

Kathleen swivelled in her chair to study her distinguished Minister of Finance. She remembered when, more than a year ago, Carter Warden had come to her with others of the Seven to persuade her to challenge Jacques' leadership. His advice had been consistent ever since then—to distance herself as quickly as possible from her predecessor. It occurred to her that Carter Warden must be saying to himself, "I told you so."

Warden's colleague in the upper chamber, Senator LaCroix, protested, "Surely there's some other way. What will Quebec think if you abandon Jacques?"

Kathleen turned back to face LaCroix. "It's not as if *I'm* tying the can to him, Gabriel. It would be the Opposition's fault, if he has to resign. Surely Quebec would understand that?" And then warming to her argument, she added, "Anyway, Jacques has the option of defending himself. What's made the Opposition so angry is his persistent silence in the face of these charges. I'm confident that if Jacques goes into the debate and makes it clear he's not involved in anything scandalous, they won't vote to reduce his salary, and the crisis will pass. You're his oldest and closest friend among us. Can't you persuade him to defend himself?"

Gabriel LaCroix shifted under Kathleen's intent gaze. Most of his colleagues were looking at him eagerly, encouraged by this slender ray of hope.

"Well, I can try," he said at last, doubtfully. "But you know how stubborn Jacques can be, especially on what he sees as a matter of principle. I'll try, anyway, I promise. If that's the only way out. . . ."

"And I'll try again, too, Gabriel. Perhaps between us we can succeed," his leader said.

And so, on a slightly more optimistic note, the meeting broke up. If Jean Jacques Charles could be persuaded to speak, the crisis might yet be averted.

In the end, they had agreed to call the Estimates of the Department of External Affairs later in the week. The Undersecretary was alerted to be prepared to brief his Minister, and messages were left everywhere demanding that Jacques attend on Kathleen immediately he surfaced.

Kathleen and Andrew were at dinner at 24 Sussex Drive when Jean Jacques Charles at last appeared at the door, still dressed in well-worn ski clothes. She invited her predecessor to join them at their unfinished meal, but he declined, offering to wait for her in the small study. Kathleen joined him there almost at once, followed by Marilou, the red-haired maid, who lowered a coffee service for two to the low table in front of Jacques. She smiled at the former master of the house, poured each a cup, and then withdrew.

Kathleen explained, briefly and rapidly, what had happened in his absence—the confrontation with Sorenson, the Cabinet's decision.

Jacques listened to her in silence, although far back in the blue eyes, a small flame flickered. Finally, he interrupted her with an impatient gesture.

"You want me to deny my involvement?" he asked in a harsh voice.

"Yes, Jacques. You can make them believe you, if you'll only explain. It's your refusal to speak that makes them so suspicious, so determined." She realized that she was not getting through to him. "Jacques, you must! There's no other hope."

"Suppose I can't convince them?" he asked.

Kathleen spread her hands, palms up. He understood full well what would follow.

"I'd have to resign," he said flatly.

Wordlessly, she nodded confirmation.

"Why should I go through all that, and *then* resign?" His tone was cold. "Why don't I quit right here and now? Just say the word," he challenged her.

For a moment, the Prime Minister was tempted, remembering how brutal Jacques had been when he had fired her from his own Cabinet, not too many years past. But Kathleen controlled the impulse. The whole country would read that as his admission of guilt. And the Estimates had already been called. She couldn't change that, on pain of being charged with double-crossing the Opposition. And they would use their alternative plan to come right back with the non-confidence motion.

"Jacques, you *must* speak."

His expression hardened. "No, Kathleen, I can't and I won't."

She looked at him, unable to believe that he could be so stubborn, when the life of her Government depended on his cooperation, on his considerable ability to dispel the air of suspicion and wrongdoing.

As if sensing her incredulity, Jacques got impatiently to his feet.

"I told you this, months ago. Nothing has happened to make me change my mind."

At last Kathleen accepted that it was useless to argue with him. She had tried—and she had failed to move the proud, stubborn man. He was adamant.

Chapter Eleven

Kathleen was dumbfounded. Never, in her wildest imaginings, never, in her worst assessment of the situation, could she have believed what her eyes were telling her. She sat in her chair as if she too were carved from oak, her shaking fingers plucking at the two sheets of paper that Anthony Whiteside had placed before her only moments before.

"How can you be sure this is genuine?" she asked, groping for straws. "How did you come by it?"

"I couldn't tell you that, even if I knew. The CIA I expect," the Ambassador said, compassion in his voice.

Anthony Whiteside hated his mission, but he had no choice at all. This was his job. He had delivered the President's brutally brief message. It and the damning evidence which was clipped to it were there on the desk before her.

He looked at Kathleen, whose eyes were glazed with shock.

Whatever the President and the State Department think, he told himself, I *know* Kathleen Marshal couldn't have been aware of this before.

Kathleen's eyes again sought the photocopy of the memorandum that trembled in her hand. A memorandum of agreement with Fidel Castro, the Cuban President. On the letterhead of the Prime Minister of Canada. Dated over a year ago.

The memo was an undertaking, given on behalf of the government of Canada, that if Cuba purchased a package of one or more nuclear reactors, plus continuing supplies of uranium and a Canadian-built production facility for heavy water, Canada would join in a program of expansive nuclear research. To facilitate the purchase, it further agreed to a substantial, long-term, low-interest loan.

The final, hand-written paragraph of the memo dispensed with compliance with the standard conditions of safeguards.

The handwriting and the bold signature below were undoubtedly penned by Jean Jacques Charles.

Her eyes moved to the attached sheet, emblazoned with the US President's seal. Kathleen's spinning brain struggled to accept and evaluate the curt note from Washington clipped to the memorandum.

"In view of the enclosed, our Ambassador is herewith recalled. A full range of economic sanctions will be imposed against Canada, at the direction of the President."

Stunned, Kathleen looked up at Anthony Whiteside. "Does anyone else know about this?" she asked.

"My instructions were to deliver it to you. But the leaders of the Opposition will also get copies," he replied.

"You mean to say that you're going to give copies of these to Adam Sorenson and Terry Malloy?" she demanded, unable to believe he would betray her so callously.

"Sorenson's copy has already been delivered. Malloy and the Social Credit leader will get theirs today. I wanted to give you your copy personally." He caught the stricken expression on her face. "Kathleen, I'm so sorry. I did try to warn you. There has been a contingency plan in effect—an 'insurance policy' they call it in Washington—for months now. We had to be certain that our interests were not ignored."

"And you knew about this, this . . . insurance policy?" she asked incredulously.

"Yes, but I tried to . . . Oh, what's the use, Kathleen. That memorandum between Charles and Castro," he gestured to the paper she still held in her hand, "exists, and must be dealt with."

"But, Tony, surely the memo must be a forgery?"

"Kathleen, that's utter nonsense! Do you think the President would impose sanctions on Canada without being absolutely certain of the validity of that memo?"

"But it can't be real. I *tell* you, I've had it checked out repeatedly here. No one knows anything at all about this."

"No one?" he said drily. "It seems pretty clear your External Affairs Minister knows. Have you any doubt at all that you're looking at Charles' signature?"

"No," she admitted, but with great reluctance.

"Look, Kath, I believe you when you say you knew nothing of this. It's obvious to me that Jacques has been lying to you all along, hoping no one would ever see that memo. But I'm not so sure anyone else will believe that. President Thompson obviously doesn't, and I suspect your Opposition won't believe you either, unless Charles goes into the House and makes a clean breast of things. Now, if they believe him, I should think that would clear you—at least from any personal involvement—but I'm not at all sure they won't suggest you were careless in not getting to the bottom of this a lot earlier."

"But, Tony," she protested, "I did everything I could. I checked out the Cabinet minutes. I spoke to Jacques. He told me there was no deal. I asked LaCroix to keep an eye on it and report to me—and he came up with nothing." Her explanation sounded desperate, even to herself.

"It isn't as if you weren't warned—by the President, for one," he admonished her.

"Yes, I know," she said impatiently. "But when I spoke to Thompson there *was* no deal. It was totally stalled. It was only this summer that negotiations were revived, and I had no idea, until this very minute, that it was finalized without safeguards. I told the House that on my word of honour, months ago. Don't you see? I've told the truth, all along. Or at least the truth as I knew it," she said in a defeated voice.

"Surely you must have heard rumours?" he suggested.

"Oh, there were rumours around the International Agency, yes. But I told my Ambassador to try to kill them, because they were baseless. Baseless! My God, if I'd only known!"

"Isn't there someone else you could have checked it out with?"

"Who?" she asked. "If AECL didn't know, if my Energy Minister didn't know, who else could I have asked?"

"Don't you have friends in the finance community or in the nuclear industry? Maybe the West Germans could have told you. Or even Castro himself."

"Oh, Tony, I don't know them. Maybe if I did, I could have called them and got it sorted out. But you can't just call up a stranger, or a head of state you've never met, and start fishing for information. You have to know who you can trust before you do that, and I never have belonged to that kind of old-boy's network. It's pretty exclusively a male club," she said in despair, aware once again of the limitation imposed by her sex.

His silence expressed his sympathy as clearly as words. Then he said briskly, "No use crying over spilt milk. Your best bet is to have Jacques make a statement right away, clearing you of any prior knowledge of this deal. Then maybe

I can persuade President Thompson to reconsider imposing sanctions, especially if you repudiate the deal."

"Repudiate it? How? Go back on the undertaking given on behalf of the country, in writing? By a Prime Minister with *carte blanche* from his Cabinet? That's a matter of the nation's honour. I don't see how I could repudiate it," she replied, her voice rising.

"You'll have to, Kathleen, in the face of these threatened sanctions. Surely your Cabinet will have something to say about being bound by a term they never authorized, a term that flies right in the face of your policy?"

"But they gave Jacques a free hand, don't you see? How can that be retracted now?"

"Surely Jacques can explain all that—that he did it without anyone's knowledge, without the express approval of Cabinet?"

Kathleen looked at Whiteside with dull eyes. Her tone encouraged no hope.

"Tomorrow, Tony, his Estimates will be debated in the House, but Jacques has refused to deal with the Candu sale to Cuba. He *refused,* don't you understand? Categorically. I must go into the House and deal with it myself. I had counted on the fact that there was nothing hidden in the deal. It was on that basis that I intended to defend him and my Government. Now what am I going to say? I'll have to admit I was wrong. That I was lied to, and that I'm trapped. Do you *understand* what that will mean? They'll vote no confidence in Jacques, and he'll have to resign." She sighed, collecting herself. "Well, he deserves it. I can see that now. But if he won't speak out, they may not believe *me.* Day after tomorrow, there'll be a confidence vote, and this time it will be me and my Government they'll be after.

"This is probably the end, Tony," she said bitterly, bowing her head, acknowledging the defeat to come.

On Wednesday, after the party caucuses, the House met at eleven. Question Period was ominously brief. Before noon, the House moved into Committee of the Whole. The Speaker left his dais, and the mace was ceremoniously placed below the level of the table. The Deputy Speaker, as Chairman of the Committee of the Whole House, took his place at the head of the Clerk's table, and the Estimates for the Department of the Secretary of State for External Affairs were called.

Surprisingly, Jean Jacques Charles was not in his place. Instead, Kathleen Marshal's desk was burdened with piles of material provided by his department. Menzie MacDonald, the Under-secretary of State, sat at a small desk on the floor of the House in front of Kathleen, ready to assist her on details of the unfamiliar Estimates.

The Prime Minister rose, the speech prepared by the department for Jacques' delivery clutched in her right hand. But before she launched herself into the speech, a desiccated review of the past year, she cleared her throat.

"Mr. Chairman, I regret to inform the Committee that the Secretary of State has this morning tendered his resignation to the Governor General. As First Minister, I will undertake to respond to questions from the Honourable Members opposite, in his stead. I trust that will be satisfactory to members of the Committee."

A buzz at once arose. Not even the Liberal caucus had been advised of this in advance. Jacques' resignation had taken members on all sides by surprise.

Adam Sorenson, seated directly across the House from the Prime Minister, thought to himself: So she knows. It will be interesting to see what she does now. But whatever she does, it won't change my strategy. We'll still reduce the Minister's salary. Whether we leave it at that will depend on what she says.

He turned to his seatmate, the Energy critic of his shadow cabinet. "This doesn't change anything. Tell our members there'll be no change of strategy; we'll vote against the Minister's salary as we planned to. That will put the last of the nails in Charles' coffin." His black eyes flashed. "It will depend on the Right Honourable Lady's attitude today, whether we have to nail it shut *with her in it.*"

Kathleen was ready. Except for the ritual introductory speech, she had held her fire all day, waiting to answer the speech she knew must be coming. And about five o'clock it did, as the Clerk called for consideration item number one of the Estimates—the Minister's salary.

Adam Sorenson made a long, vicious speech, denouncing Jean Jacques Charles. His detailed bill of indictment was a minor masterpiece, fact and innuendo interwoven into a devastatingly persuasive condemnation. He laid the groundwork by reminding the House members of the widely commented upon rapport between the President of Cuba and the previous Prime Minister of Canada. Sorenson recalled to mind the jovial pictures that had filled the press last year and the year before when Jean Jacques Charles had lingered on Dr. Castro's lush island during his trade-oriented tours of South, Central American, and Caribbean nations. The Opposition leader followed by reciting, almost verbatim, the testimony the president of AECL had given before Tolliver's Standing Committee, laying particular emphasis on the sums of public money expended for commission fees and expenses. Sorenson speculated at length, most damagingly, about what these expenses could have been, and to whom they might have been paid.

"And Honourable Members will remember," he thundered, "that half a million tax dollars—half a million, I repeat—were paid out for these expenses *without* an accounting."

Then he swept on to the employment by AECL of Willis Cranston and Stanley Findlay, characterizing the two as "another couple of Charles' buddies." He then recounted every recorded innuendo critical of the Montrealer's murky business affairs. From *The Parliamentary Guide,* he read the published biography of the late Minister of Energy. Then he dropped the small red volume resoundingly to his desk and, in a scathing voice, asked the attentive House, "And where in that background, I pray the Right Honourable Lady to tell me, does there appear any qualifications at all to undertake such negotiations? Only, I put to the Committee, that he was the responsible Minister for AECL. Stanley Findlay knew Castro, and he was Jean Jacques' well-known errand boy.

"And when the deal was finally clinched by this bunch of buddies, secretly working together to rob the Canadian taxpayer where was the commission—three million dollars I remind you again—to be delivered? Why," and he flourished a copy of the transcript of the last hearing of the Standing Committee, "it was to be paid to an offshore company in the Cayman Islands. And where are they? About as close to Cuba as you can get! And to what company was the money to be paid? Why, the Evangeline! And where," with heavy irony, "have we heard *that* name before?"

A convulsive shudder rippled through the House. But Adam Sorenson had not yet finished his denunciation.

"Now why," he asked the hushed chamber, "should Jean Jacques Charles be paid off so handsomely? Why should he be involved? Well, let's look at that. We all know Canada is a signatory to the non-proliferation treaty. We all know that Canada had a long-standing policy never to sell any of our technology without rigid safeguard conditions, ensuring that the purchaser can't use it to make bombs. We demand guarantees that they will use it solely for energy purposes. And, I remind all Honourable Members, we've been as tough on our friends as we have been on our enemies in enforcing these conditions. Or at least we were until Fidel Castro and Jean Jacques Charles got their heads together," he said ominously.

"Dr. Castro, it seems, wanted the Candu very badly. Mr. Charles, his buddy," again he gave heavy ironic emphasis to the words, "wanted to sell him the Candu. Unfortunately, Cuba couldn't afford the price. 'No problem,' says his Canadian buddy, 'we'll lend you the money.' 'Okay,' says the bearded Commie President. 'But look here, none of this inspection stuff, old buddy. All I want is electric power. You can trust me.' 'Yeah,' said the Canadian PM, 'I guess that's right—gotta trust a buddy.' And he gave his buddy his word. Canada's word, that is, in writing. That he could have it all *without safeguards!*"

The members were stunned. Aside from a handful close to each of the party leaders, no one else yet knew of the secret memorandum. But not for long. Adam Sorenson picked up an envelope from his pile of papers and slowly drew from it a single sheet of paper. His gaze swept the House, then leisurely, the press gallery. There wasn't a sound in the vast chamber. Every eye was riveted upon the leader of the Opposition.

"Let me read you what those two bosom buddies agreed to. Let me reveal what Jean Jacques Charles was lately paid three million of our tax dollars for." Dramatically, he read the brief memo into the record, and then he said, with an actor's delicate sense of timing. "It's hard to believe—it's almost incredible, I know—that a man who has occupied the highest elective office in the land, a man who for many years has enjoyed the confidence of the country and of this House, could *sell us out.* But there it is, in his own writing!"

A clamour began, but the Opposition leader held up his hand. Quiet fell at once.

"Now if what I say is not true, Mr. Chairman, then let the Right Honourable Gentleman stand in his place and say so. But no, he won't. The Secretary of State for External Affairs has persistently refused to answer questions in this House. He had his chance today to come here and defend himself. *But he didn't.*"

The declamatory voice was contemptuous now. "He quit, resigned, left the Government, rather than try to explain. Well, if that, Honourable Members," he pounded his desk to drive home his point, "isn't proof of his guilt, I don't know what else could be. Jean Jacques Charles is a disgrace to Canada. This House should be glad to be rid of him. He should be hounded out of the country."

Adam Sorenson sat down, exhausted and drenched with sweat, but nonetheless exhilarated.

Before a watchful and hostile House, Kathleen rose to speak, to defend, as well as she could, her former colleague. She hoped she would be able to separate the fact of the now-revealed memo from the naked innuendo that Jacques had been paid off for his concession on the safeguards, a concession that, as she now knew, he had been previously authorized by his Cabinet colleagues to make as he saw fit. But she knew that the likelihood of doing so was slight since she could only repeat to the House the denials Jacques had made to her and her Cabinet. Kathleen would have to rely on the shaky word of a colleague who now stood exposed to her, if not yet to the House, as a liar. The House would have to decide if Jacques had lied to her and if she had, on that basis, inadvertently misled the House, or if Kathleen had known all along of the secret memo, and thus deliberately misled the House. She was back into the terrible nightmare.

The Prime Minister took a deep breath, to begin her defence. To her chagrin, before she could speak, she was interrupted by the Chairman of the Committee of the Whole.

"Six o'clock. By the rules I must now put the motion moved by the Honourable Leader of the Opposition, seconded by the Honourable Member for Tushingham. The question is on item number one, to reduce the salary of the Secretary of State for External Affairs. All those in favour?"

Within twenty minutes, the motion had carried, the Opposition voting without exception against the Government benches. In itself, the result was meaningless, since the Minister's post had been vacant since morning. But it was ominous, a portent of the mood of the House. By careful design, Sorenson's speech had lasted exactly long enough to give the Prime Minister no opportunity to reply to the full list of his devastating charges. Kathleen Marshal's Government hung on a thread. Would the Opposition return tomorrow to the attack? Having tasted Jean Jacques Charles' blood, would they now be satisfied with anything less than hers?

There was a long, anguished night ahead for Kathleen Marshal. Until the House sat again tomorrow, there was no way of telling what the Opposition planned to do. In the next thirty hours, the fate of her Government would be sealed.

By the time Kathleen reached her office, most of her staff had already left, sharp at six o'clock, before the vote had even been taken, confident in the knowledge that the Government could not be defeated today. Kathleen dismissed those who remained.

As she herself was leaving the building, one of the House messengers, breathless with urgency, caught up to her, thrusting into her hand an envelope addressed to her in the hasty writing of her House Leader. She tore it open.

> Bad news. Have just learned tomorrow's confidence vote will condemn the Government for attracting US sanctions through a sale without safeguards. G. P.

Kathleen spent a difficult evening marshalling all the arguments she might use to forestall defeat. During the long hours, she had consulted several times by telephone with Geoff Pratt, with Bonnie Costello, and with wily old Harry Williams. Each was already hard at work preparing to make a contribution to the debate tomorrow. Kathleen hoped that others of her ministers would want to speak as well, but ministers, like members, were hard to reach on a Wednesday night. Some would be out of the city, attending to constituency or departmental business. Others would simply be treating their families to a quiet dinner out or a movie on this weekly break from tiring night sittings. The Government Whip had instructions to persuade as many members as he could to be ready with interventions in support of the Government. The Prime Minister had urged that he pay special attention to the Quebec members.

Shortly before eleven that rainy night, Senators LaCroix and Warden dropped by unannounced, at 24 Sussex.

"My friend LaCroix insisted upon coming," the Minister of Finance explained.

They had dined together, trying desperately to discover

some way to persuade Jacques to make a public statement to exonerate Kathleen and her Government from responsibility for the threatened sanctions. The two old warriors, not always friends, had gone to Jacques' home with their pleas, but he had curtly refused to see them, closing the door in the affronted faces.

Kathleen now welcomed the two seasoned politicians and invited them to join her in the family sitting room where she had been going over her notes for the next day.

As soon as he sat down in the rocker that Kathleen always thought of as Evangeline's, Gabriel LaCroix turned to Kathleen and pleaded, "Please believe me, Prime Minister. I knew nothing of that memorandum. I swear. I've always had a sense that Jacques knew more than he let on about the Cuban deal, but I had no idea what it was. He did ask me, as an old friend, to let him know if his name came up in connection with any deals, but I assumed he just had a continuing interest in work he had begun as Prime Minister. And I still believe him. I'm sure he only referred Findlay to Cranston to help Stan out and that he had no idea Findlay would get involved with a Candu sale to Cuba. And I'll *never* believe he had anything to do with that offshore company or the money. Jacques doesn't need money. He has plenty of his own. And he's an honourable man."

"Then why didn't he tell me about the memo?" she asked wearily.

"My guess is that he thought the Cuban sale had fallen through, so the question of safeguards didn't matter any more. Anyway, he really likes and trusts Castro. He considers him an honest man too, and his word would be good enough for Jacques. It was between friends. But I'm only guessing. I know no more than what I've told you. And I'm sure AECL didn't know either, although they must have been surprised that safeguards were never even discussed.

"Anyway, P.M., I want you to know I'm behind you all the way now. I haven't always been, but now I'll do whatever I can. Just tell me what!"

Kathleen was touched by this display of loyalty, however late it was. The shaggy man was clearly distraught, but just as clearly sincere in his belated pledge of support. But there really isn't anything Gabriel can do now, she told herself resignedly. What I need right now is a Minister of Energy in the Commons, not the Senate. And I need the two votes I've lost through Charles' and Findlay's resignations. If only I'd called a general election last winter. . . .

"I'm going to speak tomorrow, against the sanctions," offered her Minister of Finance.

Kathleen thanked her respected elder colleague, but privately she thought another Senate speech, even by Carter Warden, would no longer help. It would neither deter the American President from imposing the dreaded sanctions, nor dissuade the Opposition in the Commons from condemning her. It was just too late.

Tossing restlessly in her broad, lonely bed, Kathleen was still wide awake when, much later, the bedside telephone trilled. She answered quickly. It was Andrew, on an unclear long-distance line. Kathleen, close to tears of exhaustion and despair, told him of her parliamentary predicament. He promised to be in Ottawa by early next afternoon, and begged her to hold off her contribution to the debate until after his arrival. There was excitement in his voice as he explained the reason.

"I followed a hunch. I've found out something down here in the Caymans—proof that Jacques had nothing to do with the Evangeline Company. Buck up darling! Maybe this will help you through."

On Thursday, not long before the buzzer sounded for the two-hour dinner recess, the Prime Minister began her speech. She opened with a careful recounting of her efforts to learn the details of the rumoured Candu sale. For the first time, she revealed publicly the substance of her meeting in Washington with President Thompson. Although she feared that such an admission would be damaging—as it undeniably was, she realized, when she became aware of the stir in the House after she mentioned it—she felt honour-bound to make the explanation, as a background to the President's unprecedented statement on sanctions. Her judgement told her that it was better for the information to come from her instead of from the US President in a later press conference, when she would be accused of trying to conceal his warning from the country.

Over the dinner recess, Kathleen dined in her office, alone except for Andrew. They discussed at length what he had discovered—that Stanley Findlay had been the sole recorded shareholder of the offshore corporation, although instructions to set up the Evangeline Company had come from a Montreal businessman. The lawyer for the corporation had given his affidavit to that effect, although he had refused to disclose the name of the businessman who had engaged him.

"And the amount deposited to the account, and never touched since, was *two* million Canadian, not three."

Presumably, Kathleen and Andrew agreed, Cranston had raked a million dollars off the top. It seemed unlikely to either of them that Jacques would have received any of that money. In any event, to Kathleen's legal mind, the proof Andrew had brought her was at best equivocal.

"Sure, I agree, it clears Jacques of any implication in the offshore company, but it doesn't necessarily follow that he hasn't shared in the one-third skimmed by Cranston."

But for whatever it was worth, Kathleen resolved to use the affidavit, deeply grateful that Andrew had, on his own initiative, gone to such lengths to offer her something more concrete than his loving support.

At eight o'clock, Kathleen resumed her speech. She attacked Sorenson's carefully drawn picture of a venal, dishonourable Charles, calling up all her formidable forensic skills to punch holes in the fabric of his argument in Wednesday's debate.

With generosity, she extolled the contribution Jean Jacques Charles had made to Canada, reminding the House members of their past pride in his international accomplishments, underlining the warm personal nature of his relations with a number of the world's heads of state, smudging the isolated relationship with Fidel Castro, seeking to demolish the basis of Sorenson's "buddies" argument.

"The Right Honourable Gentleman has proved, over and over, that he is just that." She looked up over the top of her reading glasses. To leaven her remarks with a little humour, she said wryly, "Some Honourable Members will recall that my predecessor and I have had our rather public differences. But," and her tone returned to the serious, "I challenge any member of this House to recall one incident, even one, where Jean Jacques Charles has been less than the soul of honour.

"Honour," she said quietly to a spellbound House, "is the fundamental basis of our system of parliamentary democracy. My young friend, the leader of the Official Opposition, will recall the lesson he received in the rump session of this

House, in the spring, on how jealously Parliament protects the honour of its members, and how severely it deals with any charge of a breach of that honour."

Sorenson's face flushed a dull crimson. He remembered all too clearly the ignominy of his retreat when he had been required to back down on his charge that the Prime Minister had deliberately misled the House.

Kathleen went on, disregarding his scowl. "As a man of honour, the former Prime Minister accorded to other heads of state that same lofty attribute. I applaud such a good-will approach, as I believe all Honourable Members here do, as well. I can only suggest that, in signing the memorandum which the leader of the Opposition has produced, the former Prime Minister was relying upon Dr. Castro's personal word of honour that our nuclear technology would not be used for other than peaceful purposes. I do not believe for a moment that Jean Jacques Charles, in doing so, intended to neglect our obligations under the international treaty. He was *assured* that he had Cuba's word. He thought it unnecessary to require more."

Her tone changed, hardened. "Now, let's take a closer look at the allegations of those opposite. They have tried to make us believe that this man of recognized honour stooped to the level of the commonest crook, that he bartered his cherished honour for the dross of gold. A million dollars, or two, or three. I will vouchsafe that's a lot of money, a powerful lure—to many of us. But what incentive for wrongdoing could that be to a man of honour who happens also to be—as it is well known that the former Prime Minister is—a man with a personal fortune greater than that many times over? I suggest to Honourable Members that it makes no sense at all to believe that Jean Jacques Charles would be party to such a loathsome scheme for *any* sum, much less one that would be to him a mere pittance."

She paused to let that branch of her argument sink in.

"Well, what about the Evangeline Company, you may ask? There can surely be no one here who can have forgotten the lovely Evangeline, the former Prime Minister's beloved wife? But I have nothing but contempt for those who charge that a man who would stoop to profit personally from his public office would openly deposit those ill-gotten gains to the credit of a company with a name so indelibly linked in the public mind with his own! Even if they refuse to grant that Jean

Jacques Charles is a man of honour who could never contemplate such a nefarious scheme, who is there who can refuse to grant that Jean Jacques Charles is anything but *stupid?*"

Kathleen paused to look around her. Her argument, she thought, was having its effect. Even among the now-silent PC's there were doubtful faces, and along to her right, in his front-row seat, Terry Malloy of the NDP was watching her with, it seemed to her, an expression of reluctant admiration.

"But if there are those who doubt, I have proof." The Prime Minister motioned to a page, who scrambled up from his seat on the steps of the Speaker's dais. The Chief Page motioned him back and stepped forward himself. She handed him several copies of the affidavit. He delivered one to each party leader, and the final one to the Clerk at the table.

"Honourable Members, this is a sworn affidavit that Jean Jacques Charles had no interest whatsoever in the Evangeline Company, registered in the Cayman Islands. It was entirely owned by the late Stanley Findlay. Clearly, any allegations against the former Prime Minister on that count cannot be supported by the facts.

"I suggest to the Honourable Members of this House that there is no basis whatsoever for the regrettable vote that was taken yesterday to condemn the former Secretary of State for External Affairs. Had an opportunity been given to me before that vote, I would have said then what I have said to you tonight."

Kathleen paused yet again, and then resumed, cutting now to the heart of the debate.

"The motion before this House tonight differs slightly from yesterday's. It condemns the Government for making a Candu sale without safeguards to Cuba, and by doing so, calling down upon Canada sanctions by the government of the United States.

"I have explained to the House that the Government was—until yesterday—totally unaware of the exemption regarding safeguards pledged by the former Prime Minister. I have, however, now explained that the Right Honourable Gentleman did not thereby agree that Cuba could use our nuclear technology for any purpose it chose, other than peaceful purposes. He relied upon Dr. Castro, as another man of dependable honour, to keep his own word that nuclear technology would be used only to advance the Cuban people in *peaceful* ways. Regrettably, President Thompson has taken a drastic and, to us, potentially disastrous step in his announced intention to impose sanctions against Canada, presumably because he fears that Cuba will turn the nuclear technology it acquires from us against the United States for something other than peaceful purposes."

She paused again, for emphasis, and then said, her voice clarion-clear, "I believe that, given time, I can dissuade him from such sanctions. If you will reject this motion tonight and give me the grace of time, I pledge to the House that I will, at once, arrange to see Dr. Castro to obtain his iron-clad assurance that he will honour the word he has given to the former Prime Minister." More slowly, she continued, "Armed with that assurance, I am confident that President Thompson, himself an honourable man, will stay his hand against Canada. I *beg* the House for that precious time to avert what all will admit would otherwise be a catastrophe."

Kathleen sat down, totally drained. Several of her nearby colleagues thumped her lightly on the back, whispering congratulations. Above her, in the Senate gallery, Gabriel LaCroix beamed down at her.

"Good girl," he mouthed. The aging minister's eyes misted as he thought with satisfaction that whatever the result of tonight's House vote might be, the Prime Minister's stunning defence of her francophone predecessor would lose her no votes in Quebec.

Terry Malloy was on his feet. The cocky little redhead spoke for over half an hour. He scarcely referred to Kathleen's speech, but concentrated on a scathing condemnation of the American President. He sketched a frightening picture of the vulnerability of the Canadian economy, with repeated backhand swipes at the Liberals for letting the country become so dependent upon the United States. Finally he concluded with a mighty denunciation of President Thompson for his threats, and a ringing call to the House to ignore them. It was impossible to tell how he and his followers would vote on the motion.

The leader of the tiny Social Credit group—like him, all representatives of Quebec seats—rose next, to laud Jean, Jacques Charles. He spoke in country French, and only briefly. Nor did he reveal how his group would vote. When he resumed his seat, it was only 10:45. All eyes now swung to Adam Sorenson. The Opposition leader sat motionless. He did not rise to speak. Nor did any other member of the House.

From his dais, Speaker Ludvic scanned the rows of fidgeting members as the pause lengthened. Then he stood to put the question. In moments, bells were ringing all over the environs of Parliament to call in the members.

Kathleen, waiting in her seat, received many congratulations, even a surprising note or two from members of the jammed press gallery. She was hopeful that it had been enough.

But it was not enough. The Government was defeated by the slender margin of three votes. The Prime Minister rose as soon as the result was announced, and lifting her chin, spoke clearly in a firm, steady voice.

"Mr. Speaker, I shall attend upon the Governor General in the morning to advise that the Government has lost the confidence of the House. I will recommend dissolution."

Kathleen pushed her way through the ranks of Liberal members who had spilled into the Government Lobby and were now clustered together in groups of twos and threes. From a scattered few came words of sympathy and encouragement. The rest were too shocked, too uncertain to essay comment. Some were resentful that their leader had not somehow found the means to stave off her Government's defeat, but most were satisfied that she had done her best. Later, she knew, most of them would rally to the party's standard as they headed for the hustings, but they must already sense what she herself knew—that whatever the forthcoming election's outcome, Kathleen Marshal's days as leader were numbered. As she passed, a white-faced Bonnie Costello squeezed her arm in wordless compassion.

Beyond the lobby, her sympathetic staff formed a flying wedge to get her through the wildly clamouring press. With determination they pushed their way up the steps towards her office.

Inside that sanctuary, Andrew awaited her. Wordlessly, he enfolded her in his strong, comforting arms. The tall couple stood, silently holding one another, afraid to entrust their feelings to words. Almost immediately, they were interrupted by a knock. The door swung open, and Anthony Whiteside stepped inside.

The American Ambassador stood, taking in their embrace. He said, slowly, "I've come to say good-bye, Kath. As you know, I've been recalled. I thought for a moment you had pulled it off, and I'm sure you could have convinced the President."

Kathleen released herself from Andrew's arms and turned to face Whiteside. Her tone was reproachful.

"I think I could have convinced the President, too, but that's no longer possible, is it? How could you do it, Tony? You could have let me know earlier about the memorandum—or you could have kept it from the others long enough to give me some time. And yet you didn't. How could you do that? To me?"

Whiteside flinched, hearing the hurt in her words. With an effort he kept his own voice under control.

"Kathleen, you of all people should understand. It was my duty. I did what I had to do in the best interests of my country. In my place you would have done the same." He took a step towards her, reaching out a hand in a mute plea for understanding. "Tonight you spoke so movingly of honour—of how necessary an ingredient it is in public life. That's as true for me as it is for Jean Jacques Charles—or for you. We all serve our countries in the best and most honourable way we know."

As she faced him, Kathleen was aware that there was more than compassion in Whiteside's eyes.

"And what of friendship?" she asked, sadly. "Isn't it possible for friendship and duty to go together?"

"Sometimes we have to choose." Briefly, he reached out and held her shoulders, as if they were alone in the room. "What brought you down wasn't anything I did. It was your own honour. As your title says, you are a right honourable lady—and the honourable ones aren't necessarily life's winners.

"You didn't need to keep Jacques beside you. You didn't need to defend him when he refused to defend himself. You didn't need to tell the House of your meeting with the President. But you did all those things—for the best and most honourable of reasons. We do what we have to do, my dear, even if we can't foresee the results. And sometimes we do it when we *can* foresee those results—and find them unbearable." His hands dropped from her shoulders.

"Good-bye, Kath," he said, his voice low. "I'm sorry. Truly sorry." Then he turned and was gone.

For a moment Kathleen stared unseeingly at the closed door. Then she heard a movement behind her, and felt her husband's hands resting where Whiteside had held her just a moment before. With a long, shuddering sigh she turned and buried her face in his chest, wordlessly asking for the comfort of his arms around her. Andrew held her gently, protectively.

"Kathleen. . . ."

Her own arms tightened around him as she raised her head. Her smile was tremulous.

"Kathleen Wickstrom now," she said. "Kathleen Marshal is gone—probably forever. I don't really mind, Andrew. I hope you don't."

ABOUT THE AUTHOR

JUDY LA MARSH, born in Chatham, Ontario, graduated from the University of Toronto and Osgoode Hall, then practiced law until she was elected a Member of Parliament in 1960. A stormy but distinguished political career followed. From 1963-65 she served as Minister of National Health and Welfare, and as Secretary of State from 1965-68 before resigning from office. After quickly establishing a new career as a broadcaster and columnist, she published *Memoirs of a Bird in a Gilded Cage,* a candid, often sharp-tongued reflection on her experiences as a Cabinet minister under Lester Pearson. The book was an instant bestseller in hardcover and later in paperback. *A Very Political Lady,* one of the most controversial novels to come out of Canada in recent years, also dominated the bestseller lists. *A Right Honourable Lady* is in that tradition. Judy La Marsh lives in Toronto, where she practices family law.

SEAL BOOKS

Offers you a list of outstanding fiction, non-fiction and classics of Canadian literature in paperback by Canadian authors, available at all good bookstores throughout Canada.

The Canadian Establishment	Peter C. Newman
A Jest of God	Margaret Laurence
Separation	Richard Rohmer
Bear	Marian Engel
Lady Oracle	Margaret.Atwood
There's a Raccoon in My Parka	Lyn Hancock
The Doctor's Wife	Brian Moore
The Fire-Dwellers	Margaret Laurence
The Snow Walker	Farley Mowat
René	Peter Desbarats
Bloody Harvest	Grahame Woods
The Lark in the Clear Air	Dennis T. P. Sears
Act of God	Charles Templeton
The Stone Angel	Margaret Laurence
A Whale for the Killing	Farley Mowat
The Edible Woman	Margaret Atwood
Emperor Red	William Stevenson
Dancing Girls and Other Stories	Margaret Atwood
A Gift To Last	Gordon Pinsent & Grahame Woods
A Bird in the House	Margaret Laurence

The Mark of Canadian Bestsellers